Sometimes bad thi
to good people . . . especi
in the wrong place at t

"ANDREA KANE
EXPERTLY JUGGLES
SUSPENSE
AND ROMANCE."
Iris Johansen

NEW YORK TIMES BESTSELLING MASTER OF THE ROMANTIC THRILLER

"[IS] COMPELLING AND SURPRISING."
Linda Howard

"[WRITES] KEEPS-YOU-UP-ALL-NIGHT ROMANTIC SUSPENSE."
Karen Robards

"COMBINES ROMANCE WITH AN ELEMENT OF DANGER."
Dallas Morning News

"CRANKS UP THE TENSION."
Fort Myers News-Press

"[RATCHETS] UP THE SUSPENSE."
Publishers Weekly

"[CREATES] ABSORBING TALES OF ROMANTIC SUSPENSE."
Booklist

By Andrea Kane

WRONG PLACE, WRONG TIME
I'LL BE WATCHING YOU
SCENT OF DANGER
NO WAY OUT
RUN FOR YOUR LIFE

And in Hardcover

DARK ROOM

andrea
kane

Wrong Place, Wrong Time,

This is a work of fiction. Names, characters, places, and incidents are products of the author's imagination or are used fictitiously and are not to be construed as real. Any resemblance to actual events, locales, organizations, or persons, living or dead, is entirely coincidental.

AVON BOOKS
An Imprint of HarperCollins*Publishers*
10 East 53rd Street
New York, New York 10022-5299

ISBN: 978-0-06-074133-4
ISBN-10: 0-06-074133-3
www.avonbooks.com

First Avon Books paperback printing: March 2007
First William Morrow hardcover printing: January 2006

Printed in the U.S.A.

10 9 8 7 6 5 4 3 2 1

TO THE ENTIRE VETERINARY COMMUNITY—*those amazing professionals who dedicate themselves to the health and well-being of animals and to the advancement of veterinary medicine. You have my profound respect and my personal gratitude.*

And to two very special inspirations:

Rascal—your loving heart, feisty nature, and dauntless spirit rallied. You're a hero in the true sense of the word.

And to the real Stolen Thunder—I hope I captured your majesty on the pages of this novel.

ACKNOWLEDGMENTS

As always, I owe thanks to a handful of people who devoted their time and expertise to me and to the creation of *Wrong Place, Wrong Time*. Their input was invaluable.

Peggy Gordijn, my guide through the world of professional equestrian show jumping—I still can't get over the depth of your knowledge, from breeding and training to showing and Olympic events. My appreciation abounds!

Special thanks to Adrie Gordijn for supplying firsthand details of running a warmblood farm, for the names and lineages of his magnificent horses, and for Gran-Corrado, the ultimate last-in-his lineage champion.

The founders and staff of the Veterinary MRI + Radiotherapy Center of New Jersey, whose cutting-edge technology, dynamic personalities, and caring hearts make miracles happen.

Dr. Paul Sedlacek, who's way too humble to know what an incredible doctor he is, and to his entire staff at the Animal Clinic of Morris Plains. I created "Creature Comforts & Clinic" with all of you in mind. Dr. Joel Sedwell's name is a fitting tribute to two great vets: Dr. Paul Sedlacek and Dr. Joseph Powell.

Detective Mike Oliver, who helped make the sights and sounds of Brooklyn's Seventy-fifth Precinct come alive by taking me on patrol through East New York and providing me with a firsthand look at a day in the life of an NYPD detective, and whose quick mind and dry humor helped me create Monty.

Hillel Ben-Asher, M.D., always my quintessential source of medical information.

Andrea Cirillo, quite simply the finest and the best.

Carrie Feron, for being there in the clutch with editorial and conceptual direction, and for supplying the color, flavor, and back roads of Dutchess County.

Caroline Tolley: Welcome back, CT. You haven't lost your touch.

And last but always first, to my family—you're my foundation, my strength, and my inspiration.

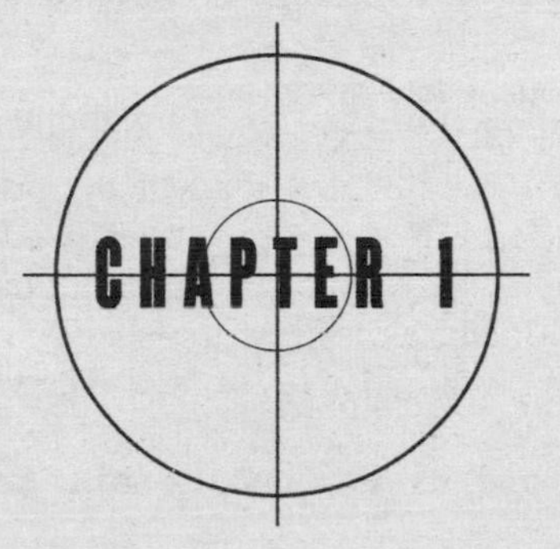

CHAPTER 1

The skies were that harsh shade of gray that signified winter in upstate New York.

Sally Montgomery's secondhand Chevy truck jostled along the narrow, snow-covered excuse of a road that led from her house to the sprawling horse farm a mile down the way. She would have hiked it—she usually did—even at this ungodly hour of 6:30 A.M. Everyone at her nursery school thought she was crazy. A fifty-two-year-old woman, choosing to trek two miles round-trip by foot, and before sunrise, no less?

But, hey, she was in great shape, she loved the outdoors, and the truth was, the hike cleared her head, made her feel alive.

Except on days like today. Even Sally drew the line here. It was frigid outside, January making its presence known full force. Subzero temperatures, high winds, and not a hint of sunlight. Plus, it had snowed again last night, just a couple of inches, but enough to make the as-the-crow-flies path she normally walked a disaster.

Hiking would be hazardous at worst and miserable at best.

So, it was four-wheel-drive time.

With a twist of the steering wheel, she turned left and drove through the gates that marked the private entrance to the Pierson farm. Rows of pine trees lined the way, and Sally's headlights caught the reflection of glistening icicles dangling from them, as well as the sparkle of fresh-fallen snow on the five hundred acres of land. The view was spectacular.

The house and its surrounding structures were even more so.

House was a misnomer, she thought as she drove past the snow-covered fenced-in paddocks and toward the buildings that defined the Millbrook estate. First came the seven-thousand-square-foot cedar-sided house. Then came the outbuildings—multistalled barn, feed and tack rooms, heated wash stalls, not to mention a massive indoor jumping arena and two smaller indoor arenas. The estate was magnificent—the largest, most elaborately designed warmblood farm in Dutchess County, with a lighted outdoor ring, exercise track and jumping arena, and grounds that included a pond and gazebo worthy of a Currier and Ives holiday card.

Sally's breath never ceased to catch when she saw the place.

But that wasn't why she loved coming here.

She loved coming here for the horses. Edward Pierson might have made his millions in the restaurant business, but his passion was right here. For years, he'd sponsored winning show horses. Now, at almost eighty years old, he not only showed but owned and bred some of the most successful and exquisite warmbloods in the country. They were extraordinary, with more ribbons than Sally could count, and personalities as individual and unique as their beauty and skill. She treasured her time with them—*all* of them, not just the three she was paid to exercise. True, she needed the extra money she earned coming over here each morning, pitching in alongside the Pierson grooms. But the truth was, she would have done it for free.

Her tires crunched in the snow as she pulled her truck up to the barn and came to a stop. She was early. Frederick wouldn't be arriving for another half hour. That worked out fine. It would give her a chance to check on Sunrise, see how her leg was faring. She'd been favoring it the other day. Hopefully by now it was on the mend.

Climbing out of her truck, Sally tromped her way to the wooden doors.

God, it was cold. Elbowing her way inside, she rubbed her gloved hands together for warmth. She could hear the horses whinnying softly and moving around in their stalls.

First things first. Sunrise.

She went down to the mare's stall, stroking her neck in greeting. Sunrise was a graceful chestnut with regal white markings and dark, expressive eyes. Warm and affectionate by nature, she responded to Sally's caress with a flick of her tail and a welcoming nuzzle, although Sally noted that her stance was still a bit stiff. Frowning, she glanced down. Yes. That right front leg was definitely bothering her.

No sooner had Sally squatted down to take a look than voices from the back of the barn reached her ears. Male voices.

". . . not just a screwup. A criminal offense. A bomb set to blow up in all our faces." It was Frederick, Edward Pierson's eldest son and Sally's morning riding partner. Evidently, he *was* here. And he sounded furious. "To hell with loyalty. He's out."

"That's my call. Not yours." The icy reply came from a voice Sally recognized as belonging to the family patriarch himself. After seventy-nine turbulent years and a recent heart attack, Edward Pierson was no less formidable than he'd been in his prime. "Stay out of this, Frederick. I'll deal with it."

"How? By paying off the right people to make it go away? That won't work. Not this time. Dammit, Father, get your head out of the sand. He's a loose cannon. He's set to go off. And when he does, it's *our* company, *our* lives that'll be blasted to bits."

"Stop being so melodramatic. I know what I'm doing."

"Great. Then clue me in. About your plans for him, and that research consultant you're pouring our money into. The whole enchilada. I've got a right to know. I'm Pierson & Company's CEO."

"And *I'm* its chairman," Edward shot back. "Until the day I die. Which means *you* answer to *me*. Not the other way around."

"How could I forget? You remind me daily. Now let *me* remind *you* that I've busted my ass for thirty years to get us where we are."

"Yes, but it was *my* ass that launched this company fifty years ago. You were still flipping baseball cards."

"Well, now I'm earning record profits. I can't do that if I'm being undermined. You obviously have an agenda. What is it?"

"You know all you need to."

Frederick sucked in his breath sharply. "In other words, butt out, and the son of a bitch stays at Pierson."

"Right."

"No, not right. This discussion is far from over." Frederick sounded as if he might snap. "Let's cut this short. Sally will be here any minute. We're going riding. After that, I'm leaving for the office. I've got a ten thirty meeting. You and I will resume this later."

That was the last thing Sally wanted to hear.

Having long since realized this conversation was not one she should be privy to, she was about to duck out of Sunrise's stall and slip away without being noticed.

That wasn't meant to be.

Frederick stormed by, muttering something about "reading him the riot act today" and nearly mowing Sally down as she exited Sunrise's stall.

"Sally." He caught her arms to steady her, his salt-and-pepper brows arching in surprise. His jaw was working and dark splotches of red stained his cheeks—vivid evidence of the argument that had just taken place. But his expression softened a bit as it settled on her, although his gaze was wary. "I didn't realize you were here. Are you all right?"

"I just arrived. And I'm fine," she assured him. Actually, she felt strained and self-conscious. Not only had she overheard some ugly words between father and son—words that implied something sketchy was going on at Pierson & Company—she'd been found hovering in the doorway like some kind of snitch.

Oh, for pity's sake, she had to stop thinking like a cop's wife. This wasn't an episode of *Law & Order;* it was an embarrassing blunder. Frederick had been expecting her. They rode together two mornings a week. Unfortunately, she'd shown up early on an inopportune day. Big deal. As for the argument she'd walked in on, whichever Pierson employee was crossing the line and getting Edward's blessing doing it was none of her business.

Time to dispel the tension and lighten things up.

Taking the bull by the horns, Sally pushed back the hood of her down parka so she could have an unobstructed view of Frederick—and he of her. "I apologize for intruding," she said, going for candor. "I'm a few minutes early. I took the truck today. It's too cold to walk—even for me. I'm sorry I interrupted your meeting."

"My *meeting*," Frederick repeated drily. "That's one term for it."

"A tactful one." Sally saw no point in pretending to misunderstand his meaning. "The truth is, I argue with my parents, too. They mean well, but we don't always see eye to eye. Still, when push comes to shove, family's there for you. So keep that in mind. Oh, and jog a couple of miles. It does wonders to dispel anger."

"Jogging's not exactly my thing."

"I guess not." Sally contemplated the fact that, other than when they went riding, she'd never seen Frederick wear anything but conservative business suits and a cashmere coat. "Racquetball?" she suggested hopefully.

He chuckled, visibly relaxing. "Nope. Work. A few hours at my desk and I'll forget I ever lost my temper."

Grimacing, Sally tucked a wisp of honey brown hair behind her ear. "If you say so."

"You're skeptical."

"I shouldn't be. Given how successful you are, you must be passionate about what you do."

"Even if that doesn't involve the great outdoors."

A shrug. "Everyone's different. I'm a nature buff. You're a business enthusiast. The world needs both."

"Tactful again. Always the lady." Frederick was speaking as much to himself as he was to her. He was a tough-looking man, with rugged features, graying hair, and a solid build. Not handsome, but charismatic, in a strong kind of way. A definite catch—rich, powerful, and reasonably attractive, not to mention available. At fifty-eight, he was a widower of two years. And while he'd been photographed numerous times with that striking blond lawyer who worked for Pierson on his arm, he'd never hidden his interest in Sally.

The last few months, he'd started spending more time at the farm, joining Sally for morning rides. She'd begun to enjoy his company. And she'd found herself responding to his overtures. It had been too damned long. At some point, she had to let go of the past.

As if reading her mind, Frederick asked, "Do you have plans for this weekend?"

"Nothing special. Why?"

He pursed his lips, a brooding expression on his face. "One of my key suppliers has a cabin in the Adirondacks at

Lake Luzerne. I'm going to head up there. I need some time to clear my head. I'd love to share that time with you."

Okay, when he'd said weekend, he'd meant the *whole* weekend. She definitely wasn't ready for that. And Lake Luzerne of all places. God, that conjured up memories.

"Thanks, but I think I'll pass," she replied.

"On me, or on the weekend?"

"The weekend." Sally drew a sharp breath. "Look, Frederick, I really enjoy your company. But if you're asking me out, I'd rather start with something uncomplicated, like dinner. A weekend away is a bit much."

Another hint of wry amusement. "Brutal honesty. Very well, I'll take this again from the top. My supplier has a *two-bedroom* cabin in Lake Luzerne. I'd enjoy the company of a beautiful and intelligent *friend* who enjoys the outdoors as much as I enjoy the boardroom. Maybe she can teach me how to unwind, and we can get to know each other in the process. As much or as little as she wants," he added pointedly.

Relenting a bit, Sally mentally ran through her limitations. "I can't leave until after three on Friday."

"Of course not. Three o'clock is when the nursery school you teach in lets out."

Her brows lifted in surprise. "You've done your homework. I'm impressed."

"Good. Then join me."

She was starting to enjoy the dance, and her hazel eyes twinkled. "Not so fast. What about the horses I'm responsible for? Who'll exercise them?"

"We've got a staff of qualified grooms and trainers. I think they can manage. Plus, my nephew Blake will be up here this weekend. He'll make sure the horses get *almost* as much expert care and loving attention as they get from you. I'll even send someone over to feed and check on your animals. Anything else?"

"Actually, yes. There's Scamp."

"Scamp?"

"My Brussels griffon. My *dog,*" Sally clarified at the blank expression on Frederick's face. "He can't stay alone. And he doesn't adapt well to strangers. I'll have to make separate arrangements for him."

"Now *that* one won't fly." With a wry grin, Frederick shot down her final stipulation. "Not when I know your daughter Devon is a veterinarian. *And* that the practice she's affiliated with is a combination Mount Sinai and Club Med for pets."

"She's not just affiliated with Creature Comforts & Clinic," Sally corrected, her eyes sparkling with pride. "Not as of January first. She's a junior partner. The youngest one in the practice." Realizing how boastful she sounded, Sally broke off with a self-deprecating expression. "Sorry. Just a burst of maternal pride."

"Don't apologize. That's wonderful news. And quite an accomplishment. I haven't forgotten that when my family bought this farm from the Wilsons, one of the reasons you asked to keep your job exercising the horses was to earn extra income. As I recall, you and your ex were putting Devon through college and Cornell Veterinary School. Well, your efforts were obviously rewarded. You have a remarkable daughter. Then again, she has a remarkable mother."

Sally accepted the compliment with a smile. "I'm flattered."

"Flattered enough to join me this weekend? I'll even alter my plans for you. I'd intended to leave Thursday, but I'll gladly wait the extra day, just to enjoy your company."

"Actually, you wouldn't need to. I just remembered that school's closed this Friday. The heating system's being fixed."

"If that isn't fate, what is?" Frederick asked, clearly pleased. "Then it's settled. We'll leave Thursday, right after school."

Sally relented another notch. "*Two* bedrooms?" she requalified.

"With a bathroom separating them. Also, a spectacular

view and incredible hiking trails. Tell you what. I'll even give ice skating a shot. But I draw the line at cross-country skiing. I'm not that courageous."

"Okay, but you don't know what you're missing." With a spontaneous rush of enthusiasm, Sally decided to go for it. A weekend in the mountains. A chance to replace old memories with new ones. She *had* to try. "It sounds like just what I need. I'll be packed and ready to leave by four."

"Consider it a plan."

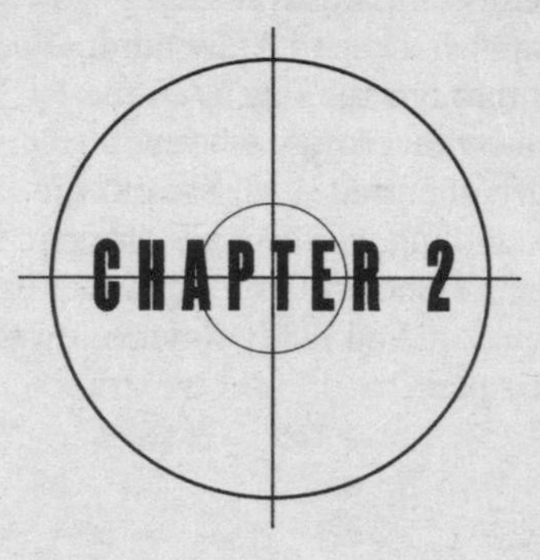

Devon Montgomery shrugged out of her lab coat and hung it away, rubbing the back of her neck. Talk about exhaustion. She'd worked a twelve-hour day, with two emergency surgeries and one emergency visit: a month-old black-and-white kitten named Marble with a urinary tract infection.

There'd been such pandemonium at Creature Comforts & Clinic today that the celebration honoring Devon's promotion to junior partner had been forgotten. By the time anyone remembered the refreshments that the office staff had arranged in the conference room, the ice-cream cake had melted down to a puddle and the pot of coffee had turned to mud.

It didn't matter. Instead of a party, Devon had the joy of saving an Irish setter's life, giving a cockatiel back her gift of flight, and diagnosing Marble's infection so she could prescribe some meds and put him back in the arms of little Amy Green, his grateful five-year-old owner.

No party could compare with that.

But now things were quiet. The adrenaline rush that had carried Devon through the day plummeted. Fatigue set in. And her personal concerns took over.

Automatically, she headed for the clinic's boarding facilities to check on Scamp, who'd been dropped off by Devon's mother early that morning. She found him well and happy, frolicking around the doggie playroom with one of the boarding techs, working off some extra energy. Not a surprise. Sandy Adams, the on-duty tech playing with Scamp, was one of his favorite people. So he was having the time of his life.

Then again, it wasn't really Scamp Devon was brooding over. It was his owner.

Dammit, Mom, what's going on with you? she mused silently, making her way down the halls of Creature Comforts & Clinic. *Why are you rushing into this weekend getaway? And if you're as upbeat as you say you are, why were you acting so weird?*

Something didn't feel right.

Devon frowned, heading back toward her office. Her footsteps echoed on the ceramic tile floor as she passed the now-empty examination rooms. Hard to believe this was the same place that not a few hours ago had been exploding with activity and vibrating with barks and meows. Now, at 9 P.M., the regular clinic facilities were silent. Not so silent, of course, in other portions of the complex. The state-of-the-art hospitalization wing was hopping, as veterinary techs checked on patients and administered medications. Adjacent to the clinic were the boarding and exercising facilities, which spanned acres of the clinic's grounds. There, skilled aides took the animals through their evening routines and settled them down for the night, while other staff accommodated late-arriving executives picking up their pets from doggie day care. As for the training center, it was quiet, since no obedience classes were scheduled till tomorrow.

Devon was proud of this place. Proud that it had been heralded by the *New York Times* as one of Westchester County's most promising new business enterprises. Prouder that they'd described it as "impressive, with top-notch medical care and obedience training, and the penultimate in boarding facilities."

Proudest of all that, at twenty-eight, she was the youngest junior partner in a practice that selected its staff from the best of the best.

She reached her new corner office, glancing briefly at the gold plate that read DEVON MONTGOMERY, DVM, to remind herself that this coveted space was indeed hers. Then she went inside and sank down behind the cherry desk. She released the clip that held back her long, golden brown hair, letting it tumble down past her shoulders. Impatiently raking her fingers through it, she leaned her head back against the chair and began massaging her temples. Talk about being stressed out.

She glanced at her watch. Dinnertime in L.A.

Of course, that didn't mean a damned thing. He could be anywhere in the world.

She picked up the phone, punched in a cell number, and waited while the call rang through.

"Hey, Dev." Her thirty-two-year-old brother, Lane, picked up on the third ring. He sounded winded but unsurprised. "I'm home. Right here in safe old L.A. So if you're calling to check in, you can stop worrying. What's the matter—you're on duty and it's a slow night?"

"Hello to you, too," she retorted. "Boy, caller ID certainly takes all the anticipation out of a ringing phone."

"That's technology for you."

Devon smiled, feeling the customary surge of reassurance at the sound of her brother's voice. He was an incredibly successful photojournalist who traveled the globe on dangerous assignments, worrying the hell out of her in the process. Then again, he had their father's affinity for living life on the edge. Danger and excitement were synonymous to them both.

Her mother was the opposite.

Devon fell somewhere in between.

"Dev?"

"I'm here. And, no, in answer to your question, I'm not on call tonight. I'm just hanging out at the clinic. And *you're* out of breath. Why? Did I call at an inopportune time?"

He chuckled at her implication. "Nope. If it was an inopportune time, I'd let your call go to voice mail. I was working out. Long day, long flight. I was in Hawaii, shooting the Kilauea volcano. The Pu'u 'O'o crater is amazing. Anyway, I just got in a couple of hours ago. I needed to unwind." He paused. "Enough small talk, doc. What's wrong?"

Devon didn't bat an eye at Lane's instantaneous zeroing-in on her mood. He knew her like a book, just as she knew him. When he'd moved to Los Angeles five years ago, she'd been crushed. She missed him like crazy. So did the rest of the family. They never let an opportunity go by without guilting him into remembering that. Poor Lane. He didn't stand a chance. He'd be moving back east before he knew what hit him.

Yup, the Montgomerys were a tight-knit bunch.

Which was why this was driving her crazy.

"Scamp's here," she announced. "Mom's boarding him till Monday. She went away for a long weekend."

"Good. She needs a little fun. So what's the problem?"

"She didn't go alone."

"I repeat, what's the problem?"

"Do I have to spell it out? Mom went away with a man."

Lane sighed. "Yeah, Dev, I figured that part out. So, as usual, this is about Mom and Dad and the never-going-to-happen reconciliation you've conjured up in your mind. Kiddo, it's been fifteen years. Aren't you *ever* going to let it go?"

"I can't. They still love each other."

"No argument. But the divorce didn't happen because of lack of love. It happened because they can't be married. That hasn't changed."

Devon's chin set stubbornly. "Dad never dates."

"He doesn't need to. He's married to his work. As for women, he probably gets whatever action he needs when he goes on those reunion weekends with his old buddies from the precinct."

"Lane." Devon protested the idea and the image it conjured up.

"Oh, come on, Dev," her brother returned impatiently. "The guy hasn't been celibate all this time."

"That doesn't mean you need to paint me a picture."

"I just call it like it is. Dad's fifty-four, healthy, and in great physical shape—not to mention a PI and a retired NYPD police detective, which are both major turn-ons for some women. As for Mom, when she ended their marriage she was—according to the testimony of all my seventeen-year-old, hormone-raging friends—young and hot. She's still great-looking. Do you honestly believe she's lived like a nun?"

"No," Devon retorted. "Of course not. But she never cared enough about anyone to go away for a weekend with him. And it's not only that. It's the way she was acting when she dropped Scamp off. Too exuberant. Too gushy. That's not Mom's style. It was like she was forcing her enthusiasm."

"Probably because she was afraid of getting the third degree from you."

"Or because she was trying to convince herself this was right."

"Maybe she was nervous. Like you said, this isn't the kind of thing she's used to doing. On top of that, she knew she'd be seeing you when she dropped Scamp off—*and* providing you with the whens and the wheres. Talk about embarrassing. I hope you didn't totally invade her privacy." A pause. "By the way, who is this guy?"

Despite her concern, Devon's lips twitched. "What is it you were saying about invading her privacy?"

"Okay, so I'm protective of her, too," Lane admitted. "Who is he?"

"Frederick Pierson. As in Pierson & Company. Apparently, they've become friendly up at the farm."

Lane grunted. "I hope Mom's not out of her league. She's not exactly the jet-set type."

"No, she's not." Devon felt that twinge of worry again. "Speaking of the whens and wheres, there's more. He's taking her to Lake Luzerne."

"You're kidding." This time Lane sounded outright stunned. "Did she say why?"

"I asked her about it. She pooh-poohed the whole thing, said it was just a coincidence. It seems a colleague of Frederick Pierson's owns a cabin up there."

"I don't care if he owns a luxury camping retreat. Frederick Pierson can afford to rent a weekend cabin anywhere in the world. But Lake Luzerne? Mom sidesteps any mention of the place. I'd think she'd avoid it like the plague for her first . . . first . . . whatever this weekend is."

Devon sighed. "Truthfully, I think she's going back there on purpose. To prove something to herself. She's trying to force Dad out of her system. And it's not going to work."

"You didn't tell Dad about this, did you?"

"No. But I was tempted."

"Well, don't. If Mom wants him to know, she'll tell him herself."

"I'm worried about her, Lane."

"She's a grown woman, doc. We're her kids, not her parents."

"I know," Devon conceded quietly. "But I'm not happy. Something just doesn't feel right."

Sally was thinking much the same thing.

The drive up had been fleetingly scenic—and painfully

familiar. The late winter afternoon had been crystal perfect, right up to a brilliant sunset. The rustic cabin was lovely, with a huge stone fireplace, comfy sofas, a modern kitchen and bath, and two small, cozy bedrooms. The conversation had been pleasant. The sleeping arrangements hadn't been questioned—at least not this first night.

But the memories were almost too excruciating to bear.

Lying quietly in bed, Sally wondered if her torn emotions were more obvious to Frederick than she realized. He'd grown progressively more quiet and pensive as the evening wore on and, following a brief after-dinner drink, had kissed her lightly on the mouth and retired to his bedroom.

Maybe this had been a mistake. Maybe it was too soon for Lake Luzerne. Maybe it would always be too soon.

She wriggled onto her side, wishing life weren't so complicated, wishing the answers were as clear as she'd thought them to be when she was a younger, more naive woman—a woman who believed love could conquer all.

It couldn't.

After a few hours of tossing and turning and a few more of fitful sleep, Sally climbed out of bed. She was used to rising with the roosters, and today was no exception.

The icicles hanging outside her window told her not to be fooled by the relative warmth of the heated wooden cabin. It was freezing outside. But she'd come prepared. She yanked on thermal underwear, a microfleece pullover, alpine ski pants, and waterproof hiking boots. Then she went out to the kitchen and brewed a pot of coffee, taking her cup out onto the screened porch.

The world was quiet. Time to breathe in the cold air and think.

And to remember.

She gazed across the snow-covered mountain scene, a myriad of past winter vacations at Lake Luzerne flashing through her mind. Lane and his skiing, progressing from his first wobbly time on the beginner slope to feeling his oats, speeding down the black diamond trail. Devon and her ice skating, zipping around the pond and trying to teach a few local dogs to do the same, helping them use the pads of their paws as skates. And little Meredith, sledding down hills with her daddy, squealing all the way, then building her first snow man—also with her daddy's help.

Pete Montgomery was the center of the kids' universe.

And of Sally's.

Whoever coined the expression *opposites attract* must have had the two of them in mind. An outdoor girl from a sheltered, home-and-hearth family, and a tough, daring Brooklyn cop who was so integrally tied to his career that it was impossible to know where the cop ended and the man began.

They'd met at a Queens deli. Sally had just finished up that evening's night classes; Pete was off duty and on his way home from the NYPD's Seventy-fifth Precinct. They'd both stopped for a cup of coffee. They met at the counter. Two hours later, they were sitting in a booth, still talking. Part of it was fascination; part was sexual attraction. The rest was a mystery. But whatever it was, the combination was enough to lead them to the altar in four months flat, and then to create and adore three wonderful children.

And, oh, how Sally loved Pete. Enough to put her education on hold and defer her career as a nursery school teacher when Lane came along right away. Enough to give up her dreams of a big stone cottage in the country, a barnful of horses she'd teach her kids to ride, and acres and acres on which to do so, and instead to settle down in a semiattached house in Queens because of Pete's crazy schedule.

Enough to replace old dreams with new ones.

All those things she could do.

But how many nights could she pace around their tiny bedroom in Little Neck, praying Pete would come home alive? How many days could she sit by the living room window, wondering what dangers he was facing while working the homicide or narcotics divisions? How many news reports could she see about a cop being shot down on the streets of Brooklyn without dying inside because she was sure it was him?

It got to the point that whenever the doorbell or the telephone rang, she'd brace herself, heart pounding, terrified it was *the* phone call—the one that would take Pete away from her forever.

Heaven help her, she wasn't cut out to be the wife of a police detective. And the kids, God—the kids. What was this lifestyle doing to them? Lane was already becoming frighteningly like his father—a daredevil who thrived on danger and was rattled by nothing. Devon worshiped the ground Pete walked on, hanging on to his every word, wide-eyed, when he told her stories about his day—stories that made Sally cringe. Meredith was her mother's daughter. She begged for a real house to live in, a pony to ride, and a school with trees and grass to play on, instead of a fenced-in blacktop playground.

Then there was the arguing. That tore the kids apart. They loved both their parents. Watching what was happening between them brought a whole new level of tension into the house.

The whole thing was too much.

Finally, Sally snapped. And ended it.

But at what cost?

She took a huge gulp of coffee, wincing as it scalded her mouth. Enough of Memory Lane. Time to work off her emotional energy.

She went back into the cabin, which remained utterly still. Then again, it was barely seven. The sun was just rising. Hardly an hour for Frederick to be up and about on his weekend away. Let him sleep. Sally would take a short hike and be back before eight. He'd never even know she was gone.

She shrugged into her goose-down parka, tugged on her insulated gloves, and headed out.

Frederick's black Mercedes was parked in the frozen driveway. An S500 luxury sedan. The Pierson & Company standard issue, driven by all the business's executives. Definitely frivolous, but the kind of status symbol that meant the world to Edward Pierson.

To each his own, Sally mused. In her eyes, the scenic beauty sprawled out beyond the sedan was far more valuable than any car. Nature at its miraculous best.

Glancing around, she took a few deep breaths of clean, mountain air, relishing the predawn quiet. She was tempted to pick up the Dude Ranch Trail and hike toward Lake George, but that would take too long. Instead, she'd walk into the village of Lake Luzerne. She'd stop at Rockwell Falls, which was breathtaking in its majestic plunge into the Hudson, then stroll a few local streets and head back to the cabin.

She took off briskly through the powdery snow.

Half an hour later, a car eased off the local road that led to the cabin and maneuvered into an alcove that was concealed by dried brush and icy tree branches. The hum of the motor went silent. The driver climbed out, scanning the ascending driveway and spotting the quaint little wooden cabin at the top of the hill.

Time for an unwelcome surprise.

It was just after eight when Sally returned to the cabin. She felt invigorated. Her blood was pumping. Her face was tingling. And her endorphins had kicked in, filling her with renewed energy and optimism. New chances. New beginnings. New resolve.

She paused at the front door, shaking off the excess snow from her boots and smiling as she wondered how Frederick would react when he awakened to a big, homemade breakfast.

Yanking open the door, she stepped inside—and froze.

The wrought-iron coat stand was overturned in the living room, lying on the floor and creating a barrier between the living room and the front hall. Outerwear was strewn everywhere.

Behind it, Frederick was sprawled on his back, blood oozing from his forehead.

He wasn't moving.

"Oh my God." Sally vaulted over the mess, kneeling beside Frederick and groping for his wrist so she could feel for a pulse. "Frederick! Are you—"

She never finished her sentence.

A rustle of motion sounded behind her. Before she could react, something heavy and solid struck the back of her skull.

Shards of pain shot through her head, and she crumpled to the floor.

It was the coughing that wrenched her back to consciousness. She couldn't stop choking, her entire body racked with spasms. And her eyes. They burned unbearably.

She jerked upright, fighting to curtail the choking as knives of pain sliced through her head. Her fingers found the massive bump at the same time as she realized what was going on around her.

The cabin was on fire.

Flames had already engulfed the drapes, and were licking their way around the room, swallowing up the cabin in record time.

Frederick.

Sally crawled over to him, shouting his name and shaking him as hard as she could. No response. She pressed her fingers to his wrist, then his neck, to feel for a pulse. Nothing. Frantic, she pulled apart the sides of his bathrobe, pressing her ear to his chest. Not a flutter. And the blood. There was a massive amount of it still pouring from the gaping wound on his head, pooling all around them. Beneath the wound,

Sally could see that his entire forehead was bashed in. And his eyes were wide-open and unseeing.

Dear God, he was dead.

A wooden beam crashed to the floor, sparks erupting next to Sally.

She struggled to her feet, feeling dizzy and close to fainting. There was so much smoke in the cabin now that she could hardly breathe, much less see the front door. If she didn't get out of here now, it would be too late.

She turned around and grabbed Frederick's legs, trying desperately to drag his body with her. It wouldn't budge. Her conscience warred with itself, sickened by the inhumanity of leaving him here to burn to ashes. But she had to be practical. He was gone. She had to save herself.

Pulling the collar of her parka up over her mouth, she flipped up the hood and staggered for the door. She shoved it open with her gloved fist.

A blast of cold air struck her, and she tumbled out, swaying on her feet and falling to her knees in the snow. Her head was throbbing horribly, but she didn't dare give in to the urge to collapse. She'd die. Either from hypothermia or from being devoured by the flames. Plus, she had no idea where the son of a bitch who'd done this had gone. He might be coming back to make sure his handiwork was completed.

She had to get out of here—now.

Shoving herself upright, she weaved away from the cabin.

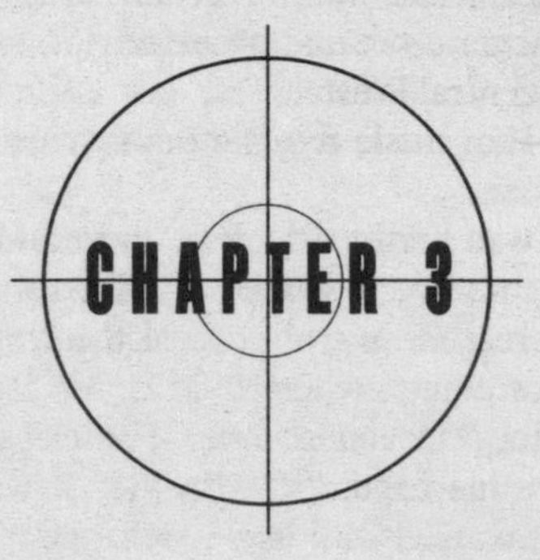

CHAPTER 3

It was rare for Devon to have a weekday morning off. When she was lucky enough to do so, she relished the event like a kid whose school was closed for a snow day. She slept late, took long baths, even went shopping or called a friend to gab over lunch.

Not today.

Today, she couldn't even relax long enough to linger over her coffee and newspaper.

She jerked awake at seven thirty, with the vague awareness that she'd been having a bad dream. She took a quick shower, yanked on some comfortable sweats, then padded downstairs to feed, pamper, and walk her various pets. That done, she headed for the kitchen, where she gulped down a cup of coffee, swallowed a bowl of cereal, then proceeded to scrub her three-level town house from top to bottom.

She'd bought the place brand spanking new last spring. It was everything she wanted—two bedrooms, two baths, and all the amenities, plus lots of grassy areas for Terror, her high-energy, several-breeds-in-one terrier, to run around in. It was also in central Westchester, just a fifteen-minute drive to the clinic. That made responding to veterinary emergencies much easier.

The house was pretty tidy, with more clutter than dirt—thanks to her three very active pets. Terror's chewed socks, Convict's chase-and-destroy squeaky mice, and Runner's food pellets were everywhere.

"You're a slob," Devon informed Runner, who was watching her restore his cage. "You may be a ferret, but you're still a man."

He returned to eating his breakfast. He didn't look the least bit offended.

"I rest my case," Devon proclaimed. She pivoted around to Terror, who was tugging at the sock she'd just picked up, trying to reclaim it. "That applies to you, too," she told him. "Considering you go to work with me every day and wear out the staff at doggie day care, you have plenty of energy left over for the limited time we spend at home to turn this place into a laundry basket."

Convict—a gray tabby whose appearance had earned her the name—rubbed up against Devon's legs, meowing apologetically and trying to make peace.

"Connie, you, on the other hand, are clearly female," Devon advised her, stooping to collect the last toy mouse and then scratch her cat's ears. "Clever and diplomatic."

Connie meowed again, this time distinctly pleased with herself.

"Don't get carried away," Devon muttered, resuming her cleaning. "I said you were smart, not neat. And the scratch marks on my kitchen cabinets have your name on them. We have to have a talk about that."

Connie rounded the corner and disappeared.

"Like I said, smart." Devon finished straightening up her pets' messes, then scoured the house until it gleamed.

It didn't help.

No matter how voraciously she cleaned, the motions of her hands couldn't keep the turmoil of her thoughts in check. She kept thinking about her mother, and the uneasy feeling she couldn't shake that something was wrong.

The telephone rang at a little before noon, and Devon plopped on the sofa, grateful for the interruption. It was probably Meredith, now a junior at SUNY Albany, who'd doubtless just opened her eyes and was eager to fill Devon in on the week's academic and social highlights.

Talking to her kid sister would be good medicine.

Devon plucked the phone off its receiver. "Hello?"

"Devon Montgomery?" an official voice asked.

A prickle of apprehension. "Yes?"

"This is Sergeant Bill Jakes. I'm with the Warren County Sheriff's Office."

Warren County? That's where Lake Luzerne was.

The prickle turned into a jab.

"Does this concern my mother?" Devon asked.

"Sally Montgomery. Yes, I'm afraid so. There's been a fire. It started sometime around eight o'clock this morning at the cabin where your mother was staying. Unfortunately, that area's fairly isolated. It took a while for someone living across the lake to spot the blaze and call it in. The air was so cold and dry that the fire spread like crazy. The cabin was already burned to the ground by the time the firefighters got to the scene. Even the surrounding woods were in flames. It took hours to bring things under control." He cleared his throat. "We're still searching the debris, but human remains have been found."

Denial screamed inside Devon's head. But she forced her thorough, analytical side to kick in. "Do you have any confirmation that any of those remains are my mother's?"

"No, ma'am." Another pause. "But, like I said, the fire destroyed everything. What's left—let's just say that it'll take dental records to make any positive IDs."

"In other words, whoever was inside that cabin was burned beyond recognition," Devon heard herself say. "In which case, we don't know who the victim or victims were. It's possible my mother wasn't even there at the time."

"Possible, but unlikely." He fell silent, clearly uncomfortable about divulging too much detail. As an officer in a small rural community, he rarely dealt with violent loss of life.

Well, he was dealing with it now.

"Go on, Sergeant," Devon pressed. "I want details. This is my mother we're talking about."

"I realize that." He blew out a breath. "Look, as I mentioned, the location of that cabin is fairly isolated. We've combed the area, by car and by foot. We even did an aerial search. No sign of your mother. We did find a set of footprints leading into the village of Lake Luzerne. We followed them. We spoke to every single shop owner and employee. The baker and the coffee-shop proprietor remembered your mother. She was in the village around seven thirty. The baker said she'd stopped in, and mentioned being on her way back to the cabin. There were footprints confirming that."

"Surely there were other sets of footprints in the village."

"Yes, ma'am, but none that led back to the cabin. Just hers."

"What about the car? Maybe she—"

"The Mercedes she came in was still parked in the driveway. There were no new tire treads. The car hadn't been moved. We traced the license plate. The vehicle belonged to Pierson & Company, which was no surprise. We'd already spoken with the owner of the cabin, who's a business associate of Frederick Pierson's. He confirmed that he'd loaned the place to Mr. Pierson and a lady friend for the weekend. So there's little doubt that he and your mother were there. I just notified the Pierson family. They gave me your mother's contact information."

Devon didn't want to talk about the Piersons. She wanted to talk about her mother. "What was the cause of the fire?"

"Undetermined. Maybe a cigarette. Maybe a candle. Maybe even a spark from the fireplace. A thorough investigation to determine the origin of the blaze is under way."

"So you're not convinced it was an accident."

"We have no reason to believe otherwise." He paused. "Do you?"

Devon gritted her teeth. "I'm not acquainted with Mr. Pierson, so I can't speak for him. But, as for my mother, she doesn't have an enemy in the world."

"And yet you're wondering if the fire was intentionally set."

"I'm a police detective's daughter, Sergeant. I ask questions."

"Fair enough. I'll try to answer them. Like I said, the cause of the fire is undetermined. The fire investigation unit is conducting its search. The coroner is on his way to the scene. Should anything suspicious be found, the investigation division of the sheriff's office will take over. Given the loss of life, the state police will probably get involved. If need be, they'll bring in specially trained dogs to sniff for accelerants. No stone will be left unturned. I hope that helps ease your mind."

"Nothing will ease my mind except hearing that my mother wasn't in that cabin."

"I'm sorry, Ms. Montgomery—pardon me, *Dr.* Montgomery," he corrected himself. "I wish that were the case. But it doesn't look good. I'd suggest you advise your family."

"I intend to." Devon was far from ready to accept what she was being told. "Sergeant Jakes . . ." She grabbed a pen and pad. "Please give me your contact information."

"Of course." He gave her his office and cell-phone numbers, and she scribbled them down.

"And your address?"

"We're on Route Nine in Lake George. But—"

"I'll let you know if I decide to drive up."

"Dr. Montgomery, I'd strongly recommend you stay put,"

the sergeant advised her. "There's nothing you can do here. Not yet. We'll give you a call as soon as we're finished at the scene and know exactly what we're dealing with."

Devon didn't respond to his not-so-subtle hint. She merely gave him her cell-phone number and her direct line at the clinic. "Please keep me posted on every detail," she requested. "I'll be in touch."

With a shaking hand, she dropped the phone in its cradle.

She sank back on the sofa, tunneling her fingers through her hair. Lane. She had to call Lane, get him on the next plane to New York. And Meredith. She'd be a wreck. She was so sensitive, and so attached to their mother. On top of that, she was in Albany, halfway to Lake Luzerne. Restraining her from rushing up there to try to find their mother was going to be a near-impossible task.

Dozens of thoughts tumbled through Devon's mind as she considered what had to be done.

But when she picked up the phone again, it wasn't either of her siblings' numbers she punched in.

Pete Montgomery, or "Monty" as he'd been dubbed since his Police Academy days, lowered his binoculars and leaned back in his well-worn Toyota Corolla. He was in a foul mood. For four days now, he'd been trailing this rich Scarsdale broad who was cheating on her millionaire husband. The case was laughably easy, since the woman had sex more often and more openly than he had lunch. The pictures he'd shot were beyond incriminating. They were his client's ticket to "bye-bye alimony."

But something was bugging Monty. He had a gut feeling that this woman and her biceps boyfriend had something else on tap, something bigger than just milking her rich husband in divorce court, then scooting off to Rio. And when he got a gut feeling, he always went with it. Because nine times out of ten, he was right. Consequently, he wasn't turning over these porn shots until he figured out what was really going on.

He flipped open his file and began scanning the seemingly insignificant aspects of his case notes.

His cell phone rang. He glanced at the caller ID, the pucker between his brows softening as he punched the send button. "Hey, sweetie. What's the matter—you're off a few hours and already going stir-crazy?"

"Where are you, Monty?" Devon asked.

He frowned, hearing the somber note in her voice. "Outside a motel in White Plains. Not far from your neck of the woods. Why?"

"I need you to drop whatever you're doing and come over. Now."

"Done." He shoved the cell phone into its hands-free cradle, then shifted the car into drive and veered out of the parking lot and onto the road. "Devon, tell me what's wrong."

"I . . ." She cleared her throat, obviously striving for control. "Let's not get into this on the phone, okay?"

"No, not okay. You're a wreck. Are you hurt? In trouble?"

"It's not me. It's . . ." Something inside her seemed to shatter. "It's Mom. She's . . . I just got a call. . . ." Devon sucked in her breath. Gone was the strong, composed woman who never exposed her vulnerability. In her place was the little girl whose tears he'd dried.

"Your mother? What about your mother?" he demanded.

"I'm not sure . . . She might be . . ." Her anguish tore at his heart. "Please, Daddy, just hurry."

Monty flinched. How long had it been since Devon had called him Daddy? And Sally—what in God's name had happened?

"I'll be there in ten."

Zooming down the ramp and onto the highway, he shot into the left lane and floored the accelerator.

* * *

Devon yanked open her town-house door the instant she heard Monty's car screech into the driveway. He was out of the driver's seat and up her walk in one minute flat, his dark gaze assessing her as he stalked inside.

"What happened to Sally?" he demanded.

Swallowing, Devon shut the front door and leaned back against it. With that simulated calm she'd learned from her father, she relayed the entire scenario to him, from Sally's trip to Lake Luzerne to the telephone call from Sergeant Jakes.

Arms folded across his chest, Monty absorbed every word, his forehead creased in concentration. Then he began pacing, his dark overcoat flapping around him, his mind clearly racing from one thought to another.

Abruptly, he came to a stop. "Human remains. That doesn't tell us much."

"It tells us someone's dead."

"Yeah, but how many someones? One? Two? And who started the fire? There's no way it was an accident. Not if Sally was there. When she's outdoors, she's attuned to every sound and smell. She'd realize the cabin was burning long before escape became impossible, and evacuate the place. The only thing that would prevent her from doing so would be if she were incapacitated."

Devon felt sick. "You think whoever set the fire trapped her inside?"

"Assuming she was in the cabin when the perp got there, he probably tried. But Sally's a fighter. And her will to live, when it comes to you kids, is strong as hell. She'd smash her way out, whether she had to shatter a window or crack someone over the head with a log." Monty scowled. "What worries me is that she'd never leave another person in there to burn to death. If this Pierson guy was with her, she'd drag him out. So why didn't she?"

"Maybe she did. Maybe the human remains the cops found belong to the arsonist."

"Nope." A hard shake of his head. "That doesn't wash. The car was Pierson's. He'd have the keys, either on him or in his possession. Probably not on him, or Sally would've found them. Anyway, if he and Sally both got out of that cabin alive, they would've jumped into that car and taken off like bats out of hell."

"Point taken. Do you think Mom was kidnapped?"

"For what? Her secondhand truck and whopping alimony checks? Pierson's the one who's a kidnapper's dream, not Sally."

"Which means Mom had to have gotten away. Unless . . ." Devon cleared her throat, forcing herself to make a verbal observation that tasted like poison on her tongue. "Monty, you're not even entertaining Sergeant Jake's theory. You and I are desperate to believe he's wrong. But what if we're deluding ourselves?"

"We're not."

"You're so sure Mom's alive?"

"Positive." Monty didn't so much as blink. "If she weren't, I'd know."

Devon choked up. Her father was a die-hard realist, one who didn't let emotion cloud facts. She could argue that in this case, he was deviating from that, letting his feelings make him irrational. The funny thing was, she didn't believe that was true. There was a connection between her parents, one that was as real as any proof.

"You're right," she agreed quietly. "You would." An overwhelming surge of comfort flowed through her. "Lane's on his way to New York," she informed her father. "I called him the minute I hung up with you."

"Where is he? In what country?"

"The U.S. He's home. He's grabbing the next flight out of LAX. He'll be here tonight."

"And Meredith?"

Devon blew out her breath. "That call's going to be harder to make."

"Sure will," Monty agreed. "She'll book herself on the next Greyhound heading for Lake George."

"Exactly. And I've got to talk her out of it." With another sigh, Devon reached for the phone.

"Tell her to hold off buying a ticket. Tell her I can get her there faster than any bus."

Devon's hand paused on the receiver. "Excuse me?"

"I'm driving up to Lake Luzerne. Now. I want to see first-hand what's going on. Jakes will talk more freely to me, cop to cop. Plus, my being there will kick their asses into high gear. There's something about the Seventy-fifth in Brooklyn that has a macho effect on cops in the boonies. Makes them want to prove they've got what it takes."

"A good old-fashioned pissing match," Devon muttered.

"Something like that. So tell Meredith to stay put. I'll pick her up in an hour and a half. She can ride up with me."

"So can I." Devon rose.

"No." Monty gave an adamant shake of his head. "You can't. Stay here. I'll call you the minute I know anything." His jaw worked. "Devon, your mother's out there somewhere. She's going to contact us eventually. You're home base. Be here to hold down the fort."

"Okay," she conceded. "I will. But, Monty . . ."

"Everything's going to be fine." He crossed over, gave Devon a quick kiss on top of her head. "You'll see."

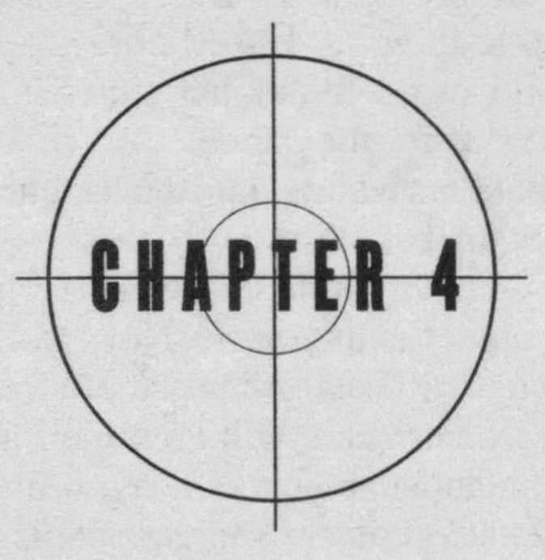

CHAPTER 4

Blake Pierson sat at the kitchen counter, his fingers steepled in front of him. He'd come up to the farm to relax, to get away from all the tension in the office. Instead, he was perched here, waiting for his grandparents to show up so they could discuss the ramifications of his uncle Frederick's death.

It was like a bizarre nightmare.

Untangling his long legs from around the stool, Blake came to his feet. He wished he could *do* something. But there was nothing to be done. Not until his grandparents arrived. Then he'd have his work cut out for him.

The immediate family had all been notified. Edward had seen to that. He and Blake's grandmother, Anne, had been the ones who'd gotten the phone call from the sheriff. That was a lousy twist of fate. Sure, Anne was one tough bird and Edward was practically made of stone. But they were nearing eighty now, and Edward's heart attack last year had thrown them for a loop—a frightening wake-up call that drove home the reality of their own mortality. Finding out that their eldest son was dead might be more than they could handle. At least if they could have heard it from a family member first, someone who could cushion the blow, it might have helped.

But that's not the way it had played out. The sheriff had done his best. Ascertaining that Frederick was a childless widower, he'd tried calling each of his brothers. He'd reached neither. Niles was in Wellington, Florida, watching his son, James, compete in the winter equestrian jumping competitions. And Gregory, Blake's father, was in Italy, vacationing with his wife at their Tuscany villa. The sheriff had even tried phoning Pierson & Company, hoping to find an available family member in the office. No luck. Having run out of options, he'd called Edward and Anne at home.

Edward had not only received the news, he'd staunchly contacted both Niles and Gregory at their respective vacation locales. Each of them was now making immediate arrangements to return home.

The only grandchild Edward had gotten in touch with was Blake.

Blake had been up here at the farm, jogging through the woods with his golden retriever pup, Chomper, when his cell phone rang. Glancing at the caller ID, he'd recognized his grandparents' home number and assumed there was some business crisis at Pierson & Company. He'd never imagined this. But he'd taken it in stride. He had to. If Frederick was dead, the fallout would be monumental.

The front door slammed and footsteps sounded—footsteps that were every bit as sure as they'd been for all thirty-five years of Blake's life.

"Blake?" Edward Pierson walked into the room. Beneath his thick shock of white hair, his features were taut, the lines on his face more pronounced. His voice was rough, just as it had been when he called from the limo to say he was on his way up to the farm. But his composure was intact. He nodded curtly when he saw his grandson. "Not exactly the relaxing weekend you planned."

"No, but under the circumstances, I'm glad I'm here."

Edward unbuttoned his coat and loosened his collar. "I had to get out of my apartment, and out of the city. I breathe better up here." He rubbed the back of his neck. "Plus, I needed someone with a level head to help make arrangements. You're it."

"I'll do whatever I can." Blake scrutinized his grandfather's hard amber gaze—the color of his eyes so unusual, so compelling, and such a mirror image of his own—wishing he were the kind of man who'd accept comfort. "Where's Grandmother?"

"She stayed home. She wasn't up for the trip. She's taking this news very hard."

Evidently, she wasn't the only one. Edward's breathing was a little too shallow to suit Blake. "Grandfather . . ."

"Don't start that invalid crap again. I had enough of it when I was in the hospital. I'm fine."

"All right." Blake bit back his concern. "Do we have another update?"

"Yes." Edward shrugged out of his camel-hair overcoat and tossed it on a stool. "Only one body's been found so far. Male. I'm having Frederick's dental records faxed up there." He averted his head, a muscle working in his jaw.

"Come into the living room and sit down." Blake put a hand on his grandfather's shoulder.

Edward stiffened. "Like I said, I'm fine. I'm not having another heart attack."

"That's a relief," Blake returned drily. "There's enough drama going on without adding a coronary to the mix. Humor me. Sit down. Take it easy. I'll get you something to drink."

"Bourbon. Straight up."

"Forget it. Ice water. On the rocks." Blake waited until

Edward relented and walked into the living room, lowering himself unsteadily onto the sofa. Then he went to the sideboard and did the honors. "What did you decide to do about James?"

"I told Niles to keep his mouth shut. The last thing I need is for James to hear news like this two days before the Wellington Classic. It'll screw up his concentration—and his performance. That Grand Prix is too damned important. He needs to win or at least to place. Not just this Sunday, but every damned Sunday between now and the U.S. Open Jumper Championship in March. He and Stolen Thunder are going to win that cup. *And* be one step closer to Olympic gold."

No surprise there, Blake thought, bringing the glass of ice water over to the couch. Edward's oldest grandchild was the apple of his eye, his one soft spot. His skill as a horseman solidified their connection. These past three years James had been showing almost exclusively on Edward's prized stallion, Stolen Thunder. The two made quite a team. James was good, but Stolen Thunder was extraordinary. The German warmblood came from a highly acclaimed, champion lineage. He was the last in his bloodline. He'd won an impressive number of four- and five-year-old championships on a national and international level before Edward bought him for a small fortune. Edward was now hell-bent on James riding Stolen Thunder to a record number of qualifying Grand Prix wins, then on to the World Games in Aachen and—their ultimate goal—to the Beijing Olympics. There was no way, after the huge financial and emotional investment he'd made, that anything was going to interfere with that.

"Besides," Edward added, taking a gulp of water, "there's not a damned thing James could do here. As it is, we're just sitting on our hands, waiting."

"True enough. And waiting's not exactly James's forte."

"No. It's not."

Blake lowered himself into the armchair across from his

grandfather. "You said the police found one body. What about Sally Montgomery?"

"She's still missing."

" 'Missing' as in they haven't found her body yet, or 'missing' as in she wasn't there when the fire started?"

"Beats the hell out of me." Edward shrugged, taking another swallow of water. "The firefighters and cops have been combing the debris for hours. There's still no sign of her. The sheriff tells me there's no way she could have been in that house and survived. That cabin went up like paper. The place was a pile of ashes in half an hour."

"Then where is she?" Blake's brows drew together. "It shouldn't take this long to search the scene. It doesn't make any sense."

"No. It doesn't." Edward rolled the glass between his palms. "But it better—soon."

Monty leaned back against his car and watched Sergeant Jakes talking on his cell. The call was from the coroner, who'd completed his initial examination. Monty had purposely walked away so Jakes could get the lowdown in private.

And so he could watch Jakes's response.

He studied the cop's expression, his gestures, his stance.

Something he was hearing wasn't sitting right. Which meant the coroner was informing him that whatever he'd found suggested this fire had not been accidental.

No surprise.

And still no Sally.

Shading his gaze, Monty glanced around, trying to figure out which path she'd taken. Had she reasoned out the safest route before she fled? Or had time been working against her? Had she been too desperate to get away from the fire—and whoever set it—to think rationally? Did the perp realize she was alive? Was he after her to keep her from identifying him? Is that why no one had heard from her? Was she hiding somewhere? Hurt? In either case, calling would be out. No way her cell phone was with her. She hated the thing, rarely carried it. And when she went out walking? Forget it. Dollars to doughnuts, her cell phone had burned to a crisp in that cabin. Which meant she was out there somewhere, alone, with only her backwoods instincts to guide her.

Still, those instincts were pretty damned amazing. They'd keep her alive and help him bring her home. They had to.

"Dad?" Meredith rolled down the car window and leaned out. "What's going on?"

Monty turned, wincing at the agonized expression on his youngest child's face. She was taking this every bit as hard as he'd feared.

"Sergeant Jakes is talking to the coroner. I'll give him a minute to process what he's being told and to share it with his team. Then I'll go over there and see what I can find out." He leaned forward, folding his arms across the open window and meeting his daughter's gaze with as much parental authority as he had the heart, or the right, to display. "I want you to stay put. No bursting onto the scene, pleading for information. It'll only piss Jakes off and make him clam up."

"I'm not a child, Dad. I'm almost twenty-one. I have no intention of freaking out in front of the cops. But I'm worried sick. I keep thinking about all the horrible things that might have happened to Mom."

"I know." Monty's fingers brushed her cheek. "I realize how scared you are. But I told you your mother is alive, and she is. I also told you I'd find her, and I will."

Meredith gave an anxious nod, swallowing back tears. She didn't look convinced. And how could Monty blame her?

"I haven't given you much reason to trust me, have I, Merry?" he murmured ruefully. "I've been out of your life more than I've been in."

"That's okay."

"No, it isn't. But it's also not the point—not now. Just know that you, Devon, and Lane mean the world to me. So does your mother. Trust me to bring her home."

With a determined sniff, Meredith brushed away her tears. "Go talk to the sergeant. I'll wait in the car. Just tell me what you learn the absolute second that you do."

It was the best he was going to get. Not a whopping show of support, but a tentative one. It would have to suffice.

Shoving his hands in the pockets of his parka, Monty strolled back over to the debris that had been the cabin. Damn, it was cold. Even with gloves and a down jacket, he was freezing. He prayed Sally had been wearing layers—warm ones.

He reached the spot where Jakes and his team were standing. "So, what light did the coroner shed on all this?"

The sergeant's lips tightened as he turned to Monty. "His preliminary exam revealed no soot particles in the victim's nostrils."

"In other words, he was dead before the fire started."

"We'll need an autopsy to confirm it, but, yeah, it looks that way. He was also the only body on the scene—or anywhere else in the vicinity. Which means things don't look too good for your ex-wife."

"She's alive. What could look better?"

"We don't know she's alive. But even if she is, things look pretty bleak."

"Why?" Monty's question was deliberately vague and provoking. He wasn't getting the full story. And he wanted it.

"You know damned well why," Jakes shot back. "The pile of ashes we're standing on is now officially a crime scene."

"Maybe Pierson was smoking a cigarette, had a massive coronary, and croaked, setting the cabin up in flames while Sally was out."

"Yeah, and maybe a frog will jump out of my left nostril. Cut the crap, Montgomery."

"If you tell me what else the coroner said, I will."

Jakes blinked, clearly surprised that Monty had seen through him. "Fine. The victim had cranial damage. Someone bashed the front of his head in before burning down the cabin. We're talking about murder and arson. Your ex-wife's missing. So she's either a criminal, a kidnapping victim, or dead."

Monty's jaw tightened. "Your first idea's complete bullshit. Sally wouldn't hurt a fly. Your second's a reach, since neither Sally nor anyone in her family has anything worth a damn; certainly not enough to cough up ransom money. As for dead—I don't buy it. If the perp was going to kill her, he'd do it here. He'd already knocked off Pierson. One body, two—what's the difference? It's the perfect spot for a murder; virtually deserted. So why would he risk transporting Sally somewhere else, where he might be seen? It's none of the above. Running away is more like it."

"Or dropping out of sight."

"Could be. But not for the reasons you're insinuating. Look, Jakes, let's put aside my personal feelings. What possible motive could Sally have for wanting Pierson dead?"

"Jealousy? Greed? I haven't checked out her history with Pierson. But I will."

"And if she was jealous or greedy and wanted him dead, she'd drive all the way up to Lake Luzerne just to bash in his head and burn down his cabin, letting everyone know they were alone up here so she'd be the prime suspect? That's a pretty far-fetched theory. Try this one instead. Frederick Pierson's a hotshot, the CEO of a major restaurant and food services company. That means he has enemies, lots of them. People he screwed over who want a piece of him. Someone came up here and got it. Sally was just in the wrong place at the wrong time."

"If that's the case, where is she? Why hasn't she contacted her family?"

Monty's gut twisted. "She's either hurt or hiding. Maybe the perp's after her. Maybe she can identify him."

"Maybe. Maybe not. That's what investigations are for."

"No arguments there." Monty forced himself to back off. He'd gotten as far as he was going to. If he wanted to stay on the inside of this investigation, he'd better keep things between him and the sheriff's office copacetic. "Do what you have to. But I want to be kept up to date."

"That goes both ways."

"Meaning?"

"Meaning that if Ms. Montgomery happens to call any of her family members, I want to be told."

"Fair enough."

Jakes yanked out a pad and pen. "I've got your daughter Devon's contact information. I'll need the same for your other kids. Also for any other friends and relatives."

"The kids are no problem." Monty gave Jakes what he needed. "But for ease of purpose, try Devon or me first. I'm bringing Meredith to her sister's place. Lane's flying in tonight, and I'm sure Devon will put him up, too."

"Fine. Friends?"

Monty blew out his breath. "Sally and I have been divorced for fifteen years. The kids would be more current on her friends. I can give you the name and phone number of the nursery school she works for. As for relatives, she's got a sister, Carol. Divorced. Fifty-one. Lives abroad, in Rome. She's bilingual, and works for some Italian exporting company. Also, Sally's parents. They live in Orange County. But go easy on them. They're in their late seventies, and this is their daughter. They don't know a thing about what's happened. I'd appreciate if you'd give me a chance to break the news to them before you drive down there and start asking questions."

Jakes nodded, glancing over at Monty's car. "I'd like to speak to your daughter before you leave."

Monty's protective-father instinct roared to life, and he had to bite back the urge to refuse. But that would be stupid. Jakes's request was a mere formality. He was going to question Meredith with or without Monty's permission. Plus, as Meredith had pointed out a few minutes ago, she was an adult now. Monty couldn't shield her from the world. On top of which, she'd want to help.

"Yeah, okay," he agreed tersely, jerking his head in the direction of the car. "Talk in there. It's warm. Meredith and I will hit the road when you're through."

None of the Montgomerys got much sleep that night.

Lane's plane landed at JFK around nine. He grabbed a taxi and headed straight for Devon's. Meredith and Monty were already there. It was a bittersweet reunion, and a toss-up as to who was the biggest emotional wreck.

Both Devon's siblings bunked at her place. They urged their father to join them, but somehow Monty wanted to be alone. So he drove the thirty-five minutes to Queens, to the little house where he and Sally had been so happy—and so unhappy—and plopped on the couch, throwing an arm across his eyes. He didn't bother turning on a light or changing his clothes. He just lay there, wide awake, trying to fit together some pieces.

It was a little after 7 A.M. when his cell phone rang. Not his regular cell phone, but his prepaid TracPhone—the "Bat Phone," as the kids called it, because it was as close to a hotline between select callers and Monty as you could get. It was damned near untraceable. Monty had paid cash for it in a drugstore, and was careful to vary the 7-Elevens he went to to buy additional minutes, also paid for in cash. There was virtually no paper trail leading to him. And very few people who had the number.

He jumped up and grabbed the phone, punching it on. "Montgomery."

"Pete—it's me."

Sally.

Her voice was raspy and weak, but it was the most wonderful sound Monty had every heard.

A flood of relief surged through him. "Thank God. Where are you? Are you okay?"

"I guess so." She coughed. "I'm shaky, dizzy, and exhausted. But I'm alive. I shouldn't be calling you, but I didn't know where else to turn. Is this line still . . . okay?"

"Yeah. And you sure as hell *should* be calling me. This way your call can't be traced. Besides, no one can do a better job of keeping you safe."

She didn't negate his words. "So you know what happened?"

"That Pierson's dead and the cabin was torched? Yeah, I know."

A shaky sigh. "I'm in a phone booth, using a calling card. It's only got fifteen minutes on it."

"Give me the number." Monty grabbed a scrap of paper and a pen. He listened, and scribbled. Judging from the area code, she was somewhere in Vermont. Good. That would make things nice and easy for the plan he had in mind. "Hang up. I'll call you back," he instructed.

He disconnected the call and punched up the number she'd given him.

"Pete?" she asked tentatively when she picked up.

"It's me. Before we get into this, how bad are you hurt and where?"

"My head. It's pounding like a drum. I'm dizzy, and I've got a huge bump. But my vision's okay, so if I've got a concussion, it's a mild one. Other than that, it's just aches, pains, and some tightness in my chest from the smoke. I'll heal."

"Thanks for the diagnosis. But I'd prefer getting it from a doctor. I'll make arrangements to have you checked out later today. Now tell me what happened."

Slowly, and with obvious physical discomfort, Sally relayed the events of the previous morning. "Once I got out of the cabin, I panicked," she concluded. "I didn't know if the killer was still around, or if he'd seen I was alive. I was terrified he'd come after me. So I took off. I cut across to Glens Falls. More people. More traffic. Less chance of being noticed. I bought a bus ticket at the diner, and took the two thirty Greyhound. I didn't get in till almost eleven."

"Into where?"

"Middlebury. I figured a college campus would be about the best setting I could pick to be invisible in."

"Smart girl. College kids don't notice anything on a Friday night. They're too drunk. And Saturday morning at seven—they're dead to the world."

"Exactly. I checked into the Marriott Courtyard. I was lucky they had a vacancy during ski season. I paid cash. I don't remember much of the night; I must have passed out. I woke up a little while ago, stopped off to buy this phone card, and came straight here." Her voice broke. "Pete, I'm scared."

"Don't be. I'll fix this."

"Did the police find the killer? Do they know who he is, or why he killed Frederick?"

"No. Not yet."

Sally picked up on the gruff censure in Monty's tone. "Do the police think *I* did it?"

"They don't know what to think. But they are looking for you—either as the perp or as a witness. I gave them my take on things. No shocker that I was right. But it's not the cops I'm worried about. It's the killer. Like you said, he's still out there. By now, he knows he screwed up and you're alive. Which means you're still a target. There's no way you can come forward, not without putting yourself in danger. Until he's found, we've got to keep you stashed away."

"Stashed away—where?"

Monty leaned forward, gripping the phone more tightly. "Remember the plan you and I talked about years ago when I was working undercover?"

A heartbeat of silence. "You mean about how the kids and I could drop out of sight if your cover was blown?"

"That's the one."

"You still have those contacts?"

"One of them's right in your backyard. I'll get ahold of him. We'll work out a time frame and I'll call you back. Give me a half hour to make the arrangements. I'll call you at the hotel. What room are you in?"

"Three forty-two."

"Okay, go back and take a hot shower. Have you eaten?"

"Uh-uh. Last night I was too out of it, and today I'm down to a few dollars."

"Spend them. Buy coffee and a muffin. That'll tide you over. You'll get everything you need, including a hot meal, soon. Okay?"

"Okay." Sally's voice was getting weaker. "Pete?"

"Enough, Sal. You sound like you're going to collapse."

She ignored his reprimand. "The kids—they're all right?"

"They will be now. They're all at Devon's. I'll drive over there as soon as I've got things set. I'll also call your folks. Now haul your ass back to that hotel. I'll be in touch in a little while."

"Thank you, Pete," she managed before hanging up.

Sally was wrapped in a bath towel, sipping a cup of hotel-room-brewed coffee when the phone on the nightstand rang.

"Yes?" she answered cautiously.

"It's me." Monty didn't mince words. "Here's the scoop. I called my contact. Rod Garner. He's a good guy and a hell of a cop. We go back twenty-five years. He retired from the Seventy-fifth a couple of years before I did, and moved to Williamstown, Mass. He's got a wife, plus two married kids, and a slew of grandkids in the area. You'll be staying with him and his wife, Molly, for as long as necessary. No one will know where you are. Rod's got ten or fifteen acres, so you don't have to worry about being spotted. Just hang close to the house and you'll be fine."

"Wait," Sally interrupted. "What about his wife? Won't she mind?"

"Mind? She'll be thrilled. Rod's like an old warhorse. Molly's heard his cop stories so many times, they put her to sleep. Besides, you two are a lot alike. She loves the great outdoors. And she's crazy about kids, especially her grandchildren. They're her life. When she finds out you teach nursery school, she'll go nuts. Anyway, she and Rod are the only ones who'll know the truth about why you're there. If the kids visit, Rod will tell them you're an old friend who's going through a rough time and needs a place to sort things out."

"But—"

"No buts. Rod's already on his way to Middlebury. It'll take him a little over two hours to reach you. So get some rest. He'll give you a call when he's fifteen minutes away. At that point, you'll head down to the lobby, turn in your key, and meet him at the back entrance. He drives a blue Ford Explorer. Any questions?"

"What about the police? You said they're looking for me."

"Let 'em look. I'll give Sergeant Jakes a call, tell him I heard from you, and explain what really went down at that cabin. Then I'll tell him you're terrified the killer's after you, and that you hung up without telling me where you were or where you were headed."

"Isn't that aiding and abetting, or obstruction of justice, or something like that?"

"Nope. Just a small twist of the truth. And only about your whereabouts. The rest is fact." Monty gave a wicked chuckle, and Sally could actually visualize that smug I-beat-the-system gleam in his eyes. "That's the great part about being a PI and not a cop. You can bend the rules a little."

"As if you didn't before," she commented drily.

"Point taken. Okay then, I can bend them even more. So, instead of wasting time following protocol and filling out bullshit reports, I can investigate on my own and track down the scumbag who smashed in Frederick Pierson's skull and nearly incinerated you."

Like an unwelcome blast from the past, Sally felt that grinding twist in her gut. "In other words, once you figure out who he is, you're going after him."

"Did you doubt it?"

"No. Are you going to elicit the help of the Warren County sheriff, or is that a stupid question?"

"It's a stupid question. I work better and faster on my own. Now go take it easy. Later, I'll want to ask you some questions about what you might and might not know about Frederick Pierson."

"Speaking of that, there's something you should know right away. It may mean nothing. On the other hand, it bugged me enough to stick in my mind. I assumed I was overreacting—until Frederick was murdered."

"Go on."

"I overheard an argument between Frederick and his father earlier this week. Frederick wanted to fire someone at his company. Edward was dead set against it. Something about a criminal offense that could jeopardize the company. At least that's what Frederick claimed. Edward obviously didn't agree. He vetoed Frederick's decision to let this person go."

"Interesting." Monty digested Sally's information. "So it could be a crooked employee. Or maybe just a disgruntled one who knew Frederick didn't trust him. As the ball-breaking CEO of the company, I'm sure he had lots of pissed-off employees. We'll just have to figure out which of them, if any, would go so far as to kill him."

"I could try to write down the exact words they—"

"Not now," Monty interrupted in that no-nonsense detective voice. "Now is about getting you settled in and checked out by a doctor. Call me when you're safely in Rod's truck."

"On the Bat Phone?" Sally asked, her lips curving slightly.

"Yeah." There was a trace of rough nostalgia in his tone. "On the Bat Phone. I'll bring it with me to Devon's. That way, you can talk to the kids when you get to Williamstown."

A pause. "Pete . . . whatever you do, be careful."

"Never mind me. *You* be careful. No hiking into town or sneaking off to hit the slopes. Be a nice, New England homebody. In the meantime, I'll start digging around to see who hated Frederick Pierson and why."

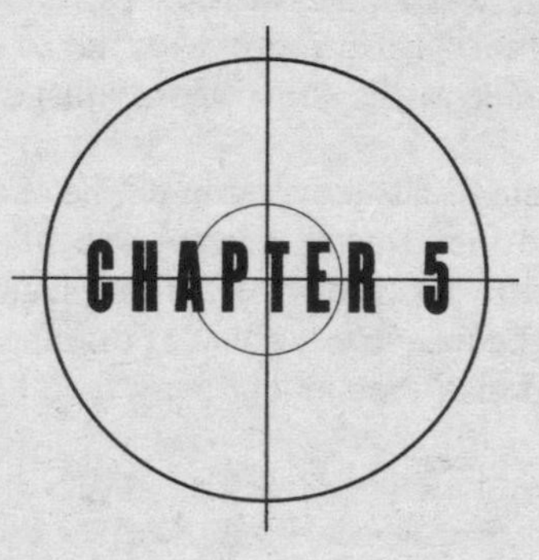

The sun was poised on the horizon, sinking slowly downward, when Edward Pierson finished his phone call and slammed down the phone in the farm's walnut-pillared living room.

"The cops still haven't found Sally Montgomery," he announced, turning to Blake. "But evidently, she's alive and hiding."

Blake extricated the shredded hem of his jeans from between Chomper's teeth and frowned. "What do you mean 'hiding'?"

"I mean she called her ex-husband. Didn't want her family to think she was dead. She got out of the cabin before the fire destroyed the place."

"Why didn't she take Frederick with her?"

"Because he was already dead." Edward dragged an arm across his forehead. Looking ill, he explained the circumstances to Blake. "She's afraid that whoever killed Frederick and whacked her on the head will be looking for her to finish what he started. So she's not telling anyone where she is."

"Did she see the guy? Is she willing to give a description?"

"I don't know." Edward filled his water glass and gulped at it, clearly wishing it were bourbon. "The cops won't give me any details. All the sheriff keeps saying is: 'It's an ongoing investigation.' Which does me a hell of a lot of good." He set down the glass with a thud.

Blake shooed Chomper away again, then gave up, letting the puppy tug at his jeans and chew the leg bottom into a soggy wad. "Grandfather, ease up. You've been pushing yourself all day. Grandmother would have your head, and so would the doctors. Let the police do their job. Concentrate on something else—like how strong James's showing will be in tomorrow's Grand Prix."

"Right." Edward's tension eased slightly. "According to our trainer, he's more than ready. His form's great and he's been clearing every jump." The scowl returned. "Of course, all that could go down the tubes before next Sunday's event. He'll have flown home to cope with a funeral and the fallout that goes along with losing not just his uncle, but the head of his branch of our company. That's bound to screw him up. You reported to Frederick, too. You and I have got to pick up the slack so James doesn't have to, and so the food-services division doesn't suffer. As it is, the staff will be in chaos, and our suppliers and accounts will be nervous as hell. It's going to be ugly." A sidelong glare at Blake. "By the way, cut out the placating, diversionary crap. It's revoltingly obvious."

"I wasn't going for subtle. And I'm not placating you. I'm helping get you through this ordeal. I'm well aware you'll fight me every step of the way. Just as you're aware that I'll fight back."

"Yes," Edward muttered, shaking his head. "Somewhere along the line I screwed up with you and James. You're not afraid of me like you should be. Everyone else in the family is."

"Except Grandmother," Blake reminded him. "*Fear's* not in her vocabulary. As for James and me, it's not a matter of your screwing up. It's a matter of your nurturing what we represent: your legacies. James is fulfilling one—your life's passion—and I'm fulfilling the other—your life's work. He inherited your hunger for Olympic gold, and I inherited your business creativity and the balls to take Pierson & Company where it needs to go."

A simple enough explanation, Blake mused. With an ocean of details omitted. It was true that neither he nor James was afraid of their grandfather. But that was for entirely different reasons. And, yes, they each represented a different priority in Edward's life. But that's where the similarities ended.

"If you're saying I'm softer on the two of you because of your likenesses to me, that's bullshit, at least where you're concerned," Edward replied, as if reading Blake's mind. "James is one story. But I'm harder on you than I am on any of your cousins, your uncles, and, certainly, your father. He's a lost cause."

Blake shrugged. "Dad's just not driven."

"Oh, he's driven all right. To sail, play golf, take vacations. You'd never know he's Pierson & Company's VP of marketing. He's in the office about three days a month. The rest of the time he and your mother are gallivanting around the world."

"He manages his end of the business."

"No, *you* manage his end of the business." Edward's gaze clouded. "But that's about to change. Everything's about to change, with Frederick gone."

"I realize that." Blake blew out his breath. "Let's take this one step at a time. The coroner has the dental records. Soon they'll make a positive ID. After that, we'll call James—*before* the news leaks out and he catches sight of a newspaper. The corporate jet will be there waiting. It's on standby, ready to fly him home, and back to Wellington after the funeral. Niles and Lynn are already back from Florida, and Mom and Dad will be landing tonight. Everyone else is home, ready to do whatever's necessary. As for the other company VPs, I'll call them after we've told James. We'll call an emergency management committee meeting for later this week, once the funeral's behind us."

Edward nodded. "Good." He rubbed his chin thoughtfully, looking peaked but, at the same time, as if his wheels were spinning a mile a minute.

"As for the cops, maybe they'll be more forthcoming once they have official confirmation of Frederick's death," Blake suggested.

"I wouldn't hold my breath." A pause. "Sally Montgomery's ex is a retired cop."

Now, *that* announcement came out of left field. "So?"

"So he was with the NYPD. Worked a tough area in Brooklyn. Retired from the force a couple of years ago. Now he's got his own PI business. He's got quite a client list, from what I gather."

"And you know this how?"

"I made a few phone calls this afternoon, too—after I found out this Pete Montgomery had driven up to Lake Luzerne to consult with the sheriff."

"Next question—why is this important?"

"Because he's got an inside track to the cops and his ex-wife. Which means he might know more than he's saying. Also, because he sounds like a good guy to have in our corner."

Blake's eyes narrowed. "You're going to pump him for information?"

"No." Edward gripped his knees, the faraway look in his eyes vanishing. "I'm going to hire him."

Devon finished the last of the dinner dishes while Terror finished the last of the table scraps.

"Starting tomorrow, you're going to have to share that food stash," Devon informed him.

Terror's head came up, and he blinked, clearly irked by the announcement.

"Relax," Devon said with a chuckle. "You won't mind your dinner partner. It's your pal Scamp. He's coming to stay with us, just until his mom gets home. Imagine the possibilities. By day, you can romp around together and drive everyone at doggie day care nuts. And by night, you can team up and destroy this place, leaving a trail of laundry in your wake. It's a veritable dream come true."

Terror barked his agreement. Then, prompted by the word *laundry,* he tore off in search of a discarded sock.

He'd have plenty of those to choose from, Devon mused. Especially now, with Lane and Meredith both staying over—and not just for a day or two, but for a week, maybe longer, depending on how quickly the Pierson case was solved. Lane had already made his requisite phone calls and rearranged his work schedule. And Meredith had e-mailed her professors, explaining the situation and asking if she could deliver her homework assignments electronically.

The extended-stay scenario was imperative, partly because they all needed to be together for emotional support, and partly to keep up appearances. Their family had to come off as worried sick, glued to the phone for any word from the police. Supposedly, they had no idea where Sally was and if they would ever see her again. As a result, they'd be too paralyzed to return to their day-to-day lives.

Devon had done her part by calling Dr. Joel Sedwell, the founder and senior partner of Creature Comforts & Clinic, and arranged for superflexible hours until this family crisis was over. And Monty had put his entire caseload on the back burner.

In private, the Montgomerys were relieved as hell. They'd all spoken to Sally, heard her voice, and knew she was okay. Meredith had called three times before she was convinced her mother was safe, settled in at the Garners' house, and on the mend. Rod had run Sally over to a local doctor, who'd treated her for a minor concussion and an irritated trachea. She was now well fed, tucked in a warm feather bed, and fast asleep.

After that, Monty had reviewed the drill with his kids. They were sworn to secrecy. If anyone asked, they had no idea where Sally was. If pressed, they'd parrot the story Monty had given the Warren County Sheriff's Office. As for talking to Sally, they'd do that only at designated times, and only on the Bat Phone.

But thank God she was all right.

Devon had promised Sally she'd take care of Scamp and make periodic drives up to the house to check on the horses, who were being fed and exercised by one of the Piersons' grooms. That promise was hardly a sacrifice. Not only did it put Sally's mind at ease, but Devon was crazy about Scamp and the house she'd spent her teens in. This gave her an excuse to enjoy both.

Having spoken to her mother, Devon had felt lighthearted enough to cook—a desire that didn't come along too often. Monty stayed for dinner, after which he made a slew of phone calls, which resulted in streams of incoming pages on Devon's fax machine, all of which he was now poring over. Lane took the opportunity to drag Meredith to a movie—a chick flick, no less—to help her relax. He looked pained at the prospect, but his concern for his baby sister won out. He did ask Devon to join them, but she refused—not because she didn't want to go, but because something told her she should stay here with Monty.

Tossing down the dish towel, she wandered into the living room, sinking down on the sofa next to her father and tucking her legs beneath her. "What did you find out?" she asked, peering over his shoulder.

"That the Pierson empire is a golden octopus with tentacles all over the place." Monty pointed at the page he was reading. "Look at this rundown on their history. Edward Pierson started the company fifty years ago as a small paper-goods distributor to the food industry. It grew like crazy, expanding into food services and catering. Evidently, Pierson pulled the right strings, because all of a sudden, his little company dominated the food-services business at major sporting arenas all across the country."

Pulled the right strings. Devon had heard her father use that expression often enough to know what it meant. "You think he bribed politicians, threatened competitors—that kind of thing?"

"Big-time. The man is smart, unscrupulous, and a corporate bulldozer. He wasn't happy standing still, even after locking up the sports venues. He wanted more than just a food-services division—something more refined. So he launched a fine dining division—those swanky Grand Prix restaurants he owns. The first one opened in Palm Beach twenty-five years ago. It's still thriving. Only now it has nineteen siblings, all located near the major equestrian competition sites: Lexington, Peapack-Gladstone, Bridgehampton, Fair Oaks, Napa Valley—you get the drift."

"Wow. That's quite an empire. Edward Pierson must be in his glory, especially since overseeing the fine-dining division means he can indulge his passion for showing horses." Devon leaned closer, reading the corporate summary. "What's this about a family-dining division?"

"That's his newest restaurant venture: Chomping at the Bit."

Devon grinned. "Cute name."

"Yeah, and another gold mine in the making. It's going to have the same horse theme as the Grand Prix restaurants, but aimed at a whole different crowd."

"Families."

"Yup. Lower prices, casual decor, kid-friendly atmosphere. The flagship restaurant is set to open this spring a block away from Yonkers Raceway."

"Yonkers Raceway—that's a far cry from Palm Beach. Then again, it's a shrewd choice. Busy area, lots of horse lovers, adjacent to a big shopping center. It'll bring in families by the droves." A pensive frown formed between Devon's brows. "Edward Pierson's almost eighty years old. Vital or not, he can only do so much. And with Frederick gone, who else is running all this?"

"Which Pierson isn't? Edward's got the whole family managing the company. Frederick ran the food services division. Niles, Edward's second son, heads up the fine dining division. And Edward's grandson, Blake, is in charge of the family dining division. It looks like Chomping at the Bit was his baby. Blake's father, Gregory, is Edward's youngest son. He's the VP of marketing. There's another grandson, James—he's Niles's kid. He's VP of sales and a champion show jumper. . . ." Monty shoved the paper aside. "I'm getting a headache."

"And I'm getting the idea." Devon leaned back against the sofa cushion. "So Edward Pierson's combined all his passions into one—family, horses, money, and notoriety. Pretty impressive." A questioning look. "All the company execs are family?"

"Looks that way. All except their attorney, Louise Chambers, and their senior VP of sales, Philip Rhodes. Oh, and their CFO, Roger Wallace, but he doesn't count as nonfamily. He's a grandson-in-law, married to Niles's daughter, Tiffany. She's VP of business development, by the way. And Blake's sister, Cassidy, is VP of human resources. Gee, I wonder how many more Piersons are out there who never made it into this report."

"Interesting." Devon ran a hand through her hair, sorting out her thoughts. "What you just described leaves lots of room for resentment. Family members resenting other family members for having more power. Nonfamily members resenting family members for having all the power to begin with. Employees who feel they'll never get ahead, that nepotism rules the day. I wonder what kind of boss Frederick Pierson was?"

"Good question."

"What about Edward's grandchildren? Don't any of them belong to Frederick?"

"Nope. Frederick was a childless widower. His wife, Emily, died of a heart attack two years ago."

"Hmm." Devon pursed her lips. "I'd love to see Edward's will. I wonder who's next in line to inherit and/or run the Pierson empire. And how the family fortune is allocated."

"More good questions. As a matter of fact, you're following my train of thought to a T." Monty shot his daughter a look. "I told you you have the mind of a cop. Cut back on your animal hours and go into business with me."

Devon rolled her eyes. "We've been through this a thousand times, Monty. I'm not cut out to be a cop. I don't have a tough enough skin. Besides, I love what I do."

"My buddies at the ASPCA's Humane Law Enforcement Department—the ones who ran those off-site training classes you took—said you were the sharpest one in the bunch. A chip off the old block. And, no, they weren't blowing sunshine up my ass. They meant it. No one believed you were in vet school going for a DVM. They thought you were in the Police Academy, joining the force."

"It was one of the best summers of my life. But that's because of the animals. And because I was spending so much time with you."

"What time? I was working a case."

"Maybe. But you showed up anyway. A couple of times each day. Kind of like you were checking up on me to make sure I was performing up to snuff. Remember?"

"Yeah. I remember."

"The pride on your face meant more to me than I can say."

Monty blew out his breath. "Devon, your instincts are dead-on. Your mind's like a steel trap. Think about how many pet owners you've helped, not in the clinic, but in the field. You've managed to locate dozens of missing animals.

Pets who were lost for weeks and no one could find—not even with flyers plastered everywhere and big rewards offered."

"Just call me Ace Ventura." Devon squeezed Monty's arm. "Seriously, that's not because I've got a cop's mind. It's because I understand animals. I know their habits. I know their minds. And I know what questions to ask to zero in on their idiosyncrasies. Then I look for clues. And, hopefully, I turn up something."

"What the hell do you think a cop does?"

Devon sighed. "Monty, you know how much I love and respect you, and what you do. And, yes, every once in a while I'd love to play Nancy Drew. But there's no brutality in her cases—not like the kind you deal with."

"Things are different than they were before. I'm a PI now. Not every case I take on has—"

He was interrupted by the ringing of his cell phone.

"It's my office line," he observed. "I call-forwarded everything to my cell while I was here." He glanced down at the caller ID and frowned. "Private. Well, that really narrows down the prospects." He punched the phone on. "Montgomery."

His brows lifted slightly, and he glanced over at Devon. "Yes, Mr. Pierson, I know who you are. My condolences on the loss of your son."

Edward Pierson? Now, *that* was a surprise.

Devon leaned forward to listen.

"Care to tell me why? I'm sure the sheriff gave you the exact same story he gave me." Monty paused. "Yes, I heard from my ex-wife. She's terrified and on the run. Whoever killed your son tried to kill her, too. She's afraid he'll try again. The only reason she contacted me is so I could bring the cops up to speed on what actually happened in that cabin, and so I could let our children know she was alive. She hung up without saying where she was or where she was going. Nope, she never saw the guy. So there's not a lot more I can tell you. Certainly not enough to warrant your sending down a limo to drive me up to your farm for a meeting."

Another pause, as Monty absorbed whatever Edward was saying. "That's very flattering, and very intriguing. But I can't imagine where you're going with this. Care to elaborate? Right. In person. Okay, I'll bite. Sure, late afternoon's fine. Four o'clock works. My office is in Little Neck—a semiattached house. One side's my home, the other's my office." Abruptly, Monty broke off, and he snapped around to face Devon.

Uh-oh, Devon thought, recognizing only too well that gleam in her father's eyes. He had a plan. And whatever it was, she wasn't going to like it.

Sure enough, Monty gave a hard shake of his head, as if negating the last part of what he'd just said. "I have a better idea, Mr. Pierson. I want to check in on my kids anyway, make sure they're holding up. They're in bad shape, as you can imagine. They're all staying at my daughter Devon's place. It's in northern White Plains. That's a good half hour closer to Millbrook than Queens is. It'll take just an hour plus to get to you. Devon's driving up to Sally's place tomorrow anyway. She wants to check on the house and the animals. I'll just grab a ride. I'm sure she could use the company." He ignored his daughter's glare. "I should be there around six. We'll continue this discussion then."

He punched *end* and turned to Devon. "Well, what do you know. Edward Pierson wants to hire me. He seems to think I can do a better job of finding whoever killed his son than the Warren County sheriff can."

"Yeah, what do you know." Devon folded her arms across her breasts. "And *you* seem to think I'm partnering up with you."

"You are."

"No, Monty, I'm not."

His hands balled into fists, made deep indentations in the sofa. "Devon, this time's different. It's your mother's life at stake."

"Dammit, Monty, that's emotional blackmail."

"Is it working?"

"You know it is. You know I'd do anything for Mom. But this is a mistake. I don't have your nerves of steel or your ability to stay objective. I'm emotionally involved. That's a detriment, not an asset. How can I possibly help you?"

"I'm not sure. But my gut tells me you can."

"How?" Devon could feel her resolve weaken.

Worse, so could Monty. He jumped all over her ambivalence, firing out suggestions as if he'd been cogitating for days, rather than devising them on the fly. "The groom who's been caring for Sally's horses. Talk to him. Maybe he can give you a feel for the players. The grandchildren. Pierson just mentioned that they're all flying in or driving up tomorrow. They're congregating at the farm to make funeral arrangements—and probably to avoid the press. They're all around your age or a little older. Strike up conversations. See what dirt you can dig up."

"In other words, be the mole," Devon responded, summing up Monty's thought process. "The innocuous veterinarian who blends in with the crowd and empathizes with their loss. My mother was seeing their uncle. She was nearly killed at his murder scene. That's our common ground."

"And your fear that Sally's still in danger—that's your jumping-off point. From there on, the conversation will take on a life of its own."

"So, while you're closeted in some private office with the family patriarch, I'll be hanging out with the yuppies, getting to know them." Devon gave a tentative nod. "It could work."

"It *will* work."

"I'll need to look at that report of yours," Devon heard herself say, reaching for the pages. "Just so I can remember which Pierson is which."

"Here." Monty thrust them in her hand. "The more I think about that phone call, the more I know Edward Pierson's got something up his sleeve. Think about it. He's about to get official confirmation that his son's dead. His entire family is converging under the worst of circumstances. That means emotional meltdown and, in this case, business upheaval. Tomorrow is going to be the day from hell. So why is Edward calling me tonight, insisting we meet ASAP? Why not wait until the storm has passed?"

Devon was used to going through these mental exercises with Monty. "Because time is of the essence. Edward's son was murdered. He's grieving, angry, and impatient. He's a man who's used to getting what he wants when he wants it. He's determined to find Frederick's killer—yesterday, if not sooner. He's banking on the fact that you can do that for him. Maybe he's also hoping to capitalize on your personal relationship with Mom and your brotherhood with the cops."

"Both, I'm sure. But there's more to it. He's done his homework, just like I have. He knows I'm good, and he's also hoping I have inside information. But he's got to know I can't be bought."

"He's counting on having superior methods of persuasion, like a six-figure check. Or maybe he's counting on outsmarting you."

"Maybe. Or maybe he likes the fact that I won't sell out. Maybe he figures it'll translate into my keeping my mouth shut with regard to whatever I turn up in this investigation. A loyal-at-all-costs Sam Spade."

"Which brings us back to the fact that he has an agenda."

"Yup. Especially when you add to the mix the argument your mother overheard earlier this week between him and Frederick."

"What argument?" Devon's head snapped up. "You didn't mention any argument."

"I was about to when my cell phone rang." Monty filled Devon in on what Sally had told him.

"Whew." Devon blew out her breath. "A criminal offense that could jeopardize the company. That's pretty heavy stuff. I wonder who's guilty. *And* why Edward didn't view him that way. Maybe Frederick's murder changed his mind."

"And opened his eyes—enough to realize he had to protect what was his. The question is, what is he protecting—a member of his family or the survival of his empire?"

"Or both," Devon added. "He said nothing to give you any indication?"

"Nope. He wants to discuss it in person. But he definitely wants to keep our meeting under wraps. I'm being escorted to his office through the back entrance. He was blunt about the fact that he doesn't want to risk any family member seeing me, or knowing I'm being hired."

"Which could mean one of them is under suspicion." Devon shrugged. "Or just that he's trying to spare them further upset."

"I opt for the first choice. Incidentally, Edward also specified that it's crucial he gets all relevant information *first*—another reason I'm his PI of choice. He went out of his way to stress my success ratio and fast turnaround time."

"First," Devon repeated. "As in before the cops?"

"Sure sounded that way."

"That would certainly support the entirety of your theory, including the issue of loyalty."

"Uh-huh. I could find the killer and help Edward Pierson keep a lid on a nasty Pandora's box he doesn't want opened."

"You'd never withhold evidence."

"He doesn't know that. I've got a reputation for bending the rules. He's counting on my willingness to do that, if not for his family, then for mine. And he's not wrong. I've already bent them. I'd do more than that if it meant keeping my family safe."

"Your family. In this case, that's Mom," Devon clarified softly.

"Yeah. It is." Monty paused, his jaw working. "Look, Devon," he blurted out. "Your sister's not here now, so I'm going to be blunt. I'm worried as hell about your mother."

"Why? Is there something I don't know?"

"You know everything—including your mother. How long do you think she's going to stay in hiding—cut off from her kids, her home, her life? A week? Two? Yeah, I've made sure she's safe. But that's a double-edged sword. Soon her fear will start to subside. She'll want to come home. There's a killer out there—one who might still be looking for her. He needs to be behind bars before Sally's restlessness gets the best of her and puts her directly in the line of fire."

"You're right." Devon dragged both hands through her hair. "I was so relieved when I heard Mom's voice, realized she was really okay, that I pushed the rest out of my mind. But Williamstown's just a Band-Aid. The wound's still there. And you're the only one who can make it go away fast enough to keep Mom safe. This meeting with Edward Pierson could be a huge step in that direction. It'll get you in the door."

"Get *us* in the door," Monty corrected. "Me in the back, and you in the front."

"How will I get in the front . . . ?"

"By introducing yourself as Sally's daughter. By thinking of yourself as Sally's daughter. Drive that bond home, and distance yourself from me. Your mother raised you. You and I are on civil enough terms for you to give me a ride up to the Pierson farm. We talk occasionally, see each other less. I care a lot. You harbor resentment. Let Meredith give you lessons. She has it down pat."

"Monty . . ."

"I don't blame her. She's right. But that's my problem. It has nothing to do with what we're facing now. All you have to worry about is connecting with the Piersons through your relationship with Sally. My name doesn't need to come up, except in passing."

"But Edward Pierson knows you're driving up with me."

"His grandchildren don't. As for Edward, I'll tell him that as far as you're concerned, I'm driving up to fill him in on what I saw at the crime scene. Simple and accurate, even if it is just the tip of the iceberg. And I'll assure him I never discuss my cases. Not with anyone. Enough said—for you and for me."

Enough said. Simple and accurate.

Monty's mantra—the one Devon had heard him repeat so many times—sprang to mind, and she uttered it aloud. "Say as little as possible. When you have to talk, stick as close to the truth as possible. You'll have less to remember. And it'll wind up saving your ass."

"I couldn't have said it better."

Devon inclined her head, met her father's gaze. "You really think I can pull this off without losing it, and screwing things up?"

"There's not a doubt in my mind."

It was all she needed to hear. "Then I'm in."

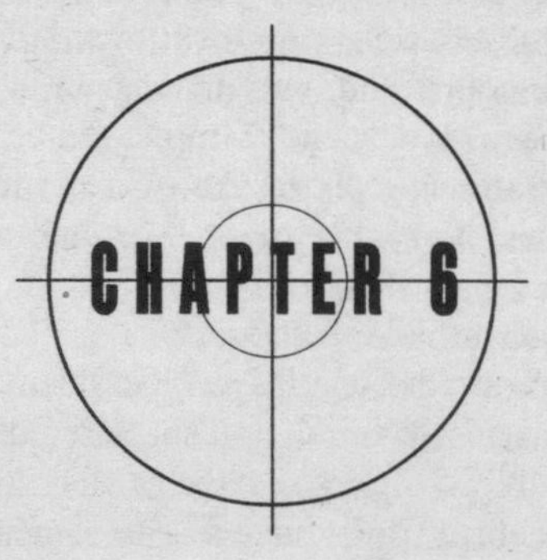

Edward Pierson looked pretty much like his photos. Tough. Lines etched on his face. Like an age-old rock that had been exposed to the elements and endured. Been-there-done-that-and-won kind of demeanor. Also, pretty damned steady on his feet for a guy nearing eighty who'd recently suffered a heart attack.

Monty averted his gaze long enough to take in the dark wood and expensive leather of the gentleman's-club-style office he'd been ushered into by the patriarch himself. He waited while Edward shut the door and turned the lock with a firm click.

"Have a seat," Edward instructed, gesturing at the wing-back chair across from his desk.

With a tight nod, Monty complied, studying Pierson's demeanor as he walked around and lowered himself into his matching desk chair. He was a hard man to read. He was obviously thrown by his son's death—which had been confirmed earlier that day by the coroner. His complexion was a little ashen, his breathing a little shallow. Yet, at the same time, he was brusque, all business—ready to take on and combat the world.

"I'm here as requested," Monty began, draping his arm over the chair and lounging back in a deceptively casual pose. "Although I feel like something out of *Mission: Impossible*. My daughter drops me off at the back gate. You sneak me through the house and lock me in your office. All that's missing is the catchy music. Why the drama?"

"No drama." Edward poured himself a glass of water. "Can I get you something? Coffee? Scotch?"

"Water's fine." Monty watched as Edward raised the pitcher again, filling a second glass and handing it over. He noticed the older man's hand was a trifle unsteady.

Grief, stress—or something more?

"Fine. You don't like the word *drama*," Monty conceded with a shrug. "Secrecy, then. Why?"

"Because my entire family's in shock. Because I don't want them upset any more than they need to be. And because they're only going to be told fragments of what you and I are about to discuss, and why I'm hiring you."

"And why *are* you hiring me?" Monty returned Edward's curt delivery with his own. "I don't have any more information than you have. The sheriff's office is doing their thing—and they're not interested in my help. As for Sally, we're divorced. I'm not her confidant."

"And yet she called you when she was in trouble."

"I was a cop for thirty years. She knew I could get the details she provided to the right people faster than anyone else. We also share three kids. She wanted them to know she was alive."

"Alive and on the run."

"Unfortunately, yes. I'd rather have her under police protection. But she didn't give me that option."

Edward shoved aside his water glass, steepling his fingers

in front of him. "Cards on the table. I'm hiring you for several reasons. The obvious ones you know. Your credentials are impressive. So's your client list. That list is also diverse. You've worked for both individuals and companies. Plus, you have a vested interest in finding whoever torched that cabin, killed Frederick, and tried to kill your ex-wife. I think you can resolve this faster than any official investigation. You can also give it your undivided attention, which the police can't."

"For the right price, you mean."

"For your kids. For your ex-wife. And, yes, for the right price. But before I name that price or go any further, I want your word that nothing we say leaves this room. Because this whole nightmare runs even deeper than you think—and with more potential for tragedy."

Monty's brows rose a fraction. "Sounds ominous."

"It is."

"I'm not cheap. Then again, I'm sure you already know that. Just like you know I don't discuss my cases. That's part of what you're paying for. So let's skip the confidentiality speech."

Edward opened his drawer and pulled out an envelope, sliding it across the desk. "There's fifty thousand dollars in there. Cash. Consider it a retainer. Plus I'll double your usual rates for as long as it takes to solve this case. But I want all your time and resources. Is that acceptable?"

"That depends on what you're asking me to do," Monty replied without touching the money. "Also, I won't blow off my current clients. I'll need a chunk of time to work on their cases."

"You can have late nights and weekends."

"Fair enough. I have associates who can do the additional fieldwork. Now, how about some details."

A tight nod. "You asked what I want you to do. I want you to act as Pierson & Company's head of security. I want you to go to the office every single day, figure out what's going on, and protect my company and my family."

Monty's gaze narrowed. "Does that mean you think whoever killed Frederick is after more of your family members?"

"Maybe. I don't believe in coincidences." Edward broke off, visibly agitated. "Look, Montgomery," he continued before Monty could probe into what coincidences Edward was referring to. "You don't get as rich and successful as I am without making enemies. And you don't always know who those enemies are."

"But you think they're company insiders?"

"It's possible. Either way, I'll make sure all business is conducted inside company walls. That'll keep this assignment manageable for you. You'll get a chance to check out visitors and employees alike."

"You're hedging. Who at Pierson & Company is on your suspect list?"

Edward took a gulp of water. He clearly did *not* like what he was about to say. "There's no list. It's just that Frederick and I had a different take on Philip Rhodes."

"Philip Rhodes. Your senior VP of sales."

A flicker of surprise registered on Edward's face. "You did your homework. Yes. Philip's been with us for years and years. He's a real rainmaker. And, yeah, he's bent some rules. So have James and I. That's how successful companies are built." Edward leveled a probing stare at Monty. "I'm sure I don't need to fill you in on who James is. If you've figured out Philip's role from our org chart, I'm sure you've done the same for other key players at Pierson, especially my family."

"Sure have." Monty didn't even glance at his notes. "James is your oldest grandchild; Niles's son. He's also VP of sales, reporting directly to Philip."

"*And* he's a champion show jumper," Edward added proudly. "He and my stallion Stolen Thunder are a one-of-a-kind team. Real Olympic material."

"So I hear. The reports from Wellington are impressive." A

corner of Monty's mouth lifted at Edward's startled expression. "I don't just do homework; I do *lots* of homework."

"Obviously."

"You said you bent some rules. Elaborate."

"The usual." Edward gave a dismissive wave. "A few political contributions to local politicians who wield power in communities where we wanted contracts for our food-service business. Some gifts to their family members. A few golf trips, here and there. Just some perks."

"I think they call that white-collar crime."

"No, they call that networking. The point is, Frederick thought Philip was going one step further—bribing officials, paying them off in cash to get what we wanted. He was pretty upset about it."

"I can understand why. Did he have proof?"

"Nothing I saw. And my gut tells me that Philip's too smart to channel company funds into something illegal."

"But if your gut is wrong, *and* if some proof actually existed, then Philip Rhodes would have a motive for murdering Frederick."

Edward's jaw began working. "I won't believe that."

"But you can't afford to dismiss it, either."

"I'm not dismissing anything. But, like I said, there's more to this nightmare—more that makes me believe it's someone on the outside who's trying to bring us down." He unlocked his center drawer, extracting an envelope.

"Will this explain your comment about not believing in coincidence?" Monty demanded.

"Two attacks on my family in one weekend? That's no fluke." Edward thrust the envelope across the desk. "Take a look at this. I got it on Thursday. It was mailed to me at the office."

Monty eyed the envelope without taking it. It was laser-printed, and addressed to Edward Pierson at Pierson & Company. "Extortion," he surmised aloud. "Which kind, blackmail or ransom?"

"Blackmail."

"Why didn't you call the cops?"

"Because I thought the letter was a hoax until Frederick was killed. Then I called you."

Nodding, Monty reached into his parka pockets. He groped around, whipping out his ski gloves. "No point in contaminating the evidence any more than it already has been," he said, yanking on the gloves. "I doubt we'll find any distinguishable fingerprints. But, just in case, let's not taint them." He leaned forward and took the envelope, eyeing it again. "No return address," he noted. "And a Manhattan postmark."

He slid out two folded sheets. The first was clearly a letter. The other was a computer printout of an article from *Horse Daily News*. He scanned that first.

ANTIDOPING AGENCY DISQUALIFIES TWO MORE HIGH-PROFILE RIDERS FOLLOWING POSITIVE DRUG TESTING, the headline read. The story, dated the previous October during Manhattan's National Metropolitan Horse Show, went on to describe the growing problem of drug use among equestrian riders, both at competitions and at random out-of-competition testing.

Monty skimmed the article just enough to get the gist of it. Then he turned his attention to the letter. Identical laser printing. Double-spaced. Nondescript in format.

Not so in content.

Sometimes disqualified riders aren't responsible for what shows up in their urine. Or their horse's urine. It could happen to anybody. Like James. Or Stolen Thunder. It could happen at an Olympic qualifying event. Like the US Open Jumper Championship CSIO in March. That would ruin everything. Lives. Reputations. All gone up in smoke.

Two million would keep them out of trouble. And safe, in and out of the show ring. Otherwise, who knows what might happen?

Consider the offer. I'll be in touch.

"No salutation. No signature," Monty muttered.

"And no follow-up." Edward took another shaky gulp of water. "I haven't heard word one from the scum who wrote that. At first, I thought it was some kind of sick gag. Then Frederick was killed."

"There's no mention of Frederick in the letter."

"What about the part about going up in smoke?"

Monty pursed his lips. "Yeah. There's that. It could be a reference to Friday's fire. But it still doesn't make sense. If the blackmailer wanted his cash, why kill Frederick before giving you a chance to come up with it?"

"An incentive, maybe." Tension creased Edward's forehead. "An act to show he means business."

"That's one hell of an incentive. Arson and murder. And why Frederick? Were he and James particularly close?"

"Our whole family's close. We fight. We make up. But family's family."

That wasn't an answer, but Monty left it alone. "We could be looking at payback of some kind. I'll need the names of anyone who might have a grudge against the Piersons. I'll also need to talk to your other family members. Not today, obviously. Over the next few days. I'll speak to them one at a time."

"I don't want them knowing about the blackmail letter. Especially James. He's high-strung enough. I don't want him to panic."

"I understand that. But he should be on the lookout for anything suspicious."

"He doesn't need to be. I've arranged for twenty-four-hour security around him, in New York and in Wellington. No one will get near him."

"He doesn't know about this?"

"It's not necessary. My people are discreet."

"I'll bet," Monty returned drily. "When is he going back to Wellington?"

"After the funeral."

"Make sure he comes into the office before that. I'll talk to him there. It'll seem less official, and he won't get as spooked. Don't worry—I'll only go at it from the angle of Frederick's murder. I won't mention the letter."

Edward gave a tight nod. "Fine."

"What else should I know?"

"My grandson Blake will be your alternate contact. If I'm not around, go to him. He'll be the only person I fill in on all the facets of your investigation."

"Including the blackmail letter?"

"Yes. Blake's the future of my company. He's smart. He's tough. And he's my sounding board. I'll pull him aside later and tell him about the letter."

"Good." Monty pushed back his chair and rose, pausing to scoop up his fifty-thousand-dollar retainer and tuck it in his pants pocket. "I'll need a list of your employees, and background information to go with it."

"No problem. When you get to the office tomorrow, stop at human resources. My granddaughter Cassidy can give you whatever you need."

"I'll be in around nine. Let her know to expect me."

Relief flashed across Edward's face as he rose. "I will."

Monty refolded the article and the letter and slipped them back into the envelope. "Can I keep these? I want to look them over more thoroughly."

"Go ahead." Edward was back to being the tough businessman. "Just figure out who sent them."

"I will." Monty stared him down. "Count on it."

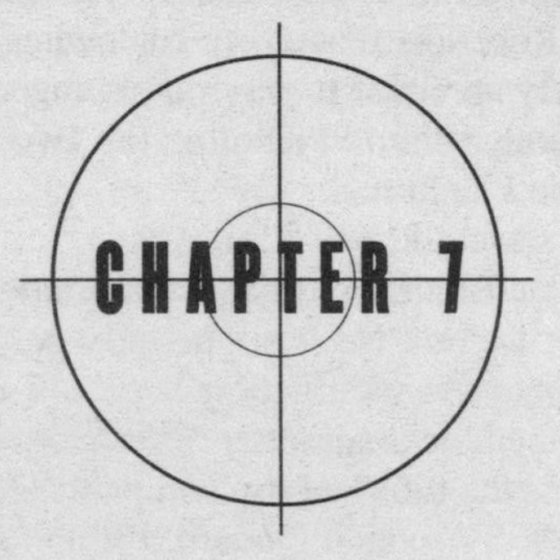

CHAPTER 7

Devon stood on the Piersons' front doorstep, hands shoved in the pockets of her camel-hair overcoat, staring at the formidable double doors.

It was showtime.

She sucked in her breath, wishing her talk with Roberto, the Piersons' groom, had yielded something of substance. No such luck. Striking up a conversation with the guy had been easy. They'd talked horses, riding competitions, and proper care of warmbloods. As for a lowdown on the Piersons, she'd learned nothing she hadn't already read in Monty's notes, other than how profound a role James's equestrian triumphs played in his grandfather's life. It seemed that James's accomplishments in the show ring had been a lifeline for Edward after his heart attack. According to Roberto, James's growth toward Olympic potential had given Edward the will to live.

The groom was clearly proud. Devon heard all about James's

extraordinary form, his unique affinity with Stolen Thunder, his drive to win. Roberto's reports were glowing. Unfortunately, they were totally unrelated to yesterday's tragedy.

So now it was time to execute step two of her plan—befriending the Piersons.

She hoped she could pull it off.

She *had* to pull it off. Monty was counting on her.

More important, her mother was counting on her.

Blowing out her breath, Devon rang the bell.

A somber-looking butler opened the door. With his wrinkled face, sucked-in stance and sallow complexion, he looked like a sour pickle with hair. "Yes?"

"I'm Devon Montgomery, Sally Montgomery's daughter," she introduced herself. "I drove up this afternoon to check on my mother's house. When I passed your farm, I noticed all the cars in the driveway. I wonder if I might pay my respects to the Piersons?"

The pickle frowned, obviously unsure if he should allow her to enter.

"Please tell them I'm here," Devon suggested quickly. "They'll know who I am. If they'd prefer not to see me, I'll leave."

"Very well." He disappeared.

A murmur of voices followed, after which Devon heard the *click-click* of high heels approaching. A minute later, a striking young woman of about Devon's age appeared at the door. She was wearing a black Donna Karan suit, and her dark hair feathered the sides of her face, complementing her high cheekbones and fair complexion, before brushing the top of her shoulders in a blunt, silky cut.

"Hello—Devon, isn't it?" Seeing Devon's nod, she opened the door wider. "Won't you come in?" She scrutinized Devon as she complied, her pale green gaze as sharp as chips of jade. Then she extended her hand. "I'm Cassidy Pierson. Frederick is . . . was . . . my uncle."

Cassidy Pierson. Devon could see the page in her mind's

eye. *VP of human resources. Twenty-eight years old. Daughter of Gregory. Sister of Blake.*

"It's nice to meet you," Devon replied, shaking Cassidy's hand. "Although I wish it were under different circumstances."

"As do I." Cassidy waved her arm toward the rear of the sprawling, dimly lit house. "Please join us."

"I don't want to intrude. I just . . ." Devon cleared her throat. "I just wanted to say I'm sorry. And maybe to be among others who understand. I didn't know your uncle, but my mother held him in high regard."

Cassidy's probing gaze softened. "You're scared. I don't blame you. Whoever did this horrible thing is still out there."

"And so's my mother."

"I know." Cassidy turned as the pickle reappeared. "Albert, please take our guest's coat."

"Certainly." He waited while Devon shrugged out of it, then draped it over his arm and walked away.

"Are you sure this isn't a bad time?" Devon felt compelled to ask.

"Not yet. Right now it's just family and a few close friends. Later, it'll be a circus." Cassidy's reply was refreshingly and, surprisingly, honest. "Come on," she urged. "I'll introduce you."

Devon followed her through the polished hardwood foyer. The house was imposing. Like the family.

The voices grew more distinct, and the foyer opened up into an expansive pillared living room with burgundy leather sofas, walnut chairs and end tables, and about a dozen chatting people.

The Pierson clan.

All eyes were on Devon as she stepped into the room. Her first thought was that she now understood what Cinderella must have felt like when she made an entrance into a royal ballroom. Her second thought was that she was glad she'd listened to her instincts and changed into a tailored pantsuit before heading over here from her mother's. The jeans and sweater she'd had on before would have stuck out like a sore thumb.

"This is Devon Montgomery," Cassidy announced—a mere formality, since everyone already knew who she was.

Actually, they weren't at too much of an advantage. Devon had very little trouble figuring out who was who. She quickly put faces to the names and profiles Monty had gone over with her last night.

Anne Pierson was a matriarch if ever there was one. The grande dame of the family, she had silver white hair, piercing ice blue eyes, and a regal carriage that nearly made Devon curtsy instead of acknowledging Cassidy's introduction with a handshake.

"I'm so terribly sorry about your loss," Devon told her sincerely.

Those frosty eyes pinned her to the spot. "Thank you. Has there been any word on your mother?"

"None since yesterday. We're trying to stay positive."

"Of course you are." It sounded more like an accusation than an acknowledgment.

"Grandmother, you should sit down," Cassidy interceded to suggest. "You look exhausted."

"You're right. I am." Anne lingered a moment longer, her gaze fixed on Devon. Abruptly, she turned away. "Please excuse me." It sounded more like an order than a request.

Next, Cassidy introduced Devon to her uncle Niles and aunt Lynn, followed by her parents, Gregory and Natalie.

No surprises there, either. Niles and Lynn were the snobs; Gregory and Natalie were the free spirits.

Devon was just meeting Philip Rhodes when there was a commotion from the hall, and a golden retriever puppy exploded into the living room. He was about three or four months old, Devon surmised; still chubby, with paws too big for his legs—a furry, adorable, clumsy ball of energy.

Ignoring the exclamations, he shook off a layer of snow, then sprinted into the center of the room, stumbling, panting, and wagging his tail all at once. His warm brown gaze found Devon and he bounded over, sniffing as he did. He jumped up, yanking at Devon's blazer with his teeth, and yipped excitedly. Just as swiftly, he was back on all fours, crouching down so he could sniff at the hem of her pants. He grabbed the material between his teeth and began to chew, just as a tall, dark-haired man strode over, snapping his fingers and commanding: "Chomper! Drop it!"

Chomper's ears went up. But he didn't miss a beat. Totally ignoring his owner, he dragged more material into his mouth, made a nice, wet wad, and settled down to chew on it.

"Chomper! I said, *drop it*!"

This time, the ears barely flickered.

Biting back laughter, Devon gazed from the enthusiastic pup to his irritated owner, who was now squatting down to take a more hands-on approach. "I don't think he's listening," she noted.

"He never does." The man began trying to physically pry Chomper's teeth away from Devon's slacks.

"That's not going to work," Devon informed him. "Not in the long run."

"So I see." Giving up, Chomper's owner leaned back on his heels. He tilted back his head and gazed up at her, a corner of his mouth lifting in a rueful grin. "I apologize. We just got in from our walk, and he took off before I could grab him. I'll gladly pay for any damage to your suit."

"No problem." Devon watched the man rise and smooth the front of his navy jacket. He made a pretty devastating package. Over six feet tall, athletic build, Brioni suit—this guy emanated power and charisma. His hair was jet-black, a few strands of which swept his broad forehead, and there was a lionlike quality to his amber eyes that was hard to look away from.

Too tall and powerfully built to be James. Hair color and texture like Cassidy's.

Must be Blake.

Sure enough, he stuck out his palm and said, "I'm Blake Pierson. This is Chomper, who's introduced himself the hard way."

Devon smiled, shaking Blake's hand. "Devon Montgomery. And don't worry about Chomper. I'm used to being slobbered on. It's a daily hazard for me."

His brows lifted. "You have a manic retriever pup, too?"

"A terrier. Mine steals socks. But that's not what I meant. I'm a veterinarian."

"So you deal with guys like Chomper all day."

"Dogs, cats, birds, ferrets . . . you name it. That's probably the reason for my popularity with Chomper. I stopped at the clinic to check on some patients. I'm sure I brought all kinds of interesting animal scents up here with me. And there's one other reason he could have been drawn to me." She reached into her pocket and pulled out one of the peanut butter dog biscuits she carried everywhere with her. "May I?"

"Please." Blake gestured at the floor, where Chomper was still occupied with Devon's pants. "Especially if it will divert him."

She squatted down, saying Chomper's name in a quiet, firm tone until she got his attention. Then she showed him the biscuit. "Not these," she instructed him, tugging away her pants. "This." He sniffed at it, caught the enticing scent of peanut butter, and snatched it up. "Good boy," Devon praised.

The praise was nice. The biscuit was better. Chomper crunched away happily.

"Diversion accomplished," Devon announced, standing up.

She came face-to-face with a willowy, attractive woman in her midthirties, who'd evidently joined them while Devon was dealing with Chomper. Stylish, blond, well put together.

This one didn't require a guess. Devon had seen her photograph, on the arm of Frederick Pierson, in the newspaper archives Monty had searched.

Louise Chambers. Pierson & Company's corporate counsel.

"Dr. Montgomery. It's a pleasure." The woman held out a manicured hand. "I'm Louise Chambers."

"Ms. Chambers." Another handshake. And more head-to-toe scrutiny of Devon. This time it seemed to be more personal. Best guess? It was because she was Sally's daughter and Sally had been dating Frederick. And, from what Devon had gleaned in the social columns, Louise and Frederick had been something of an item this past year and a half.

"Louise is a close family friend," Blake was saying. "She's also Pierson & Company's outstanding general counsel."

"Put that in my paycheck," Louise quipped, patting Blake's arm. She turned back to Devon. "You must be worried sick about your mother."

"I am." Devon trod carefully. "Very worried. I'm also very sorry about Mr. Pierson."

Genuine pain flashed in Louise's eyes. "We all are."

"Maybe Devon would like a drink." A lean guy with dark wavy hair and a Crest Whitestrips smile strolled over.

Medium height. Grandma Anne's blue eyes and aristocratic features. And Pierson charm.

James.

"What can I get you?" he asked Devon.

"I'd love a Diet Coke."

"Done. I'm James Pierson, by the way."

"It's nice to meet you."

"And it's nice to meet you." He gave her a blatant once-over, followed by a more lingering perusal. He then flashed an approving, if obvious, smile before going in search of the Diet Coke.

Bingo. James wanted to hit on her. What more natural scenario in which to initiate a personal conversation?

Swiftly, Devon scanned the room, her mind racing. She didn't have much time. People were starting to filter out. Last-minute arrangements were being made. A funeral. A business, sans a CEO. The Piersons had a lot on their plates. Till now, Devon had been a curiosity. Soon she'd become an annoyance. Before that happened, she had to secure more than formal introductions. She had to talk, really *talk*, to at least one of the Piersons. She'd met nearly all of them. The only ones left were Tiffany and Roger Wallace. And that had to be them, standing in the corner, talking quietly to a child of kindergarten age. Their daughter, Kerri, no doubt.

She'd forfeit meeting them. She had to capitalize on James's interest in her.

"Subtle, isn't he?" Cassidy murmured beside her.

Devon turned, grinning at the knowing twinkle in Cassidy's eyes. "No. But I doubt he has to be. Is he your brother?"

"My cousin."

"Frederick's son?"

"No, Niles's." Cassidy gestured in Niles's direction. "Frederick and Emily never had children."

"Then that branch of the family's gone."

A reflective nod. "I hadn't thought of it that way, but yes. Niles is Grandfather's eldest now."

"That must drop the weight of the world on his shoulders."

"In business, you mean?" Cassidy looked amused. "Niles will carry it well. He thrives under pressure. Then again, I doubt he'll get involved in the food-services division. He's a fine-dining guy all the way. Plus, with James's equestrian competitions, he's on overload already."

"Did I hear my name?" James asked, walking back over and handing Devon a crystal glass.

"Don't you always?" Cassidy replied good-naturedly. "I was just telling Devon how busy your father is, between Pierson & Company and your riding."

"Yeah, that's Dad. Always on the go."

Devon sipped at her drink, eyeing James as she did. "Cassidy mentioned equestrian competitions. What kind and where?"

"Show jumping. And wherever they'll have me."

"Ah, that's my cue." Cassidy gave a mock sigh. "James pretends to be modest—which is far from the truth—so I'll toot his horn and make him sound more impressive. He's competed at major events everywhere, including Calgary and Toronto this past fall. Right now, he's competing at the Winter Equestrian Festival in Wellington. He came in second at today's Grand Prix. We're all sure that he and Stolen Thunder are on their way to the World Games in Aachen, and from there to Olympic Gold in Beijing."

"The Olympics? That *is* impressive." Devon's brows rose.

"You're right. It does sound better coming from you," James informed his cousin. "Let's hope your predictions come true."

"Are you kidding? Grandfather wouldn't have it any other way."

"So you don't work at Pierson & Company?" Devon asked, feigning ignorance.

"Sure I do. I'm VP of sales."

"How do you manage that? Two demanding careers—I can barely handle one."

"Talent," James replied with a teasing grin. "No, seriously, discipline and commitment. It also helps that riding is my passion."

"Among others," Cassidy muttered.

He shot her a look, then turned his charm back on Devon. "I heard you say you're a vet. That must mean long hours."

"It does."

"Does it leave any time for fun?"

Devon had just opened her mouth to reply, when Chomper shot up from the floor and barked, then abandoned his biscuit crumbs and bounded across the room. Following him with her gaze, Devon saw that Kerri had perched on the edge of the sofa and was drawing a picture. Chomper, evidently, had spotted her crayons and decided they were edible. He snatched two in his mouth, then took off, with Kerri in close pursuit.

"Chomper!" Blake, who'd been concentrating on some vehement revelation Louise Chambers was in the process of confiding, broke away to go after his dog. Louise frowned as she watched him go. Her troubled stare slid briefly to Devon before she walked over to the martini pitcher on the sideboard and refilled her glass.

Devon got the distinct feeling that whatever had just been said concerned her.

"Great," Cassidy noted in disgust. "Chomper's on the run again. I hope my brother reaches him before he reaches the back door. Otherwise, Blake will be organizing the second search party of the day."

"I assume Chomper likes to take off."

"Constantly. He's either escaping or destroying something." Cassidy rolled her eyes. "And that's up here at the farm. Imagine him in a Manhattan brownstone."

"Your brother lives in the city?"

"Whenever he's not up here, yes. I'm sure you can't guess which place Chomper prefers."

"I'm sure I can." As she spoke, Devon spotted Kerri returning to the living room, sans crayons. There was no sign of Chomper or Blake.

Reacting on instinct, she set down her glass. "I'm pretty good at tracking down runaway pets. Maybe I should give Blake a hand."

James caught her arm. "Blake can manage," he assured her. "Besides, I was enjoying our talk."

"So was I." Devon hesitated, unwilling to blow her opportunity to get information out of James, yet equally unwilling to stay idle when she knew she could expedite the task of finding Chomper.

Cassidy made the decision for her.

"Let her help, James," she urged. "The sooner Chomper's found, the better. We've got guests arriving to pay their respects. You and Devon can talk later."

"Can we?" James asked, studying Devon intently.

"Yes." Devon met James's stare, giving him what she hoped was an eager look. "I'd really like that."

"So would I." Pleased by her response, he released his hold on her arm. "Go ahead. I'll be waiting."

Devon weaved her way through the living room and into the hall. No need to ask directions. She followed the racket of scurrying paws and chasing feet.

The sound of padding paws vanished. But the running footsteps continued, along with a few exasperated shouts.

She reached the back door in time to see it waving open on its hinges, with Blake standing on the threshold, glaring outside.

"Dammit." His expression was intent as he scanned the well-lit grounds.

"A few minutes too late," Devon surmised, coming up behind him.

He turned his head, noting her presence. "Yeah. And a few minutes is all it takes." He jiggled the handle on the swinging door. "We've got to get this latch fixed. The wind keeps blowing it open."

"Which is Chomper's cue to bolt." Devon stepped past him to peer outside.

"Don't bother looking for paw prints. He's too light, and the ground's too frozen for him to make any imprints."

"That's not what I was doing. I was figuring out the detours he could have taken to vanish so quickly. And I was checking out the grounds to see where he might hide."

"Any conclusions?"

"Where did you find him earlier today?"

Blake grimaced. "I see Cassidy's filled you in on Chomper's antics. I found him near the pond." He pointed. "I have no idea why he went there. It's frozen."

"It's got an eastern exposure. The sun was out this morning. He probably found a warm spot to play with whatever he'd stolen."

"That would be my glove," Blake supplied. "And the weather's a nonissue. Chomper's not picky when he's in bandit mode."

Devon shivered, hugging herself to stay warm. "Trust me, he won't like this chill. The poor little guy must be freezing. It's gotten windy, and the sun's gone down. I'd suggest we check enclosed places. Places he'd be able to wriggle his way into, like a barn or an indoor arena."

"We've got three indoor jumping arenas. They're on the western portion of the property. The barn's to the north. So are the feed and tack rooms."

"Any other heated areas?"

"The wash stalls. They're right next to the feed room."

"We've got our work cut out for us. You take the arenas. I'll take the barn area."

Blake nodded, already in motion. "I'll get our coats and some flashlights."

Ten minutes later, Devon finished a quick search of the wash stalls. Dark, deserted—no signs of Chomper. As for the feed and tack rooms, the doors were shut tight. On to the barn.

She turned up her collar and headed in that direction.

The door was slightly ajar. Devon pushed it open and hurried inside. She reached into her pocket for a peanut-butter biscuit. "Chomper!"

A few surprised horses snapped around to stare at her. But no puppy.

She checked the stalls, one at a time.

"Good boy," she called out in a voice filled with praise. "I've got a treat for you." She made a smacking sound with her lips. "Yum. Come and get it."

She heard the slightest jangling sound from the far end of the barn.

Now *that* could be a good sign. It sure sounded like a metal ID tag and dog license clinking together.

"Come on, Chomper," she coaxed, veering in the direction of the jangle. "Peanut butter beats Crayola, hands down."

Another jangle.

She reached the last stall, which was empty, and stepped inside.

There, settled on a pile of hay, surrounded by purple and green crayon wrappers, was Chomper. His head shot up when Devon walked in, and he wagged his tail proudly. His nose and snout were purple. His paws were green.

Forcing herself to keep a straight face, Devon squatted down beside him. "No, no," she chided, taking away the crayons. "Those aren't to eat."

Chomper yipped in protest, trying to snatch the crayons away from her.

"No," Devon said firmly. "No crayons." She shoved them in her coat pocket.

He paused, looking uncertain.

"Sit." Devon issued the command in an unyielding but kind tone. "Chomper, sit."

He sat.

"Good boy." She flourished the biscuit, offering it to him without hesitation.

He pounced, gobbling the biscuit with great enthusiasm.

Devon wrapped her coat more tightly around her. She was shivering. So was Chomper. But she let him finish the biscuit before scooping him up and tucking him inside her coat. "Okay, tough guy. Time to brave the cold. Let's get you back to the warm house."

He nuzzled against her, absorbing her warmth, then happily began licking her chin as she retraced her steps.

She'd left the barn door slightly ajar. She was just reaching for it, when it was pushed open from the other side.

Startled, Devon jumped backward to avoid being hit.

A middle-aged man with a medical case and notebook

strode in. "Mr. Pierson? I—" Seeing Devon, he broke off, looking equally as startled as she. "Excuse me. I assumed you were Mr. Pierson."

"No, I'm just a guest, hunting down this little guy." Devon indicated Chomper, who had poked out his head to sniff the newcomer.

"I see." The reedy fellow blinked behind his eyeglasses.

"Which Mr. Pierson did you want? They're all inside the house."

"Edward. But there's no need to interrupt him, not at this difficult time. I'll just see to the horses and be on my way."

Devon eyed his bag. "You're a veterinarian?"

"In part. Why do you ask?"

"I don't mean to be nosy. I just recognize the tools of the trade. I'm a veterinarian myself."

"Are you?" He looked concerned. "I had no idea Mr. Pierson hired someone new. When did this happen?"

"It didn't." Devon waved away the notion that she was a threat to this man's job. "I'm here for personal, not professional, reasons."

"Oh." He shifted awkwardly. "I apologize. Are you family?"

"No." Devon felt compelled to explain. "I'm Sally Montgomery's daughter. My mother owns the house next door."

"Sally Montgomery?" Anxiety transformed to sympathy. "The newspaper said . . . that is, she was the woman who . . . who . . ."

". . . was with Frederick Pierson in Lake Luzerne when the cabin caught fire," Devon finished for him.

"She survived, didn't she?"

"Yes. But she's missing." Devon kept the explanation short.

"That's what I read." He shifted the medical bag to his other hand. "I hope she's brought home, safe and soon."

"Thank you." Devon inclined her head quizzically. "I'm sorry; I didn't catch your name."

"Vista. Dr. Lawrence Vista."

"Dr. Vista." Devon acknowledged his introduction. "Are you an equine specialist?"

"I'm a genetic consultant. I'm advising Mr. Pierson on the best breeding partners for his show horses."

Devon's curiosity was piqued. "So you examine his horses and make genetic assessments and recommendations?"

"Precisely."

"That sounds fascinating. I'd love to hear more about it. . . ." She frowned, as Chomper began squirming again. "But now's clearly not the time. I'd better get this little guy inside."

Dr. Vista nodded. "The wind is really picking up."

"Another time, then."

"Certainly." He stepped aside to let her pass. "I'm sorry I startled you."

"No harm done. It was nice meeting you."

Devon walked out of the barn. Dr. Vista was right. The wind really had picked up. It blasted her in the face like ice water.

Nestling Chomper close against her, Devon hunched her shoulders and prepared to brave the elements. Dr. Vista's truck was parked directly in her path. She inched her way around it and struck off in the direction of the house.

She was halfway there when she spotted Blake emerging from a jumping arena. She called out his name, and when he turned, she aimed her flashlight beam at Chomper. Blake saw him, looked extraordinarily relieved, and walked over to meet them.

"Where was he?" he asked.

"In the barn. Feasting on crayons." Devon pointed at Chomper's purple snout, which was poking out of her coat.

Blake gave a snort of disgust, although his lips were twitching. At the same time, Chomper spotted his owner and gave a joyful yip, struggling to free himself and get to Blake.

Laughing, Devon handed him over. "He's shivering. Tuck him inside your coat."

"Yeah, that solution will work for another month or so," Blake muttered, wrapping the warm folds of his coat around the pup. "But tell me, doctor, what do I do when he weighs ninety pounds and his feet are the size of my head?"

"Nothing. Because, if you're smart, you'll put him in obedience classes now, while he's still a manageable size. Goldens are very intelligent. They're also sweethearts who are eager to please their owners. But right now, Chomper thinks he's the pack leader and you're the pack. He's confused. Train him right and you'll both be happier."

Blake tipped his head thoughtfully, examining her with those penetrating amber eyes. Only this time the examination was very thorough and very male. "Words of wisdom. Suppose I take your advice—do you make house calls?"

The remark was teasing. Maybe flirtatious. But certainly not offensive or harmful. Still, it threw Devon—a lot.

"No," she heard herself reply.

"Pity." The sleeve of Blake's coat brushed hers. "How about apartment calls?"

Even through several layers of clothing, Devon felt a surge of warmth at the contact.

She stiffened. James might be the family charmer, but there was something incredibly sexy about Blake Pierson—something she was susceptible to. She'd have to watch herself around him.

"Nope. On-site only," she quipped.

"No exceptions?"

"Not a one. But don't worry. No house calls are needed. Chomper's in perfect health."

"Physically, yeah. But not psychologically. You just said so yourself. He's confused and disobedient."

"That's easily fixed. By a trainer. Which I'm not. My clinic has a top-notch obedience and training staff. I'd recommend them, if the facilities weren't so inconvenient for you. You're in Manhattan. The clinic's in White Plains."

"Are you?"

"Am I what?"

"In White Plains."

"I live near the clinic, yes."

"But you spend most of your time at work."

"A good chunk of it," Devon acknowledged.

"So I'd see you whenever I brought Chomper to obedience school."

"Not likely. The clinic's big and spread out. It's divided into sections. I'm in the medical wing. You'd be in the training wing."

Blake shot her another of those probing looks. "I'm a good navigator. I'll find you."

Freezing or not, Devon was starting to perspire. She was glad they were nearing the house.

She glanced up to see James in the doorway, hands shoved in his pockets, frowning as he watched their approach. An elderly man with white hair—presumably Edward Pierson—was standing beside him, waving his arm and talking vehemently.

James stopped him in midsentence, gesturing toward her and Blake.

Edward's head snapped around. His gaze seemed to pin her where she stood.

Then he turned and disappeared into the house.

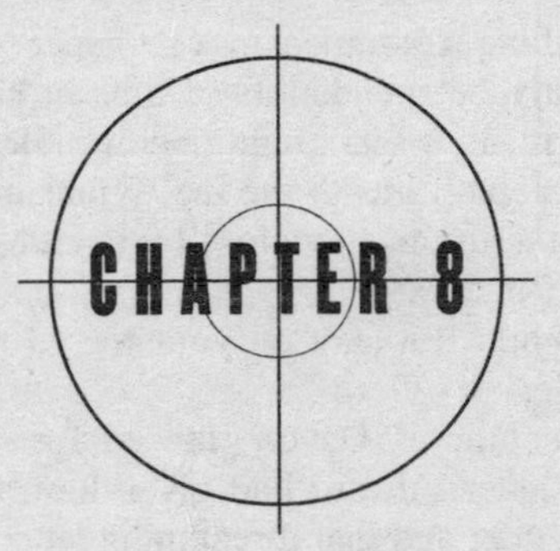

CHAPTER 8

"Two guys hitting on you. Both of them Piersons. Not bad for an evening's work," Monty commented drily, settling himself in the passenger seat and scribbling down some notes.

Devon's gloved fingers tightened on the steering wheel, and she accelerated onto the highway. "I'm glad *you're* happy," she muttered. "I feel like I just walked off a soap opera set."

"Yeah, well, you did. This family's got more drama and secrets than the Kennedys." Monty put down his pen. "How'd you leave it with James and Blake?"

"James and I were supposed to get together while I was there. That never happened. He and his grandfather went behind closed doors five minutes after Blake and I walked in with Chomper. They were still there when I left."

"But you made sure he'll call."

A sigh. "Yes, Monty. I gave Cassidy my phone number and asked her to pass it on to him."

"And Blake?"

"He's enrolling Chomper in obedience classes at my clinic. Evidently, he spends lots of time in Yonkers, getting his restaurant ready for its grand opening. He made it abundantly clear that he wants to see me. Whether that's genuine interest or just a ruse to stay close by in case Mom contacts me is anyone's guess."

"Probably both. But stay on your toes. I don't trust any of these people."

"No argument there." Devon glanced over, saw her father rereading the letter Edward had given him. "Do you think Frederick's murder and that threatening letter are related?"

A shrug. "Maybe. Maybe not. I intend to find out. In the meantime, no mention of the letter to anyone."

"My lips are sealed." Devon grinned. "I'm flattered you shared it with me."

"You're my partner."

"On *this* case," Devon reminded him.

"Yeah, yeah, on this case." Monty's forehead creased as he leaned back against the headrest. "Assuming the murder and the letter are connected, James is the logical common denominator. He reports to Philip Rhodes. Frederick didn't trust Rhodes. He suspected him of playing dirty to bolster the food-services division—Frederick's division. Now Frederick's dead and James is the target of a threatening letter. The minute Edward's pride and joy shows up at the office, I'm finding out what makes him tick. As for you . . ."

"I'll make a date with him ASAP." Devon finished her father's train of thought. "He's got a huge ego. I'll play into it. Who knows? Maybe I'll get more out of him than you will."

A scowl. "As long as he doesn't get too much out of you."

Devon couldn't help but laugh at the uncharacteristic display of paternal protectiveness. "I'm a big girl, Monty. I know how to take care of myself. But thanks for the warning."

"No thanks necessary. It's part of the job description." An odd expression crossed Monty's face. "Too bad I could never get that job right. I tried like hell. But it wasn't enough. I still don't know why. Other cops manage."

"Other cops can put a cap on their personal relationships. You can't." Devon reached over and squeezed his arm. "The way you loved Mom, and us—there's no room for intensity like that times two."

"So I've heard."

"On the other hand, it's never too late to try again," Devon couldn't help but add. "Circumstances change. Priorities change. Even people change."

Monty averted his eyes, staring out the window. "Just drive, Devon. We've got a lot to do before tomorrow."

Edward paced inside the barn, waiting and brooding.

Devon Montgomery wasn't supposed to be a problem. She was supposed to be a potential solution. Now all that had changed. How much remained to be seen.

James was taken with her. Doubly so after deciding Blake was his competition. He wasn't about to back off. That meant his performance at Wellington was in jeopardy.

And so was he.

Inhaling sharply, Edward stopped pacing and leaned back against the stable wall. His chest felt tight. Beads of sweat dotted his forehead. His health. He had to protect it. He'd get the situation in check. He'd already initiated damage control. Now he just had to find out if it was enough.

The crunch of tires reached his ears. A minute later, the barn door opened and Lawrence Vista walked in.

He stopped the minute he saw Edward. "I'm here, as promised." He slapped his gloved hands together, shifting nervously from one foot to the other. "I'm very sorry about your son."

"So am I." Edward cut to the chase. "You said on the phone that you ran into Devon Montgomery at the barn. What happened?"

"We spoke. For two minutes tops."

"What did you tell her?"

"As little as possible. My name. That I was a genetic consultant. That I was advising you on the best breeding partners for your show horses. None of that's a secret."

"And that's all you said?"

"That's it."

"Did she see anything? Anything at all?"

"No." Vista shook his head. "We never left the doorway. I came in with only my medical bag and a notebook. And our conversation was all veterinary talk."

"What the hell were you doing here to begin with? You know my whole family's gathered at the farm."

"I had the preliminary results I promised. I planned on leaving them in the usual spot. The barn was lit and the door was ajar. I checked to see who was inside. I assumed it was you."

"That was a stupid assumption. I'm in no shape to work—not even on this. My son was just killed."

"I realize that. But we set up our meeting before that happened. And it occurred to me that you might decide to show up, if for no other reason than to get your mind off your loss."

"Nothing can do that."

"I understand. And I apologize if I made a bad choice. But I still don't understand why you're so agitated. Devon Montgomery's a veterinarian, not a cop."

"Maybe not, but she's a cop's daughter."

"Huh?"

"Her father was with the NYPD for thirty years. He retired to become a PI. A damned good one, too. And his ex-wife's still a target for Frederick's killer, so he's knee-deep in this case. The last thing I need is for Devon Montgomery to say something to her daddy that starts his wheels turning."

Vista sucked in a breath. "I see your point."

"You took a stupid chance. Don't do it again." Edward

walked past him, then paused in the doorway. "Were the preliminary results what we'd hoped for?"

"Very close."

A terse nod. "The funeral's tomorrow. Give me a few days. Then we'll set something up."

The man hovered in the shadows, teeth chattering from the cold. He struck a match, peering at his watch. Ten twenty-four. Almost time.

Sure enough, six minutes later a black Mercedes sedan turned into the deserted parking lot. The headlights caught him, and for one panicky instant he imagined being struck dead and left to rot.

Abruptly, the lights were extinguished and the motor was cut. The front door slammed as the driver got out. Purposeful steps approached him, then stopped.

"Aquí." Without ceremony, a thick padded envelope was shoved at him. *"Veinte mil dólares y un billete sencillo a Uruguay."*

"Twenty thousand?" He reverted to his broken English. "You said fifty."

Furious eyes stared him down. "And *you* said you'd do this right. You're lucky to be getting anything after the unforgivable way you botched things up."

"That wasn't my fault. You said—"

"Shut up. I know what I said. And you'll get your full fifty thousand. But do you really want to risk being stopped by airport security and having to explain why you're traveling to Montevideo with enough cash to fill a suitcase?"

The man fell silent.

"I didn't think so. Take the envelope. The rest will be wired to you. *If* you follow instructions. If not . . ." A pointed glare. "Now get going. Your flight leaves in two hours. Time to disappear."

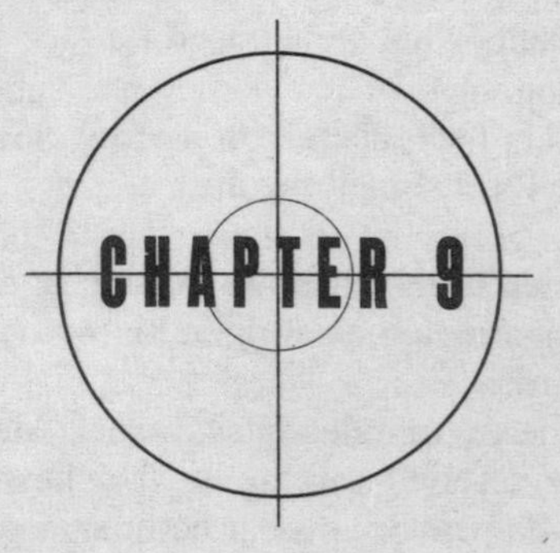

Devon was up and dressed before dawn. At six thirty, she went downstairs to brew a pot of coffee. To her surprise, the coffee was already brewed, and Lane was straddling a stool at the kitchen counter, mug in hand. Connie was rubbing up against his legs, Runner was inside his cage nibbling on fresh food pellets, and Terror and Scamp were playing tug-of-war with one of Lane's sweat socks.

"Hey," Lane greeted his sister. "I figured you'd be down about now."

Devon blinked. "Well, I certainly didn't expect to see you. It's three thirty Pacific time."

"Making quick time-zone adjustments is a necessary evil in my line of work. Besides, I wanted to touch base before you headed off to the clinic." He gestured for her to pour herself some coffee and join him. "I had a couple of impromptu get-togethers with East Coast colleagues yesterday.

By the time I got back, you were asleep and Monty was gone. So what happened at the Piersons'?"

"Nothing monumental. Just some clarification for Monty and initial feelers for me." Devon plopped down beside her brother. "Monty's the new head of security at Pierson & Company. He's going in first thing today to begin guarding Edward Pierson's future heirs."

"And interrogating them in the process." Lane set down his mug. "I'm not worried about Monty. He's a pro. But you—let's just say this danger game is new to you. So if you need me, I'm here."

"Always the big brother." Devon gave his arm a grateful squeeze. "Thanks. At the slightest sign of trouble, I promise to take you up on your offer. Right now, my part in this investigation is pretty tame."

The telephone rang.

Devon reached for it, rolling her eyes as she did. "Except in Monty's eyes. He's taking this partner thing very seriously. How much do you want to bet that's him now, doing a morning check-in? Hello?" she said into the receiver.

"Hi, sweetheart."

"Hi, Monty. What a surprise." The background noise told Devon he was in the car. "Are you heading into the city?"

"Yup. I'm getting an early start. I'm meeting Blake Pierson in his office at seven thirty. After that, I've got a long list of people to interview before everyone blows out of there for the funeral. I just wanted to give you a heads-up. Blake mentioned something about zipping up to Yonkers right after we talk—via White Plains. Seems he's arranged to check out Creature Comforts & Clinic and enroll his golden in obedience classes. Pretty ambitious, given he's got a midday funeral in Manhattan. Definitely a man with a mission. So expect to be asked out."

"Thanks for the warning." Devon's call-waiting signal beeped in her ear. "Hold on a second, Monty. I've got another call coming in." She pressed the *flash* button. "Hello?"

"Devon?"

"Yes. Who's this?"

"James Pierson. I hope it's not too early. But Cassidy said you'd be at the animal clinic before eight. I wanted to catch you beforehand. Normally, I don't wake up women at dawn to ask them out. But in this case, time's working against me, and I *really* want to see you. I've got a full day at the office, other than the few hours I'll be at my uncle's funeral. After that, I'm flying back down to Wellington, midday tomorrow at the latest. So tonight's all I've got. Is there any chance you're free?"

Devon gave a breathless laugh. "Talk about a whirlwind life. I'm flattered you thought of me."

"I've been thinking of you since yesterday. Does that mean you're free?"

"For tonight? Yes. But right now, I'm on another call."

"I see." A hint of annoyance. "Not with Blake, I hope."

"With Blake?" That was a weird conclusion for him to jump to. "No. With my grandparents," she improvised. "They're frantic for some word on my mother."

"Have you gotten any?" James was suddenly all concern.

"Unfortunately not." Devon used that concern to her advantage. "So, to be honest, I could use an evening out. It'll take my mind off my worry for a few hours."

"I could use the same. So, shall we say seven o'clock?"

"Seven's great."

"Excellent. I won't keep you from your grandparents. How about if I call later for directions?"

"Call me at work." Monty's heads-up about Blake's intentions popped into Devon's head, and she reacted accordingly, choosing a time for James's call that was in between Chomper's potential drop-off and pickup times. "I'll be in surgery all morning. And I'm sure you'll be inundated with work and with emotionally preparing for the funeral. Why don't you give me a call around four?"

"Done." James sounded smug. "What's your office number?" He jotted it down. "I'm really looking forward to this evening."

"So am I. Bye, James." Devon punched the *flash* button again. "Monty?"

"Still here."

"That was James Pierson. We've got a dinner date tonight."

"These Pierson guys don't waste any time."

"Or any tears. Neither Blake nor James seems grief-stricken over his uncle's death—at least not enough to curtail their social lives."

"So I noticed. I can't wait to find out the scoop behind that."

"Go for it. James is planning a full morning at the office. You can zero in on him as soon as Blake leaves for White Plains."

"Sounds like a plan. I'll check in with you later, in between your impromptu get-together with Blake and your hot date with James. We can compare notes."

"Want to choose my outfit for dinner?" Devon asked drily.

"Cute. No, I'll leave that to you. I do want to know where you'll be and when."

"Right. In case I need backup."

Monty chuckled. "You watch too many cop shows. Talk to you later."

With a wry grin, Devon hung up the phone.

"What was that all about?" Lane demanded.

"My part in this detective team—cajoling information out of Edward Pierson's grandsons."

"Clearly, you're well on your way." Lane raised his mug in a mock toast. "I'm impressed, doc. That was fast work."

"A little too fast, if you ask me." Devon frowned pensively. "Either I'm a lot hotter than I realized or those guys want to stick close to me for a reason."

"To find out Mom's whereabouts."

"That would be my guess." A final sip of coffee. "Plus,

there's major rivalry between James and Blake. I'm stepping in the middle of an interesting testosterone war—a fight to see who breaks down my defenses first, and who ultimately scores points with Grandpa." She set down her mug. "Wish me luck."

"Good luck. And Dev?" Lane stopped her as she headed toward the door. "I wouldn't be so quick to dismiss the idea that sexual agendas factor into their motivation. They're male. And you're a lot higher up on the hot scale than you realize. I should know. For the past ten years, I've been the one scaring off men with my stop-undressing-my-sister-with-your-eyes-or-I'll-punch-your-lights-out glare."

Devon's lips twitched. "Sorry to be so much trouble."

"Well, you are. And, as if that's not bad enough, I have to do a repeat performance with Merry. Couldn't *one* of you have inherited Dad's looks instead of Mom's?"

"One of us did—you. And, trust me, it's no deterrent. Women have been drooling over your dark, dangerous sex appeal since you reached puberty."

"We're not talking about me. We're talking about you. Be careful."

Devon snapped off a salute. "Yes, sir."

Thirty minutes later, she jumped into her royal blue Mazda Miata, backed out of her assigned parking space, and headed off to work.

A dark maroon coupe inched out from behind the snowbank that had concealed it from view. Pulling onto the road, it followed Devon's convertible at a discreet distance.

It was ten fifteen and Devon had just finished reviewing some follow-up X-rays on a collie whose leg she'd set, when Gil, her veterinary tech, poked his head in.

"There's a guy named Blake Pierson to see you."

No surprise there. "Is he with or without his golden retriever?" she asked.

"With. They're touring the place—evidently, on your recommendation. Can you break away?"

"Sure." Devon gestured at the X-ray screen. "These look good. Tell Mrs. Goble that Shep's doing fine. He'll be walking on that leg again in a few weeks."

She headed out of the X-ray room and walked down to the reception area.

Blake was standing at the desk, glancing over the clinic's brochure. Chomper was sprawled on the floor beside him, gnawing at his training leash. He spotted Devon instantly. Lurching to his feet, he yanked at the leash and barked, his tail wagging with great zeal.

Blake regained his balance and looked over at her, a slow smile curving his lips. "Hi."

"Hi to you both." Devon squatted down, scratching Chomper's ears, then reaching into her pocket as he continued to bark. "Translated, that bark means, 'You're the lady with the cookie. Where is it?' " She handed it over. "There you go. I'm not naive enough to believe you're thrilled just to see me."

"Speak for Chomper. Not for his owner." Blake's comment was teasing, but his expression was serious.

"Why? Don't you like peanut butter?"

"Sure I do. But it still comes in second right now."

Devon acknowledged the compliment with a polite nod and a murmured "Thanks." She shoved her hands in the pockets of her lab coat. "So, how was your tour?"

"Impressive. The facilities are great. So are the training classes. Chomper and I sat in on a beginner session. 'Puppy preschool,' I think it was called." Blake's lips twitched. "The name of the class might be amusing, but the instructor was all business. Talk about no-nonsense; *I* almost heeled on command."

Devon laughed. "I would have paid to see that. But, yes, our instructors are top-notch. They're crazy about dogs, but they manage to combine that love with an air of authority.

And, of course, skill. When you read our brochure, you'll see the astounding credentials everyone here has."

"You're very proud of this place," Blake noted. He picked up the brochure, glancing at it before he slipped it in his jacket pocket. "Now I know why. I spotted your name on the list of partners." He gave her another once-over, this time more assessing than intimate. "I'm guessing that's quite a coup. You're young. You can't be out of veterinary school for long."

"Two years. And, yes, I'm the youngest partner in the practice. I'm lucky. Dr. Sedwell had enough faith in me to give me this opportunity."

"I doubt luck had anything to do with it. I checked out Joel Sedwell. He's a pioneer in the veterinary field. He's made astonishing strides in animal behavior as well as surgical procedures."

Devon's brows rose. "So you *did* do some homework before coming in."

"Are you offended?"

"Not at all. I didn't expect you to take my word for the clinic's attributes. Chomper's important to you. That makes you a caring dog owner—something we love to see." Devon glanced at her watch. "How are you handling today's logistics? Your uncle's funeral is at noon. That's only an hour and a half from now. Did you want to leave Chomper with us?"

"Actually, yes. I've already made arrangement at your doggie day care."

"Good." Devon nodded. "Chomper will have the time of his life. I'll make sure he meets my dog, Terror, and my mom's Brussels griffon, Scamp. They're both super-friendly."

"I'm sure." Blake's brows had drawn together. "I don't recall mentioning that the funeral was at noon."

"You didn't. James did."

"James." Blake's tone was noncommittal. If the resentment Devon had picked up from James was reciprocated, it was well concealed. "I didn't realize you and he had spent any time together yesterday."

"We didn't." Devon tested the waters. "He called this morning. We're having dinner together tonight, before he leaves for Wellington."

"Ah." Blake looked more reflective than troubled. "And here I thought *I* was moving fast. It seems my cousin's even speedier. Kudos to him."

Devon folded her arms across her breasts. "Why do I feel like this is the NHL play-offs and I'm the Stanley Cup?"

That elicited a chuckle. "Because, in a way, you are." Blake surprised her with a bluntly frank reply. "James and I are competitive. We always have been. Two years apart in age, the only Pierson grandsons—it comes with the territory. In this case, it's also that we both have good taste."

"I'm not sure whether to be flattered or put off. I'm not into the whole macho rivalry thing. And I don't want to cause friction between you and James—especially not at a time like this."

"You won't." Blake dismissed the notion with a wave of his hand. "Have dinner with me tomorrow night."

"Why? Because James will be in Wellington where he can't find out?"

"No, because you're busy tonight, which is when I was going to ask you out for. Feel free to tell James. I'd do it myself, but a funeral's not exactly the right time to compare social calendars. If it makes you feel better, I'll track him down at the office and let him know. If you say yes to my invitation, that is."

Devon wished she knew what the full agenda here was, where the acting ended and the reality began. She also wished that the thought of having dinner with Blake Pierson wasn't so damned pleasing.

"Sure. Tomorrow night's fine."

"Great. Then I'll arrange for Chomper to spend the evening here. I'll pick him up after I take you home." Blake's fingers tightened on the leash as Chomper finished off his cookie and scrambled to his feet, ready to start bounding around. "That's my cue. What's your address, what time is good, and what kind of food do you like?"

"Fifteen Green Court, seven o'clock, and anything but sushi." Devon scribbled down a few quick directions. "It's a contemporary town-house development in northern White Plains. It's just a mile off the highway, right near the main drag. It's easy to find."

"Then I'll find it."

Blake pulled out of the clinic's parking lot fifteen minutes later, then glanced at his watch. He had to take a detour through Yonkers, check out the progress at Chomping at the Bit, and make it to the funeral service early. Time was tight.

He snapped his cell phone into the hands-free cradle and punched in his grandfather's private line.

"It's done," he announced.

"Good. Any snags?"

"Just one. James."

Philip Rhodes shut his office door and straightened his tie for the third time in as many minutes.

New head of security, his ass. Pete Montgomery was here for a lot more than safeguarding the Piersons. He was digging around for a lead in Frederick's murder.

He was still closeted with James in his office. What the hell were they talking about?

Damn, he was in trouble.

Rhodes wiped beads of sweat off his forehead. He was next on the PI's list of "chats." He couldn't give any indication that he was coming unglued. Montgomery was a retired detective. A pro. And with the funeral still an hour away, there was plenty of time for him to interrogate Philip and tear him to shreds.

He *had* to get through to Bolten.

Leaning over his desk, Rhodes punched on his speakerphone and pressed the redial button—again.

The same receptionist answered. "Paper and Plastics Limited. How may I direct your call?"

"Gary Bolten."

"One moment, and I'll connect you."

One ring. Two. Three. Voice mail.

Dammit.

Rhodes jabbed at the phone, disconnecting the call. He'd left the guy three messages already—two in his office and one on his cell phone. Where the hell was he?

Jumping up, Philip crossed over and poured himself a glass of ice water, lifting it to his lips with a shaking hand. He had to get it together, now, before Montgomery walked in.

Talk about setting a new low in bad luck. The situation would be comical if it weren't so harrowing. Sally Montgomery. Of all the women in the world, why did it have to be Montgomery's ex-wife whom Frederick had taken up to that cabin? Why hadn't he taken Louise? *Anyone* but a cop's ex.

The intercom buzzed.

"Yes?" Rhodes answered.

"Mr. Montgomery's ready to see you," Alice, his secretary, informed him. "And Mr. Bolten's on line three. Should I tell him you'll call back?"

"No." Rhodes snapped out the answer a lot more harshly than he'd intended. "No, Alice," he repeated, this time more calmly. "It's a quick call. And, with all that's going on today, I won't have a chance to get back to him. Tell Mr. Montgomery I'll be with him in a minute."

He didn't wait for the reply. He pressed the flashing light on line three.

"Gary?"

"Yeah, Phil. Sorry I didn't get back to you sooner. I was at my daughter's college for parents' weekend. The police tracked me down there and filled me in on what happened at the cabin. I still can't believe it. Poor Frederick. Did the cops find out who did it? Is that why you're calling?"

"What? No." Philip's mind was racing. "When you spoke to the cops, what did you say?"

"I confirmed that the cabin was mine and that I loaned it to Frederick for the weekend. What else could I say?"

"That loaning it to him was my idea."

"What difference does that make?"

"To me? A big difference. Did you tell them?"

"No."

Philip felt a pang of relief. "Good. Don't. I mean it, Gary. Don't say a word."

A prolonged silence.

"This is nuts, even for you," Bolten finally said. "You think that because you wanted your boss to enjoy a weekend getaway, the cops are gonna think it was a murder setup?"

"I don't know *what* they'll think. But I don't need to plant any seeds."

"What seeds? Does someone at Pierson actually think—"

"Let it go, Gary." Rhodes cut him off. "I can't get into it. It's politics. Let's leave it at that. Just don't bring up my name when you talk to the cops."

"Okay. Fine. But I think you're the one who needs a vacation."

"You're right. I do. And I'll take it. When all this is over."

Monty rubbed the back of his neck, glancing casually at Rhodes's secretary. Middle-aged. Sensible clothes. Quick and efficient. But on the serene side. Certainly less domineering than Frederick Pierson's secretary, Marjorie Evans. That woman was a bulldozer—and smart, too. Monty hadn't gotten squat out of her.

But this Alice Jeffers was worth a try.

"Is Mr. Rhodes still tied up?" Monty asked.

The secretary glanced at the telephone, then looked up from her computer and nodded. "I apologize for the delay."

"No problem. The call must be important. Mr. Rhodes sounded upset."

"Everyone's upset." A quick rise to her boss's defense. "I'm sure you can understand why."

"Of course I can—Ms. Jeffers, isn't it?"

Another nod.

"Your CEO was just killed. That's a huge blow to your company *and* to staff morale, considering how family-oriented Pierson & Company is. It would be strange if everyone *wasn't* on edge."

Ms. Jeffers's defensiveness eased. "I'm glad you recognize that."

"It would be hard not to. There are major reorganizational meetings taking place, and a ton of press hovering outside, ready to pounce on the Piersons. I feel sorry for them—for all of you, in fact. I'm sure Frederick Pierson was held in high regard."

"He was well respected. No one was more diligent or more dedicated."

Well respected. Nothing about being well liked.

Monty pretended to glance through his notes. "From what I've been told, he worked Guinness book hours."

"He did." The secretary relaxed a bit. Clearly, she was on more comfortable ground now. "He was always at his desk when I arrived, and when I went home. No matter how early or how late. He gave his all to the company."

"I'm sure that was especially true these past few years since his wife died."

"Losing her hit him hard. He devoted even more of his energies to the company after that."

"I can relate. Work is a great outlet when there's no one to go home to." Monty blew out a reflective breath. "With me, it was divorce. But becoming a widower? After decades of marriage? That must have really shaken him up."

"It did."

"I don't blame him for practically living at the office. I'm assuming that's how he and Ms. Chambers got together. She seems to put in long hours as well. It's a typical scenario for two lonely workaholics to start dating."

Ms. Jeffers's guard was back up. "I suppose so. I don't know much about their relationship. They worked well together. And, yes, they socialized. Any more than that, you'll have to ask Ms. Chambers."

"I plan to—after the funeral. The poor woman was too upset to talk this morning. I respected her request for some space. She and I are meeting later today." Monty cleared his throat. "Just so you know, I don't enjoy sticking my nose where it doesn't belong. I'm not expecting you to gossip about your colleagues. But my job is to keep everyone at Pierson & Company safe. I'm just trying to figure out where I should focus my energies."

"I'm not following."

"Let's just say that if someone needs extra security, I mean to provide it."

Ms. Jeffers's gaze widened as Monty's meaning sank in. "And that 'someone' might be a person Mr. Pierson was close to or confided in."

"Now you're getting the idea. You're a smart woman, Ms. Jeffers. And a discreet one, too. Don't alarm the staff by mentioning this. I doubt Ms. Chambers is in danger. I'm just covering all my bases."

"I understand." There was new respect in her eyes. Good. That's what Monty had been hoping for.

Time to zero in on the real subject he wanted to pursue with her.

"Let's get to Mr. Rhodes," Monty suggested, his concern over the staff's well-being still fresh in the secretary's mind. "He's practically a lifer here. How many years have you worked for him?"

"Sixteen."

"Wow. So you're his right hand. As he was Frederick Pierson's." A quizzical lift of his brows. "Right?"

"I suppose so." Ms. Jeffers propped her elbows on the desk, folding her hands beneath her chin. "Although I'm not sure I'd describe it that way. Mr. Rhodes reported directly to

Frederick Pierson, yes. But the sales department works as a team, not a two-man show."

"And who heads the team?"

"Now *that's* a tough call." Ms. Jeffers smiled faintly. "Because no matter how you slice it, Edward Pierson runs the show. You'll hear that from anyone you ask. God bless that man, at almost eighty he has more moxie than most thirty-year-olds."

"So I've noticed. He's a formidable guy. He also thinks a great deal of Mr. Rhodes."

"That's not a surprise. He hired him—it must be twenty-five or twenty-six years ago."

"Just a few years after Frederick came on board."

"That's right."

"Philip and Frederick were about the same age. Were they friends?"

"Not socially, no. But as colleagues, they worked extremely well together. In many ways, they built this company. Along with the senior Mr. Pierson, of course. Back then, the company was solely a food services business. Many of its key contacts were made during that time—by Frederick and Edward Pierson, and Mr. Rhodes. They established the foundation of the company, then built on it. Now we've got three divisions, all of which are still expanding."

"Would you say the food services division is the mainstay of your organization?"

"I'd say so, yes."

"So its sales team is front and center. Where does James fit into that team?"

Ms. Jeffers's smile was indulgent. "James fits into *every* team. Certainly sales. He's sharp as a tack. He's a first-class charmer. What better assets for someone in this department to have?"

"Good point. And you're right. I just spoke at length with James. He's quick. Not to mention versatile. After hearing everything he does—and apparently excels in—I feel like a slug."

"We all do," Ms. Jeffers said with a chuckle. "No one can keep up with James. He never wears out, not in business or on the show circuit."

"He's got endurance, all right. I envy him. Smart, talented, and unfazable."

"Not so unfazable," Ms. Jeffers amended in a placating tone. "Oh, I know he comes off that way. Like I said, he's quite the salesman. But beneath that cool veneer, he's very intense. He pushes himself hard. That's how he manages to excel at so many things."

"It's nice to know he has at least one fault."

Monty was ready to abandon the subject of James. After spending an hour with the guy, he'd already formed an opinion. The rest he'd learn tonight, after James's dinner with Devon.

Right now, he had other fish to fry.

Putting on a concerned expression, Monty lowered his voice. "Did Mr. Rhodes have any unusually long or intense meetings with Frederick Pierson last week? Anything that you noticed?"

Ms. Jeffers got his message loud and clear, and worry creased her forehead. "Oh, dear. You don't think Mr. Rhodes is in danger, do you?"

"I can't be sure. But it stands to reason that if Frederick Pierson's murder was triggered by something business-related, his closest in-house colleagues might be at risk. In which case, I plan to protect them."

"Of course." Ms. Jeffers gave a firm nod, then turned to the computer, punching up her electronic calendar. "Mr. Rhodes and Frederick Pierson had three meetings last week: Monday afternoon at three, Tuesday morning at ten, and Wednesday late afternoon. I don't have an exact time on the final one. Mr. Pierson set it up last minute. If I remember right, it started around four. I have no idea when it ended. They were still in Mr. Pierson's office when I left for the day."

"What time was that?"

"Six, maybe six fifteen."

"Who else attended that meeting?"

"It was just the two of them. James was in Wellington. Edward Pierson was up at the farm."

Monty was on the verge of asking Ms. Jeffers if she remembered any particular tension prior to that meeting, when he was interrupted by the buzz of the intercom.

Ms. Jeffers lifted the receiver. "Yes, Mr. Rhodes? Of course. Right away." She hung up and gestured toward the door. "You can go in now."

"Thanks." Monty rose, gathering up his notes.

"Mr. Montgomery?" The secretary's expression was still troubled, and she leaned forward to touch Monty's arm as he passed by her desk. "If there's anything else I can do, please let me know."

"I will. In the meantime, keep this conversation between us, all right? The last thing we need is for people to panic."

"You can count on me."

"Good. I will." With a warm, grateful smile, Monty walked over and knocked on Rhodes's door.

"Come in."

In the blink of an eye, Monty's smile vanished.

Different people. Different tactics.

He stepped inside and shut the door.

Philip Rhodes was sitting at his desk, a manilla folder lying open in front of him. His tie was as straight as his posture. Every one of his neatly styled gray hairs was in place. His concentration was fixed on the file he was perusing.

Ostensibly, the essence of composure. Clearly, anything but.

"Mr. Rhodes. Thanks for your time." Monty started the dance, subtly calling for Rhodes's attention.

The other man's head snapped up. "Oh. Yes, of course. Have a seat." He indicated a leather chair. "Edward mentioned he'd hired you, and that you'd be stopping by to get some information from me. What can I help you with?"

Monty kept his expression carefully blank. "I'll keep it brief," he said, sitting down and flipping open his notes. "It's a difficult day, and you have a funeral to get to."

"Right." Rhodes nodded, stealing a quick look at his watch. "It starts at noon. I have to be there early, for Edward and Anne."

"You're close with the Piersons."

"I've worked for them most of my life, so yes, I'm close with them."

"Personally? Or just professionally?"

Rhodes slid forward in his chair. His right leg was pumping, the heel of his shoe making a rat-a-tat sound on the floor. "To the Piersons, it's all one and the same. There's no dividing line. Not with Edward. And not with Frederick. This company's everything to them. That's why their family makes up most of the board."

"And you're a part of that family."

"I like to think so."

"I'm sure you do." Monty jotted something down. "You said you were expecting me. So you know what my job here is."

"To safeguard the place." Rhodes fiddled with his pen. "That's your official role, at least on paper."

"You don't believe it?"

"Oh, I believe it's *part* of why you're here. The other part is to figure out if someone here killed Frederick—or has any idea who did." Beads of perspiration dotted Rhodes's brow, but he pressed on, determined to expose Monty's hand. "I'm not an idiot, Montgomery. Edward didn't hire any old security guard. He hired a PI, a retired police detective who's worked every kind of violent crime, including homicide, in one of Brooklyn's worst crime districts. He didn't do that just so you could patrol the halls and make sure no bad guys with machine guns storm the place."

Monty didn't so much as blink. "That's a pretty dramatic assessment."

"Are you saying I'm wrong?"

"Nope. You're dead-on, although I think you're underestimating how worried Edward Pierson is about his family. As for the rest, my credentials aren't a secret. Neither is what I've been hired to do. I'm just keeping a low profile so no one here freaks out. But, yeah, I'm not only patrolling the place, I'm investigating the murder. So's the Warren County Sheriff's Office. I'm just doing it a little more up close and personal. That's the way Mr. Pierson wants it. Is it a problem?"

Rhodes's jaw worked. "No. No problem. In fact, knowing Edward, I should have expected it. I'll help in any way I can."

"Good. And I'll keep an eye out for your safety." Monty paused. "Any thoughts as to who'd want Frederick Pierson dead?"

"Not a one. He was a tough businessman. A real ball-breaker when he had to be. That causes friction, jealousy, and resentment. But murder? No way."

"What about in-house?"

"That's even more far-fetched. We haven't had so much as a resignation in the past several years. So it's a leap to think an employee killed the company CEO."

"Speaking of employees, what was the scoop with Louise Chambers and Frederick Pierson?"

A shrug. "They dated. Steadily, over the past six months. But they weren't—what's the word?—exclusive. They each saw other people. Obviously you knew that, since one of those people was your ex-wife."

"True." Monty nodded. "So, to your knowledge, there was no animosity, no lovers' quarrel, going on?"

"Frederick was a private person. He kept his feelings to

himself. As for Louise, she's the consummate professional. So I wouldn't know if they were on the outs. But, even if they were, Louise is no cold-blooded killer. You're barking up the wrong tree."

"I hear you." Monty shut his notebook and rose. "That's it for now. You've got a funeral to get to. I'll find you later, and we can get down to brass tacks."

"Brass tacks?"

"You know, the things that produce leads. Details of your current business ventures. Specific events and phone calls. Recent discord among family members. Special favors that went sour. Nothing the cops won't ask."

Rhodes didn't reply. But his silence spoke volumes.

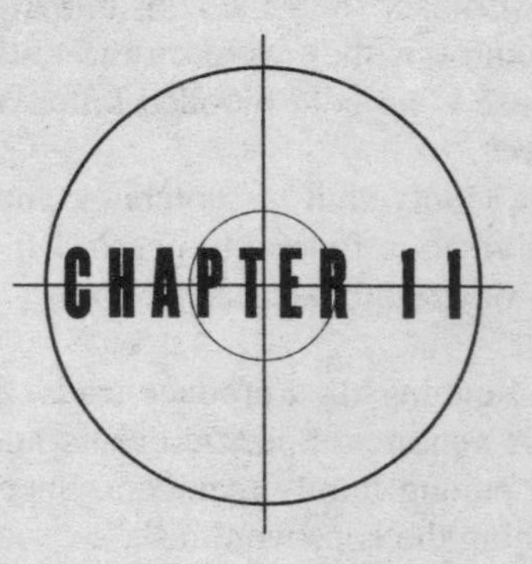

CHAPTER 11

Devon put on a touch of mascara, then stepped back to assess her reflection in the bedroom mirror.

Not too done up. Not too casual. Classic black silk slacks and a pale pink cashmere sweater.

Perfect for a date with the oh-so-smooth James Pierson.

A quick glance at the clock. Six forty-seven. Almost showtime.

Turning back to the dresser, Devon picked up her brush and ran it through her hair until it tumbled down her back like a silky curtain.

The telephone rang. Someone else in the house picked it up.

A minute later, there was a knock on Devon's door and Meredith poked her head in. "For you. It's Dad."

"Of course it is." Devon grimaced. "I'll be with him in a minute."

Meredith walked in and plopped down on the bed, reaching for Devon's phone. "Dad? Hang on." She was about to push the hold button, then paused, the receiver still pressed to her ear. "What? I'm fine. Yes, I got your message. I have a ton of work to do. We'll see. Maybe. Yes, I'll get back to you tomorrow. Here's Devon." She handed her sister the phone. "You look beautiful," she told her.

"Thanks." Devon studied Meredith pensively. "Can you wait here a sec? I'll be off as soon as I'm prepped for battle."

"Sure." Meredith settled herself more comfortably and propped a pillow behind her head.

"Hey, Monty." Devon tucked the phone under her chin and applied her lip gloss as she spoke.

"Hey, yourself. All set?"

"Yup. Dressed and ready. And you're in the car—again."

"On my way to Edward Pierson's apartment. I was summoned. Time to report in on my first day."

"How'd it go?"

"As expected. No major surprises. Except Louise Chambers, who was too broken up to talk to me. She went home right after the funeral. I'll have to track her down tomorrow. It's too bad, too. Funerals make people vulnerable."

"And easier to interrogate."

"Right." Monty went on to fill Devon in on his chats with Marjorie Evans, Alice Jeffers, and Philip Rhodes. "That was my morning. My afternoon wasn't productive. No one got back from the service until three. And even then, they arrived in a trickle. The major players showed up for an hour or so and then took off. Again, more to come tomorrow."

"What about James and Blake?"

"As expected. James is the center of the universe. He's also insecure as hell when it comes to his cousin Blake. With good reason. James has the flair. Blake has the substance. He's got great instincts and a big-picture mentality. There's no doubt that Blake is the future of Pierson & Company. And that's a lot more long lasting than a gold medal. By the way, did Blake ask you out?"

"Uh-huh. Dinner tomorrow night. I haven't done this back-to-back weeknight thing since college."

"Yeah, well, at least you'll get some good food out of the deal. Where's Blake taking you?"

"To be decided. We're talking tomorrow."

"What about James?"

"We're going to the Gedney Grill, right here in White Plains."

"Good choice. Get the baby back ribs. You'll be covered in barbecue sauce. Too slimy to touch."

Devon chuckled. "I like their sirloin. But thanks for the thought."

"No problem. I'm not worried anyway. You two won't be alone."

She blinked. "You plan on being there with your binoculars?"

"Nope. Not necessary. Edward's got security on his grandson, remember?"

"That's right. I'll keep that in mind, even though James has no idea he's being guarded like Fort Knox. I'll check out the place, see if there's some burly guy with a toothpick in his mouth peering at us over the top of a newspaper."

"Like I said, you watch too many cop shows. More likely, he'll be a young punk who's wolfing down a sirloin and guzzling imported beer so he can charge an expensive meal to Edward Pierson."

"Good point." Devon finished applying lip gloss. "Anyway, I appreciate the reminder."

"Sure thing. Now go figure out what makes Golden Boy tick. Use the personal angle. Poke around about his family relationships, his view of Philip Rhodes. You know the drill. But soft-pedal it. I'll do the heavy-handed stuff."

"I'll be cuddly as a kitten."

"Just keep your claws ready."

"Yes, Monty."

"Explore his other world—the show circuit. What's his

mind-set in the saddle? Who are his competitors? Who'd have an ax to grind?"

"I get it, Monty."

"Call me when you get home. I don't care what time it is."

"I will, Monty."

"Oh, and one more thing—"

"Good-bye, Monty." Devon hung up the phone.

"That sounded like fun," Meredith noted drily.

"It was just Dad being Dad." Devon eyed her sister. "I take it he asked to see you?"

"Yeah, he wanted to get together. I can't. I have a huge paper to write and three exams to study for. As it is, I've been ignoring my friends. They've been IM-ing me since I left school. I have to go online and answer them."

"Ah, Instant Messenger. How did Lane and I get through college without it?" Devon's tone was teasing, but her gaze was serious. "Merry . . ."

"The cable guy was here," her sister piped up. "He came by this morning and cleared up the problem you were having with the upper channels. Apparently, it wasn't just you. It was your whole town-house development."

"That's nice." Devon wasn't fooled by the attempted distraction. "We have to talk about this."

"No, we don't."

Devon sat down beside her sister. "Try to cut Monty a little slack. He screwed up. He realizes that. He didn't mean to. He loves you."

Meredith sighed. "I know that, Dev. I get the whole picture—better than you and Lane think I do. I'm not a kid. I'm an adult. I understand mistakes. I also understand consequences. I'm not angry at Dad. I just don't have the same bond with him that you and Lane do. It's no one's fault. It's just the way things turned out."

"Mom's forgiven him."

"So have I. That doesn't erase all the years in between.

Besides, don't compare me to Mom. She's hardly objective. She's still crazy about him."

"I know." Devon traced the geometric pattern on her comforter with one fingertip.

"And *you* still think there's a chance they'll get back together."

"Guilty as charged," Devon freely admitted. "I've never seen two people so much in love—even fifteen years after getting divorced."

"No arguments. But love doesn't conquer all. Not in real life."

"You sound like Lane."

"Well, Lane's right. The fact is, Mom's an incredible woman. She deserves someone who'll put her first. Dad never did."

"His life's different now."

"Is it? He's all gung ho about this case. He's got you working it with him. Is this really about Mom and her safety? Or is this just Monty, doing his Dick Tracy thing?"

Devon blew out a weary breath. "You really are bitter."

"No, I'm realistic. I see Dad for what he is."

"Then maybe it's time you *accepted* him as he is," Devon suggested softly. She gave Meredith's arm a squeeze. "Grab a sandwich with him. Talk. Get to know each other. Monty missed out on your childhood. Don't deprive him of getting to know you as an adult. You're a terrific, sensitive young woman, Merry. Give him a chance."

Downstairs, the doorbell rang.

"That's your date." Meredith scrambled to her feet. "I'll let him in."

"Merry?"

Her sister paused in the doorway. "I'll think about it. Okay?"

"Okay."

Monty assessed the Park Avenue penthouse, wondering if the butler who'd taken his coat earned more a year than he did. Talk about living your money. If anybody doubted how much Pierson & Company raked in in profits, one glance at Edward Pierson's four-thousand-square-foot, floor-to-ceiling windowed palace would change their mind.

The king himself was in the sunken living room, pacing around restlessly and glaring at the glass of ice water in his hand. On one of the antique sofas, Blake Pierson sat, engaged in quiet conversation with the regal-carriaged, elderly woman who had to be his grandmother.

An interesting combo of personal and professional.

"Mr. Montgomery," the butler announced.

Edward veered around, waving Monty in. "You made good time."

"I aim to please." Monty stepped into the room and waited for Edward to set the stage.

"You've met Blake." Edward paused while the two men acknowledged each other. "And this is my wife."

"Mrs. Pierson," Monty responded with a respectful nod of his head. "My condolences on your loss."

"Thank you." Anne Pierson didn't rise, but extended a polite hand to him in greeting. Her tone and expression were cool, but there was pain behind those piercing light blue eyes. "I understand you're working for my husband."

Monty shot Edward a quick, questioning look.

"I know everything," Anne supplied before Edward could answer. "I pried it out of these two. I won't be protected. Not when it comes to my family. Frederick was my son. You're looking for his killer. And for whoever's threatening James. I want to know what you've found out."

Monty wasn't particularly surprised by her spunk. Anyone married to Edward Pierson had to be a tough broad. She'd climbed the ranks with him from paper-goods distributor to food-industry giant. You had to respect that. Sixty years ago, she'd been a salesperson at Macy's. Now she was a matriarch.

"Not much," Monty answered her question. "Not yet."

"Nothing?" Edward snapped. "That's no better than the cops."

"Murderers generally don't want to get caught. That's why finding them takes a while."

"Why don't you have a seat, Mr. Montgomery," Anne suggested, clearly trying to ease the tension. "Would you like a drink?"

"No, thanks. I'm fine." Monty perched at the edge of a chair. "What did the police have to say?"

"Very little we didn't already know," Blake provided. "They found a few more tire treads down by the road. Turned out to be a dead end. They belonged to Frederick's Mercedes, just like the others. Gasoline was the killer's accelerant of choice. He splashed the stuff around and then probably lit the drapes. The whole cabin was torched in minutes. No other clues were found in the debris." A pause. "Of course, the hunt is still on for your ex-wife."

Monty got the message loud and clear. "No one knows that better than I do. My kids are a mess. But judging from what Sally said on the phone, she's as clueless as we are. Traumatized, but clueless. And scared to death."

"She hasn't called again—not even her kids?"

"Nope. They would've let me know."

"So you check in with them often?" Blake asked carefully.

"Every day." Monty met Blake's probing stare. "Sally raised them. But they're my kids, too. Grown or not. Since this happened, I keep tabs on them, make sure they're okay." Putting an end to that obvious fishing expedition, Monty turned to Edward. "Any follow-up on the blackmail letter?"

Edward shook his head and gulped down some water. "Not a word. No phone calls. No mail. Nothing."

Monty frowned. "Strange."

"Maybe they're waiting for James to go back to Wellington. Up here, he's no threat to his competitors."

"That would only make sense if the extortion was an isolated incident. But if it ties into Frederick's murder—as we both assume it does—that theory doesn't fly. My money's still on a business or family vendetta. That would encompass the whole enchilada, from Pierson & Company to the show ring to your family members themselves."

"You're saying we all could be in danger?" Anne demanded.

"I'm not trying to alarm you, Mrs. Pierson. I'm just calling it as I see it." Monty's gaze returned to Edward. "I questioned some of your staff today. I'll be doing more of that tomorrow. I've also started rundowns on your potential enemy list. So far, no red flags. But I'll keep at it. In addition, I'll start digging around inside Pierson & Company for a paper trail. Which reminds me, I put in a call to a forensic accountant I work with. Alfred Jenkins. He's top-notch in his field. He knows what to look for in situations like these. He'll leave no stone unturned. Acceptable?"

"Yes, acceptable," Edward agreed.

"Good. I want to bring him on board as soon as possible. In the meantime, I'll need free access to correspondence, telephone and e-mail records, and financial accounts, both personal and professional. When can that be made available to me?"

"Right away," Blake answered for his grandfather. "I'll log you in with my password. That'll give you access to pretty much everything."

"Including the high-security stuff? Blocked personal and/or confidential material that's protected by extra security passwords? Because I'll need access to all that, too."

Blake remained silent, deferring to his grandfather.

"Fine," Edward replied. "Blake will give you everything."

"Then I'll be in his office at eight A.M."

Before Blake could reply, his cell phone rang. He pulled it out of his pocket and glanced at the number, a pensive expression crossing his face. "Excuse me a minute." Rising, he walked over to the panorama of windows. "Hi," he said quietly into the phone. "Are you all right?"

Edward eyed his grandson for an instant, then turned back to Monty. "What did you think of Philip Rhodes?"

"I just scratched the surface." Monty responded to the question on autopilot. He was straining to hear Blake's conversation. "First impressions? Rhodes is dedicated to his job. He's loyal to you. And he's got something he doesn't want to talk about."

"Now's not a good time," Blake was saying. His words were low, but Monty could make them out. "I'm in a meeting. I'll check in with you later."

He punched off the phone, just as his grandfather reacted to what Monty had said about Rhodes.

"What do you mean, something he doesn't want to talk about? Something about Frederick?"

"Don't know. Could be something totally unrelated. But whatever it is, I intend to figure it out." Monty studied Blake as he rejoined the group. "Woman problems?"

Blake's brows rose. "Pardon me?"

"Judging from your tone, I assumed that was your girlfriend, and she was giving you a hard time."

"No hard time. And no girlfriend. Just a friend who happens to be female."

"Ah. Those can be high maintenance, too."

"Yup." Blake didn't bat an eye. "Sure can."

In her luxurious apartment on East Sixty-eighth Street, Louise Chambers hung up the phone and gritted her teeth in frustration.

A meeting. One he wouldn't excuse himself from. Not even to come by and offer her a shoulder to lean on. That didn't bode well.

Dammit. She wasn't going to let things fall apart. Not after all her planning, all her careful orchestration and infinite patience. She hadn't endured all she had just to lose out in the end.

Damn Frederick. It had been first one obstacle, then another. Now he was dead.

This was her last chance.

And no one was robbing her of it.

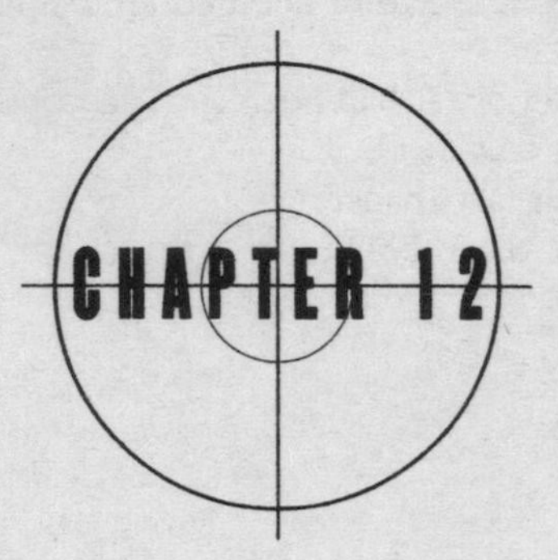

The Gedney Grill was a little more subdued than usual, most likely because it was a Monday night. Which was fine with Devon. The less boisterous the atmosphere, the easier it was to talk.

She and James had been here long enough to polish off a glass of wine, eat their salads, make a dent in their entrées, and cut through the niceties. During that time, Devon had spotted a grown-up street kid whom, after careful scrutiny, she'd determined was James's "bodyguard." He'd been watching them nonstop from across the room. So if Edward Pierson didn't already know about this date, he'd know by tomorrow.

"How's your steak?" Oblivious to his lookout, James was focused totally on Devon. He wrapped her up in his gaze, concentrating on every word she said, saturating her with attention. At the same time, he spoke freely about himself, emphasizing all the right things, downplaying all the flaws.

The center of the universe, Monty had said. Well, he was dead-on.

"Devon?" James repeated over the rim of his glass of Cabernet.

"Sorry." She put down her fork and knife. "My steak's delicious, as always. It's also superfilling. I can barely move. It's breather time."

James chuckled. "I know what you mean. I could use a time-out, too." He pushed his plate aside and indicated her half-filled goblet. "More Cab?"

"No, thanks. Two's my limit. Otherwise, I get a massive headache. But you go ahead."

"Uh-uh. Two's my limit, too. I usually don't drink at all when I'm competing. So, after this glass, it's club soda for me."

"I didn't think of that." Devon was thrilled for the opening he'd given her. Time for equestrian chitchat. "Your abstinence, is that because of potential drug testing?"

"Nope." James shook his head. "When it comes to equestrian events, the Antidoping Agency doesn't concern itself with alcohol. Booze would only retard a rider's performance. The agency is more worried about the presence of coke or steroids, neither of which I do. As for drinking, I just choose to err on the side of caution. I plan to win. I don't want anything, not even the slightest mental cobweb, to screw up my timing or my form."

"You demand a lot of yourself."

"That's the only way to become number one. Anything less is unacceptable."

"A perfectionist. *And* a very competitive one."

"Is that bad?"

Devon's shoulders lifted in a shrug. "I'm guessing it's necessary when you're riding for the kind of stakes you are." She leaned forward. "Tell me what it's like. The people. The anticipation. Riding in a Grand Prix—I can't even imagine—it must be an amazing adrenaline rush."

"It is." James rolled his goblet between his palms. "It's intense. It's disciplined. And it's consuming. The talent you're up against is daunting. The mentality is 'win at all costs.' There's big money and big egos on the line. Mine included."

"When you say 'win at all costs'—I assume that some participants would cheat, bribe, or even sabotage to win."

"Some would *kill* to win."

Devon started. Was James trying to impress her, or was he actually stating a fact?

"Okay, now that's got to be an exaggeration," she probed lightly.

"Does it? Sometimes I'm not sure." James's tone and expression were hard.

"Whew." Devon blew out her breath. "Clearly, your show-circuit crowd's just a little too intense for my tastes."

"Some of them. Not all."

"Is it mostly the riders or the sponsors?"

"Both."

"Anyone in particular you've come up against?"

James's jaw tightened a fraction. "Over the years? More than I care to recall."

"This go-around, too?"

"Uh-huh."

Devon gave a troubled frown. "That must really mess up your concentration. How do you handle it?"

"I block it out. And I steer clear of those types."

"But you're competing in the same events. How can you—?"

"The events are *inside* the ring," he interrupted flatly. "There, I deal with whoever I have to. Outside's another story. I pick and choose."

Devon couldn't miss the note of finality. She'd pried pretty deep. If she pushed James any further, he'd get suspicious.

"I'm glad to hear there are some normal types, too," she

tried instead. "With such a supercharged atmosphere, you'd go nuts if you didn't have a few friends to hang out with."

"I get enough downtime. As for friends, I don't know if I'd call them that. They're more like comrades in arms."

"It sounds like war."

"At times, it is." James's jaw was still working. "Being the victor is everything. How you get there is secondary. It's easy to lose all sense of perspective; to see nothing, care about nothing, but the prize." Abruptly, he relaxed—or forced himself to. "That's why I like my double life; part-time at Pierson, part-time on the circuit. It keeps me grounded."

"Your family must help with that, too."

"Some members of it, yes."

Very pointed inference. Time for Devon to take a risk. "You don't like Blake much, do you?"

James's brows rose. "Why? Do you?"

She blinked. "I hardly know him."

"But you're going out with him."

Now *that* caught her off guard. "He told you?"

"He made a point of it, right before I left for the day."

Devon caught her lower lip between her teeth. "That's my fault. I insisted that it be out in the open. I didn't want to cause problems between you two."

James snorted. "No worries on that score. Any problems between my cousin and me started years before you came on the scene. Blake and I have been one-upping each other since we were kids. It's partly because we're the only two male grandchildren, partly because we're both overachievers, and partly because we have different personalities, different goals, and different ways of going after those goals."

"Sounds pretty normal to me. It also sounds as if you have one goal in common: pleasing your grandfather. Which I find commendable."

A grin that could melt ice. "When you put it that way, I come off as noble." His grin faded. "You didn't answer my question."

"About liking Blake? As I said, I hardly know him. He seems like a pleasant enough guy. And, yes, we're having dinner tomorrow night. He brought Chomper into my clinic for obedience training. We chatted. He was very nice."

" 'Nice.' That's not a word I'd use to describe Blake. Ambitious. Deliberate. Single-minded when he wants something. Relentless when he goes after it. Those are better choices."

"Those same adjectives could be used to describe you."

James gave a thoughtful nod, his good humor restored. "Touché. Maybe that's the problem. Maybe, when it comes right down to it, Blake and I are just too damned much alike. Looks like we're even attracted to the same women."

"Why, has this happened before?"

"That we both date the same person? No. Then again, it's not often that a woman as beautiful, intelligent, and charming as you just strolls through our front door. We'd have to be stupid not to react. And that's one thing neither Blake nor I is—stupid."

"A gross understatement, I suspect." Devon took another sip of wine. "What about you and your sister—Tiffany, isn't it? Are you two close?"

"When we both stand still long enough to connect, yeah. Tiff's a whirlwind. She's got this motherhood–career-woman combination down pat. But it doesn't leave time for much else. Not that I'm complaining. Kerri's fantastic. Then again, I'm biased. She's crazy about horses. And she's a natural in the saddle. I'm glad I don't have to compete against her. By the time she takes the equestrian world by storm, I'll be retired."

"Somehow I can't imagine you retired."

"You'd be surprised." James resumed slicing his steak. "A couple of gold medals. A big windfall at Pierson. I might be persuaded."

"In other words, leave your mark on both worlds, then fade off into the sunset?"

He laughed aloud. "Fade off? Nah. I'm not the fading-off type. More like the constant-burst-of-fireworks type."

"Ah." Devon followed his lead, cutting her sirloin as she spoke. "A hedonist. So retirement will be one unending party."

"Sounds good to me." His brows rose. "What about you?"

"I haven't thought that far ahead yet. I just bought into my veterinary practice. I like to flatter myself into thinking they couldn't get along without me." Devon chewed and swallowed. "In my case, that's wishful thinking. But in your case, it's probably fact." A weighted pause. "Especially now. I'm sure you're on overload after what happened to your uncle."

If the reference upset James, he didn't show it.

He shrugged, continuing to eat. "The burden falls mostly on Philip Rhodes. Senior VP of sales," he added by way of explanation. "I don't know if you met him yesterday when you dropped by the farm. He's my boss. After that, the buck stopped with Frederick. I've got to crank things up a notch—do a little extra hand-holding with our key suppliers and contacts. But Philip's the one who'll have to do the major juggling act until things settle down. Then again, he's always had that role. Remember, I'm away a lot. He's used to this."

"It sounds as if your family's lucky to have him on board."

"I suppose we are."

Devon picked up on the odd note in James's voice. "Am I missing something? Is Mr. Rhodes a problem in some way?"

"Phil? The only problem is getting him to go home. He's a die-hard workhorse. It's just that I never viewed us as lucky to have him on board. I doubt he has, either. He's been with us for so long, he's like family."

"In that case, maybe your grandfather will appoint him the new CEO."

A short, derisive laugh. "Not *that* much like family. No, my grandfather would never let a non-Pierson head up the company. Technically, my father's next in line for the CEO spot. I doubt he wants it. Not that it would matter if he did. My grandfather's long since decreed that it'll be Blake who takes over the throne. This will just accelerate his ascension."

"Does that bother you? You're older, right?"

"I've got two years on Blake. But, no, it doesn't faze me in the least. I've got zero desire to run Grandfather's empire. I've got a different legacy to fulfill."

"Capturing the Olympic gold."

"You got it."

"I think it's great that you and your father are both so accepting about Blake becoming Pierson & Company's head honcho." Devon pursed her lips thoughtfully. "But, as you said, you're family. Philip Rhodes isn't; not really. You'll reap the long-term benefits of Blake's leadership. He won't. Is he really that magnanimous? I know I'd hate working my tail off if I knew there was a dead end at the finish line."

James stopped chewing. "This is starting to feel like an interrogation."

Mentally, Devon kicked herself. Too pushy. Too obvious. Time for damage control.

She launched into the speech she'd prepared if something like this happened.

"Sorry." A rueful smile. "Force of habit. My dad's a retired cop. I guess being nosy is in my blood." She stared at the tablecloth. "And I admit there's a part of me that is interrogating you. I want to know who killed your uncle. I want him behind bars. I miss my mother. I'm scared for her. I want this nightmare to be over. I want my mother home, safe and sound."

Her ploy must have worked, because James covered her hand with his. "I understand. Everyone's focusing on what a horrible time this is for my family. Well, it's a pretty horrible one for yours, too. Your mother's out there somewhere. You must be a mess."

"I am."

"What can I do to help?"

"You're doing it now, just offering your support. And forgiving me for grilling you."

"No forgiveness is necessary. And, for the record, if I had any idea who did this to Frederick, I'd offer the SOB up on a platter. Frederick and I had different styles—God knows, we didn't always see eye to eye—but he was my uncle. I get sick when I think about how he died."

Devon wasn't letting that admission go without a try. "Different styles?" she repeated quizzically. "Why, was he closed-minded, or overly conventional?" She rushed on, determined to keep the harmonious moment from disintegrating back into wariness. "I'm not interrogating, not this time. My question is strictly personal. Your uncle was dating my mother—seriously enough for her to go away with him for a weekend. That's not something she'd do lightly. I guess I need to feel as if I knew him."

"I suppose I can understand that." James didn't release her hand. "Frederick was a workaholic. When I said we didn't see eye to eye, it was because we handle things differently. I combine work and play. Frederick is—was—all about work. He's as serious as a heart attack. Our goals are the same. I just enjoy the means as well as the end."

"Meaning you wine and dine the players."

A grin. "Smart girl. It's a winning combination, at least for me. Sales is all about people. Win their hearts, and their wallets will follow."

"People." Devon's lips curved. "Why do I get the distinct feeling that most of those *people* were women?"

"Because, like I said, you're a smart girl."

"And Frederick didn't approve?"

"Let's just say he wasn't a big fan of living on the edge. Then again, he had the weight of the world on his shoulders.

He answered to my grandfather. That couldn't have been fun."

"Especially if your methods were more successful than his." Devon processed that and continued. "Was your grandfather upset by the way you went about doing things?"

"He was happy as a clam. I won over the accounts. That trumped all else. And if you're asking if Grandfather would blast Frederick if he was pissed off at me, the answer is no. My grandfather's not a subtle guy. If he was pissed at me, he'd call me in and read me the riot act—right to my face."

"Where did Philip Rhodes fit in? He must have been caught in the middle."

"Not really. Philip liked seeing profits rise. Plus, he was tight with my grandfather. So things were copacetic."

"It sounds as if your uncle was a hard guy to get along with. Were any of the accounts put off by him?"

One brow rose. "Back to interrogating?"

"Fishing is more like it. If you could think of anyone who had an ax to grind with Frederick . . ."

"I would have given his name to the cops," James finished. "They have a complete list of family, friends, and business associates, along with notes about their specific relationships with Frederick."

"I guess." Devon lowered her gaze.

"Devon." James's grip on her hand tightened. "I know you're eager to have your mother home. But the cops will figure this out. Unless your father beats them to it." A pause. "You did know he was working at Pierson, didn't you?"

Devon had to give him credit. He'd turned the tables in a hurry. Now it was his turn to test her.

She nodded. "Yes, I knew. I was Monty's ride up to the farm yesterday. He was in there too long just to be rehashing what your grandfather already knew. So I quizzed him about the meeting on our drive home. All I got out of him was that he'd taken a security job at Pierson & Company. No surprise that he wouldn't elaborate. He never discusses his cases. But given the circumstances, I'd have to be an idiot not to figure it out."

"You're no idiot. Then again, neither is your father. We spoke for a chunk of time this morning. He's a sharp guy."

"I know. I'm glad he's working this case—not only for your family's sake, but for mine. We're worried sick about our mother."

"I met your sister, Meredith, when I picked you up. Any other siblings?"

"An older brother, Lane. He's thirty-two. Merry's almost twenty-one. We're all holding on to one another to get through this."

"What about your father? Does he factor into this family support system?"

My, James was interested in Monty. "Not really," she stated flatly.

"So you're not close with him?"

"No one's close with Monty. His work is his life. Always was. Always will be. In this situation, that's good. He'll find your uncle's killer. You'll have closure. And we'll have my mother back. In the meantime, I can't stop myself from asking questions. It's all I can do—and I have to do something."

James studied her for a long moment. Then he brought her fingers to his lips. "You're a fascinating package. Independent and self-assured one minute, sensitive and vulnerable the next. The most intriguing woman I've met in a long time."

Devon wondered how many women had heard that particular speech.

"I sound like a Tootsie Pop," she responded drily. "Hard on the outside, soft and chewy on the inside."

At first, James looked startled. Then he began to laugh. "Ouch. I think my ego just took a hit. Add 'painfully honest' to that list of qualities."

"Sorry." She mustered a wry grin. "That comes from years of eavesdropping on my brother's conversations. He's got a dozen seduction speeches down pat."

"And that sounded like one of them?" James gave a self-deprecating shake of his head. "I'd better work on my technique, then. The last thing I need is to be figured out."

"Relax. Not every woman has a big brother. And very few of them have one like Lane. He's the whole package—looks, brains, magnetic charm, financial success, and an exciting lifestyle." A purposeful pause. "Actually, I think I just described you."

That did the trick. James's eyes glinted with satisfaction. "Now that's a comparison I can live with. I'd like to meet this brother of yours sometime."

"Then you're in luck. He'll probably be there tonight when you take me home."

"At your place?"

"Uh-huh. He's staying with me until we get news about Mom. So's Merry. Like I said, we're keeping one another together."

"I see. Well, that certainly puts a crimp in my plans for the evening. I was hoping you and I would be alone."

Devon wasn't going to play games, not when she knew damned well what that comment meant. "It's a little too soon for what you have in mind. I don't live life in the fast lane the way you do. Besides, don't you have to be up early for your flight back to Wellington?"

James nodded, taking her not-yet message gracefully. "The Gold Coast Classic's this week. I'm competing on Wednesday. I'm riding one of my grandfather's younger stallions, Future. It's an intermediate-level event, but it keeps me in shape for Sunday's Grand Prix." He caressed her palm before releasing her hand. "I'm assuming that was a 'later' and not a 'no'?"

"That was a combination 'let's see what happens' and 'let's give it time.' "

"Fair enough." James seemed satisfied with her answer. He sat up and glanced around for the waiter. "If this is the only alone time we're going to get tonight, let's prolong it. Coffee and dessert time."

The bat phone rang.

Sitting in his living room, Monty responded instantly to the expected call. He pressed the mute button on his TV remote, silencing the eleven o'clock news. Then he shifted his La-Z-Boy recliner into the upright position and punched on the phone.

"Right on time," he greeted.

"And that surprises you?" Sally returned lightly. "I'm not the one who thinks punctual means a half hour late."

"Ouch." Monty grinned. "That hurt."

"You can take it. You're tough."

Monty wasn't fooled by Sally's banter. He heard the underlying strain, and his grin faded. "You okay?"

"I guess." Sally drew an unsteady breath. "Physically I'm fine. A dull headache and a scratchy throat are the only lingering effects from the fire. Emotionally's another story. I hate being cut off. I feel helpless." She coughed. "Anyway, I'm calling in, as ordered."

"Good. Now get some sleep. Call in again tomorrow, same time."

"Pete—wait." Sally broke in. "Where do things stand? What did you find out?"

"Not a hell of a lot," he replied, keeping it vague. He couldn't undo what Sally had been through so far, but he damned well intended to keep her out of the line of fire from here on in. "It'll take time. Today was just my first day at Pierson & Company."

"Stop placating me." Sally's impatient words told Monty he wasn't getting off that easily. "Your whole macho protective strategy isn't going to work. Not anymore. I'm a cop's ex-wife. I'm too smart. And I know you too well. So stop hedging and answer me."

"Fine." Monty relented. "Right now, I'm focusing on

Philip Rhodes, trying to figure out if he's the one Edward and Frederick were arguing about at the barn. He's jumpy. Could mean something; could mean nothing. Tomorrow, I'm digging into financial, phone, and e-mail records. And Devon's picking James Pierson's brain as we speak."

"Did Devon really want to do this, or did you twist her arm?"

"No arm-twisting was necessary. Devon would do anything to ensure your safety. And don't worry. I'm watching her back every step of the way."

"I know you are." Sally's voice was getting weaker and raspier. "I just wish—" She broke off to dissolve into a spasm of coughing.

"Go to bed, Sal," Monty instructed. "You need your rest. I'm on top of this. I'll fill you in when there's something to say."

"I'll hold you to that."

His lips curved again. "I never doubted it. Talk to you tomorrow. Same Bat time, same Bat channel."

A hint of laughter. "Good night, Pete."

An hour and a half later, James left Devon's town house, having exchanged polite greetings with Lane and chatted for a minute with Meredith. He climbed into his Beemer and pulled away.

The punk who'd been scrutinizing him all night waited until the sports car had rounded the bend. Then he threw the gearshift of his beat-up Chevy into drive and followed close behind.

From his surveillance spot in the cluster of bushes near Devon's town house, the driver of the maroon coupe watched the Chevy drive away. Reaching over, he diddled with the controls on his audio equipment before settling himself behind the wheel and clamping on his headphones.

First—silence.

Then a telephone number being punched in.

Montgomery answered on the first ring. "You're home."

"Safe and sound," his daughter replied. "A few personal tidbits to report. Nothing major. How about your meeting?"

"The same. You sound beat. Wanna talk in the morning?"

"Yeah. Believe me, there's no case cracker tonight. I'll call you as soon as I get up."

"Unless I call you first."

A shared chuckle, and then a dial tone.

Okay. He'd get the lowdown in about six hours. He could use a nap anyway.

He leaned back against the headrest and shut his eyes.

Monty was poring over a month's worth of Pierson & Company e-mails, his stomach growling for lunch, when Alfred Jenkins returned his call.

After hearing Monty out, the forensic accountant gave a low whistle. "Now that's what I call a high-profile case."

"High profile enough to get you to shift your schedule and haul your butt into Manhattan?"

"How does tomorrow morning sound?"

"Like the answer I was hoping for."

"Thought so." Jenkins paused. "Are the cops having any luck tracking down your ex?"

"Nope."

"Now why doesn't that surprise me?"

Monty didn't bat an eye. "Because you know she learned from the best."

"And the most modest." Jenkins cleared his throat. "I hope you get her home safe."

"I plan to. See you in the morning."

Monty scarfed down a sandwich, then headed down to Louise Chambers's office for the third time that day. She'd been in morning meetings, then out to lunch. It was time to lie in wait.

He greeted her secretary, then seated himself next to her station. "I'll wait for Ms. Chambers."

It wasn't a request.

Ten minutes later, the woman in question walked in. "Diana, please hold my calls. I have some legal documents I have to—" She spotted Monty and broke off, her brows arching in surprise. "I didn't realize Mr. Montgomery and I had an appointment." A quick glance at her secretary.

"Don't blame Diana," Monty interjected smoothly. "I didn't give her much choice. You're a busy woman, Ms. Chambers. Getting in to see you is a real challenge. So I decided to grab you first thing after lunch. You can spare ten or fifteen minutes, can't you?"

"Of course." She was definitely ticked off. But she kept it under wraps. "Come on in."

He waited while she picked up her messages, then followed her into the elegant cream and chocolate brown office. Modern. Classy. Expensive.

"Have a seat." She gestured at the swivel chair across from her desk.

He complied, waiting until she'd settled herself in the plush leather desk chair.

"I'm sorry it's been so hard for us to connect." Clearly, she was going for the penitent approach. "Yesterday, I wasn't myself. Today, I'm inundated. This whole situation hit me like a ton of bricks."

"Losing someone who's important in your life will do

that to you. Especially when it's coupled with the shock of knowing he was murdered." Monty flipped open his notebook. "I'll make this as quick and painless as possible. Let's start with the obvious. You're one of the few VPs at Pierson & Company who's not a family member."

"That was a lucky break on my part. None of Edward's grandchildren chose to become lawyers. So I was offered an opportunity I otherwise wouldn't have received."

"It looks to me like you deserved it. Your credentials are strong: academic scholarships, top of your class at law school, published in *Stanford Law Review*—the whole nine yards. And then, ten successful years at Pierson & Company. Pretty impressive." A heartbeat of a pause. "You and Frederick Pierson were personally involved, right?"

Louise's brows arched. "You certainly get right to the point, Mr. Montgomery."

"It saves time."

"Very well. Yes, Frederick and I were involved."

"Interesting. You're thirty-four. Frederick was fifty-eight."

"And that's a problem?"

"No, just a puzzlement. From all accounts, Frederick was a staid and serious workaholic. Not your typical dazzler of younger women."

"There was nothing typical about Frederick. Then again, there's nothing typical about me."

"Yes, I can see that." Another pause. "When did you two start dating?"

"About a year and a half ago."

"Hmm. Frederick's wife, Emily, died six months before that. Did you know her?"

"Of course. She was a lovely woman. Frederick was very devoted to her, especially after she developed a heart condition. And, to answer your next question, no, Frederick and I didn't become involved until after Emily passed away."

"Thanks for filling in that blank."

Louise interlaced her fingers on the desk and leaned forward. "Before we get into the nature of Frederick's and my relationship, may *I* ask *you* a question?"

Monty glanced up. "Shoot."

"Can you be objective about this subject? After all, it's your ex-wife who was at the cabin this weekend. Which means she's not only right at the heart of Friday's arson and murder, she's also clearly involved with Frederick."

Monty looked amused. "I think I can manage to hold on to my objectivity. The operative word here is *ex*-wife. Sally's social life stopped being my business a long time ago. I want her to be safe. I don't give a damn who she sleeps with. Does that answer your question?"

She gave a tight nod.

"Good. Then tell me about you and Frederick. Were you on good terms?"

"Always." Louise gave a fond smile. "We weren't always on the same page, but we were always on good terms. We ebbed and flowed. Sometimes we were exclusive, sometimes we weren't."

"And now was one of the 'weren't' times?"

"Actually, yes. We've both been seeing other people. But that didn't change our history, or my feelings for him. I still can't believe someone killed him."

"Any thoughts as to who that someone might be?"

"No."

Monty scanned his notes again. "I see you were home alone on Thursday night and that you worked at home all day Friday. Saturday, too. I guess it wasn't one of your 'seeing other people' weekends."

"I guess not." Louise tapped a manicured fingernail on the desk. "If you're concerned about my alibi, check with my doorman and the parking attendant at my garage. I arrived home around eight o'clock Thursday night. I was exhausted. I slept in. I brought work home. I didn't leave my building Friday until after Blake called me with the news."

She peeled off a Post-it and reached for a pen. "Shall I write down my address and the appropriate names for you?"

"That won't be necessary. I already have them."

"I suppose I shouldn't be surprised."

"Nope. I'm a good detective. And you're a good lawyer."

Louise put down the pen. "I cared deeply for Frederick. I also respected him as a CEO. He was the most dedicated man I ever met."

"And you miss him."

"Yes, I miss him."

"What about Blake Pierson?"

"What about him?"

"Are you two friends? Outside the workplace, I mean."

Clearly, the question struck a chord. "I'm not sure I understand your implication."

"No implication. A straight-up question. You're about the same age. You're both smart, good-looking, and ambitious. You're close colleagues. I noticed that you left for and returned from Frederick's funeral together. So, are you friends?"

"That depends on what you mean by 'friends.' Blake's been very supportive of me, and I of him. We're both reeling from Frederick's murder. And, yes, we get along well—personally and professionally. So, if that's your description of friends, I guess we fill the bill."

"I guess you do." Monty went with his gut. "Tell me, Ms. Chambers, did you happen to call Blake Pierson on his cell phone last night—say, at around seven thirty?"

She looked a little taken aback. "As a matter of fact, yes. Why? Did Blake mention it?"

"Actually, no. But I was with him when he got the call. From his end of the conversation, I got the feeling it was you."

"I don't recall his saying my name."

"He didn't. Like I said, it was a gut feeling."

"I see." She swallowed, then spoke slowly and distinctly. "Yesterday was a horrible day, Mr. Montgomery. I was emotionally raw. The funeral threw me a lot more than I anticipated. The pain. The finality. Blake was equally unnerved. I needed to lean on someone. So did he. That's why I called."

"Did he drive over to your place after our meeting?"

"As it turned out, no. He spent some time with his grandparents. After that, we were both exhausted. We stayed in our respective apartments and spoke on the phone before turning in. Separately," she added with a pointed stare. "Is this line of questioning going somewhere special?"

"Nope." Monty shut his notebook and rose. "I appreciate your time. If you think of anyone—*anyone*—who might want Frederick Pierson out of the way, let me know." He stared directly at her. "You'll do that, won't you?"

Not even a flinch. "Of course. No one wants Frederick's killer caught and punished more than I do."

"Good. Because that's exactly what's going to happen to him—or her. You have my word, Ms. Chambers."

Devon had been edgy all day.

And that edginess had a name: Blake Pierson.

Their date was tonight. And she had no idea what she was walking into.

Despite his warm and outgoing demeanor, Devon's gut told her there was a lot more to Blake Pierson than he'd allowed her to see. He was a complex guy, one with an agenda that was still murky. He was clearly running interference for his grandfather. Devon knew she was part of that interference. But that was the case with James as well. The difference was that Blake was harder to read.

And she was attracted to him. Tonight was going to be a challenge.

Monty's late-afternoon phone call hadn't helped.

Devon had been wrapping up her last appointment of the day when the clinic's receptionist had poked her head into the examination room to announce that Devon's father was on the phone.

Monty was terse. He'd called to give her a heads-up about Louise Chambers. After his chat with her, he had the distinct feeling she and Blake were involved. Whether that involvement was romantic, platonic, or conspiratorial, he didn't know. But it bugged him.

Another dark corner to explore.

By the time Devon arrived home, she was tight as a drum. Blake was due at six thirty; it was already six. She jumped in the shower, then hurried into her bedroom to pick out an outfit.

Merry nearly collided with her in the doorway. "Sorry." A rueful grin. "Bad timing, good timing."

"What does that mean?" Devon began vigorously towel-drying her hair.

"It means I didn't mean to plow you down, but I'm glad I reached your room before you got dressed. Blake called while you were in the shower. He said to wear jeans."

"Jeans?" Devon lowered the towel, her brows drawn in puzzlement. "I don't get it. I thought we were going to some elegant seafood place."

"Not anymore. A change in plans, he said. Jeans, a sweater—over lots of layers—and boots."

"Where are we eating, in the Arctic Circle?"

Merry laughed. "No idea. I'm just the messenger."

"Okay. I'll bite. Jeans and layers." Devon yanked the appropriate apparel out of her closet.

The doorbell rang at six thirty on the dot. By that time, Devon's hair was dried, and she was dressed in a light blue cable-knit sweater and jeans. She trotted downstairs and opened the door herself.

Blake was leaning against the doorjamb. He'd adhered to the same dress code as she—jeans, sweater, and boots—all topped off by a down parka and gloves.

He assessed her with an approving grin. "Good. You got my message."

"Confusing as it might be, yes." Devon folded her arms across her breasts. "So we're not eating seafood?"

"Nope. Not even close."

"Care to tell me what we *are* doing?"

"Driving down to Central Park. It's a beautiful night—cold, but beautiful. First, we'll go sledding down Pilgrim Hill. Next comes ice skating at the Wollman rink. And don't worry. We won't starve. After that, we're going to Serendipity. We'll get dinner and frozen hot chocolates."

Devon blinked. "You're kidding."

"No, I'm not kidding. The past few days have been nightmarish for us both. We need stress relief. You've already done the wine-and-dine thing with James. So this is kick-back-and-have-fun night." He paused. "Unless you're not up for it?"

Devon heard his note of challenge loud and clear. "Now that's a dare if ever I heard one."

"So, are you taking it or wimping out?"

"I've never wimped out on a dare in my life." Devon was already in motion, walking over to the coat closet. She grabbed her down jacket, then squatted down to fumble around on the floor. "Give me a sec to find my skates."

"No problem. Oh, and I brought two sleds. Just in case you don't have one."

"How thoughtful." Devon was smiling when she rose, skates in hand. "As a matter of fact, I do have one. But it's in the basement, so I'll use yours. I don't want to waste a minute during which I could be wiping that smirk off your face. Let's go."

Whatever Devon had expected her evening with Blake to be, it wasn't the lighthearted banter and childlike romping that composed the next few hours. They had races down the hill, ice-skating contests, and snowball fights in between. They were drenched, winded, and weak with laughter by the time they tumbled into Serendipity.

The experience hadn't been just stress relieving. It had been downright liberating.

Devon warmed up on a bowl of corn chowder, then gobbled down her salad, cheddarburger, and fries and made an enthusiastic dent in her frozen hot chocolate—all in record time.

"You have whipped cream on your nose," Blake commented, digging into the healthy slice of blackout cake he'd just ordered.

"I know." Devon kept a straight face. "I'm saving it for later, when I'm hungry again."

Blake's lips twitched. "That's physically impossible. You just devoured half the menu in fifteen minutes."

"You did it in ten. Besides, I was starving. No lunch. A puny Nutri-Grain bar for breakfast. And a heavy-duty exercise workout I didn't plan on."

"Would you have preferred the more conventional dinner and a movie?"

"Not on your life. Especially since I won six out of ten sled races, outclassed you on the ice, and creamed you with my professional snowballs."

"I let you win."

Devon rolled her eyes. "Yeah. Right."

A chuckle. "Okay, fine. You kicked my butt. Is that what you want to hear?"

"The truth hurts."

"Not as much as the snowballs. You pack quite a wallop, Doctor."

"I'll take that as a compliment." Devon used the edge of her napkin to wipe the cream off her nose. "Better?"

"It doesn't matter." Blake's grin vanished, and he studied her intently, with an expression that left no room for misinterpretation. "You'd look gorgeous no matter what."

Devon's insides tightened. He could be playing her like a fiddle. The past few hours could have been a careful scheme to lower her guard and loosen her tongue.

She had no intention of letting him do either. But that didn't change her gut reaction.

Blake Pierson got to her.

The question was, how was she going to use that to her advantage?

"That was a compliment," Blake broke into her thoughts to clarify. "Not a brainteaser."

She swallowed, snapped back to the here and now. "Sorry. I've always been awkward when it comes to looks-related compliments. You want to commend me on my rapport with animals? Great. You want to flatter me on my ice-skating talent? Flatter away. I'll eat it up. But my appearance? That's something I can't take credit for. It's either the luck of the draw or genetics."

"Fair enough." Blake was still gazing at her with that provocative look in his eyes. "Then I'll rephrase. You're incredible with animals. Chomper's proof of that. You're the epitome of grace on ice skates. But like it or not, you're also a knockout. Not to mention sexy as hell—even with whipped cream on your nose."

Somehow, even the teasing seemed intimate. "Thanks," Devon managed. "I think."

At that moment, an onslaught of teenagers piled into the restaurant. They were howling with laughter and shouting back and forth to one another.

Blake frowned. "So much for quiet conversation."

"It seems that way." Devon was just as unhappy as he was. She had a full agenda yet to delve into. She was far from ready to call it a night. "Maybe we could take a walk?"

"Bad idea. Our clothes are still damp, and it's even colder now than it was earlier." Blake pushed aside his dessert. "I have a better suggestion. It's not that late. Let's go back to my place. I'm on Seventy-eighth just off Third. That's less than a mile from here. I've got a great bottle of Merlot I've been wanting to try. We'll have a glass and talk."

Devon's brows arched.

"You don't like Merlot?"

"I like Merlot." A measured look. "I just want to be clear on what goes with it."

"Ah." Blake didn't avert his gaze. "I'm not staging a seduction scene. Luring women into bed isn't my style. And I'm smart enough to know that being lured isn't yours. That having been said, I do want to be alone with you. To *talk,* and get to know you better. That's why I didn't suggest your place. You've got a full house."

"True." Devon weighed her options and decided to take the risk. "Okay, then, your place it is."

CHAPTER 14

A half hour later, seated on the taupe leather sofa in Blake's oak-paneled living room, Devon wondered what she'd let herself in for. There was something warm and cozy about the three-story brownstone, despite the daunting fact that Blake owned the whole damned building. Everything was done in earth tones with rustic accents, including a wall-to-wall brick fireplace. It was very male, and very Blake.

Also very quiet and very private.

"Where's Chomper?" Devon asked, half hoping the pup would come bounding into the room and lighten the atmosphere of intensity hovering around them.

"He's staying overnight at your clinic," Blake replied. He was standing at the sideboard, opening the bottle of Merlot. "He hates being alone. And I knew I'd be out late, so I arranged to pick him up tomorrow. Which works out fine, since he and I have an obedience class at eleven. I've got an eight thirty meeting at the office. Then I'll shoot up to White Plains."

An eight thirty meeting. That would be with Monty.

Devon kept her expression nondescript. "I'm sure Chomper's being spoiled rotten. Our boarding staff prides themselves on that."

"I got that impression." Blake poured two glasses of wine and carried them over to the sofa. "Did you always want to be a vet?"

"Since I was a kid. I loved animals. I was fascinated by medicine. So I found a way to do both." With a nod of thanks, Devon took the glass of wine, waiting until Blake had settled himself on the other side of the sofa. "What about you?" she asked. "Have you always wanted to be a bigwig in a family-owned, multimillion-dollar company?"

A chuckle. "Maybe not always, but close to it. I've always been fascinated by the restaurant industry. And I've always had a flair for business management, along with a thousand creative ideas. Combining all that into one career was too good to pass up. So I went for it."

"Straight to Pierson & Company?"

"Nope. Not before paying my dues. My grandfather believes in family, but he also believes that busting your ass builds character and leads to success. He made it clear I needed the education and the experience before I'd be considered for a high-level position. So, off I went to Providence, Rhode Island."

"Johnson and Wales?" Devon guessed.

"Uh-huh. Their food-service management program's top-notch. I got my bachelor's degree and went to work for the food-services division of Marriott for two years. After that, I went to NYU business school and got my MBA. *Then* I joined Pierson & Company. That was nine years ago. I've worked in every division."

"Sounds like a great way to find your niche. Where'd you end up?"

"In none of them," Blake returned drily. "No surprise. I've never been content with what is. I'm always envisioning what could be."

"So you started something new?"

"Yup. Food services addresses the en masse crowds that go to sporting arenas. Fine dining addresses the limited, elite crowd who have sophisticated palates and deep pockets. That leaves a huge chunk of the population unaddressed—namely, families."

"I see your point."

Blake rolled his goblet between his palms. "I'm starting up a whole new division. Family dining." He proceeded to explain Chomping at the Bit and where things stood on the project.

Even though Devon had read the basics in Monty's notes, it was far more interesting hearing it from Blake's perspective. "It sounds like a surefire winner," she said sincerely. "The kids will be thrilled. The parents will be thrilled. Soon you'll have restaurants all over the country. And the coffers at Pierson & Company will be even fuller."

"That's the plan." A shadow flickered across his face. "At least it was. Right now, expansions are on hold. Other priorities trump them."

"You're talking about Frederick's death."

"Yes. His death leaves a gaping hole at Pierson & Company."

That opened the door. Devon stepped through it carefully.

"I can't imagine how debilitating this tragedy must be for you. Your personal and professional worlds, both thrown into chaos."

"That pretty much sizes it up."

"Did you report directly to Frederick?"

"Yes. But that's the least of it. Besides being CEO, Frederick headed up the food-services division. I've been tapping into their resources—suppliers, contacts—anything to get Chomping at the Bit off the ground. With Frederick gone . . . let's just say the situation's bound to become complicated."

Something in Blake's tone made Devon press on. "Complicated how? I'm sure you can still access those contacts. Unless someone's standing in your way," she added, verbalizing her hunch as it dawned on her. "Someone like James, for instance."

Blake shot her a sideways look. "Now *that's* a loaded question. What exactly did you and James discuss last night?"

"Lots of things. Including you." Now was the time for wary candor. "He said you'd be running Pierson someday, and that he's fine with that. But I'd be lying if I said I didn't sense some underlying resentment. Or maybe 'resentment's' too strong a word."

"No, I'd say it's dead-on accurate." Clearly, Blake wasn't bothered by her assessment. "James is a good salesman and an exceptional rider. But he's not great at sharing the limelight. He has a problem with my place at Pierson. How big a problem? Who knows. Especially now that his insecurities are being fed by my interest in you."

"Great." Devon grimaced. "I don't want to escalate the tension."

"Don't worry about it. I can handle James. And he can handle me."

"He said something similar."

"What else did you two talk about?"

"The usual stuff. Work. Family. Oh, and the cutthroat world of competitive show jumping."

"What business isn't cutthroat? Mine's just as bad."

"Well, mine isn't. It's rewarding, humane, and honest. Maybe that's why I like animals better than people."

A corner of Blake's mouth lifted. "Makes sense."

"You, on the other hand, like being on the fast track."

"If wanting every day to be a challenge is the fast track, then I'm on it."

Devon took a sip of wine, deciding which road to take. She couldn't just grill him about his family and/or Philip Rhodes. He'd see through that in an instant.

Maybe a one-eighty would catch him off guard.

"You're a cut-to-the chase kind of guy," she stated.

A wry grin. "You noticed."

"It's hard not to. You aren't exactly subtle."

"If you're referring to my approach with you, subtle wasn't what I was going for."

"What were you going for?"

"Convincing. Is it working?"

"That depends." She leaned forward, scrutinizing his expression. "Is your interest in me genuine, or is it put on so you can figure out if I know more than I've admitted about my mother's whereabouts?"

A prolonged pause, during which Blake set down his goblet. "And you think *I'm* direct?"

"Fine. We're both direct. Now, are you going to answer my question?"

"We're also both loyal to our families."

"Is that your way of intimating that you're in this to spy for your grandfather?"

"And you? Are you here to pump me for information to share with your father? I'm sure you're well aware of his role at Pierson."

He was turning the tables on her, trying to turn her offense into a defense.

She had no intention of letting him.

"I know that Monty is your new head of security," she responded without hesitation. "And I know he'll bust his tail to find my mother. What else is it I'm supposed to know?"

"You tell me."

"Frankly? My father and I aren't exactly tight. He doesn't confide in me. But if I know one thing, it's that he's a crackerjack investigator. If he's working on solving Frederick's murder, he'll solve it. Your turn. Because you and your grandfather *are* close. Which means it's far more likely you're doing his bidding."

"I don't do anyone's bidding. Not even my grandfather's. However, you should know he's stubborn as a mule. So, if your mother was in any way involved in Frederick's death, he'll find out—*and* he'll find *her,* wherever she is."

Devon set down her goblet with a thud. "My mother is *not* a killer."

"Maybe not. But she did go up to that cabin with Frederick. Which means she's the only living witness to the crime."

"She didn't witness anything." Despite her rising anger, Devon realized she was being baited. "My father's the one who spoke to her," she continued, choosing her words carefully. "From what he said, she never saw the killer. Unfortunately, *he* saw *her*. Which is why she dropped out of sight, and why we're all beside ourselves with worry."

"I'm sorry for what you're going through. But you can't blame my grandfather for leaving no stone unturned. Frederick was his son."

"I know. But the idea that my mother was in any way involved is insane. She's the kindest, gentlest human being on earth."

"From my own observations, she's also down-to-earth and outdoorsy. Not really Frederick's type."

"As opposed to whom—Louise Chambers? I agree. Although I really can't visualize your corporate counsel hiking in the Adirondacks. Still, I was surprised your uncle didn't ask her, rather than my mother, to go with him. Unless, of course, Louise is unavailable to him now because she's seeing someone else. You, for example."

A glint of amusement lit Blake's amber eyes. "Nice shot. Unfortunately, not a slam dunk. Why would you think Louise and I are involved?"

"She was on your arm when we met. The vibes were there. Am I wrong?"

"Yeah, but I like the fact that you're jealous. It bodes well for what I have in mind."

Devon sidestepped the innuendo. "Next you're going to be telling me that you and Louise Chambers are 'just friends.' "

"Hmm." Blake considered the idea and shrugged. "Nope. We're not that, either. We're just good, old-fashioned business colleagues. So tell me, did James get a good-night kiss? Or did you send him away with a handshake?"

"Excuse me?" Devon started. "That's none of your business."

"Ah. My social life's your business, but yours isn't mine? Or were you asking about me and Louise for another reason?"

Devon gave a hard shake of her head. This battle of wits was turning into something as challenging and blood pumping as their snowball fight.

"Another reason?" she returned. "Like what?"

"Oh, I don't know. Checking out alliances and alibis, maybe."

"Why? Do you have any to share?"

"Not a one. Now that we've settled that, let's get back to James. Did you or didn't you kiss him?"

Half laughing, half-exasperated, Devon waved an imaginary white flag. "Okay. I give. Just be advised that I'm *not* a good loser."

"Then I'll quit while I'm ahead." Abruptly, Blake stood, tugging her to her feet. "I want you in a good mood. Otherwise, you might slug me when I do this." He drew her closer, tilted back her head, and covered her mouth with his.

It was meant to be an overture, an initial exploration of the physical attraction that sizzled between them.

The overture never happened. The kiss was out of control before it began.

Their lips brushed, circled—then fused, currents of sensation barreling through them. Blake muttered something indistinguishable and tore his mouth away, scrutinizing Devon with a burning gaze. Then he gave up the fight. He hauled her against him, nudged her lips apart, and took her mouth.

Devon was trembling, inside and out. She couldn't begin to think, much less object. And the truth was, she wanted to do neither. What she was feeling was just too damned good. Resistance wasn't an option.

She gave a low moan of pleasure, gripping handfuls of Blake's sweater and following his lead.

The kiss took on a life of its own.

Like Blake, it was consuming, his mouth eating at hers, possessing her with an intensity that swirled through her in dizzying waves. His tongue swept inside, rubbing against hers in slow, erotic circles. His arms locked around her, drawing her closer, deeper into the wildness.

Long moments passed. The kiss went on and on, growing more heated, more intense, like a wildfire blazing out of control.

Devon wasn't sure who grabbed hold of reality first. One minute the two of them were locked together, the next they were an arm's length apart, staring at each other with dazed eyes and ragged breathing.

"What was that?" Devon finally managed, running a shaky hand through her hair.

"I'm not sure." Blake's tone was husky, his expression as clouded as hers. "But whatever it was, it was about to move to my bedroom."

"I know." Devon wasn't surprised by the realization. What surprised her was her reaction to it. "I don't do this," she supplied inanely.

"Yeah, I guessed. For what it's worth, neither do I."

She stepped backward, trying to put what had just happened into perspective. "Things like this don't happen. Not in real life."

A corner of Blake's mouth lifted. "Apparently, they do."

Unacceptable. Especially in light of what she was trying to accomplish for Monty, and for her mother.

"I'd better get home." Devon blurted out the first mundane thing she could think of. She followed it up by glancing at her watch. It took three tries to actually make out what the dial said. "It's almost one o'clock."

Blake nodded his agreement. "I'll get our jackets."

"No." Devon stopped him. "Just get mine. I'll grab a taxi to Grand Central and take the train."

"Not at this hour, you won't. I'm driving you home, as planned." Blake frowned, waving away the refusal she was about to utter. "Look, I understand you want to be alone. You're freaked out. So am I. We both need space. And you can have yours—*after* I drop you off."

He looked freaked out, too. And preoccupied as hell.

Idly, Devon wondered if the lip-lock they'd just shared had screwed up his agenda as much as it had hers.

"Okay," she replied. The truth was, she was too frazzled to argue. Talk about complications. She'd just entangled herself in a huge one.

The problem was, she didn't know if she really wanted to break free.

Sally's call came as promptly that night as on the two previous nights.

"Okay, now this is overkill," Monty announced into the Bat Phone. "Plus, you tipped your hand. Punctuality's great, but no one times their calls down to the second. You're doing this to get a rise out of me."

"Is it working?" Sally's voice was stronger and clearer tonight.

"Sure is. My tail's between my legs."

Her laughter brushed his ear. "Now *that's* an image. Anyway, no tail hanging necessary. Just a simple confession. Admit you're lousy at time management. That'll be enough to make my day."

"And if I don't?"

"I'll hire a different PI."

Monty chuckled. "You drive a hard bargain. But, okay, I suck at time management. Happy?"

"It's a start. Now tell me you've made some progress on figuring out who Frederick's killer was."

The banter vanished. "Some. I had an interesting talk with Louise Chambers today. She's a real barracuda, and an operator. Wanted to know if I could be objective about Frederick's murder, since the two of you were involved."

A long pause. "Was she asking because she wanted to know how deep that involvement ran, or because she thinks I killed him?"

"In my opinion? She was trying to tip the scales in her favor. It didn't work. I'm staying in her face. I don't trust her."

"You think she killed Frederick?"

"I doubt it. But I'm not ready to write her off as a suspect. She was tight with Frederick. Now she's sniffing around Blake. The whole thing smells rotten." Monty contemplated his own words. "Did Frederick ever mention Louise?"

"Not to me. I knew they had some kind of relationship. But whether it was all business, or business and personal, I'm not sure." Sally hesitated, and Monty could picture her forehead creasing in thought. "I keep reviewing the day before the fire in my mind. The drive up was pleasant; no red flags. Frederick was himself. But later, as the evening wore on, he got quieter, more pensive. I assumed it was a reaction to my ambivalence. On the other hand, maybe it was related to whoever ended up killing him."

Monty couldn't bite back his question. "What ambivalence?"

"Oh, come on, Pete." A sigh. "I don't need to spell it out for you. Being up at Lake Luzerne was a lot harder than I expected. I guess I'm not as mature as I gave myself credit for."

"When it comes to Lake Luzerne, neither am I."

There was a long silence.

"I'm going to turn in now," Sally said at last. "I'll call tomorrow. Hopefully, you'll have made a breakthrough. The sooner I can get back to my life, the better."

"I'll bust my ass to make that happen."

"I know you will."

Monty's grip tightened on the phone. "Good night, Sal."

"Good night, Pete."

He stared reflectively at the phone before punching it off. He wouldn't be falling asleep anytime soon.

Then again, neither would Sally.

Monty's cell phone rang.

He fumbled for the alarm clock on his night stand, and squinted at it. Three forty A.M. Shit.

It wasn't the Bat Phone, so it wasn't Sally. And Devon had checked in around two. So who the hell was it?

He snatched up the phone and punched it on. "Montgomery."

"It's Edward Pierson." The older man's voice was shaky. "He called."

"Who did?"

"That son of a bitch who's blackmailing me."

Monty was suddenly and completely awake. "Tell me exactly what he said."

"He told me to wire two million dollars to an account in the Cayman Islands. He gave me the number—and twenty-four hours. If I don't come through, the people I care about will start getting hurt. The last part's a direct quote."

"How did you respond?"

"I didn't. I didn't have a chance. He hung up."

"You got this call at home. Interesting."

"Why? Where else would he call at three thirty in the morning?"

"That's not the point. It's a snap to reach you at Pierson & Company. The number's listed. Your home phone's not."

"Well, apparently he got it."

"Actually, I'm wondering if he already had it. That would level the playing field in terms of where he called."

"You think it's a close acquaintance?"

"You tell me. Did you recognize the voice?"

"I couldn't. He used one of those voice scramblers."

"No surprise." Monty's wheels were turning. "Did you hear any background noise? Anything that might tell you where he was calling from?"

"A couple of honking horns."

"Car horns or truck horns?"

"Car, I think."

"What about road noise? Could you tell if the vehicles were traveling at high speed or low? Zipping along quietly, or rumbling heavily?"

"What difference does any of that make?"

"The difference between a city and a highway. Eighteen-wheelers make one kind of racket. Manhattan taxis make another." Monty paused. "I'm assuming you didn't tape the call?"

"I wasn't expecting it, so no. The letter came to my office. I assumed he'd continue to contact me there. If he had, I would have been ready for him."

"We'll put a wiretap on your home phone. Not that it'll do us much good. If he's using a voice scrambler, he's probably taking other precautions to make sure he can't be made. Like a convenience store cell phone with prepaid minutes, cash and carry."

Edward blew out a frustrated breath. "Twenty-four hours. Damn. There's no way I can liquidate two million in assets fast enough."

"Even if you could, you don't know if that'll make the extortionist shut up and go away. He could try shaking you down for more. Remember, once you pay him, you're his."

"So what do you suggest I do?"

"Go through the motions. Start liquidating. If this person

is someone connected to you or your company, he'll be paying attention, and it'll appease him. Also, expect him to contact you late tomorrow to make sure everything's set. I'll prep you for that call. In the meantime, I've got Jenkins coming in at eight and Blake giving us access to your computer systems at eight thirty. I've got a day to dig around. I know what to look for. So does Jenkins. As for your family, I'll make a few phone calls and arrange for added security to protect them. Stay calm. We'll get the guy."

"We better. Before he gets someone else I love."

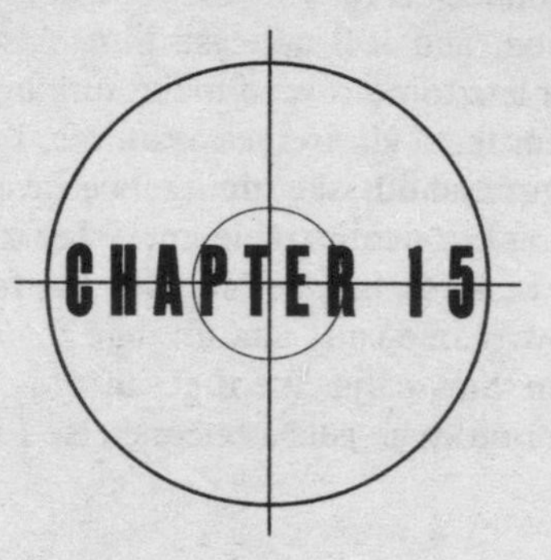

CHAPTER 15

John Sherman, PI, was shaving in the bathroom of his apartment in Astoria, Queens, when his cell phone rang.

He tossed down the razor, patted his face dry with a towel, and flipped open the phone. "Sherman."

"Boy, do you sound out of it. You must have just woken up. Work or a woman?"

Sherman grunted. "Gimme a break, Monty. What woman would put up with my hours? I'm out of it because you dumped a whopping caseload on me. I spent all day yesterday on follow-up, and all night tailing that rich broad and her boyfriend to see if your hunch about them was right."

"And?" Monty queried. "Did you see anything?"

"Just a few sex moves even *I've* never dreamed up. Unfortunately, now that I learned them, I don't have time to try them out."

"Forget it, Sherman. The woman's a contortionist. If you tried any of her moves, you'd be stuck in that position for life."

Another grunt. "You're probably right. Anyway, I'm on them like tar. If they're planning anything more than a screwing marathon, you'll be the first to know."

"Thanks. Listen, I know I left you with a full caseload. But before you head out now, do me one favor. Call the precinct. See who's got time in their schedule for a security gig. It's for Pierson, so the money's good. Starts tonight. Ends when I solve this case."

"How many guys do you need?"

"Plenty. There are four generations of Piersons to protect."

"I'll get on it now, and call you back."

It was 9 A.M., and already eighty degrees in Wellington.

Soon thousands of people would be arriving at the winter festival, eager to watch the competitions, shop, or catch a glimpse of the rich and famous.

James rolled over in his bed and plumped his pillow. No riding today. Not for him. He was a mess. The necessary arrangements had been made. Now it was just him, his family's lavish Wellington hacienda, and the central air-conditioning. A welcome reprieve from crowds, kids, and pressure.

Tonight, he'd call Devon. He'd be feeling better by then. His grandfather would be pissed as hell, but he'd get over it. No way she'd blow his concentration. If anything, she'd be a great picture to hold in his mind when he won.

Frowning, he wondered if Blake had made any inroads with her by now. Well, there wasn't a damned thing he could do about it from here.

Actually, that wasn't true.

He reached for his cell phone and called FTD.

"Anything?" Monty leaned over Alfred Jenkins's shoulder as the accountant studied the computer monitor. He'd been closeted in Frederick's office for four hours now, poring over months and months of business records. And Monty had popped in three times already.

"Still no red flags." Jenkins shook his head. "The guy looks clean. He's got some hefty corporate credit-card bills, but that's not unusual. Especially if he was the kind of CEO who schmoozed people over expensive meals and high-priced wine."

"Great." Monty grimaced.

"Hey, I'm just getting started. There's a lot of territory to cover here."

"In other words, chill out." Monty stretched and headed for the door. "I'll check in with you later."

"Yeah. I'm sure you will."

Monty stepped into the hall and practically collided with Philip Rhodes.

"Oh . . . excuse me." To say Rhodes was flustered would be a gross understatement. "I need a file from Frederick's office. Is it off-limits?"

"Only if it involves accessing his computer." Monty kept his expression and tone nondescript. "I've got someone working there."

"Doing what?"

"Just some routine accounting stuff. Go on in and get what you need."

Rhodes looked ill. "Thanks."

Devon was restless.

It was a little past noon. The hustle-bustle at Creature Comforts & Clinic had reached a midday, midweek lull. Devon's morning appointments were finished, as was the surgery she'd performed on Rocky, a boxer with a disk problem. She'd checked her schedule, only to find that her afternoon was quiet.

The truth was, she didn't want to run into Blake when he came out of Chomper's obedience class.

She poked her head into Exam Room 3, where Dr. Joel

Sedwell was finishing up with a long-haired tabby kitten who'd been abandoned and was now a permanent resident of the clinic.

"Joel? Any problem if I run out for a few hours? I want to ride up to my mom's house and check on the animals. If I leave now, I'll be back in time for the late-day craziness."

"No problem." Joel nodded, simultaneously scratching the kitten's ears until it purred. "Any word from your mother?"

"Nothing since she called my dad on Saturday." Devon hated lying, especially to the senior partner she so admired and who'd given her the chance of a lifetime. But there was no choice. Her mother's safety was at stake.

"Get going," Joel urged her. "That way you'll avoid rush hour and be back before dark and before those winding roads become icy."

"Thanks."

Devon left the building. Before climbing into her car, she scanned the parking lot. No sign of Blake's silver Jag. Maybe he'd already left for Manhattan.

She turned her key in the ignition, pulled out of her parking spot, and drove around to the exit.

She was just about to accelerate onto the road when she spotted Blake in her rearview mirror. He was walking through the parking lot, leading Chomper along by his leash.

Puzzled, Devon stepped on her brake and waited, watching Blake stride purposefully toward the row of cars she'd just scrutinized. Had she missed his?

He stopped beside a black Mercedes sedan, unlocking the door and opening it. He waited until Chomper had jumped in. Then he hopped into the driver's seat and backed out of the spot.

Something made Devon wait until she'd gotten a full view of the vehicle. When she did, her eyes widened in surprise. It didn't make sense. But it required a proactive move on her part.

Accelerating into traffic, Devon punched a few buttons on her cell phone, until she'd initiated a call to: "Monty's cell."

One ring. Two.

"Yeah?" Monty sounded distracted.

"Bad time?"

"Today's been one long bad time so far. What's up?"

"Just a question. Did the police release Frederick's car?"

"Doubtful. They'll probably keep it awhile. If a new lead turns up, they'll want to sweep it again for forensics. Why?"

"Because I'm confused. Last night when Blake picked me up, he was driving a silver Jag. But just now I saw him leave the clinic driving a black Mercedes S500 luxury sedan. If it's not Frederick's, whose is it?"

"I don't know. But I will. Thanks, honey." Monty paused. "Are you okay?"

"Sure," Devon returned lightly. "Why wouldn't I be?"

"Because my gut tells me you have more than a professional interest in Blake Pierson."

"I'll get over it."

The words tasted like sandpaper on her tongue. Suspecting Blake of poking around to get information for his grandfather was one thing. Suspecting him of being involved in Frederick's death in a more hands-on way was quite another.

Just how used was she being?

"Don't jump to conclusions," Monty advised her. "Another trick of the trade."

"I'm not. I'm just steeling myself." Devon cleared her throat. "Anyway, just so you know, I'm headed up to Mom's place to check on the animals. I'll eyeball the Pierson farm when I cruise by."

"Drive safe. And, Dev, hang tough."

"I plan to."

Monty didn't waste time.

He went straight to his most cooperative source.

Alice Jeffers looked up from behind her desk as Monty approached. "Mr. Montgomery," she greeted him cordially. "How can I help you?"

"I'm on my way to examine the execs' cars. I want to make sure they're all safe and no one's tampered with them. Can you get me a list of who drives what?"

"Certainly." She frowned. "Did you want a list of personal cars as well as company cars?"

"I'd appreciate it, yes." Monty paused. "How many company cars are there?"

"About a dozen. Each of the top-level executives has one."

"And they're all Mercedes S500s." It was a statement, not a question.

"Yes." Ms. Jeffers smiled. "That's Edward Pierson's car of choice."

"I'm sure it is."

"What the hell are you babbling about?" Edward stared blankly at Monty.

"Your company cars. Why didn't you tell me there are a dozen of them that are identical to Frederick's?"

"What difference does it make?"

"Did you give that information to the police?"

Edward's shoulders lifted in a puzzled shrug. "Maybe. I don't know. Why?"

"Because the tire treads found at the crime scene belonged to a Mercedes S500. We all assumed they came from Frederick's car."

"Yeah, well, they must have. There was only one set of tire treads in the driveway."

"True. But there was also a set of treads in the alcove off the road. What if those were made by another car—more specifically, another S500?"

Edward went very still. "Then someone I trust at Pierson & Company would be a murderer."

* * *

The intermediate-level competition at the Gold Coast Classic started right on time.

The International Arena at the Palm Beach Equestrian Club was full, thousands of spectators filling the stands. Anticipation hovered in the air and rippled through the crowd.

Bill Granger, a groom at the Pierson stables, eagerly waited his turn. He was a good rider, especially on Future, Edward's prize six-year-old stallion. Future was a winner; Bill had no doubt he'd amass a sterling record over time—even if he wasn't the Olympic champion that Stolen Thunder was. Bill knew this horse. He had heart, and he had grit. That was something Bill and Future had in common.

They were a good team. Bill knew Future's abilities like the back of his hand. He exercised the stallion every day, and dreamed about getting a chance to compete.

His day had finally come.

He felt bad that James was sick. But he'd do him and Mr. Pierson proud. He'd place in this competition. He just had to stay focused.

His fingers brushed the saddle pad on Future's back—just once for good luck. It was something he always saw James do, and he understood why. The saddle pad represented a win. It brandished the colors of the Pierson stable: white with a blue border and, in the center, a red emblem of two stallions, squared off and facing each other. James called the saddle pad his lucky charm.

Bill was counting on that luck extending to him.

He dragged an arm across his forehead. Damn, the sun was strong today. Maybe that's why he felt dizzy. Or maybe it was because he was so pumped up. Either way, it wouldn't affect him. He wouldn't let it.

With pride, he rode Future out of the warm-up ring, under the overpass, and into the arena. They were announced. He urged the stallion into a trot, leading him down the center of the ring, then around, pausing only when they reached the jury box so he could tip his cap to the judges.

The time bell sounded.

Bill urged Future into a left lead canter. The first jump was a single fence and low. Horse and rider took it beautifully, timing and all. But Bill's head was woozy. And it was getting worse.

He pushed Future on the second jump. He could feel the pacing error starting from six strides away. Not a huge error, but enough for Future to overjump the double fence. That would cost them points. And the third jump, coming up fast, was the dolphin jump—high, blue gray, with the figure of a dolphin on either end. Well known as a major challenge.

By the time they reached it, Bill was sweating profusely. He could hardly think past the buzzing in his head. Little black spots were dancing before his eyes.

He saw the dolphins. They flickered in and out of his vision, obscured by those damned black spots. He hunkered down as he and Future approached the fence. He felt Future gather his legs beneath him. He felt the momentum of going up and over. And he felt the ground rush up at him.

Then he felt nothing at all.

Devon finished up at her mother's house, pleased to see that all the animals were in great shape. They'd been fed, their pens and stalls cleaned, and the horses had been exercised. Reading the note that was taped to the barn door, Devon realized she owed the great care the animals had received to the Piersons' groom, Roberto.

She decided to stop next door to thank him personally.

Maneuvering her car down the winding driveway, Devon admitted to herself that she had two reasons for this visit. One, to thank Roberto, and two, to see if any of the Piersons were around so she could talk to them.

To her surprise, Dr. Vista's truck was parked near the stables. It was hard to miss—the truck was a giant Suburban with an extra-wide trailer hitched to its rear.

Devon hesitated. The genetic consultant hadn't been too

thrilled the last time she showed up here; he seemed to regard her as some kind of competition. Maybe she'd thank Roberto another time.

She was about to pull away when the stable door opened and Vista walked out. Collar turned up against the cold, he took a few steps toward his truck. Then he spotted Devon.

He walked over to her car, and she rolled down the window.

"Dr. Montgomery," he greeted her, no sign of his earlier tension present. "This is a surprise."

"Hello, Dr. Vista." She had no idea why she felt compelled to explain herself. But she did. "I dashed out of work to ride up and check on my mom's barn. Roberto's obviously been caring for all its occupants. I stopped by here to thank him."

An understanding nod. "I'm sure he'd appreciate that. I didn't see him in the stables. That doesn't mean he isn't around. He could be exercising one of the horses in the indoor arena."

"I'm due back at my clinic anyway. I'll just jot down a quick note and tape it to the inside of the stable door. That way, Roberto will find it."

"Good idea." Vista gave a wave of his hand and stepped away from the car. "I'm heading out myself. Have a good day."

"You, too."

Devon watched him drive away, the truck and trailer crunching heavily in the snow. His progress was slow. No surprise, given the Suburban's cumbersome weight. Vista must have some serious medical equipment stored in there.

Pulling out a sheet of paper, Devon scribbled a note to Roberto.

Monty stopped by Philip Rhodes's office late in the day. Ms. Jeffers had already gone home, but Rhodes was still there.

With a purposeful knock, Monty swung open the door

and walked in, not giving Rhodes a chance to school his features. The man's head jerked up, and he stared at Monty as if expecting him to slap on cuffs and lead him away.

"Did you find the file you were looking for in Frederick's office?" Monty asked.

"What? Oh, yes. It was on the top shelf of his credenza." Rhodes was flushed, and he loosened his collar as he spoke. "I also talked to that Jenkins guy. He said he's a forensic accountant."

"Yup. Best in the business. He's sweeping all the financial records to see if Frederick was in any trouble."

No response.

"By the way," Monty continued. "I checked out your company car. It was clean."

"Clean?"

"Yeah, you know—not tampered with."

Rhodes half rose from his chair. "Were you expecting that it had been?"

A shrug. "Don't know. Then again, I didn't know you had a Mercedes S500, either. Were you aware that was the make of the only tire treads found at the crime scene?"

"I assumed as much. Frederick drove the same make and model."

"Just like all the other execs. Quite a coincidence." Monty flattened his palms on the desk and looked Rhodes straight in the eye. "I understand the cabin Frederick died in belonged to one of your suppliers. A Gary Bolten, president of Paper and Plastics Limited."

"That's right." Rhodes didn't avert his gaze, but a vein throbbed at his temple. "Gary loaned the cabin to Frederick for the weekend."

"So he said. Apparently, he thought Frederick could use some R&R. Any idea who conveyed that idea to him?"

Rhodes's pupils dilated. "Obviously, you already know the answer to that. So let's cut to the chase. What is it you're accusing me of?"

"Just curious why you never mentioned that fact, to me or the police. Too insignificant? Or too incriminating?"

"Too misleading. It was an innocent gesture of friendship, meant with the best of intentions. I never anticipated—" Rhodes broke off. "I have nothing more to say."

"And I have nothing more to ask." Monty turned. "Night, Rhodes."

Monty was halfway down the hall when Frederick's bulldozer of a secretary, Marjorie Evans, rushed up to him.

"Mr. Montgomery." She didn't look like a bulldozer now. She looked frazzled and panicky. "Wait!"

He stopped in his tracks. "What's up?"

"Edward Pierson needs you in his office right away. There's been an accident."

Edward was pacing behind his desk, his complexion ashen.

"Ms. Evans found me," Monty announced, walking in and shutting the door behind him. "She said there'd been an accident."

"Yes." Edward stopped, taking a gulp of water. "At Wellington. During today's competition."

"Was James injured?"

"No. He wouldn't have been, even if he'd been riding. What he *would* have been is disqualified."

Monty frowned. "Explain."

Edward leaned heavily against his desk. "James was scheduled to ride my stallion Future in the intermediate level of today's event. He called me this morning and said he was sick—too sick to even get out of bed, much less compete. So I pulled a few strings, got a doctor's note and permission to sub in another rider—Bill Granger, one of my grooms. He was the logical choice. He's a damned good rider. He exercises Future every day. He and Future make a great team. The switch should have been no big deal."

"But?"

"At the third jump, Granger collapsed and fell off Future. He's in the hospital now. I'm waiting to hear how bad his injuries are."

Monty's eyes narrowed. "What was the cause of his collapse—pressure? Heat?"

"Neither." Edward took another gulp of water. "The drug testing turned up positive for hydrochlorothiazide. That's a diuretic."

"Yeah, it's taken for high blood pressure."

"That's the thing. Granger doesn't have high blood pressure. Just the opposite. His pressure's low."

"Which explains why he collapsed. So why did he take the stuff?"

"He didn't. Someone must have slipped it in his water or his coffee. And whoever did it thought he was sabotaging James."

"Why? Does James have low blood pressure, too?"

"No. That's why I said he wouldn't have been hurt if he'd been in the saddle. But injury wasn't what the SOB who did this had in mind. Disqualification was."

"You lost me."

"Diuretics are categorized as masking agents. If a rider's taking any other drug—performance enhancing, narcotic, you name it—diuretics can flush them out of the system faster."

"Which would keep them from showing up in a drug test."

"You got it. So if James had been riding today, and if he'd been subjected to a routine drug test, he'd be out. And not just out of this competition. We could kiss the Beijing Olympics good-bye."

"So whoever did this didn't find out about the substitute rider in time," Monty mused aloud.

"Exactly." Edward set down his glass with a thud. "Granger better be okay. He's been with me for years. He's as decent and loyal as they come."

Monty folded his arms across his chest. "You obviously think that whoever's blackmailing you is behind this."

"What else is there to think?"

A shrug. "It's a stretch that so many unrelated disasters could happen to one family all at the same time; I'll give you that. But if the events are related, this extortionist's tactics are bizarre. Why wouldn't he wait until your twenty-four-hour deadline had passed before he acted?"

"The same reason he didn't wait last time. He murdered Frederick before giving me instructions on how to turn over the money."

"Exactly. And, like I told you Sunday, that's weird, too. The sequence of events doesn't fit." A pause. "Unless money's just part of what this guy's after. Maybe he's got another motivation, like revenge."

The phone rang.

Edward jumped on it. "Yes?" His entire body sagged with relief. "That's great news. Tell him to take it easy and not to worry about anything, including expenses. Get him a private nurse. Keep me updated. Oh, and put an extra guard on James. Make sure you two check every drop of food or liquid that goes into his mouth."

He hung up. "Granger's okay," he informed Monty. "He's got some ugly gashes, a broken wrist, and bruised ribs. The hospital's keeping him overnight for observation, just in case there's any sign of concussion. Otherwise, he's fine."

"And James?"

"Hmm?"

"You said James was sick. What's wrong?"

"Oh." Edward snapped back to himself. "He's got some twenty-four-hour stomach bug. He was bent over the toilet all night."

"And now?"

"Now he's just shaken. He knows that diuretic was meant for him." Edward massaged his temples. "I've got to calm him down, or he'll lose it before Sunday's Grand Prix."

Monty didn't reply. He just continued scrutinizing Edward, his expression pensive.

Devon couldn't wait to get home.

She'd returned to the clinic at four fifteen, just in time for the late-day chaos. The nonstop activity had been good for her. It kept her from thinking. Because when she thought, she thought about Blake. Not about the wonderful time they'd had last night, but about the car she'd seen him driving this afternoon. What did it mean, and how did it factor into Frederick's murder?

Blake had an alibi. Sort of. He'd been at the farm all weekend. On the other hand, he could have slipped out without anyone noticing, driven up to the cabin, committed the crime, then driven back and—

No. She wasn't letting herself go there. Not without grounds. As of now, there was no motive. There wasn't even basis for suspicion—just something that might very well be a fluke. Monty would find out what the story was with the second Mercedes. Once she heard it, she'd decide how to play things with Blake.

In the meantime, she was beat.

She left work at seven fifteen. It was dark. Cold. On tap for tonight was checking in with Monty, eating a Lean Cuisine, and hitting the sheets.

It didn't happen that way.

Within minutes of veering off the main drag, Devon got the disturbing sense she was being followed. She checked her rearview mirror repeatedly, but she saw nothing suspicious. Easing from the single-lane road onto the shoulder, she slowed down to a crawl and let the thin smattering of cars pass her. Not a single driver gave her a second look.

Still, she couldn't shake the feeling.

She pulled back onto the road and accelerated, heading toward home as quickly as caution would allow. The air was bitter cold, leaving the side roads icy and dangerous.

The feeling persisted.

A half mile before reaching her condo, she pulled off onto the shoulder again. This time, she cut the engine and turned off her lights so she could see without being seen.

Other than Terror and Scamp giving her puzzled looks from the backseat, she saw nothing.

Maybe she was becoming paranoid.

With a disgusted sound, she started her car and steered back onto the road. Minutes later, she turned down her winding street and into her driveway.

Gathering up the two dogs, she hurried up the walk that led to her town house.

"Hi," Merry greeted her, glancing up from the computer she'd been working on. "Everything okay?"

"I guess." Devon squatted down to deposit Terror and Scamp on the floor. "I'm a little strung out. Probably overtired. I need some sleep."

"Who wouldn't after two hot nights on the town?"

"Very funny." Devon rose and shrugged out of her coat. "How about here? Everything all right?"

"Pretty quiet. Oh, except for your flower delivery." Merry made the announcement in a slow, exaggerated tone. "An exquisite bouquet—orange lilies, yellow roses, and assorted purple sprays. I've been dying to read the card all afternoon."

Devon chuckled. "So why didn't you?"

"I'm nosy, but I'm not totally intrusive. I waited for you. But now let's find out which one of your avid suitors is trying to impress you." She jumped up and led Devon into the kitchen, where the flowers were displayed in a designer vase.

"You're right. They are impressive." Devon tugged the tiny envelope free of its plastic tine holder and slipped out the card. She wasn't sure what she was hoping to see. And she wasn't waiting to figure it out.

She scanned the card, which read: *You're in my thoughts. Hope I'm in yours. I'll break away as soon as I can, and we'll pick up where we left off. Till then, look at these and think of me. —James.*

"Well?" Merry demanded.

"They're from James." Devon realized as she said it that she wasn't surprised. This kind of grand gesture screamed "James" at the top of its lungs.

And Blake?

Blake's idea of a postdate gesture would probably be lining up a sled rematch on Pilgrim Hill.

The thought made her smile.

"I guess you're happy," Merry observed.

"They're beautiful," Devon replied. "And, yes, flattering."

"Good. You can tell that to James. He called twice. So did Blake. James left his number in Florida. Blake said to call his cell. So, the contenders are running neck and neck. The tension is mounting. I can't wait to see who crosses the finish line first."

"No one's crossing *any* line," Devon retorted. "This is a plan, remember? I'm helping Monty figure out who killed Frederick Pierson. Period."

"Yeah. Right." Meredith rolled her eyes. "I believe the helping Monty part. But the 'period'? No way. You're into this. Or into *them*. You've got those Pierson grandsons chomping at the bit—excuse the double entendre. And you're chomping right back. No way this is just business."

Devon shot her a look. "Go back to your econ assignment. I have to call James and say thank you."

"Don't forget Blake," Merry reminded her good-naturedly as she headed back to the living room. "He's waiting, too."

The doorbell and the phone rang simultaneously.

"You see which contender's calling in," Merry instructed. "I'll see who's at the door." She scooted off.

Devon scooped up the receiver. "Hello?"

"Did you get them?"

"James." From the corner of her eye, Devon saw Monty enter the house. "I was just about to call you. They're gorgeous."

"So are you," James replied. "Did you just get home?"

"Two seconds ago. I took off my coat and found your flowers." Devon's brows drew together as Monty stepped into the kitchen, clearly intent on hearing this call. "They're a welcome sight after a long day."

"Yeah. A *very* long day." James sounded strained. "It's good to hear your voice."

"Yours, too." Devon was watching Monty scribble something on a slip of paper, which he then shoved in front of her.

Put him on speakerphone. Ask how Wellington went today.

Devon nodded. She had no idea where Monty was going with this, but she followed his instructions, pressing the speakerphone button and hanging up the receiver. "How did today's competition go?"

A hollow laugh. "It was a disaster."

"Why? From what I recall, you said it was an intermediate-level event on a younger horse. Did he give you trouble?"

"*Life* gave me trouble. I picked up some kind of twenty-four-hour stomach bug. I couldn't ride. My grandfather subbed in someone else."

Monty waved his hand in a keep-him-talking gesture.

"And that upset you?" Devon pressed quizzically. "I thought it was only the Sunday events you're focused on."

"It is. I was relieved as hell that my grandfather got Granger to ride Future. I sure couldn't do it."

"Who's Granger?"

"One of our grooms. He's also a very strong rider. He was a good choice—or he should have been. He blacked out right before the third jump."

"Blacked out?" Devon didn't have to feign her shock. "He fell off the horse?"

"Uh-huh. He's okay, other than some minor injuries. He's lucky. We're all lucky. I don't think I could have lived with myself if it had been serious. Someone slipped him a diuretic. It was meant to disqualify the rider—me. Granger has low blood pressure, so it did a lot more than that."

Devon sank down on a kitchen stool. "Someone tried to sabotage you?"

"Big-time. It turns out there was a random drug test scheduled for today. If the Antidoping Agency had found that stuff in my blood, I'd be banned from the circuit, maybe for good."

"That's horrible. Do you know who did it?"

"Not a clue. It could have been a dozen different people. I told you, the equestrian world's pretty brutal."

"Is there an investigation under way?"

James gave a humorless laugh. "There's *always* an investigation under way, especially when drugs are involved. That doesn't mean anything will be uncovered, much less proven."

Devon glanced at Monty, who scribbled down the words: *Ask how he's feeling.*

"What about your stomach bug?" she inquired. "Is it better?"

"More or less. I managed to hold down some tea and dry toast. So I'm on the mend. Although the news about Granger made my stomach turn all over again."

"I can imagine. Is there someone down there with you? Someone who can check on you, or bring you what you need?"

"Not to worry," James assured her. "We've got an entire staff, including a family doctor, here in Wellington. I'm in good hands. But thanks for caring." He paused. "How was your date with Blake?"

"Fine." Devon saw her father grimace. "Very lighthearted and fun."

"Fun? What did you do?"

"Sledding, skating, and snowball fighting."

"You're kidding."

"No. Actually, it was good to unwind. This week's been a nightmare, as you well know."

"And Blake gave you a reprieve. I'm glad. Listen, I was thinking of flying up Sunday night. Are you free?"

Devon blinked. "Sunday's the Grand Prix."

"Which I plan to win. And, since there are no Monday events, Sunday night is party time. I'd rather party with you. I don't have to be back until Tuesday. What do you say?"

"Will you feel up to it?"

"To seeing you? I already do."

"I guess I'm a great cure for a stomach virus."

He chuckled. "Guess so. Is it a date?"

Monty nodded.

"Sure," Devon responded.

"Great. Since I liked that answer, I'll press my luck a little bit. Would you consider flying down next weekend and watching me compete? I'd arrange for the corporate jet to be ready and waiting Friday night. Wellington's got a private airstrip. You'd be here in the blink of an eye. What do you say?"

Monty was already shaking his head vehemently.

"I'd like to, but I can't," Devon hedged. "Not unless my mother's safely out of hiding. My sister and brother are here with me, remember? I can't desert them. Plus, I'd be lousy company. I hope you understand."

"I'd be lying if I said I wasn't disappointed. But of course I understand. Just tell me you'll take a rain check. For right after your mother comes home."

"Rain check taken." Devon's gaze followed Monty, who'd spied the floral bouquet and crossed over to examine it. An anticipatory look crossed his face, and he searched the countertop until he found the card. Glancing at it, he gave a hard, satisfied nod.

He gestured for Devon to wrap up her call. Then he flipped open his cell and stalked out of the room.

By the time Devon had hung up and gone out to the living room, Monty was thanking someone on the other end of his cell phone and saying good-bye.

He whipped around to face Devon. "Interesting. James Pierson ordered these flowers personally. From Wellington. Early this morning. While his lips were supposedly glued to the toilet."

Devon processed that. "You think he's lying about being sick."

"I think this story has too many holes in it. It felt wrong before, and it feels even more wrong now. James gets a convenient, disabling, but intermittent stomach bug. Granger, the ideal rider to take his place, just happens to have low blood pressure. There's a random drug test scheduled for exactly the right date and event—a test that ends up not mattering because Granger blacked out and required independent blood tests anyway. And the drugging procedure—if someone wanted to target James's drink, wouldn't he make damned sure it *was* James's drink before he plopped some meds in?"

"Points taken," Devon said thoughtfully. "I'm just not sure where your rationale is taking us."

"Me, either. But here's another inconsistency: James's reaction. It's way out of character for him to be so blasé about getting to the bottom of this. Edward's preoccupied with the big picture. But James doesn't know squat about the extortion scheme. So why isn't he hell-bent on figuring out who did this to him?"

"Okay, so you're suggesting this was all staged. Why? Granger's no threat to James, not personally or professionally."

Monty gave a tight nod, then began pacing around. "That's the part that doesn't fit. Granger's the only one who stood to get hurt."

Devon sank down on the sofa, her expression pensive. "You knew about all this before James called."

"Yeah. I found out a few hours ago. Edward summoned

me into his office. He was pretty worked up. Once he heard Granger was okay, he calmed down. But he didn't seem surprised or worried that James, the avid equestrian, was sick enough to bail out of an event. That bugged me. But not as much as what James just said. Edward didn't mention anything about a scheduled drug test. He just tossed out the possibility like a what-if, not a fact. So, either he didn't know as much as James did, or he did a damned good job of covering. Either way, you can be sure I'm going to poke around and find out how far ahead this drug screening was planned, and who knew it was going to take place."

"Do you have anything to go on?"

"From what I've learned, Edward is a pretty big sponsor at Wellington. Maybe James used Grandpa's clout to pay someone off. Maybe that someone told him about the drug test in advance."

"Maybe James knew he was being targeted, so he opted out."

"That's the nice conclusion. The uglier one is that James is using and intends to keep that under wraps."

"I hope not."

"Yeah, well, the James who just called you isn't the emotionally frayed nervous wreck his grandfather described. He was barely ruffled." Monty shook his head. "I'm not sure what's going on here. *Yet*. What I *am* sure of is that I don't trust James Pierson."

"What about Blake Pierson?" Devon felt compelled to ask. "Do you trust him?"

Monty heard her question loud and clear. He stopped pacing and looked at her. "There are a dozen company cars with the same make and model as Frederick's. All the execs have them—from Edward to Philip Rhodes to Louise Chambers. And, yeah, to Blake. He must have used his this morning when you saw him at the clinic. But he's a very bright guy. If he'd driven up to Lake Luzerne and torched his uncle, he wouldn't be parading around in the car he drove up in. Feel better?"

"Actually, yes."

"Well, don't. I might not think Blake's a killer, but that doesn't mean I trust him. And you shouldn't, either."

Devon nodded. "Don't worry. My guard is up." She massaged her temples. "This case is getting more complicated rather than less."

"They always do. That's when we solve them." Monty leaned forward and scooped an apple out of the fruit basket on the coffee table. "Where's your sister?" he asked, taking a bite. "She let me in, then vanished."

"Probably in the guest room, on the computer. She's battling her way through a big econ assignment." Devon glanced over at the deserted living-room computer. "She was working here when I came home."

"Until she saw me. Then she took off."

Devon sighed. "Monty . . ."

"Don't worry." He waved away her words of appeasement. "I've got thick skin and a will of iron. I'm not giving up. So, since you two haven't eaten, how about I whip up some of my famous linguini in Montgomery sauce?"

That conjured up a warm, nostalgic memory. "Wow," Devon replied, snippets of childhood flashing through her mind. "Talk about a blast from the past. We haven't had linguini in Montgomery sauce in years. Even Lane might be persuaded to stay home for dinner."

"Where is he?"

A shrug. "Who knows? He's met with a few colleagues and made a couple of trips into Manhattan. But he's being very vague about what his reasons are." Devon crossed her fingers and held them up. "I'm hoping he's putting out feelers for East Coast assignments. That way we'll get him back home where he belongs." She rose. "I'll find Merry."

"No." Monty stopped her. "You make sure we have all the ingredients I need. I'll find Merry."

Devon nodded her understanding, then headed for the kitchen. "Good luck to us both."

"Don't forget the chili peppers," Monty called after her.

"How could I?" she called back. "They don't forget me—not for three days after I eat your famous Montgomery saucc."

Philip Rhodes locked his office door and flipped on the light.

It was after nine. No one was in the building. Still, he had to ensure he was alone. Especially if he found what he expected to. Then the walls would come crashing down.

He logged onto his computer and punched up a security code.

Access.

He knew which file to look for. He'd read snatches of it earlier in the day. But he kept getting interrupted. Coworkers. The police. Montgomery.

Especially Montgomery. He was getting suspicious.

Bingo. There it was—the ticking bomb.

Rhodes highlighted the file. Opening it, he pored over the data.

Twenty minutes later, he sat back in his desk chair, sweat dripping down his face.

It was worse than he'd feared. Totally incriminating.

There was only one course of action for him to take.

He slid open his top drawer, groping around till he found what he needed.

His fingers closed around it.

Then he reached for the telephone.

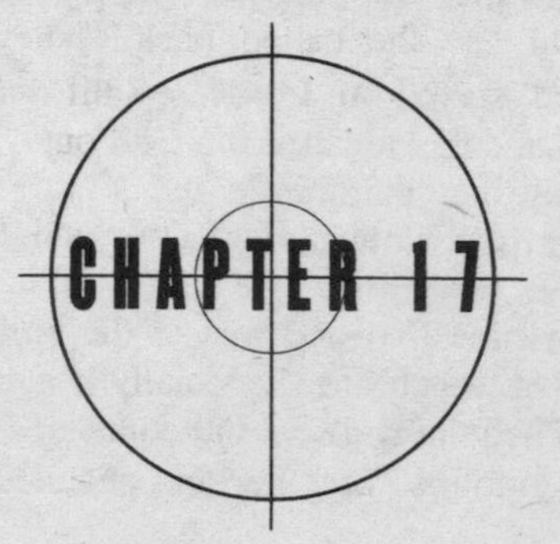

Devon woke up feeling more relaxed.

A family evening. How long had it been since she'd had one of those? Ages. They'd eaten, talked, even laughed. Merry had definitely thawed—especially when Monty whipped out the Bat Phone and suggested they all call Sally together.

There had been tears in her mother's voice—bittersweet tears, of happiness, longing, and loneliness.

She wanted to be home.

Monty would make it happen. More and more, Devon believed it. She also believed he was right about Sally's growing impatience. No way would she stay in hiding much longer. Five days and already she was fidgety, like a caged bird ready to soar. The more time passed, the farther away the threat seemed to be. And the farther away it seemed to be, the more likely she'd be to wing her way home and screw the consequences.

This murder investigation had better be wrapped up, and soon.

Monty had stayed at Devon's until midnight, during which time Lane had cleaned them all out in a poker game. Like old times, they paid him with IOUs for Snickers bars.

Devon had drifted off at twelve thirty, more content than she'd been in a long time.

Only when she was half-asleep did she realize she'd never returned Blake's calls.

He rectified that at 7 A.M.

Barely had Devon stepped out of the shower when her telephone rang.

"Hello?" she said breathlessly.

"It's a good thing I've got a strong ego. Otherwise, I'd be concerned that you were blowing me off."

Devon felt her lips curve. "Hi, Blake. I'm sorry. I didn't get home last night until seven something, and then the night just got away from me. By the time I sat down, it was midnight. I didn't know if you'd still be up."

"I was up," he assured her, the thrumming background noise telling Devon he was in the car. "I usually am. I don't need much sleep. Which is good, because I rarely get any." A pause. "Speaking of which, I know it's early. Did I wake you?"

"Nope. I'm an early bird, at least on workdays. I like to get into the clinic by eight. The animals scheduled for surgery arrive between eight thirty and nine. I try to meet with their owners before I conduct the presurgical physical exams. It gives everyone a little extra peace of mind."

Blake digested that. "That's very sensitive of you."

"It's my job. Pets are family members. They deserve to be treated with care and respect. Of course, so do their owners. They're going through a trauma as well."

"It's good to hear someone speak so passionately about what they do," Blake replied. "Maybe I'll forgive you for not calling me back. Or maybe I won't. Tell you what. Have dinner with me tonight and we'll discuss it."

Devon hesitated, for a whole host of reasons. She was still feeling off balance from the sizzling kiss they'd shared. Monty's warning about Blake's trustworthiness—or lack thereof—was still ringing in her head. And she still wasn't sure how much of Blake's interest in her was real and how much of it was part of Edward Pierson's grand plan.

"I don't know," she replied, ducking the invitation. "It's been a pretty crazy week. I'm really dragging—"

"Too much sledding? Or too much, too soon?" he interrupted.

"Both." She abandoned evasiveness and went straight for honesty. "I've got a demanding career. I'm not used to non-stop social engagements topping off my hectic workdays. I'm also not used to being on acute emotional overload from so many different sources at once."

"And I'm one of those sources."

"Yes."

"Good. Then I know I got to you."

Silence.

"If it makes you feel better, you got to me, too," he added.

Yes, it made her feel better. She wished it didn't.

"I have to go, Blake. I've got patients waiting. And you've got a business to run."

"Fair enough." Clearly, he wasn't taking no for an answer. "Here's the deal. I'll let you off the hook for tonight. But tomorrow's Friday. I'll pick you up at seven."

"I'm working Saturday."

"So am I. That doesn't change the fact that it's the weekend. We need some downtime."

"Downtime," Devon repeated, her tone amused. "Let me guess—a rematch of our snowball fight?"

"Nope. A quiet evening at home for two tired workaholics. I'll cook. I make a mean poached salmon with dill sauce."

"You're kidding."

"Uh-uh. I'm a man of many talents. So, do we have a date?"

"Yes." She gave up and gave in. "We have a date."

Blake was pleased with the way his morning had started.

The call to Devon had opened on an ambiguous note and closed on a positive one. With any luck, the rest of the day would go as well.

He left his car in the parking garage and headed up Fifty-fourth Street to the office. Entering the building through the revolving doors, he nodded at the security guards, then strode through the lobby to the elevators.

He stepped out on the twenty-seventh floor, the executive level of Pierson & Company. The place was dark. Not a surprise, given it was 7:20 A.M. He made his way through the corridor. The light sensors picked up his presence, illuminating each section of hallway as he crossed it. He was the first one in. That wasn't unusual. Not since Frederick's death.

Instinctively, he shot a passing glance at his uncle's office. It was dark. Barren. Seeing it that way still felt surreal. Somehow Blake half expected Frederick to be hunkered down at his desk, making phone calls or reviewing sales projections.

Shoving aside the thought, Blake continued on to his own office, where he dropped off his briefcase and scanned the contents of his desk. His "Priority To Do" pile was sky-high. Plus, after yesterday's incident at Wellington, there'd be damage control to initiate.

He headed down the hall and around the bend, his destination the kitchenette, his goal a cup of strong, black coffee.

From the corner of his eye, he spotted Philip Rhodes's office and came to a surprised halt. The door was tightly closed. That was unusual. Rhodes worked long hours, but was never in before seven thirty. He was a creature of habit. Early mornings were spent at the gym.

The guy must really be sweating it, Blake thought grimly. He'd been a wreck ever since Frederick's murder. Not that he blamed him. Keeping James on track had been hard enough before. Now it was brutal. And after yesterday's fiasco at the Gold Coast Classic . . .

Drawing a sharp breath, Blake put his coffee quest on hold and headed toward Rhodes's office. They had some details to iron out regarding Chomping at the Bit. Now was as good a time as any.

Reaching the door, Blake knocked.

No response.

"Philip?" he called.

Again, no reply.

That was odd.

Frowning, Blake tested the handle. Unlocked.

He pushed open the door. The hum of the computer told him it was on. Rhodes's coat was hanging on the brass coat-rack, and his briefcase was placed neatly beside it.

"Philip?" Blake stepped inside, looked around, and stopped dead in his tracks.

Behind the curved mahogany desk, Philip Rhodes was crumpled in his chair. The side of his forehead was bloody. Some of the blood had oozed down, leaving an ugly red stain on his shirt and a small puddle on the rug beneath him. His arms hung limply at his sides.

Below his right hand lay a pistol.

"Jesus Christ."

Edward Pierson sank into his chair, sheet white, as Monty faced him in his office a short while later.

"Drink," Monty urged, indicating the glass of water Blake had poured him.

"Water's not going to help," Edward snapped. "It won't bring Philip back. Or make any sense of this lunacy."

"Grandfather, you've got to relax," Blake instructed. "Dr. Richards is on his way."

"I don't need a goddamned cardiologist. I need an explanation." Edward loosened his tie, wiping perspiration off his brow. "What made Rhodes do this? Why was he so over the edge?" Despite his protests, Edward lifted the glass to his lips and drank.

"The police are reviewing the evidence now," Monty replied. "There'll be an autopsy performed. But given what we know—the gun, the call to you, and the presence of a typed note—the medical examiner is preliminarily ruling this a suicide."

"That much I comprehend. Rhodes blew his brains out. But why?"

"Good question." Monty eyed Edward intently. "You knew Rhodes had a gun?"

"Yes, I knew."

"So did I," Blake added. "It wasn't a secret. He bought it a couple of years ago for protection."

"It didn't do much of a job, did it?" Monty noted drily. His gaze returned to Edward. "You said Rhodes called you around eleven o'clock last night?"

"A little past. I was watching the news."

"He didn't sound desperate?"

"Desperate? No." Edward set down his glass with a thud. "He sounded upset. Maybe a little out of it. I asked if he'd been drinking. He said no. He said the pressure had gotten to be too much, and he had to leave. I thought he meant the company. I asked if this pressure was connected to what happened to Frederick. He said I'd have a full explanation in the morning. I assumed he wanted a private meeting. I said I'd be in at eight sharp. He said good night. I tossed and turned all night. Then I came in to find this."

"There was no finality to his tone or his words?"

"No. Maybe. I don't know." Edward planted his palms on the desk, clearly trying to calm himself down. "At the time it didn't seem that way. Now when I think back, his choice of words was strange. But, Jesus, who'd expect the guy to kill himself?"

"Yeah. Who would?" Monty muttered. He glanced at Blake, who was watching his grandfather with a brooding expression. "You saw the suicide note on the computer screen. Do you remember what it said?"

"Not verbatim," Blake replied. "Then again, I was reeling from finding Philip like that. My focus was on calling 911, not scrutinizing Philip's last words. I remember something about him not being able to forgive himself, something about Frederick's death, and something about a slush fund he'd been siphoning money out of."

"Did he say he killed Frederick?"

"I don't think so. Not that I saw. He referred to Frederick's suspicions about his activities and how cornered he felt. He might have said more. I just don't remember. I guess I was in shock."

"Probably," Monty agreed. "It's not every day you find a dead body at your workplace. Even rarer that it's the body of a valued employee and longtime friend—*and* one who died a violent, if conveniently timed, death. Don't bother with your water. I'd advise having a stiff drink."

Blake's gaze narrowed. "Is that some kind of cryptic accusation?"

"No accusation. Just thirty years of experience. I'm still on the fence as to whether or not this was a suicide. I'll reserve judgement until I've talked to the crime-scene investigators, the M.E., and Midtown North."

"What are you saying?" Edward demanded. "You think this was murder?"

"I'm saying I'm a tough sell." Monty shrugged. "Especially with everything that's gone down this week." He turned and walked to the door. "I'm heading over to the precinct to have a word with the detective assigned to this case. Hopefully, he's someone I know, and he'll share a few of the facts. If nothing else, I'll get a glimpse of the alleged suicide note." He paused in the doorway, looked at Edward. "No other phone calls last night?"

"Hmm—what?" Edward's blank expression transformed to hollow awareness. "You mean the extortionist? No. He never called. Does that mean he is—*was*—Rhodes? That Philip was our blackmailer?"

Monty shrugged again. "Maybe. Or maybe our blackmailer framed and killed Rhodes. We'll see." He reached for the doorknob. "I'm out of here. You follow your doctor's instructions. Try to take it easy. I'll be in touch."

Devon stepped out of surgery at one thirty-five to find a healthy pile of morning lab reports to review and the usual number of pink message slips.

She wasn't expecting three of those to be from Monty. She certainly wasn't expecting them to say things like *sooner than ASAP* and *urgent*.

She darted into her office and punched up his cell.

"Yeah," he answered. "Devon. Good."

The instant she heard his voice, she knew something was very wrong. "What is it?" she asked. "Is it Mom?"

"No. No news about your mother." Monty was responding to her question and subtly reminding her that they weren't on the Bat Phone. "It's Philip Rhodes. He's dead. Gunshot to the head. It happened in the office. The media's swarming all over the place. I didn't want you to hear the news and freak out. I'm fine."

"*Another* death linked to the Piersons?" Devon sank into her chair, her mind quickly processing this. "Was it murder or suicide?"

"That's the million-dollar question. I'm outside Midtown North now, swallowing a hot dog. I'll know more later. Can you grab dinner with me tonight?"

"Just us?"

"Yeah."

Devon understood. Monty wanted to bounce the situation around with her. And he didn't want to do it in front of Merry, who'd always been too sensitive to sit in on these crime-solving brainstorming sessions.

"I can grab a train to the city as soon as I finish here," Devon said. "That should be around six, unless we have an emergency."

"No. I'll drive up to you. It'll save time. I'll pick you up at the clinic. We can eat at the diner on Main Street."

"Done." Devon paused. "You don't think it's suicide, do you?"

"Nope. See you later."

Monty munched on his double-burger platter while Devon picked at her chef salad.

They didn't waste time with small talk, but got right into the back-and-forth case analysis they'd perfected when Devon was in her teens.

"Okay, so we have a thirty-eight revolver, registered to Rhodes, a typed suicide note, and no witnesses—except Edward Pierson, who spoke to Rhodes by phone a half hour before he died." Devon summarized the basics Monty had provided. "What about the autopsy report?"

"Officially, it's being released tomorrow. But I spoke to the M.E. who performed the autopsy. The ruling's going to stand. There's no solid evidence this is anything but a suicide."

"But there are inconsistencies."

"A truckload."

"Let's hear them."

"Where do I start?" Monty scowled. "To begin with, the note was typed and unsigned—strangely impersonal for a suicide. The telephone call to Edward Pierson was vague. Not a gut-spilling confession. Just some ambiguous fragments. Not even enough to make Pierson call the cops—which he'd do in a minute if he suspected Rhodes was involved in Frederick's murder. Then there's the slush fund Rhodes mentioned in his note, the one he was supposedly stealing from. Jenkins, my forensic accountant, never found a trace of it. And he's the best there is."

Monty paused to stick a french fry in his mouth. "There were no burn marks and no gunpowder residue on Rhodes's face. Which suggests the thirty-eight wasn't pressed to his temple. Also, crime scene didn't find any powder residue on his hand."

"I didn't think they tested for that anymore," Devon interrupted.

"They don't. Too many false positives. But the absence of it tells me Rhodes didn't fire that gun."

"His prints were on it?"

"His and only his. That's consistent with a homicide staged to look like a suicide."

"What about the angle of the weapon?"

"Slightly downward."

"Upward is more consistent with a suicide," Devon remembered aloud. "Still, none of this constitutes proof."

"I'm a PI now. I don't need proof. And you know my old saying. . . ."

"If it looks like a duck, waddles like a duck, and quacks like a duck, it usually *is* a duck," Devon recited. "And I agree with you. There are way too many discrepancies. So now what?"

"Now we figure out why Rhodes was killed and by who."

"Probably the same person who killed Frederick." Devon put a forkful of salad in her mouth, chewing and swallowing thoughtfully. "That lets James off the hook."

"He never left Florida," Monty agreed. "I already checked that out. Which doesn't mean he's not involved. It just means he didn't pull the trigger." A frown. "You're seeing him Sunday night."

"And Blake tomorrow night," Devon added in reminder.

"Assuming he's up for it. He's the one who found Rhodes's body. He was pretty shaken up." Monty's frown deepened. "I got the feeling the suicide ruling wasn't sitting right with him, either. I'm not sure why."

Devon put down her fork. "The other night, Blake mentioned that Chomping at the Bit needed to tap into the contacts and suppliers of the food-services division. That meant his working closely with both Frederick and Philip." She leaned forward, propping her elbows on the table and interlacing her fingers. "He implied that James might try to sabotage his efforts and undermine him now that Frederick's gone. I have no idea if any of this is connected, but it does put all three people who were targeted this past week center stage."

"True. It's worth looking into. So are the surveillance tapes from the Pierson building—the ones taken last night. Although I'd bet my bottom dollar they won't show anything."

"You think the killer was already inside."

"Yup. I think he or she works at Pierson. I think he or she framed Rhodes for Frederick's murder, then killed him, leaving the building via the delivery entrance. I don't know if Rhodes was squeaky-clean or not, but I'd be willing to bet he planned to tell Edward Pierson everything. The killer couldn't have that. Which reminds me. I'm going to see if I can get someone to check out Rhodes's hard drive. Assuming he had something incriminating, the killer might have deleted it."

Monty paused, leveling a hard stare at his daughter. "Back to Blake Pierson. Given the rapport you two have, do you think you can get him to open up to you?"

"If you're asking if Blake's attraction to me is going to make him spill his guts, the answer is no."

Another pause, this one longer and more intense. "You're in pretty deep."

"*I* don't know that." Exasperation laced Devon's tone. "How could *you*?"

"Call it father's intuition."

Devon averted her gaze, fiddling with the edge of her napkin. "Let's leave your intuition out of this, okay? In fact, let's avoid the whole subject of my personal life—especially since I'm not sure yet if Blake Pierson factors into it. My focus right now is helping you solve this case, and getting Mom safely home. It's possible that Blake is actively involved in keeping that from happening. Until I'm sure how deep his role in all this goes, I'm not thinking ahead."

"In that case, you should be eager to get him to lower his guard tomorrow night. The sooner he tells you what he's not saying, the sooner you can decide if he's worth thinking ahead about."

The driver of the maroon coupe eyeballed the diner, then flipped open his cell phone and punched up a number.

"Still having dinner with Daddy," he reported. "Probably strategizing. No problem. I'm sure they'll have a follow-up call tomorrow. I'll get the audio."

CHAPTER 18

The drive to Blake's brownstone was nothing like Devon had imagined. It wasn't because of her nerves, although she had major butterflies in her stomach. And it wasn't because of Blake's mood, although he was obviously on edge, thanks to the media circus following the second violent death striking Pierson & Company this week.

No, it was because of Chomper.

Blake had picked up his pup right before swinging by Devon's place. And between Chomper's high energy level and his sheer delight at seeing Devon, he was a virtual jumping machine all the way from White Plains to Manhattan. So rather than tension, the silver Jag was instead filled with playful scuffling and fits of laughter.

"We're lucky we didn't have an accident," Blake declared when they were finally inside his building. "Chomper's a menace."

"He just needs some car rules," Devon returned, shrugging out of her coat and bending down to scratch Chomper's ears. "And a designated area in the car that's his—one that has a fixed perimeter. You might think of trading in your Jag for a nice SUV. Chomper will thank you for it."

Blake hung their coats away, his lips twisting into a grin. "I have a truck up at the farm. Chomper's partial to it. Before I enrolled him in obedience classes, he didn't spend much time in the Jag. We usually walk here in the city. But I'll take your suggestion under advisement."

"Do that." Devon stepped farther into the foyer, crossing her arms and vigorously rubbing the sleeves of her angora sweater to warm herself up. "It's freezing out tonight."

"Easily remedied." Blake led her into the living room, where he turned on the gas fireplace. "Sit," he invited, gesturing toward the sofa. "I'll pour you a glass of wine, then get dinner started."

"What can I do to help?"

"Entertain your biggest fan." Blake indicated Chomper, who'd followed Devon into the living room and plopped down near the sofa, gazing expectantly in her direction. "The fish is all seasoned and ready to go into the oven. And I made the dill sauce before I drove up to White Plains, secret ingredient and all. It's in the fridge, along with the rest of dinner. I only need a few minutes to get things together. We'll be eating in a half hour."

Devon inclined her head, running her fingers through her hair and watching Blake with a bemused expression. "Now this is a side of you I didn't expect," she confessed. "The homebody and gourmet chef."

"Don't get carried away," Blake retorted, going to the sideboard and opening a bottle of Sauvignon Blanc. "Until I got Chomper, I was rarely home. Now that I am, takeout's the name of the game. I cook about once a month, if that. As for the gourmet part, reserve judgment until you've tasted the fish."

"Fair enough. Actually, I'm the same way. I'm home at

night for my pets, and because after a day of work I'm too tired to move. Even so, I rarely cook. But when I do, I'm pretty good."

"Great." Blake handed her a glass of wine as she sank down on the sofa. "Next meal's on you. We'll see who does better."

Devon rolled her eyes. "I knew it. Another competition. And here you'd almost convinced me that this was nothing more than a nice, quiet dinner meant to help me relax."

"It's both." Blake set his glass down on the coffee table. "Be right back." He headed off to the kitchen.

Devon leaned back, sipping her wine and scratching Chomper's ears.

Five minutes passed, then ten.

The fire felt good, warming Devon's skin as the wine warmed her senses. A soothing, lethargic feeling settled over her, and she yawned, wriggling more comfortably on the sofa and sinking back into the cushions. She could scarcely keep her eyes open. Obviously, she was more worn-out than she'd realized.

A faint perception drifted through her mind. A noise of some sort—an insect maybe? She frowned, swatting at her ear.

There it was again. That annoying buzz.

Chomper exploded into action—barking, leaping up from her feet, and taking off.

The buzz wasn't an insect. It was someone at the door.

Devon jerked upright, groggy and vaguely aware that she'd fallen asleep. Chomper was nothing more than a golden streak disappearing around the corner. Blake was at his heels, striding through the hall and toward the front door.

An instant later, Devon heard it swing open.

"Hello, Blake." A woman's voice. "I thought you could use some company. When you left the office, you looked like death. Not that I blame you. Finding Philip the way you did . . ." Revulsion laced her tone. "Anyway, I thought I'd drop over and—"

"Now's not a good time," Blake interrupted.

Devon was suddenly and completely awake. She recognized that voice. It belonged to Louise Chambers.

"You're wrong," Louise was saying. "It's the perfect time. We've both had a hellish week. We're both dodging the media. We can do that together."

"I have company," Blake bit out.

"Company." Louise digested that news with more than a little irritation. "Family or friends?"

This was too good to pass up.

Devon rose, combing her hair with her fingers and marching to the foyer. "Blake?" she called as she rounded the bend and Louise came into view. "I think I smell something burning. Should I check on the—oh, excuse me." She came to a halt, her expression rife with fabricated surprise. "I didn't realize anyone was here. Ms. Chambers, isn't it?" She gave Louise a bright smile. "We met the other day."

"Yes, we did." Louise was clearly choking on her words and on her smile. "Dr. Montgomery. Nice to see you."

"Please—it's Devon." Devon shifted her innocent gaze to Blake. "I didn't realize Ms. Chambers would be joining us for dinner."

"She's not." Blake's lids were hooded, his jaw set. He was pissed off. Whether it was because Louise had intruded or because her unwelcome timing was a glaring proclamation that there really was something going on between them and he'd lied through his teeth—that remained to be seen.

"I appreciate your concern, Louise." There was a definite note of finality in his tone. "But I'm hanging in. We all are."

Enough time had passed for Louise to regain her composure. "Of course we are. There's no other choice." She flashed another, equally plastic smile at Devon. "I'm sorry I intruded—Devon. Enjoy your dinner."

"Thank you—Louise. And you enjoy your evening."

Blake shut the door and turned around, arms folded across his chest. "What was that?"

"You tell me," Devon shot back. "I think it was the woman you're not seeing and not friends with, dropping by to offer you comfort in bed."

"I know what *that* was. What was your little one-woman show? If I didn't know better, I'd say you were staking your claim, and warning Louise to back off."

Devon bristled. "That goes to show how arrogant you are. This has nothing to do with staking a claim. It's exposing a lie. Being cryptic is one thing. Lying is another."

Blake glared back. "I wasn't lying. Louise and I are colleagues. Before last week, we never spoke outside the office. But she was pretty freaked out by Frederick's death. So she's called a couple of times. We've talked. Period."

"And this impromptu visit?"

"Her first. She's never been here. I've never been to her place. And, for the record, I resent like hell being interrogated. If I didn't want to get past these ridiculous misconceptions of yours, I'd be ripping mad. So, for the last time, I'm not sleeping with Louise, seeing Louise, or palling around with Louise."

"She'd obviously love to change that."

"I'm not responsible for Louise's agenda, only my own. Now, do I go back to the kitchen and make dinner, or do I take you to bed the way I've wanted to since last Sunday?"

Devon's mouth opened, then snapped shut. "What?"

"You heard me. Which is it?"

"Bed." The word was out before Devon could censor it. Not that she would have. She wanted Blake as much as he wanted her.

His gaze darkened at her reply, and he leaned forward, yanking her against him. He tilted up her chin and covered her mouth with his in a kiss that blew their last one out of the water.

Sensation roared to life, and Devon gave a soft, shaky moan, wrapping her arms around Blake and throwing herself into the moment. She pressed closer, slanting her lips against his and deepening the kiss.

Blake's mouth ate at hers, and his hands slid under her bottom, lifting her and fitting the contours of her body to his. She wriggled against him, raising her legs to hug his flanks, whimpering at the friction of his erection rubbing against the sensitive skin between her thighs. Even through their layers of clothes, the sensation was exquisite.

Muttering something hot and unintelligible, Blake backed Devon to the staircase, half walking, half carrying her up to the second floor and around the bend to the master bedroom. She was tugging at his sweater as he crossed the threshold, and he set her on her feet beside the bed, dragging the sweater over his head and flinging it aside. They stared at each other for one burning moment, their breath coming in short, hard pants.

"You're sure?" he managed in a gravelly tone.

"Very." Devon tugged off her own sweater, dropping it onto the carpet.

"Let me." Blake moved closer, unhooking her bra and gliding the straps down her shoulders. Sparks glinted in his eyes, and his hands followed his gaze, molding her breasts in a lingering caress that sent lightning bolts of heat shooting through her.

Devon's eyes slid shut, and a hard shudder ran through her as his thumbs grazed her nipples. She reached for his slacks, fumbling with the zipper as he pulled her against him, rubbing her naked breasts across his bare chest.

"Blake—don't," she choked out. "This is torture."

His response was to lower her onto the bed, breaking away long enough to shed the rest of his clothes. He chucked them aside, then turned his attention to Devon, who'd just squirmed out of her slacks. He made quick work of her thong, then lowered himself onto her, pressing her into the mattress and touching every inch of her body with his.

She arched to increase the sensations, biting her lip at the enormity of the physical pleasure. It was almost painful in its intensity. Blake muttered her name, his mouth hot against her skin, kissing her neck, her throat, her breasts. He went very still, then abruptly pushed up on his forearms, staring down at her with a burning amber gaze.

"I have to get inside you." Sweat beaded his forehead, and his thighs were already wedging hers apart.

She nodded fervently, too aroused to speak. She was as wild for this as he was, her lower body lifting for his, her legs shifting to accommodate him.

His penis probed at the entrance to her body—once, twice—then pushed inexorably inside. He didn't go slow. She wouldn't let him. Her hands balled into fists, pushing at the base of his spine, urging him into her. He didn't pause until he was all the way there, and even then, he pushed deeper.

Devon would have screamed if she hadn't been so focused on the exquisite point of pleasure coiling tight inside her. It was just out of reach, and she'd die if she didn't get there.

"Blake . . ." She heard the frantic plea in her own voice, felt the helpless arching of her body.

So did he.

With a muffled groan, Blake withdrew, then pushed back into her, gripping her bottom as he deepened his presence inside her, going that infinitesimal distance farther, closer to where she needed him to be.

Abruptly, he swore, muscles tensing as he went deadly still. "Dammit . . ." His teeth were clenched against a peak that was roaring down on them with the force and speed of a tidal wave. "Not yet . . . Not . . . yet . . ."

"Yes . . . now." Devon negated his intentions, her head tossing back and forth on the pillow. She was frantic, so desperate for release she was shaking with it. "Now, now, *now*."

The first tiny spasms began deep inside her, and Blake lost the battle in a rush. He withdrew a fraction, only to thrust all the way back in and then some. Devon cried out, her climax slamming through her with dizzying force. She convulsed again and again, her body shuddering helplessly as the pinnacle spun out in hot rings of sensation, draining her, milking him.

Blake lost it. With a low animal sound, he crushed their bodies together, erupting in a mind-numbing orgasm. He came in hard, pulsing spasms, his body jolting under the impact. Reflexively, he timed his rhythm to match hers, pushing into her contractions, matching them with his own.

He collapsed on top of her.

Neither of them moved. Their breath came in harsh pants, their bodies still trembling from the exertion of the past few minutes.

Blake swallowed hard, turning his lips into Devon's hair. "Are you okay?" he asked hoarsely.

"I'm not sure," she murmured. "I might be dead."

His lips curved. "Trust me, you're not."

"If you say so."

"I do. But if I keep crushing you, that might change." He made two valiant attempts before finally managing to lift himself off of her, rolling onto his back with a groan. "I think I just reverted back to my teens. No, I take that back. I never lost it to that degree, not even then."

A faint smile. "I'm flattered." Devon paused, cracking open her eyes so she could see Blake. "And you're amazing."

"So are you." He frowned as he saw her shiver, another level of awareness sinking in. "I don't believe this. I didn't even pull back the damn covers. Bad enough rushing you *into* bed. I rushed you *onto* bed." He reached over, tugging her against him so he could wriggle the comforter and top sheet out from under her. "There." He laid her down, climbing under with her. "Better?" He settled her against him.

"Ummm." Devon nodded, her head pillowed on his chest. "Much."

From where he'd sprawled in the bedroom doorway, Chomper barked, scrambling to attention.

"Shit," Blake muttered. "He thinks it's bedtime. Which means he wants to go out and do his business."

Devon's shoulders began to shake with laughter. "I'd suggest getting dressed. It's ten degrees outside. Your teenage parts might freeze."

"Cute." Blake hesitated, visibly reluctant to leave. "You know," he murmured, threading his fingers through her hair. "I should be offended. You fell asleep while I was slaving away in the kitchen."

"I apologize."

"You're forgiven. You made up for it."

"Consider it dessert first. Which reminds me, is dinner burned to a crisp?"

"Nope. It never made it into the oven. I'll rectify that now, when I take Chomper out. I'll just make a few minor adjustments to my serving plan. Instead of fine china and candles, we'll do snack trays and paper, and we'll have dinner in bed."

"That sounds wonderful. I'm ravenous."

"I wonder why."

Devon's eyes twinkled. "Guess I'm a teenager, too."

Another bark, this one more insistent.

"You're being paged."

"So I heard." Blake climbed out of bed, yanking on a pair of sweats and snapping his fingers at Chomper. "I'll be back soon," he told Devon.

"I'll be here." She snuggled into the bed, feeling boneless and replete, her muscles as weak as if she'd run a marathon. She wondered if she had enough strength left to eat.

Or to do what she'd come here to do.

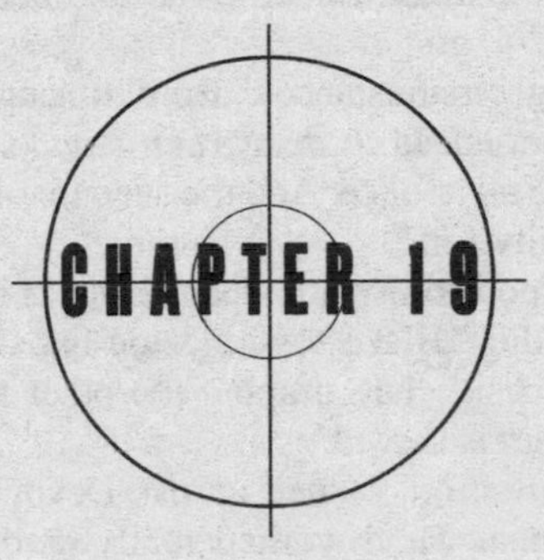

Devon was half-asleep when, thirty minutes later, Blake strode back into the bedroom, Chomper at his heels. It didn't take a scholar to figure out why the pup was glued to his master. Blake was carrying two snack trays of food. Chomper was sniffing the air and waiting for the great aromas to translate into great table scraps.

"Wake up," Blake announced. "Dinner is served."

"I'll try." Devon squirmed into a sitting position, plumping a pillow and propping it behind her. "Okay. I'm fully conscious," she determined, settling herself against the headboard, the comforter tucked around her.

"Glad to hear it." He placed a tray across her lap. "By the way, you owe Chomper an apology, too. He was really put out earlier when you fell asleep on the sofa and started dripping wine on him. I took your glass before it hit the floor."

Soberly, Devon regarded Chomper. "Sorry, boy. I'll make it up to you. I'll share." She gave a bemused shake of her head. "I've never fallen asleep on a date before. Tonight I did it twice."

"Extenuating circumstances. Both times. The first because you've never had so many high-stress stimuli exploding in your face all at once. And the second—hey, that I take full responsibility for."

"Not *full* responsibility. I had some say in it."

"Yeah, you did." Blake tossed aside his sweats and slid back into bed beside her, draping the other tray across his own lap. "Dinner is served."

Startled admiration flashed across Devon's face as she regarded the meal. He'd worked really hard, she thought, feeling touched. Dinner was salmon fillets garnished with basil and parsley, all over rice, beside which were dollops of dill sauce, fresh green beans, and a mixed tossed salad.

"This is lovely," Devon murmured. "A veritable feast. Really." She glanced up at Blake and smiled. "Thank you."

"My pleasure."

Chomper barked, tugging the comforter with his teeth.

"Don't worry," Blake assured him. "There's a little of everything saved for you. After that, you'll have to settle for your food."

Another bark, this one in protest.

"Sorry. We can't go totally people food. Not when we're trying to impress your doctor with our healthful habits."

Devon began to laugh. "I'm already impressed. But I have to agree, Chomper. Your food is best. It'll help you grow strong and healthy."

Chomper didn't look convinced. He did, however, dive into the small plate of table scraps Blake leaned over and placed beside the bed, making quick work of it. He then bounded off to the kitchen to his own bowl, hunger winning out over pickiness.

"Maybe we'll have a few minutes of peace," Blake said, turning his attention to his dinner—and his dinner partner.

"So, what's the verdict?" he asked as Devon dipped a piece of salmon in dill sauce and tasted it.

"Delicious." Devon didn't have to fake her enthusiasm. "You might just win this contest."

"You'd never allow that."

"You're right. Which means I'll have to come up with an amazing recipe to trump yours."

"I'll give you a week. Not a day more. And this time, *I'll* bring dessert. We'll have it first again."

"Same kind I brought?"

"Similar. Only this time hotter, so we have to savor it slowly."

A tiny shiver went through Devon. "Savor it, maybe," she murmured. "But hotter? I don't think it gets much hotter than it just did."

"We'll find out, won't we? Next Friday. Your place."

"Next Friday." Devon repeated his words, the provocative aura of the past hour eclipsed by a harsh dose of reality. "I'm not sure I'll have the place to myself yet."

The silence that ensued was a vivid reminder of the events defining the past week—events that had brought them together.

"Is your family staying until your mother's home?" Blake inquired carefully.

"I think so, yes." Devon took a bite of salad. If Blake was going to start pumping her for information, she'd better jump the gun first. "Not just my brother and sister," she added, forcing herself to address the issues she'd come here to address. "But also my mother's dog. You met Scamp."

"Uh-huh." Blake nodded. "At your house and at doggie day care."

"That's right. So it's SRO at my place right now. Fortunately, Scamp and Terror get along well. The only place they have territorial battles is in the car." Devon paused to chew and swallow a forkful of green beans. "Speaking of the car, we never finished our earlier conversation. Are you going to drive your truck down to Manhattan or take my advice and buy an SUV?"

"Probably the SUV."

"Good. Because Chomper's going to grow fast. And a Jag's no place for an eighty-pound dog."

"I agree." Blake popped a piece of fish into his mouth.

"I looked for your Jag in the clinic's parking lot a couple of times this week," Devon continued, her tone conversational. "I was hoping to catch you so I could say hi. I didn't spot the Jag anywhere."

"Didn't you?"

"No. Did you and Chomper cut class?"

"We were there."

"Really? Jag and all?"

Blake put down his fork and eyed her with an amused expression. "Nice poker face. Not bad delivery. But overkill. Let me help you. You're trying to get me to mention the Mercedes. Okay, I'll bite. I drove the Benz up to White Plains. Chomper prefers the roomy interior. Does that answer your question?"

Devon tried to hide her surprise. "I have no idea what you're talking about."

"Sure you do. You want to know if I'm hiding info on the make and model of my company car. I'm not. Anything else you're unclear on? If so, go for it."

She took the bait. "Okay, fine. Let's bypass the automotive argument. Let's switch to a subject we've both stayed far away from. Philip Rhodes. I heard about his death. I'm sorry."

"Me, too. Philip was a good man."

"From what I hear, so was your uncle."

That hit home.

"I don't believe Philip had anything to do with Frederick's murder," Blake stated flatly. "Or with your mother's disappearance."

Devon's brows arched at the adamant tone of his words. "You sound certain."

"I am. I'm also certain Philip didn't kill himself. So's your father." Blake's lips twisted into a wry grin at her startled expression. "Gotcha."

She wet her lips. "Actually, you've lost me."

"No, I haven't. You understand me perfectly. Someone murdered Philip. Probably the same someone who murdered Frederick. That someone tried to make it look like a suicide, thereby framing Philip and getting rid of him in one fell swoop. What I don't know is who or why. But your father will figure it out. Tell him if he needs my help to just ask for it. *Not* via his daughter. Face-to-face."

Clearly, Blake was waiting for a reaction.

He got it.

Devon twisted around and stared up at him. "I have no idea where your theories are coming from. Are they based in fact, or are you a frustrated PI?" She waved away his response. "Before you answer that, let me say this. I resent your implication that I'm here as some kind of carrier pigeon. And I more than resent my realization that whatever's happening between us is just a cover for your version of Spy versus Spy." She started to get up.

Blake's hand snaked out, his fingers wrapping around her forearm, keeping her in place. "Wrong," he said with a hard shake of his head. "What's happening between us is the only honest part of all this. So let's stop playing Spy versus Spy. Let's lay our cards on the table. Fair enough?"

"That depends. What cards are we talking about?"

Another glimmer of amusement. "You're good. I see a lot of Pete Montgomery in you."

"So I've been told." *Stick to the truth,* Devon reiterated silently. *There's less to remember.* "I might have been a cop or an investigator, if I'd had the guts. I don't. So I'm not."

"I'll feed your competitive spirit. We'll play an adult version of truth or dare. Only sans the dare. There's no way we'll outdo the one you took downstairs. Besides, we're past that point."

"Meaning?"

"Meaning what just happened in this bed."

"I got the dare part. I was questioning what it is we're past."

"I'll spell it out, then. What's between us is real. So whatever mind games we play, our personal involvement doesn't factor into them. It's separate and apart. Agreed?"

"Okay. Agreed."

"Fine. On to our game of truth. I'll ask you a question. You either answer frankly or tell me to go to hell. No lies. We'll see who capitulates first."

"It sounds more like chicken," Devon observed.

"Maybe." His brows rose quizzically. "So, are you game?"

"I'm game. Ladies first?"

Blake made a wide sweep with his arm. "Sure. Go for it."

She nodded, a challenging glint in her eyes. "Did you start pursuing me because your grandfather asked you to? Was he hoping I knew where my mother was and I'd tell you?"

"That's two questions," Blake pointed out. "But they're related, so I'll let them slide."

"How very generous of you. Are you going to answer them?"

"Yup." Blake traced the curve of her shoulder with his fingertip. "I went after you because I wanted you. *And* because my grandfather hoped you'd spill the beans about your mother's whereabouts. He also wanted me to act as a distraction, so you'd lose interest in James. My cousin's easily diverted by a beautiful woman. Grandfather wants his concentration to be focused on the show circuit."

"Oh." Devon hadn't thought of the last part. She'd been too centered on the murders.

"My turn," Blake reminded her. "Are you officially working with your father on this case? Or did he just ask you to keep your eyes and ears open when you're with me or James?"

"That's two questions," Devon parroted drily. "But they're related, so I'll let them slide."

"Thanks."

"Anytime. I can't officially work with my father. I don't have a PI license. But I do have a great head on my shoulders. And I'd do anything for my family. So if I had a way of figuring out who killed Frederick and put my mother's life in danger, I'd do it in a heartbeat."

"Meaning, yes, you're in this with your father."

"Meaning I have faith in Monty. He'll get to the bottom of this. I'm just the icing on the cake."

"You're hedging. And, for the record, you're a hell of a lot more than just icing."

Devon wasn't about to be sidetracked. "So, are you going to call your grandfather now, or wait till I'm home?"

"Is that your next question?"

"No. It's a follow-up to yours."

Blake looked amused. "That sounds like a rule breaker to me. But I'm in a generous mood. The answer is, I'll wait till you're home. Then I'll report in. What you really want to know is, what am I going to say. Guess that'll have to be your next question."

"Uh-uh." Devon plunked her snack tray on the nightstand, folding her arms across her breasts. "That'll come later, when I've given you something worthwhile to report. Right now, all you've got is confirmation of what you already knew."

"True," Blake acknowledged. "The same applies to you." He set aside his own tray. "Okay, here's something you don't know. I've wanted to meet you for months. Ever since last August. It was a Sunday morning, around six. I was up at the farm for the weekend. I'd gone riding. I was walking back to the house when I spotted you exercising the horses with your mother. You were wearing a light blue shirt and tan riding pants that fit you like a glove. I ogled you like a horny teenager. I planned on asking your mother for your phone number. Then Chomping at the Bit swung into full gear, and my personal life went on the back burner. So last weekend, even though the timing sucked, I was thrilled to see you walk through the door."

Devon couldn't help but smile. "Was I worth the wait?"

"Oh yeah. And then some."

She licked her lips, blurting out a question she didn't even realize she'd formulated. "Blake, do you know who's following me?"

His amusement vanished, his eyes narrowing. "What do you mean?"

"Ever since last weekend, I've had the feeling I'm being watched. At home. At work. I thought maybe you knew something about it."

"Not a thing."

She tilted back her head and gazed at him. "Is it something your grandfather would arrange without telling you?"

Blake fell silent.

"I'm not trying to entrap you," Devon clarified. "I'm just . . . a little unnerved."

"Have you mentioned this to your father?"

By opening up, she was taking a risk and she knew it. But she'd just slept with this man. She had to trust her instincts a little. "No. I didn't want to worry him. Not without evidence. Why? Should I?"

"Yes," Blake surprised her by saying. "I don't like the idea that someone's shadowing you. Sure, my grandfather might be behind it so he can find out if your mother shows up at your door. But whoever killed Frederick could be behind it, too."

"That's what I was afraid of," Devon said tonelessly.

"Hey." Blake caught her chin between his fingers, held her gaze with his. "Yes, I want to get at the truth. And yes, I want to protect my family and my company. But that doesn't mean I'd endanger you. I wouldn't. Trust me on that much."

"I do." She didn't look away. "But I need to trust you on more."

"Such as?"

"Such as, how do you know so much about the inner workings of Monty's investigation? He's not big on sharing. Yet you're aware of his questions about the company cars, about Philip Rhodes's supposed suicide, and probably a whole lot of other things I'm not mentioning. How?"

Blake didn't seem one bit fazed by her probing. "Number one, I'm smart. Number two, I stay on top of everything that goes on at Pierson & Company—including who gets questioned and why. Oh, and number three, I'm your father's point person when my grandfather's not around. But I assumed you already knew that."

"And that's it?"

"No, actually that's not it. I was pretty annoyed at myself for not realizing that another Mercedes S500 might have made that set of tracks down by the road. Not that it changes much. A dozen of us drive that car, and lots of other people have access to them—not just Pierson employees, but garage attendants, valets, you name it."

Devon couldn't argue that. "What about Louise Chambers? She's one of those who has a company car."

"What about her? She's ambitious as hell. I'm sure she has a personal agenda, too—maybe even one that includes me. That doesn't make her a killer. Take my word for it, her feelings for Frederick were genuine."

"Frederick was seeing my mother. That can't have sat too well with Louise. Ambitious women don't take kindly to second place."

"They also don't get rid of the competition by killing the prize they're both vying for. Louise is shrewd, not emotional or irrational. What would she gain by killing Frederick? Money? Professional status? No. So it doesn't fit. Louise wouldn't risk a life sentence to satisfy some sort of jealous rage."

Blake's point was well taken. Monty had made a similar one the other day.

"You've given this a lot of thought," Devon murmured.

"I've considered the same suspects you have. I want the killer caught—no matter who he, or she, is."

That was Devon's entrée—if she gambled and took it.

Rolling the dice, she stepped further into the realm of Pierson family secrets. "Can we talk about James?"

Blake's jaw hardened. "What about him?"

"He's the common denominator in this equation. Frederick, Philip Rhodes, the incident at Wellington—James has connections to all of them. You two grew up together. You know his character. How much of him is real and how much is a facade?"

"I'm not sure what you're asking."

"I think you are." Devon went for it. "Why didn't he ride Wednesday? Was he really sick? Or was it something else? Because he called me three times that day. He also sent me flowers. And all while he was too sick to compete in the Gold Coast Classic."

Blake scowled. "What an idiot."

"For being so obvious?"

"Or for being so reckless. Either way, he took a stupid risk."

"Is he afraid? Is that what this is about? Or is it something else, like drugs? Is he into them?"

"You're very interested in my cousin," Blake said quietly. "Is that for personal or investigative reasons?"

She forced a smile. "Jealous?"

"Should I be?"

Slowly, Devon shook her head. She wasn't going to lie, not about this. "No."

Blake's jaw relaxed. "Good."

"Although on the personal front, James is doing a hard sell on me. Dinner, phone calls, flowers. He asked me to fly down to Wellington next weekend to watch him compete."

"I'm sure he did. You're not going."

"Because I'll throw off his concentration?"

"Because you'll be busy. With me."

"That's just Friday," Devon reminded him.

"Our date *starts* Friday," Blake corrected. "It extends through Sunday. Blow James off. Not just for next weekend. For good."

"Pushy, aren't you?"

"Possessive. A quality I've only just discovered in myself. Surprised?"

Devon shook her head. "Not after tonight. Talk about discovering new, unknown qualities in oneself. I didn't recognize myself these past few hours. So how can I be surprised about your feeling that way, too?" A pause. "I told James no, by the way."

"Wise choice."

"But I'm seeing him Sunday night."

"Cancel."

"I can't."

"Why's that?"

"Because I made a commitment."

Blake digested that thoughtfully. "Which commitment is that—the one to James, or the one to your father?"

Devon didn't pretend to misunderstand. "Let's just say that James's objectives don't factor into my decision."

"Then I'll try to live with it. But after what just happened in this bed, don't expect me to be open-minded."

Devon searched Blake's expression, her own filled with amazement. "It was pretty intense, wasn't it?"

He nodded slowly. "*Very* intense. And not *was—is*."

She heard his intimation loud and clear. "A relationship between us is going to complicate an already tense situation."

"No argument." Blake paused. "Are you okay with that?"

"I guess I'll have to be. You?"

"Fine. Risk doesn't frighten me. I've got good instincts. I've learned to rely on them. And to fight for what I want."

"As opposed to James, who's more self-indulgent and spoiled," Devon surmised.

"You said it, not me."

"You didn't answer my question. Was James really sick? Because his virus was nowhere to be found when we spoke. He sounded in good spirits."

"He knows how to lay on the charm. He wants you. He's not about to expose his weaknesses when he's trying to win you over." Blake paused, his brows drawing together. "To my knowledge, he's not doing drugs. As for his fears, he doesn't confide in me."

They were dancing around the blackmail issue, each of them waiting for the other to address it first. Devon knew it was her call, since her awareness, or lack thereof, was the wild card. She wasn't ready to go there. Not without first getting Monty's permission. She'd already pushed the boundaries of her obligations to him tonight. She'd breached confidentiality by discussing the details of her involvement with this case. She couldn't compound the matter by telling Blake she'd been fully apprised of the extortion letter and phone call.

"Does James know about Philip Rhodes's death?" she asked instead.

"He knows."

"How did he take it?"

"The way he takes everything. With a grain of salt. He was upset. He'll get over it."

"You don't like him much, do you?"

Blake shrugged. "We have different values. What we have in common is our sense of family." A wry look. "And obviously our taste in women."

Devon's lips curved. "I'm sure I'll regret telling you this—but, for the record, it was never a contest. You got to me from the minute I saw you when you freed my soggy pant leg from between Chomper's teeth."

"That was a turn-on, huh?"

"Big-time."

"Good to know." Blake reached out, threaded his fingers through her hair. "What else has that effect on you?"

She felt the sexual electricity between them crackle to life, shimmer through her. "Blake." She pressed a restraining palm against his chest. Pragmatism was urging her to use these moments of intimacy to learn as much as she could. But pragmatism was being drowned out by desire. "We still have a lot of territory to cover," she tried.

"Uh-huh—I know." He leaned forward, nibbled on her shoulder.

"Verbal territory, I meant." Her eyes slid shut.

"It'll wait."

"Till when? I have to get home at a reasonable hour. I have a shift at the clinic tomorrow."

"Hmm." He paused long enough to eyeball the nightstand clock. "You're right. It's getting late. The way I see it, we have two choices—finish our game of truth, or give a repeat performance of dare. Well, maybe not an exact repeat performance. A variation. Slower, more thorough, lengthier. But just as stimulating." He moved Devon's hair aside, kissed her neck, her throat. "Take your pick," he muttered against her skin.

Devon was having trouble breathing. "We can play truth in the car," she reasoned aloud.

"Good point."

"And continue it on the phone."

"Right."

"And . . ." She had no idea what she was going to say next. Nor did she care.

"And . . . ?" Blake prompted, raising his head and gazing at her, sparks of amber fire glinting in his eyes.

"And nothing."

His smile was darkly seductive. "So what's the verdict?"

Devon lay back against the pillows, reaching for Blake as she did. "Let's go for dare."

Monty and Lane were perched at the kitchen counter, drinking coffee, when Devon flew down the stairs the next morning. She was concentrating on twisting her still-damp hair into a French braid and simultaneously zipping up her boots, when she stumbled into the kitchen.

Spotting her brother and father, she came to a halt. "Hi." She noted their dour expressions, and her stomach knotted. "Is Mom okay?"

"She's fine," Lane assured her.

"Then why is Monty here at eight o'clock on a Saturday morning? And why are you both glaring at your coffee like it's poison?"

"I'm running interference," Lane supplied.

"And I'm waiting for you." Monty set down his cup with a thud. "Have a late night?"

"Excuse me?"

"What time did you get in?"

"I already answered that one, Monty," Lane reminded him, looking more amused than annoyed. "Three seventeen. Give or take a minute."

"You time-stamped my arrival?" Devon asked in amazement.

"Hey, waiting up is what big brothers do."

"I don't believe this." Devon finished braiding her hair, then opened the cabinet and reached for a mug. "My daddy and my big brother lying in wait like a posse." She poured herself a cup of coffee. "Last time I checked, I was an adult. Has that changed without my knowledge?"

"Adults remember to call in," Monty stated flatly. "So do partners. Especially if that partner is the other partner's daughter, and she's been out with a guy who's key to their investigation."

A twinge of guilt intruded on Devon's irritation. "I meant to call. But as Lane pointed out, it was late. And this morning, I overslept."

"Yeah, well, you're not going anywhere until you tell me what went on last night."

"On that note, I'll leave you two alone." Polishing off his coffee, Lane rose and flashed Devon a wry grin. "I'd suggest omitting the sordid details. I don't think Monty's open-minded enough for that."

"Gee, thanks." Devon's glare was blistering. "Why is it I wanted you home again?"

"Because I keep life interesting." Lane tugged her braid and headed for the door. "Play nice, you two."

Devon watched him go, then turned back to her father. "I didn't mean to worry you."

Monty took a gulp of coffee. "And I didn't mean for you to get involved with Blake Pierson."

"I know. Neither did I." She sank down onto a stool. "I just have a few minutes. So let's get right down to what I learned. Blake knows I'm working with you. He also knows that you have doubts about Rhodes's death being tagged a suicide. In fact, he knows pretty much your whole MO on this case—with a few exceptions."

Monty's jaw tightened. "How?"

"Mostly by asking the right people the right questions, then drawing his own conclusions," Devon answered honestly. "The rest he got from me. I took a calculated risk. In my opinion, it paid off."

"This had better be good."

"It's bits and pieces of the puzzle, and securing a bunch of loose ends. Louise Chambers, for instance. She showed up at Blake's door while I was there. She's definitely angling for him. She turned green when she saw me. Blake sent her on her way. I grilled him. He's not involved with her. That doesn't mean she's not the killer. Although Blake doesn't think so." Devon filled Monty in on Blake's rationale.

"Same thoughts I had," Monty acknowledged. "Still, there's something about that woman. . . ." A frustrated grunt. "I don't trust her as far as I can throw her. I'm not ready to cross her off the suspect list. She's a barracuda."

"I agree. Speaking of trust, Blake doesn't trust James any more than we do—although he's hesitant to slam him outright."

Monty's brows rose. "How much about James did you get into? Did you discuss the extortion?"

"No. That's one of the things I held back on. I knew from you that Blake was privy to the blackmail scheme. On the flip side, he wasn't sure how much I knew. He was waiting for me to broach the subject. I didn't. I needed your permission first."

Monty studied her intently. "You really trust this guy."

"In the ways that matter most, yes, I do."

"You're about as objective as Juliet was about Romeo."

"Cut it out, Monty." Devon waved away his comment. "I'm not a starry eyed girl. Nor am I wearing blinders. Yes, Blake is a Pierson through and through. And, yes, he's determined to protect his family. I can't exactly fault him for that. If I did, I'd be a hypocrite, since I'm doing the same for my family."

"What about the fact that he went after you hot and heavy? Did he admit it was Edward's idea?"

"It was more complicated than that. But yes, Blake admitted that his grandfather told him to stick close to me, in case Mom showed up at my door. Blake's keeping tabs on me, just like I'm keeping tabs on him."

"Go on."

"He's dead set on finding out who killed his uncle and Philip Rhodes." Devon paused. "Like I said, he has a good handle on you. He spelled out the whole theory he believes you're operating on—and he was right. What's more, he agreed with it. He asked that you go to him directly, and he'll do what he can to help."

"You're kidding. What made him . . . ?" Monty rubbed a palm across his jaw. "Never mind. I'm not going to ask what prompted Blake's unexpected burst of candor. Lane's right. I don't want to know."

Devon hid her smile. "With regard to what else I *didn't* tell Blake, I kept quiet about Mom, except to reiterate what he already knew. Anything pertaining to her whereabouts stays in this house."

"Damn straight it does."

Interlacing her fingers on the counter, Devon turned to Monty. "That's it in a nutshell. What's the verdict?"

Monty swished the coffee in his mug around, staring broodingly into it. "You're a maverick like your father. Also like him, you're lousy with rules. But you did good. Let me meet with Blake and call him on his offer. The conversation I have planned will tell me if he's for real."

"Explain."

"There's a big piece not fitting here. It got lost in the shuffle after Rhodes's death. But it's bugging me. It should be bugging Blake, too."

Devon inclined her head, waiting. Late for work or not, she had to know where Monty was going with this.

"The extortion. It's way out of whack."

"That's bothered you since the beginning."

"Yeah, but now it's a glaring red flag." Monty pivoted on the stool, his hand slicing the air as he spoke. "Bad enough that the timing was off on Frederick's murder and James's near miss at Wellington. But what about the extortionist's demands? It's been three days since I prepped Edward for that phone call. None came. Why?"

"The logical assumption would be that Rhodes was the blackmailer, and now he's dead."

"That assumption sucks. Rhodes called Edward the night he died. He never mentioned any demand for millions. Plus, suicidal people don't stock up on money before blowing their brains out."

Devon nodded. "So whoever killed Rhodes wants him to look like the blackmailer."

Monty's gaze narrowed. "That theory falls flat, too. In order to frame Rhodes, the blackmailer would have to give up on his windfall. Any attempt to collect would mean Rhodes was innocent."

"You're right." Devon's mind was racing. "You think the blackmail was staged."

"I sure do. And I know just the guy who'd do it."

"James."

"Yup. Golden Boy himself."

Devon held up her palms in a quizzical gesture. "But why? To get his uncle and Rhodes out of the way? It doesn't fly. James doesn't want the company; he wants Olympic notoriety. Plus, Rhodes was no threat to James's rise to the top. He wasn't even a Pierson."

"True. But he might have had damning information that would screw James out of his place in Grandpa's life. The same goes for Frederick." Monty pursed his lips. "What if the argument your mother overheard at the Pierson barn wasn't about Rhodes? What if it was about James? What if James was the one Frederick didn't trust?"

"That's not the picture Edward painted when he hired

you. You think he was protecting his grandson?" Devon shook her head, negating her own question. "No way. Not if James killed Frederick. He was Edward's son." A pause. "Besides, we confirmed that James never left Wellington on Wednesday night. So how could he have shot Rhodes?"

"He could have hired someone. As for the first part, you've got too soft a heart. Edward Pierson would protect his grandson no matter what—even if he committed murder. And, yeah, even if the victim was Edward's own son. James is the light of his grandfather's life. No way he'd let him rot in jail."

Devon blew out a breath. "That's a pretty tough scenario. You plan to run it by Blake?"

"Yup. It's a great way to test the sincerity of his commitments."

"What commitments?"

"To find the killer. And to you."

"Monty . . ."

"Don't bother. I'm not listening." Monty waved away her objection. "You're my daughter. You're falling for this guy. Which means I'm allowed to play macho dad. End of story."

"Great," Devon muttered. "Do you plan to wave your Glock in his face or just flash the holster at him for effect?"

"Give me a little credit for finesse." A hint of amusement lit Monty's eyes. "Although I like the image. I might use it if he pisses me off."

"You'd better be joking."

"I'll let you know afterward." Monty's grin faded as his thoughts reverted back to the investigation. "I'll lay out the James theory for Blake. I want to see how he reacts, and how much he spills to Grandpa. Oh, and I'll tell him you know about the blackmail aspect of the case. I'll do that when I inform him you're keeping your Sunday night date with James."

Devon's head came up. "You *want* me to see him?"

A nod. "Right here in this very house. For dinner and alone time. He'll be thrilled. It's just what he's been angling for."

"Monty, what are you cooking up now?"

"Lane and Merry will go out for the evening. You'll be wearing a wire. And I'll be outside in my car, listening. You and I can write your script beforehand. I'll record every word that's said. If James is our guy, we'll find out. And we'll nail him."

Edward slammed his car door shut.

Turning up his collar against the cold, he glanced around, ensuring he was alone. The frozen acres of land that composed his farm were deserted. The house was far enough away, and occupied only by his staff. And the stables were shut tight.

He made his way toward them, marching up to the trailer that was parked there.

A decisive knock. "Vista, it's me," he announced.

Shuffling sounds came from within.

The door opened, and Lawrence Vista poked his head out. "Come in."

Edward climbed inside.

Other than being antiseptically clean and free of clutter, the place looked like any other veterinary trailer belonging to an equestrian specialist. Medical equipment, examination stalls, and floor-to-ceiling closets.

It's what was inside those closets that made all the difference. That, and what was hidden behind the curtain.

Edward shoved his hands in his pockets and leveled a hard stare at Vista. "How close are we?"

Behind his glasses, the other man blinked. "You know the answer to that. The preliminary results were positive. We're almost there. A few more weeks, maybe."

"That's not good enough. Not anymore."

"What do you mean?"

"I mean, we've got to speed this process up. I need immediate results."

Beads of perspiration broke out on Vista's brow. "Why? Has something happened?"

"Not yet. But we've run out of time."

"This isn't a race. We can't arbitrarily speed things up. Not without major health risks. Plus, I need to wait a reasonable amount of time to ensure there are no adverse reactions."

"I don't give a damn," Edward snapped. "I'm almost eighty. My heart's in lousy shape. I've got no idea how long I'll be here. And I need to secure my legacy. That's what I pay you for."

"I still don't see the urgency—"

"You don't have to see it. You have to get results. Now." Edward dragged a shaky palm over his face. "Two people close to me are dead. The cops are crawling around Pierson & Company. How long do you think it'll be before they extend that investigation to my apartment, and then to my farm? What the hell are we going to tell them when they knock on your door for questioning—and when they can't reconcile your extravagant lifestyle with what I'm supposedly paying you?"

All the color drained from Vista's face. "Why would they question me? How do I factor into a murder investigation?"

"*Everything* factors into a murder investigation," Edward shot back, struggling to keep his temper in check. "Look. Let's not waste time bickering. Just get this done. I don't care how. Take pills. Drink coffee. Do whatever you have to. But pick up the pace. Work twenty-four/seven. I want this finished, tested, and ready in a week. That'll give us a month before Wellington's big CSIO Olympic qualifying event. James *will* be winning that."

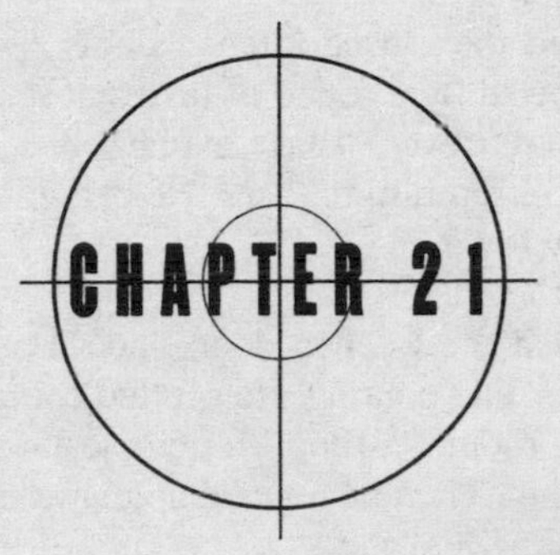

CHAPTER 21

Blake's brows rose as he opened his front door. "Detective Montgomery. This is a surprise."

"I doubt it." Monty pulled off his gloves, looking past Blake and into the foyer. "You weren't at the office. So I assumed you were here. Are you alone?"

"Yup. Catching up on paperwork."

"Good. Then you can take a short break."

Amusement tugged at Blake's mouth. "Looks that way." He stepped aside. "Come in."

Monty was already past him.

"Can I take your jacket?" Blake inquired. He waited while Monty shrugged out of his down parka and handed it over. "I just brewed a pot of coffee. Want a cup?"

"Sounds good—thanks." Monty glanced around. "Nice place."

"I like it." Blake led Monty into the living room, gesturing for him to have a seat on the sofa.

Monty complied.

From behind the closed kitchen door, a series of barks sounded, followed by a round of insistent scratching.

"My golden retriever," Blake explained.

"No need to keep him in there. He can join us."

"He's pretty rowdy."

"So am I. It's fine."

Blake opened the kitchen door, and Chomper exploded out, bright-eyed and panting. He spotted company and raced into the living room, sniffing Monty's jeans and boots with great enthusiasm. Then he jumped up, paws on Monty's lap, and began licking his face.

"Down, Chomper," Blake commanded.

Reluctantly, Chomper obeyed, landing on all fours. He brightened up when Monty leaned over and began scratching his ears.

"Hey, boy. You're a real ball of energy, aren't you?"

Chomper barked. Then, bored by the inactivity, he crouched down, eyeing the bottom of Monty's jeans.

"Don't even think about it," Blake warned.

The pup stopped in his tracks, turning to look at Blake.

"Sit," Blake instructed.

Chomper scrambled around. Facing Blake, he plunked his bottom down to the floor and sat up tall, gazing expectantly at his owner.

"Good boy," Blake praised. He walked over and stroked Chomper's head, handing him a peanut-butter biscuit. The pup snatched it between his teeth, then rushed over to the rug by the fireplace. He lay down, giving the reward his full attention.

"Not bad," Monty commented.

"That's Devon's doing."

"Really? Does it work on men?"

Blake's lips twitched. "I wouldn't know."

"Well, I would. She's had me wrapped around her finger since the day she was born."

"I'll bear that in mind. Although with Chomper it just meant enrolling him in puppy pre-K. He's finally learning some manners."

"He got off easy."

"Seems so." Blake jerked his thumb toward the kitchen. "I'll get the coffee. How do you take it?"

"Black."

A minute later, Blake carried out two steaming mugs, handing one to Monty and taking his own over to the leather wing-back chair positioned across from the sofa.

"What can I do for you?" he asked, sitting down.

Monty took a deep swallow of coffee, gazing steadily at Blake. "You asked for a face-to-face meeting. Here it is."

"That was fast." Blake glanced at his watch. "Eleven fifteen. You must have ambushed Devon as soon as she woke up. Is that standard procedure, or just when she's been out with me?"

Monty's brows arched. "Don't flatter yourself. It's standard procedure. Especially when I'm not sure if I trust the guy she's out with."

"I'm hoping to change that."

"So I gather. Is that to catch the murderer, or to score points with me?"

"The truth? I wouldn't mind accomplishing both."

"Honest and direct. Good start." Monty gave an approving nod. "Okay, let's hear what you've got."

"What I've got?"

"Uh-huh. You've obviously given it thought. Enough to come up with what you think is my take on things. If you had time for that, you had time to work it through. Where'd you come out?"

Blake met Monty's challenging stare. "I didn't. I'm not objective enough. Not when my family members top the list of suspects."

"Fair enough. So where do we go from here?"

"You talk. I fill in blanks, give you perspective, and offer insights. Together maybe we can paint a picture that neither of us could paint alone."

Monty reflected on that for a moment. "We could give it a shot. Let's start with your cousin James."

A faint smile. "Now, why doesn't that surprise me?"

"Because you're smart. Otherwise, I wouldn't be here."

"What do you want to know?"

"How much is Golden Boy capable of? Cheating? Doing drugs? Bribery and fraud? How about murder?"

Blake frowned, giving an ambiguous shrug that told Monty he'd already contemplated all this. "I don't know. James is shrewd, ambitious, and insecure. I've seen him straddle the line between legal and illegal. I've never seen him cross it. Would he? Maybe. Depending on how high the stakes were."

"Stop being vague. Talk specifics."

"James wouldn't do drugs for kicks. But performance enhancers? I can't dismiss the idea. He's determined to win. Is he capable of committing the crimes you just mentioned? I suppose. All except murder. I just can't visualize him as a cold-blooded killer."

Monty took that in without comment. "What was James's relationship with Frederick like?"

"Strained. Frederick was more by the book than either James or my grandfather. He wasn't thrilled with James's cavalier approach to business. Even Philip Rhodes reined my cousin in, and Philip was a rule bender." Blake set down his coffee mug, steepling his fingers in front of him and regarding Monty thoughtfully. "Devon knows about the extortion scheme, doesn't she?"

"Yes." Monty didn't hedge. "That's one of the things she and I talked over this morning. She wanted my okay to break confidence so she could discuss it with you."

"And you agreed?"

"Not happily. But my daughter seems to trust you." A weighted pause. "I hope that trust is warranted."

"It is," Blake answered quietly. "You'll have firsthand

evidence of that—soon. Reserve judgment till then. Establishing trust takes time."

"Yes, it does." Monty took another gulp of coffee. "To be blunt, I'm not convinced we have any blackmail scheme here. I'm leaning toward it all being a setup."

"You think James staged everything."

"In a word? Yes."

"I can't say that shocks me. But even if it's true, how does it tie into Frederick's murder?"

"Not just Frederick's. Rhodes's. And I'm not sure it does. The MO was wrong for blackmail from the beginning." Monty cleared his throat. "Let's digress for a minute. While I was questioning your grandfather, I got the distinct impression that you had your own doubts about Rhodes's death being a suicide."

"I did and I do. The pieces just don't fit."

"I agree." Monty lay another of his cards on the table. "I've had Jenkins at Pierson & Company all morning. He brought in a computer whiz, who's analyzing Rhodes's hard drive as we speak. I'm hoping they find something."

"Something the killer deleted."

"Right. Rhodes's uptight manner, his paranoia, and his phone call to your grandfather—he knew something. Something that got him killed." Monty blew out a breath. "Tell me about Louise Chambers and your uncle."

"They were involved. On again, off again for more than a year."

"Did it start when your aunt was alive?"

"Not to my knowledge. But can I swear to it? No. I wouldn't put it past Louise. She goes after what she wants. But Frederick—he's less clear-cut. Very ethical. Not the type to have an affair. Plus, he was consumed by Pierson & Company. Between that and my aunt Emily, he had his hands full."

Monty motioned for Blake to wait. "What's the scoop with your aunt? Was she a shrew?"

"Not at all." Blake shook his head. "She was frail and sickly, for as long as I can remember. Especially those last couple of years, when her health took a rapid nosedive. During that time, Frederick was totally devoted to her." A frown. "On the flip side, I doubt they had a viable marriage during those final years. Emily's failing health prevented it. So, could Frederick have taken up with Louise? I suppose so."

"I didn't know your aunt was chronically ill."

"She had a heart condition. Even as a kid, I remember her popping nitroglycerin tablets. Toward the end, it was really bad. She was frail and weak, to the point of being housebound."

"For how long?"

"A couple of years, I'd say. She became a total recluse. She stayed in their apartment and saw no one."

Something was nagging at Monty. He just wasn't sure what—yet.

"What about Pierson & Company?" he asked. "Was Emily involved in the business?"

"Nope. Not even when she was stronger. She never walked into the building."

"Okay." Monty processed that. "I think we've covered enough for now. Oh, except for one thing. Devon's going through with her date with James tomorrow night."

Blake's eyes narrowed slightly. "Why?"

"Because I asked her to. She'll be wearing a wire. And I'll be listening."

"I see," Blake replied slowly. "She's hoping to get some kind of confession."

"Uh-huh." Monty set down his cup. "Here's the part where you earn your trust wings. Not a word to anyone—especially your grandfather. Not about tomorrow night, and not about my suspicions that James set up the whole blackmail scheme. Edward will move heaven and earth to protect James. I won't. Will you?"

"I'm being tested," Blake assessed flatly.

"Damn straight." Monty didn't mince words. "What's more, you can't open your mouth even if tomorrow night turns up something incriminating. I'll need time to get my ducks in a row."

"And if I agree?"

"Then you pass the test."

"Screwing my family in the process."

Monty's jaw set. "No one's getting screwed. If James is innocent, he'll walk away smelling like a rose. If he's guilty, it's better that I find out before the cops. I can help with damage control."

Reluctantly, Blake nodded. "I'm counting on your discretion."

"You've got it."

"Also, I want to be kept up to speed."

"Fine."

Monty's acquiescence was just a little too quick.

A corner of Blake's mouth lifted in a wry grin. "More opportunities to test my integrity?"

"You bet. Worried?"

"Fascinated. You'd move heaven and earth for her, wouldn't you?"

"Devon? You bet your ass. Heaven, earth, and then some. So don't hurt her."

"I don't plan to."

The fervent exchange was interrupted by the ringing of Monty's cell phone.

He whipped it out and glanced at the display. "It's Jenkins. Hang on." He punched the Talk button. "Hey, Jenkins. Got something for me?" A weighted pause. "I'll be right there." He punched off the phone, vaulting to his feet. "Want to start keeping your mouth shut sooner than expected?"

"Yeah." Blake was already grabbing their coats. "Let's go."

Fifteen minutes later, they were gathered in Rhodes's office, along with Jenkins and his computer whiz, Len Castoro.

"It's an Excel spreadsheet," Monty pronounced, peering at the computer monitor over Castoro's shoulder.

"A *deleted* Excel spreadsheet," Castoro amended. He was seated at the desk, flanked on either side by Jenkins and Monty.

"Detailing what?" Blake demanded, striding behind the desk so he could scan the information. "And how did you find it?"

"Detailing the transactions of an offshore bank account," Castoro replied. "As for how I found it, fortunately no one's used this computer since Rhodes's death. I simply used special 'undelete' software." He pointed to the floppy disk drive. "In layman's terms, the software scans and restores all possible deleted files on the computer's hard drive. I monitored the process, undeleting any file that looked even remotely suspicious. I've been at it since seven this morning. Finally, I hit pay dirt." He stood up, whisking the hard copy out of the laser printer and stepping away from the desk. "This transaction ledger was deleted the night Philip Rhodes died."

Monty snatched the pages. "Receipts. Disbursements. All from an account in the Cayman Islands." He shot Blake a look. "What a coincidence. That's where our blackmailer wanted his millions deposited."

"It's not exactly an unusual spot for an offshore bank account," Blake reminded him.

Monty blew off the comment, shoving the pages in Blake's direction. "Recognize any of those names?"

Blake looked. Abruptly, he sucked in a sharp breath. "Yeah," he said in disbelief. "Some local bureaucrats and politicians we wined and dined to win contracts."

"Pretty expensive wining and dining." Monty pointed at a couple of entries. "Two hundred thousand dollars. A hundred and fifty thousand dollars. Not what I would call a little palm greasing."

"Shit," Blake muttered, dragging a palm over his jaw.

"They're payoffs. Big ones. The question is, who made them? James? How'd he get them by Frederick? By embezzling? If so and if Frederick found out, did he threaten to take him down, nephew or not? Is that why he's dead? Did Rhodes stumble onto all this? Is that why he became a threat?"

Blake didn't respond.

"Let's start with the basics," Monty said. "Did you know this account existed?"

"Not a clue."

Monty nodded, glancing over the other entries. "These two names show up repeatedly—Lawrence Vista and Gerald Paterson. Mean anything to you?"

"One does," Blake supplied in a flat monotone. "Vista. He's an equestrian vet and genetic consultant. He works for my grandfather. From what I understand, Vista's advising my grandfather on the best breeding partners for his show horses."

"And getting paid a king's ransom to do it. A dozen monthly payments of twenty grand each, during last year alone. Quite a hefty consulting fee. Not bad for equestrian matchmaking. What about Gerald Paterson? Know him?"

Blake shook his head. "Never heard of him."

Monty studied the details more closely. "The payments were transferred to Paterson's bank in Colorado Springs. Castoro, start there. Do an extensive computer search on this guy. Find out who he is and what he does."

"Okay." Castoro's fingers flew across the keyboard. "Let's start simple. Just what's publicly available." A few seconds passed. "Looks like Paterson's an average Joe with a house and mortgage. Nothing too exciting. Now let's wake up the feds and some IT security weenies. Hacking time." He fired up some programs and responded to their prompts, gaining access to the restricted systems. "Here's something interesting. He's an IT guy. And his employer is the US Antidoping Agency."

Blake swore again, turning his back to the group and glaring out the office window. "If he's being paid off, it must be to relay advance information on event testing."

"Yup," Monty agreed. "That way whoever's paying him will know which events need fixing. It's a different kind of hands-on approach. Very clever. There's no need for James to take drugs. Instead, he makes sure others take them, at just the right time and place. I'll bet if we check, we'll find a few of his closest competitors were disqualified for drug usage—even though they probably swore they never used."

"If you're right, then Wednesday's accident at Wellington was rigged," Blake said woodenly. "Which would fit your theory that James set up the whole extortion scheme."

Monty nodded, turning his attention back to the accounting pages, this time with a new slant in mind.

"What's this horse farm in Uruguay?" he asked, jabbing his finger at the page. "There was a payment made to them this week."

"That's one of the farms my grandfather deals with. They sell him sperm specimens to inseminate his mares." Blake gave a baffled shrug. "But those are legitimate transactions. So why pay them from a secret account?"

"Additional business," Jenkins muttered.

"Maybe conducted by an additional person," Monty concurred. "Someone who's paying off an illegal debt."

"What kind of debt?" Blake demanded.

"I can't answer that. But I'll bet James can."

Blake made a frustrated sound. "We've got to strong-arm the bank," he pronounced. "We need confirmation of James's connection to this account."

"Don't hold your breath. The bank won't reveal that information." Monty pursed his lips. "We'll have to dig it up through another, more subtle source. A source who's got immediate access and an emotional in with James."

"Devon?"

"Yeah. Devon. My daughter's going to be a busy girl tomorrow night."

The telephone woke Monty up.

He jumped to his feet, dropping the notebook he'd had on his lap onto the floor. Papers spilled everywhere, and he swore as he stepped over them to scoop up his office phone.

"Montgomery."

"You sound worse than I do," John Sherman informed him. "Once you solve this Pierson case, it's time for a vacation."

"Hell, yeah." Monty rubbed his eyes, blinking as he glanced around the side of his house that served as his office. "What time is it?"

"Ten after four. P.M., if you need to know."

"I've been staring at the samc page for the past three hours. I'm beat." Stretching, Monty got his bearings. He planted his hip against the desk and turned his attention to the conversation. "What's up?"

"Raymond Carlburgh wants to see you," the other PI said. "He sounds like hell."

Carlburgh. He was the pathetic rich guy whose wife was banging her boyfriend like there was no tomorrow.

"Why? Did he walk in on them?"

"No idea. He sounded pretty out of it. All he said was that he wanted a meeting with you ASAP, complete with report and pictures. He tried your cell. When he couldn't get through, he called me."

"Great." Monty massaged the back of his neck. "The shit's hitting the fan here. I can't break away."

"He's expecting you tonight. Tomorrow morning at the latest."

"You're kidding."

"Nope. Neither is he."

Monty sighed. "Fine. Have his chauffeur drive him here."

"No can do. He says he's too sick to leave the house. You've gotta drive up to Scarsdale."

That was odd. Being a pain in the ass was out of character for Raymond Carlburgh. He was usually dignified and patient. Something must have really freaked him out.

"Yeah, okay," Monty agreed. "I'm heading up to my daughter's place tomorrow. Carlburgh's mansion isn't too far out of my way. Do me a favor. Get his file together. I'll swing by and pick it up first thing in the morning. And call Carlburgh back. Tell him to expect me around nine."

"You got it."

Monty hung up and went back to his notes. He had a half hour before Devon arrived. They had a lot to go over.

In the meantime, something was still bugging him. It had been since his meeting with Blake. Until now, he'd been too preoccupied with the file Castoro had uncovered to give it much thought. But he needed to see if his suspicions had merit.

Backtracking to his notes of a few days ago, he found

the interview he was looking for and sought out the inconsistency.

It didn't take long to find it.

The front-door buzzer sounded.

Startled, Blake sat up. He'd been flopped on his living-room sofa, polishing off a second glass of bourbon and scratching Chomper's ears. Now Chomper was scrambling up, barking excitedly and making a beeline for the door.

Blake blinked back to awareness. The living room was dim, and shadows stretched across the walls. Sometime between when he'd arrived home and now, the sun had set.

He glanced at his watch. Six thirty-five.

Again, the buzzer sounded, this time more insistently.

"I'm coming." Blake stumbled to his feet and made his way through the foyer. He was still half out of it from his thoughts and the bourbon. He rubbed the back of his neck and opened the door.

"Hi." Devon was standing outside, shivering, her hands shoved in the pockets of her jacket. "Bad time?"

"I . . . No." Suddenly wide-awake, Blake blocked Chomper from lunging outside to greet Devon. "What are you doing here?"

"Nice greeting." She glanced pointedly into the hall.

"Sorry." Blake stepped aside, opening the door wider. "Come in."

"Thanks." Devon hurried in, wrapping her arms around herself as she stomped on the mat, kicking snow off her boots. "It always feels ten degrees colder in the city than in the suburbs. Which is pretty bad, considering it was twelve degrees when I drove out of the clinic's parking lot, and ten when I left Little Neck. Plus, now the sun's down. So it's like Iceland out there." She stooped down to rub Chomper's snout and ears. "Hey, boy. At least *you're* happy to see me."

"I'm happy to see you, too," Blake said. "Just surprised."

"So I gathered." Devon rose and unzipped her parka. "Tell you what. Hang up my jacket, pour me whatever you're having, and I'll tell you why I'm here."

One dubious brow lifted. "You want straight bourbon?"

"Yuck. No." Devon shuddered. "How about a Thoroughbred Cooler?"

"What the hell is that?"

"Your bad." Devon's eyes twinkled. "Opening a restaurant chain called Chomping at the Bit, and you don't know what a Thoroughbred Cooler is? Looks like having a party animal for a big brother trumps having a family in the horse business." She handed Blake her parka. "It's bourbon, sour mix, and orange juice, plus a dash of grenadine, lemon-lime soda, and ice. A lot more palatable than straight bourbon. Think you can manage?"

A wry grin. "I can try."

"Good." Devon ran her fingers through her hair and headed toward the living room. "Were you asleep?" she asked, glancing around the semidarkened room.

"Nope." Blake walked in behind her and flipped on a light. "I was thinking."

"From what I heard, you have a lot to think about."

Blake studied her face. "You saw your father."

"I just left his office. He filled me in. You must be reeling."

"Did you drop by to check on me?"

"In part, yes. From what Monty said, you had a rough day all around. Some disturbing revelations implicating your family and an inquisition from my dad. Lucky you."

"The inquisition wasn't bad. At least I understood where it was coming from. But the rest . . ." Blake blew out his breath. "Speculating that a relative of mine is into something criminal is one thing. Having the reality shoved in my face is another. And murder? That's unfathomable. I feel like a stranger in my own family."

"It's not your whole family, Blake," Devon reminded him. "It could be just one person."

"Yeah. The person you'll be alone with tomorrow night."

"That's not a concern. Monty will be right outside." Devon sat down on the rug near the fireplace. Chomper plopped down beside her, his snout in her lap. "How about a nice, warm fire."

"Consider it done." Blake flipped the wall switch, and the flames licked to life. "The wonders of gas. Should I make you that drink?"

"I have a better idea. Let's open a bottle of wine and order a pizza with everything on it." Devon tilted her head. "I promise not to eat more than half."

"That's a relief." Blake's lips twisted into a grin. "And here I thought I'd have to fight you for a fifth slice. I appreciate your restraint."

She smiled. "No problem. Although restraint isn't what I had in mind—at least not this minute."

Her tone was teasing. But her meaning was clear.

The mood in the room shifted abruptly.

"Is that so?" Blake asked, sexual tension crackling to life.

"It's so."

"Thanks for the warning."

"Can you handle it?"

"Definitely." Blake's gaze swept slowly over her, his eyes darkening. "Just tell me this—when do I have to have you home by?"

"Breakfast." Devon leaned back on her elbows. "Merry's feeding the pets. Monty's got an early-morning client meeting. If he shows up at my place early, Lane will entertain him—and tie him up with duct tape, if necessary."

"Your brother's resourceful," Blake replied, still studying her heatedly. "Remind me to thank him."

"Thank me instead."

"My pleasure." Blake pulled off his sweater and tossed it aside, lowering himself onto the rug beside her. "You know, this day is turning out a lot better than expected."

"I thought you might feel that way," she murmured, unbuttoning her blouse. "Of course, I still expect to be fed."

He took over the unbuttoning job. "It's early."

"That's true." Devon lay back, feathering her hair out around her. "On the other hand, I skipped lunch. I'm pretty hungry. And if we push dinner off for a while *and* I exert tons of energy, I'll probably be ravenous. I might eat a whole pie myself."

Blake was making quick work of the rest of their clothes. "Tell you what. I'll be a sport. I'll spring for two pizzas."

Devon's smile was pure seduction. "That's all the incentive I need."

An hour later, they were wrapped in blankets, munching on pizza and sipping wine by the fire.

"Now *this* is what I call a great end to a day," Devon announced between bites.

"Better than great." Blake caught her hand, brought her palm to his lips. "You're exactly what I needed. Thank you."

"You're more than welcome." Her lips curved. "The funny thing is, I didn't plan this part. It just sort of happened."

"That's the best way." Blake kissed her bare shoulder. "You said you wanted to talk. I assume it's about the deleted file."

"Specifics of it, yes." Sobering, Devon stared into her glass. "Lawrence Vista," she clarified, not mincing words. "Turns out I met him. Twice, as a matter of fact."

Blake's brows rose. "When? And where?"

"This week. At your farm." She elaborated on her two encounters with Vista. "He seemed uneasy. Especially after I told him I was a veterinarian. I assumed it was a question of job security, that he felt threatened by the thought of your grandfather hiring the competition. But maybe that wasn't it. Maybe he was afraid I'd pick up on something. I have a trained eye. If he's involved in something illegal to benefit James, and that something is medical, I might very well notice it."

"Did you?"

Devon shook her head. "I wasn't looking. This time I will be."

"This time?"

"Yes. I'm taking Monday off. I'll be driving up to my mom's house. After that, I'll go by your family's place and look for Vista. Hopefully, he and his truck will be there, and we'll have a talk. Maybe there's a tie-in between him and that Uruguayan horse farm. If not, I'll have something else to check out. I'll poke around the stables if that's what it takes."

Blake shook his head, his eyes narrowing in thought. "There's a snag to that plan. My grandparents are up at the farm. They'll be there through midweek. Which means James will probably stay up there while he's home. It also means that there'll be business meetings going on, and Pierson staff members will be zipping in and out all day. It'll be too hard for you to get to Vista—at least without a deluge of questions." A pause. "I have an idea. But first things first. Tomorrow night, I want you to tell James about us."

Devon stopped eating. "Does that request relate to your idea, or is it just another burst of possessiveness?"

"Both. Plus, it's the only way you'll retain credibility. What's going on between us is out of the bag since Louise walked in and saw us together. You'll have one shot at getting information out of James before he hears that you and I are involved. And that shot's tomorrow night. He won't have spoken to anyone yet. He'll go straight to your place from the airport. Once your date's over, someone will clue him in. Nothing this juicy stays a secret for long."

"That makes sense. How does it factor into your idea?"

"It clears the way for it. I'll escort you up to the farm on Monday. My family will have already heard about us from James, so it'll seem perfectly natural. We're in a new relationship. We're both in the middle of family crises. We need to chill out. What better place to do it than the farm?"

"I see your point." Devon nodded. "And you're also right about James. It's better he hears about us from me. But not until *after* I finish delivering the script Monty's preparing. I need to catch James off guard and get him to admit something." Her brows knit. "It's still hard for me to picture him as a killer."

"He probably doesn't view himself as one. Remember, even if he's guilty, he didn't commit the crimes firsthand. He has an ironclad alibi for both the morning of Frederick's murder and the night of Philip's. He was in Wellington. So he'd have to have hired someone to do the dirty work. That way, his hands—and his conscience—could stay clean. Typical James—self-indulgent, self-serving, and cowardly."

Devon looked up from her wine. "You're still hoping he's innocent."

"I'm hoping a lot of things, and not counting on any of them," Blake answered roughly. "Besides, I've got my own demons to fight."

"Your grandfather," Devon surmised quietly. "It must be hard not sharing this with him."

"Hard? I feel like Benedict Arnold." Blake shoved aside his food. "If James turns out to be guilty, it'll destroy my grandfather. Then after that, to find out I betrayed him, too? I'm lucky if it doesn't kill him."

"You're not betraying him."

"Not in your mind. In his, I'm screwing my family. That's the ultimate betrayal." Blake blew out a breath. "Let's not go there. Not yet. One step at a time."

Leaning forward, Devon lay her palm against his jaw. "I'm sorry."

"Don't be. I'm doing what I have to." He met her gaze. "And tonight, I'm doing what I want to."

She understood. Tonight was for losing himself. For losing both themselves, in something that felt good and right.

Her expression softened. "Does this mean I'm not getting a chance to polish off my third slice?"

Blake's hand slid beneath her hair, cupping the nape of her neck and pulling her closer. "You'll eat it cold."

The maroon coupe slid slowly by Blake's apartment.

Inside, the man punched up a number on his cell phone.

"She's still in there," he reported. "A hundred bucks says she's spending the night."

"You have the plan down pat?" Monty demanded as he finished taping the audio transmitter to the small of Devon's back.

"Down to the last word." Devon peered down the front of her sweater, checking to make sure the microphone was securely attached to the front clasp of her bra. "Are you sure this will stay put?"

"Positive. Just make sure Golden Boy keeps his hands to himself, and you'll be home free." Monty straightened, tugging down the back of Devon's sweater. "The receiver will be in my car. It has a built-in microrecorder and incredible audio quality. No matter what room you and Golden Boy are in, I'll hear every word you say. And if you need me, I'll come running."

"I'll be fine, Monty," Devon assured him. "James isn't going to attack me. And I'm not going to give him reason to. I'll stick to the script. With any luck, we'll have what we need in a few hours."

"You've become quite the pro."

Devon knew that tone. Her father wasn't issuing a compliment.

"What does that mean?" she asked.

"Only that your social life is certainly hectic these days. Filled with Edward Pierson's grandsons."

"That's the angle you told me to pursue, remember?"

"I don't remember telling you to make overnight house calls."

Devon got the message loud and clear. "Where are you going with this, Monty?"

"You spent the night at Blake's."

"You're right. I did. Although I didn't think you noticed. You were late arriving here this morning."

He snorted. "Yeah, well, my meeting ran longer than expected. I had to show my client some unpleasant photos. I never thought he'd take it so hard—not when he already knew what his gold-digger wife was doing. I felt like a bastard. The guy crumbled right in front of me. He was popping nitroglycerine pills like they were going out of style."

"He's ill?"

"A bad heart. That seems to be the theme of the day."

"Speaking of which, you still haven't told me what's bugging you about Emily Pierson."

"Later. Right now, let's concentrate on James." Monty glared at her. "Which brings me back to the original subject."

Devon rolled her eyes. "Drop it, Monty. My relationships are off-limits."

Monty ignored her protest. "I like Blake. He's a smart, decent guy. But the jury's still out on whether he's good enough for you."

"Well, I'm the jury."

"And I'm the judge. I can overturn your verdict."

Devon couldn't help but laugh. "I'm glad I lived with Mom during my teens."

"Me, too. I might have shot one of your dates and wound up in prison."

Monty's cell phone rang.

"It's Jenkins," he announced, checking the caller ID. "I told him to call ASAP if he turned up anything else we could use tonight." Monty punched on the phone. "Yeah, Jenkins, what've you got?" A long pause. "You're sure? Damn straight it's good. It's exactly what we need. Thanks." He disconnected the call and gave Devon a thumbs-up. "Bingo. We hit pay dirt."

"I'm all ears."

"Seems our friend Gerald Paterson has a gambling problem. Not with horses, with casinos. He's in the hole for thousands, and that's just from the preliminary info Jenkins has dredged up so far. Also, he's managed to pay back some creditors in substantial chunks. The dates of those payments coincide with the dates payments were issued to him from that offshore account."

"So we've got motive and opportunity." Devon pursed her lips thoughtfully. "That helps. It gives me direction when I broach that part of my conversation with James."

"Right." Monty glanced at the wall clock. "It's seven thirty. Golden Boy should be here in an hour. Anything you want to go over?"

"Nope. I'll just fix my makeup, put out the fruit and cheese platter I ordered, and do some deep-breathing exercises. Wish me luck."

Monty shot her a quick wink. "No luck's necessary. The guy's toast."

Eight thirty on the nose.

Devon carried out a tray of crackers and placed it beside the fruit-and-cheese platter. She then stood back to assess her handiwork. Everything was set. The food, the wine, and her.

She adjusted the neckline of her sweater, reaching

around back and groping beneath it until her fingers brushed the transmitter. It was firmly in place. It wasn't going anywhere. Neither was the microphone. She'd checked it five minutes ago.

The rest of the stage was set, too. Lane and Merry had left for a local concert, Monty was poised outside in his car, and James had called to say his plane had landed.

Now it was up to her.

She mentally reviewed the topics she had to delve into. Getting at them was only part of the challenge. She had to come across as relaxed, casual, not suspicious or prying. James was a shrewd guy, one who was used to manipulating others. He'd see through her in a minute if she didn't play this exactly right.

The doorbell rang.

Devon turned, inhaling slowly, then blew out her breath. "Okay, Monty," she muttered into the scooped neck of her sweater. "It's showtime."

She walked to the door and pulled it open.

James was leaning against the doorjamb, wearing a cashmere overcoat and leather gloves, his collar turned up against the cold. He was carrying an overnight duffel.

"Hi," Devon greeted him.

"Hi yourself." Giving her an appreciative once-over, James smiled his approval. "You look beautiful. Worth braving the frozen tundra for."

"It is freezing," Devon agreed. "Come on in." She stepped aside, gesturing for him to enter.

He stepped into the house, dropping his bag. He captured her shoulders in his hands and bent down to kiss her. Devon was prepared. She kissed him back—lightly—breaking away when he tried to deepen the kiss.

"The weather must be quite a contrast to Florida," she said, plucking a hanger out of the hall closet. "I don't know how you tore yourself away."

"I was inspired." James didn't try to kiss her again. Instead, he handed her his coat and walked into the living room, taking in the spread she'd laid out. "Everything looks great."

"I had planned to cook." She followed him in. "Then I thought better of it. You competed today. I didn't think you'd want a heavy meal."

"You're right. I don't."

"I also didn't know how you'd feel about wine, so I didn't open the bottle yet. Would you like some, or are you abstaining?"

A corner of his mouth lifted. "I'm not riding for three days. So, absolutely, let's open a bottle. But not wine. Champagne."

Devon wrinkled her nose in disappointment. "I'm sorry. I don't have any champagne."

"No problem. I do." He strode back to the door, unzipped his duffel, and yanked out a bottle of Dom Pérignon. "Shall I do the honors?"

"Please," Devon replied, flourishing two champagne flutes. "What a lovely surprise."

"I pride myself on those." James uncorked the bottle and poured, handing her a flute. "To this evening," he said, raising his glass. "May it yield one surprise after another."

"To this evening," Devon echoed. She took an appreciative sip, then gestured toward the sofa. "Please, have a seat."

"After you." He stood beside the sofa and waited.

Devon sank down on the cushion, angling her legs toward him to keep a conversational distance between them. "How was the Grand Prix?"

"No complaints." He perched on the adjoining cushion. "Stolen Thunder and I took first place."

"That's wonderful. Congratulations."

"Thanks." He flashed his dazzling smile. "Today's just my day. I sensed it the minute I woke up. Probably because I knew I was seeing you." He glanced around. "Your family's out?"

"For the evening, yes."

"It's very quiet. Where are your pets?"

"Terror's upstairs with a stack of socks to chew on, and my mom's dog, Scamp, to play with. Connie's in the laundry room sulking because I'm with you instead of her, and Runner's in his cage in Merry's room."

"All for me? I'm flattered."

Devon's lips curved. "It's hard to concentrate with chaos erupting. I wanted to give you my full attention." She paused, smile fading. "I know what a difficult week this has been for you. First, that horrible accident involving your groom. Then Mr. Rhodes's death. This nightmare never seems to end."

Soberly, James nodded. "It's hard to believe so much can happen in so short a time. Frederick, your mother, the Wellington fiasco, and now this." He leaned forward, taking her hand in his. "Still no word from your mother?"

"None." Devon's lips thinned into a grim line. "I'm worried sick about her."

"Of course you are." James's grip tightened. "I wish there was something I could do."

"There is. You can be honest with me."

A hint of wariness. "I'll try."

Lowering her gaze, Devon studied their clasped hands. "I apologize in advance if I offend you, but I have to ask someone or I'll burst."

"Go on."

"I didn't know Mr. Rhodes. Maybe he was a fine man and I'm reaching. But the timing of his suicide . . . is it possible he's the one who murdered your uncle, and the guilt was too much for him?"

James shrugged. "I'm not offended. You'd have to be a fool not to wonder if the incidents are connected. The truth is, I just don't know. Philip felt guilty about something, that's for sure. It could have been strictly financial. On the other hand, it could have gone deeper. The idea that he murdered Frederick turns my stomach. But I can't swear that he didn't." A pause. "What does your father think?"

"He won't tell me anything. I guess he's trying to protect me. But it's not working." Devon tucked a strand of hair behind her ear. "My mind's gone crazy this week. So many crimes and no solution to any of them." She looked up, her forehead knit with concern. "Was there any progress in figuring out who tried to sabotage you?"

"No. I didn't expect there to be. The people who do things like this cover their tracks well."

"You're more accepting than I am. Not only could you have been disqualified, you could have been hurt, or worse. How's your horse? Is he all right?"

"Future's fine. He got really spooked when Granger collapsed. He took off, bolted out of the ring. But my trainer calmed him down. I checked on him later in the day. He was back to himself."

"So were you, I hope."

"Yup. Good as new. Stomach bug gone."

Devon gave a resigned sigh. "Like I said Monday night at dinner, the show circuit is too rough for my tastes. I'll stick to healing animals. Oh, which reminds me, I met Dr. Vista this week. His work sounds fascinating."

That caught James off guard. "Where did you meet Vista?" he asked, his tone undeniably strained.

"At your stables. Twice. Once when I was searching for Chomper, and once when I was searching for Roberto. Both times I ran into Dr. Vista instead. And I'm glad I did. I learned a great deal."

"About?"

"Genetic consulting. It's an area I was totally unfamiliar with. I'm sure that lack of knowledge doesn't apply to you."

Tension creased James's forehead. "Actually, that's my grandfather's area. I don't get involved much."

Her brows rose in disbelief. "Cassidy was right. You *are* too modest. When it comes to anything horse-related, I'm sure your grandfather asks for your input. After all, you're the guy who's going to ride his way to a gold medal—probably more than once. Who better to consult on what qualities matter in a show horse?" Devon kept her expression open and friendly. "Dr. Vista mentioned acquiring specimens from a horse farm in Uruguay. Are the stallions there superior to the ones in Germany or the Netherlands?"

A startled look. "Vista discussed that with you?"

"Only in passing. Why? Is it a secret?" Devon drew her fingers across her mouth in a zipping motion. "If so, my lips are sealed."

"It's not a secret." A rapid recovery. "We just like to keep our sources confidential. Otherwise, we'll tip the competition."

"That makes sense."

James sipped his champagne. "So what else did you and Vista talk about?"

"That's about it. He was in a hurry. He drove off in that monster truck of his. Although 'drove off' is an exaggeration." Devon modified her words, weaving bits of truth into her fiction. "That Suburban is so weighted down it can barely crawl. I was afraid it would bottom out in the snow. There must be some serious equipment in there."

She was hoping for some sort of reaction.

She got it—subtle, but visible.

James's hand jerked, and a few droplets of champagne trickled down his chin.

He wiped them away, giving a tight cough.

"Are you all right?" Devon was eager to ascertain if James's reaction was due to her comment about Vista's truck.

"Fine," he assured her. "Just paying too much attention to you and not enough to the amount of champagne I'm drinking." A practiced smile— one that was visibly forced.

"I'm flattered." Devon wasn't letting this opportunity slip by. "Although my guess is you're more captivated by my words than you are by me."

The smile froze on James's face. "I'm sorry?"

"Dr. Vista's truck," Devon explained smoothly. "And his heavy-duty veterinary equipment." A resigned sigh. "You know, boys and their toys—nothing can compete."

"Yeah. Right." James took another sip of champagne. He set down his glass, roughly clearing his throat. "Maybe I should eat something."

"Of course." Devon's mind was racing as she prepared a plate of fruit and cheese. James was rattled. She'd definitely hit a nerve.

She handed him the plate. "Here. Enjoy."

"Thank you." He ate a cracker topped with Brie, chewing slowly, then swallowing. By the time the cracker was gone, his composure—and his charm—were fully restored. "You're wrong, you know. It is you I'm captivated with." He draped an arm over the back of the sofa.

Devon leaned forward and helped herself to a plate of food, aware that James wasn't just trying to seduce her, he was trying to change the subject. The latter wasn't a bad idea. She'd crammed a lot into the first hour. James's guard was up. She'd be wise to let some time pass before she touched on the next subject.

With that thought in mind, she lapsed into her warm, friendly mode, keeping just a touch of nervousness in her demeanor. She had to seem edgy about something, otherwise the culmination of this evening wouldn't fly.

The next hour passed in pleasant conversation as she and James chatted about work, play, and general nothingness.

Translated: He was working up to getting her into bed.

She, on the other hand, was working up to getting him out the door—after she touched on her final point.

Intermission over.

"I can't stop thinking about what a close call you had on Wednesday." She gave a disconcerted shudder. "It upsets me terribly. I don't understand why someone can't find out who was responsible. Aren't there judges or people from that Antidoping Agency you mentioned who are in charge of things like that?"

James gave her an indulgent smile. "You're a sweetheart. I appreciate your concern. But don't hold your breath. The Antidoping Agency only goes whole hog when they choose to. Kind of like cops who let three speeders go by and then grab the fourth. Who knows what motivates them?"

"I guess." Devon still looked troubled. "Who administers the drug tests? Are they specially trained?"

"The labs that process them are, yes. As for the doping control officers, they file an application, pass a test, and get a territory. They're not in the medical field, if that's what you mean."

"Then any Tom, Dick, or Harry could apply. Some of them might be corrupt. And if they are, what would stop a rider or trainer from bribing them to fix the tests, or even to leak information on when the tests are scheduled to occur?"

A definite guardedness had settled over James. "Fixing the tests would mean swapping samples. I can't imagine that happening with so many people around. I guess it's possible. *Anything's* possible, bribery included. Like I said, this is a cutthroat industry—and a wealthy one. So, yeah, illegal stuff goes on."

"I'm sure. Not only that, but a sport like yours must breed all kinds of scandals. Alcoholism. Sex. White-collar crime." Devon raked a hand through her hair. "The doping control officers have all that wealth shoved in their faces while they're pulling down modest salaries. A lot of people would jump at the chance to make extra cash. Especially if they lived above their means or had a nasty habit to feed—say, compulsive gambling. What better provocation for blackmail?"

James spilled his champagne on the table, then grabbed his napkin and dabbed at the moisture. "Sorry about that."

"No problem." Devon cleaned up the mess. "I didn't mean to upset you. It just amazes me that the drug-testing process has so many loopholes. I feel horrible for you and for your groom."

"I'm not upset. But you do have quite an imagination."

"I'm a cop's daughter."

He shot her a quick look. "Did you conjure up that scenario out of thin air, or have you heard rumors I should know about?"

"Rumors?"

"About people taking bribes or squandering their money in casinos."

Funny he should mention casinos. She hadn't.

"Current rumors, you mean? No. And certainly none involving the show circuit, since I'm an outsider. Believe me, if I had, I'd make sure whoever did this to you was arrested. I'm just reflecting on stories my father's spouted over the years. I apologize."

"Don't." Relief flooded his face. Relief—and something more. "I enjoy hearing you stand up for me."

An abrupt shift in mood. A heightened sense of intimacy. James's fears had abated, and in his mind, he was back on track. On the road to seduction.

Warning bells sounded in Devon's head.

Sure enough, James plucked the champagne flute from her hand and set it down on the table along with his. "I think we've talked enough, don't you?"

He reached for her.

Devon would have leaped off the sofa if she hadn't been fully aware it would make James suspicious. Fending him off wasn't a concern. Monty had taught her self-defense when she was ten. But the wire—if James found it, she was screwed.

"Excuse me for a minute." She said it calmly, without blurting it out. Easing away from him, she rose. "I'll be right back."

Anticipation glittered in James's eyes. "Of course."

Great. He thought she was readying herself for wild sex.

Devon went to the powder room, checked on the microphone and transmitter. Still in place.

Fruit and cheese was not going to deter James. This interrogation had gone as far as it could. Time to call it a wrap.

Prepping for the last act, Devon pasted a contrite look on her face and walked back out.

James was lounging on the sofa, a suggestive gleam in his eye. "Welcome back."

She remained standing, launching into her speech without prelude. "We need to talk."

He patted the cushion beside him. "Didn't I just say that we've talked enough?"

"Yes. But trust me, we haven't." Devon rubbed her palms together. "This is my fault. I let it go too far. It's just that I really like you. And I'm not good at drawing a line in the sand."

One brow rose. "Are you about to tell me you're still not ready?"

"Yes. No. Not in the way you mean." She swallowed. "James, you're a fantastic guy."

Now he was frowning. "Why do I sense a 'but'?"

"Because there is one." She shifted uncomfortably. "I have to tell you something, now, before this gets totally out of hand."

"I'm listening."

"Blake and I . . . we're . . . we've become involved."

Icy silence permeated the room.

James just stared at her, his expression a literal version of the phrase *if looks could kill.*

"Since when?" he demanded.

"It just happened." Devon gave a helpless shrug. "We didn't plan it. It—"

"Yeah, I heard you," he bit out, rising from the sofa. "It just happened. When did you plan on telling me—in bed?"

Devon felt like kicking him in the groin. "Of course not," she forced herself to say as he glared at her. "I planned to tell you now, while we ate. It didn't occur to me that you'd move so fast."

"Obviously not as fast as my cousin."

"Don't be that way."

"Which way should I be—understanding? Next you'll be saying you want to be friends."

"The thought had occurred to me."

"Then get rid of it. I'm not ready to be that magnanimous. Not yet."

"I understand." Devon's tone was pained. "I'm sorry if I handled this badly. It wasn't to lead you on; it was to try to salvage some kind of relationship with you."

"Does Blake know you're seeing me tonight?"

She nodded. "I told him."

"And he was okay with it?"

"Not really," she answered honestly. "But he understood."

"Why shouldn't he? He won—again. That's the story of Blake's life." Eyes glittering with resentment, James stalked out of the living room and grabbed his coat and duffel bag. "There's no point in dragging this out," he announced from the doorway. "Let's just call it a night."

Devon followed him to the door. "I feel terrible about this. Especially if it hurts your relationship with Blake."

"Not to worry. I'll survive. As for Blake, nothing between us will change. It never does." James yanked open the door. "It's still early. You've got the house to yourself and half a bottle of Dom Pérignon. Call Blake. I'm sure he'll be glad to pick up where I left off. Good night, Devon."

The driver of the maroon coupe was dozing behind the wheel when James stalked out, jumped into the waiting limo, and took off.

He punched up a number on his cell phone. "He just left. No way he'll be back. He was pissed off. I'm surprised, too. I assumed—" He broke off, peering intently out his front windshield. "Wait. Talk about split-second timing. Montgomery's back. No, not a chance it's a coincidence. He must've been watching the place this whole time. It could mean a lot of things. Don't worry. I'll find out."

CHAPTER 24

It was three thirty the next afternoon when Devon and Blake hiked across the grounds of the Pierson farm, heading from the house to the stables.

They'd driven up to Dutchess County at lunchtime and gone straight to Sally's place. There, they'd checked on the animals and dropped off their overnight bags. They'd decided in advance to stay there rather than at the Pierson farm. Not only for privacy, but because it would eliminate the tension that would result from staying next door with both James and the elder Piersons around.

"Your grandparents looked less than thrilled to see me," Devon commented as they crunched through the snow. "I guess they must associate me with Frederick's death."

"They'll get over it." Blake waved away her concern, then reached for her gloved hand, gripping it in his.

"And James looked like he wanted to choke me," she added.

"That's part jealousy, part hangover. I suspect he downed an entire bottle of booze last night before crashing. Needless to say, he doesn't take rejection well." Blake gave an offhand shrug. "Besides, the way he looked at you paled next to the way he looked at me. He would have beaten the crap out of me if he wasn't seeing double."

Devon blew out her breath, watching it emerge as a frosty mist. "I'm glad you made up that excuse about us going riding. The tension in there was so thick I could hardly breathe. Especially after Louise showed up with those legal documents. It's like the gods conspired to make this day as tough as possible."

Blake digested that thoughtfully. "You've been subdued since we left your mother's place. Visiting there's tough on you, isn't it?"

"Yes." Another sigh. "I lived there as a teenager, and during my breaks from college and vet school. The place was always vibrating with activity. Now it seems so quiet, so eerily deserted. I just want things to go back to normal. I want my mother back." Devon shot Blake a self-deprecating glance. "That sounds juvenile, doesn't it?"

"Uh-uh. You had a happy home life. You want to keep it that way."

"Well, not *exactly* the same way. I'd like one major change." Devon's smile was wistful. "As long as I'm making embarrassing, juvenile admissions, what I really want is for my parents to get back together."

Blake's brows arched. "Is that in the cards?"

"I don't know. What I *do* know is that they're crazy about each other. No matter how much they pretend otherwise." Devon stopped talking and stiffened, peering ahead toward the stables. "Vista's truck is there. Your phone call worked."

"No surprise. When my grandfather says jump, Vista says how high. All I had to mention to Vista is that he was needed. I didn't specify by whom. Oh, I did let it slip that

James is up for a few days from Wellington. I'm sure that was the cake topper. Anyway, let's get down there before someone clues him in to the fact that I'm the only Pierson coming to meet him and that you're here with me. I don't want to give him any prep time."

"Good idea." Devon nodded. "He's either in the stables or in his trailer. Let's start in the stables so I can poke around a little. If we run into him there, we'll deal with him sooner rather than later. If not, I can check out the horses and see if Vista's done anything unorthodox. Then we'll check out his trailer and go for broke."

"We should have the stables to ourselves. I called ahead and told the grooms to leave early."

"That was smart. It'll give us the freedom to thoroughly examine the horses without providing any explanations."

They reached the stables, easing by Vista's Suburban and trailer and making their way to the barn door.

"Look how low this thing is," Devon hissed, pointing at the trailer. "It's got to mean something. James nearly hit the ceiling when I mentioned it."

"We'll find out." Blake pulled open the wooden doors, and the two of them hurried inside. "Watch what you say," Blake muttered. "In case Vista's in here."

A silent nod.

"Introduce me around," Devon said aloud. "Last time I was in here it was to find Chomper. I haven't met any of your horses."

"I'll rectify that now. Unfortunately, you won't be able to meet five of our best. They're down in Wellington, competing. But we've got two dozen more, ranging from colt and filly to stallion and mare. I'll introduce you to them, and we'll do a second round of introductions this spring." Blake pointed to a portrait hanging just inside the barn. Its subject was an imposing stallion the color of dark chocolate. He was classically beautiful, with a thick, glossy tail, long legs, and tiny white markings on each of his hind legs. He stood tall and correct, his carriage as regal as any monarch. "That's Stolen Thunder. I'm sure James mentioned him."

"Yes, he did. With glowing praise." Devon studied the painting. "He's breathtaking."

"Stolen Thunder is one subject James and I agree on. He's extraordinary—truly one of a kind. He's a German warmblood from a champion lineage. He's the last in his bloodline. My grandfather paid an obscene amount of money for him. But he was worth it. By the time Grandfather bought him at age five, he'd won a long list of four- and five-year-old championships on national and international levels. Now he's eight and priming for the World Games and the Olympics."

"Wow." Devon was genuinely impressed.

"We've got two more stallions down in Wellington. Gentleman, who's also at the advanced level, and Future, who's at the intermediate level. He's Gentleman's son, and he's shaping up to be another winner."

"He's the stallion your groom was riding in Wednesday's competition, wasn't he?"

"Yup. Luckily, he's got a great temperament. Spooked or not, he was back to himself in no time."

Devon's brows knit. "You said he's Gentleman's son. What about Stolen Thunder's legacy? Since he's last in his bloodline, wouldn't it make sense to inseminate one of your mares with his sperm?"

"It would, and we've tried. So far none of his sperm has resulted in conception."

While Blake spoke, he and Devon scrutinized the stables, trying to assess whether Vista was inside. There was no sign of him. They strained their ears, but all they heard was the whinnying and stomping associated with horses.

Expanding their search, Blake led Devon from one stall to the next, introducing her to the Pierson warmbloods. They were exquisite animals, and Devon enjoyed the diversion of seeing them, stroking their necks and muzzles, and speaking softly to them—all the while checking to see if there was any telltale evidence of foul play.

"Do you know what you're looking for?" Blake murmured.

"Not yet," Devon replied softly. "But I will when I find it."

The last stall on the left was the one where Devon had found Chomper two Sundays ago. At the time, it had been empty. Today, there was a beautiful chestnut mare inside, standing in the corner.

"Who's this?" Devon asked, leaning forward to caress the mare's neck.

"That's Sunrise," Blake said. "She was scheduled to compete at Wellington. My grandfather changed his mind and withdrew her. I'm not sure why."

"Because she's ill," Devon supplied.

"Not to my knowledge."

"Then no one's filled you in." Devon pushed open the stall gate and stepped inside. "Poor baby," she said soothingly, continuing to stroke the mare's neck. "It's all right. Everything's going to be all right." She turned toward Blake. "She's definitely ill. She's standing in the corner. Her head is hanging, and she's lethargic. And look—her water's low. She's been drinking a lot. I'll bet if I took her temperature, she'd have a fever." Devon stooped down, studying Sunrise's limbs. "She's favoring her right front leg."

"Why?" Blake demanded.

"Her hock is badly swollen. She's had some injections." A frown. "More than some. A lot. It had to have been in order to produce this much swelling. The entire region from stifle to hock is inflamed. The tendon area's been injected repeatedly." Devon rose. "I don't like this. Why would she be undergoing this kind of veterinary treatment?"

Blake's eyes narrowed. "Not a clue."

"Well, Dr. Vista better have one." Anger glinted in Devon's eyes. "I'm going to speak with him."

She blew by Blake and out the stable door. This time she didn't try to muffle her approach. This time she wanted to be heard.

She tromped up to the trailer door and knocked.

"Just a minute." There were shuffling sounds, followed by a couple of thuds—cabinet doors closing. Then footsteps. "Is that you, Mr. Pierson?" Vista called out.

Devon had opened her mouth to reply when Blake's voice resounded from behind her. "Yes, it's me." He gave Devon a tight smile when she spun around to face him. "He didn't specify *which* Mr. Pierson he was expecting," he told her in a low, hard tone. Obviously, he was as angry as she was.

A lock turned, and Vista pushed open the door. His eyes widened when he saw Devon, and anxiety flashed across his face. He looked only slightly mollified when he realized Blake was with her.

"Blake, hello. I thought your grandfather would be with you."

"He's in the house," Blake said. He was already easing Devon inside the trailer and walking in behind her. "So is James. They'll be out to see you later. But I was just giving Dr. Montgomery a tour of the stables. She asked to speak with you."

"I see." Vista didn't sound happy. "About what?"

"I'll let her explain."

While Blake had been laying the groundwork, Devon was assessing the trailer. A typical veterinarian's quarters, with two examining areas, X-ray equipment, a water bucket, disinfectants, and floor-to-ceiling cabinets that were each labeled. The trailer was neat—too neat—without a speck of clutter or even discarded medical supplies in the trash.

"Dr. Montgomery," Vista pressed. "What can I do for you?"

Devon turned to meet his gaze. "You can tell me what's wrong with Sunrise."

"Wrong?"

"Yes. She's ill. I'm sure she has a fever. Clearly, you've been treating her. What's the diagnosis?"

"I have no idea—"

"Then you're not treating her. Fine. Tell me which veterinarian is."

Silence.

"Numerous injections have been administered to her right front leg. The entire limb is inflamed. Would you care to explain?"

A vein was throbbing at Vista's temple. But he fought like hell to hide his nervousness. "With all due respect, I don't discuss my work, not even with another professional. Everything I do for Mr. Pierson is confidential."

"Everything you do. Does that include experimenting on horses? Because I can't think of any other reason for a healthy mare like Sunrise to show these symptoms, or to need treatment by a genetic consultant."

More silence.

"I'd like answers, too, Vista," Blake interjected. "Since you're uncomfortable providing them, tell me who can—my grandfather or my cousin?"

Vista stiffened. "Leave James alone. The last thing he needs is an interrogation."

"Meaning he's the one who hired you to treat Sunrise?"

"Meaning he's in the middle of a major competition. He needs to stay focused."

Without waiting for an invitation, Devon marched farther into the trailer. She scanned the labels on the cabinets. They all consisted of an odd combination of letters and numbers, unlike any medical references she'd ever seen. C#124DW, L#830IN—they were all cryptic symbols that looked more like code than labels for medication.

"I've never seen such an immaculate veterinary facility," she declared aloud. "Where do you keep your files? Or that thick notebook you were carrying when I met you? In here?" In one motion, she twisted the handles of two cabinets and pulled them open.

Bottles. Shelves and shelves of them. All filled with liquid medication. All labeled with the same code as the corresponding door. And all with their brand names torn off.

"What do you think you're doing?" Vista barked, storming over and shutting the closet door.

"Trying to figure you out," Devon retorted. She folded her arms across the front of her down parka. "Are those illegal drugs?"

"Of course not." The genetic consultant bristled. "I'm a scientist, Dr. Montgomery, not a drug trafficker. I deal in facts. I conduct cutting-edge research. But I obey the law. And I resent your implying anything else."

He planted himself firmly in front of the cabinet. "The reason those codes look foreign to you is because I buy drugs you're unfamiliar with for testing. The kind I do on rats, not horses. And those cabinets . . ." He pointed toward the back, where a cluster of unmarked cabinets formed an L with a curtain that spanned the width of the trailer, hiding the rear third of it from view. "Those cabinets contain all the traditional drugs you're accustomed to seeing in a veterinary practice." He glared at Devon from behind his glasses. "I hope that satisfies you. Not that I owe you any explanation."

Devon was barely listening. She was trying to figure out a way to catch a glimpse of whatever was behind that curtain.

"If there's nothing else, I'd like you to leave," Vista said. "Blake, anything else you're interested in, I'd suggest you speak with your grandfather."

"I intend to." Blake made eye contact with Devon. "Let's go."

Reluctantly, she complied. She wouldn't get another shot at this. Whatever was back there, Vista would get rid of it the minute she left. Dollars to doughnuts, his trailer would be squeaky-clean the next time she stepped inside.

If she wangled her way into it a next time.

She hesitated, aware of how adamant Blake was, weighing it against how close she was.

"Devon." Blake waved her toward him as he shoved open the door. "Let's head back to the house. Once the sun goes down, it'll be freezing." He glanced at Vista. "Keep an eye on Sunrise."

Rigidly, Vista nodded. "I will."

"Yeah, I'm sure," Devon muttered. She crossed over and left the trailer with Blake.

They marched across the snow toward the house.

"Why did you drag me out of there?" Devon demanded, the minute they were out of earshot.

"Because you were about to rip open that curtain," Blake responded calmly. "Which would mean shooting yourself in the foot. Right now, Vista thinks he has the upper hand. That gives us leverage. He still has something to hide—and something to lose. Once that changes, we're screwed. And I don't plan to let the scales tip until we have everything we need to lock him up."

That got Devon's attention. "So you agree with me."

"That Vista's doing something criminal? Hell, yes. I'm just trying to figure out how much of this is his initiative, and how much of it is being orchestrated by James."

"Good question."

"I'll have an answer as soon as we get back to the house. I'm pulling my grandfather aside and having a talk with him. I don't care if he's signing papers for Louise, or meeting with the board. I'm getting to him before Vista does. Otherwise, James's tracks will be covered, and we'll be dead in the water. I won't accuse James right out. I'll just feel out the situation and see where it takes me. But I'm not letting this go." He twisted around to look at Devon. "Will Sunrise be okay?"

She nodded. "Vista won't dare inject her again. He's

probably in her stall now, frantically working to get her well before your grandfather finds out what he's up to." A pause. "Unless he already knows."

Blake's jaw tightened.

"Blake, I know you don't want to hear it, but Monty thinks your grandfather would do anything to protect James. Maybe he's doing that now."

"I hope not. And you're right—I don't want to hear it. That doesn't mean I haven't thought of it. So I'm not speculating. I'm finding out."

What Devon and Blake walked in on wasn't a business meeting. It was cocktail hour.

Everyone was in the living room. Edward and Anne were seated on one sofa. James sat across from them on the other. And Louise stood by the windows. All of them were nursing drinks.

"Blake, there you are." Edward waved him in. "Come in and join us." He turned to the butler, who was standing at the sideboard. "Albert, pour Blake a Jack Daniel's on the rocks."

"Very good, sir." Albert reached for the bourbon.

Blake angled his head slightly toward Devon. "Will you be okay alone?" he asked quietly.

"I'll be fine," she assured him. "Do what you have to."

"Join us, Dr. Montgomery," Edward added. He looked less than thrilled. But, clearly, he thought Blake was annoyed at the omission. "Just tell Albert what you'd like to drink."

"Thank you. I'd love some water." Devon entered the living room, trying to ignore the twin icy stares being leveled at her by James and Louise.

"You don't drink?" Edward inquired.

"I do, sometimes."

"And tonight's not one of those times?"

"No," Blake interceded. "It isn't. And it shouldn't be for you, either. Jack Daniel's wasn't on the list your cardiologist gave you."

Edward snorted. "If I followed that list, I'd die of boredom. I'd rather take my chances with life."

"Suit yourself." Blake met his grandfather's gaze head-on. "I need to speak with you."

"About my drinking habits? No thanks. I don't need a lecture."

"It has nothing to do with that. But it's important."

Edward's brows shot up. "I'm listening."

"Not here. In private. It'll only take a few minutes."

"All right." Edward rose and set down his glass. "Let's go to my office."

Blake nodded, and the two men left the room.

Silence hung behind them.

"Great," James muttered, reaching for his gin and tonic. "More drama. Just what we need."

His grandmother gave him a reproving look that screamed don't-air-our-dirty-laundry-in-front-of-strangers. He got the message loud and clear, and bit back whatever else he'd been about to say.

Another silence, this one more uncomfortable than the last.

The clock in the hall chimed five.

"I wonder what's keeping Cassidy," Anne murmured. "She was due here a half hour ago."

"She's probably tied up in a meeting," Louise surmised. She turned to give Devon a cool, inquisitive look. "You take Mondays off?"

"Not usually, no," Devon replied, taking the glass of ice

water Albert handed her and nodding her thanks. "Today's an exception. I needed a break."

"I'm not surprised. You've had quite a hectic week." Sarcasm laced Louise's tone. She didn't wait for Devon's reaction, but averted her gaze, glancing from James to Anne. "Excuse me a moment. I'd like to freshen up for dinner." She breezed out of the room and headed for the powder room.

"I'll call Cassidy and make sure she's on her way," Anne announced. She eased to her feet, her sharp blue eyes flickering over Devon as if she were invisible, then fixing on James, silently ordering him to control himself. "I asked Frances to have dinner on the table at six so we can make it an early night."

"Thanks, Grandmother," James responded. "I appreciate it. I'm beat."

"I realize that." Anne laid a hand on his shoulder as she passed by. "You'll rest tomorrow. The plane will take you back to the competition tomorrow night." She paused, glancing back at Devon almost against her will. "You and Blake will stay for dinner." It wasn't a request. "I assume you like chicken." Without waiting for an answer, she went down the hall.

"So, it looks like it's just you and me," James observed. He indicated the now empty sofa across from him. "Have a seat. My headache's too bad to get into anything heavy. Besides, there's already enough tension in this room to blow the roof off."

Skeptically, Devon perched on the edge of the sofa.

A corner of James's mouth lifted. "You look like a frightened bird about to take flight. Like I said, the fireworks are over. Last night was the emotional scene. Today's the dawn of a new day. New beginnings and all that." He sipped his drink. "Did you intend to stay for dinner, or did my grandmother just put a crimp in your plans?"

Devon kept her expression nondescript. "No crimp. Blake

and I didn't have any ironclad plans. Besides, I'd enjoy seeing Cassidy again."

"Cassidy. Right." James gestured for Albert to fix him another drink. "Any idea why Blake was so hell-bent on talking to my grandfather?"

"You'll have to ask him."

"Did you?"

"No." Devon shook her head. "I make it a point not to interfere. Whatever Blake has on his mind is between him and your grandfather."

"How magnanimous of you."

"Not magnanimous. Respectful. I understand Blake's commitment to his family. I have the same commitment to mine. We all do what we have to, to protect the people we love."

"I'll drink to that." James held up his glass, regarding Devon with a pensive expression. "This dinner should be fascinating. I can hardly wait."

Down the hall, Edward shut his office door and turned to face Blake.

"Okay, what is it?"

Blake shoved his hands in his pockets. "Devon and I were at the stables. We planned on going riding. I showed her around first. She noticed Sunrise looked sick. When she checked her out, she found that Sunrise's right front leg was swollen. Apparently, she'd been given injections. We think Vista administered them."

Edward had sunk down into a chair. "What makes you think that?"

"We spoke to him."

"When?"

"We just came from his trailer."

"At the Best Western?"

"No. At our stables. I called and asked him to come by. I implied that you wanted to see him. So he came running.

We confronted him about Sunrise. He didn't admit anything. But he reacted like he was guilty."

"Great." Edward rubbed the back of his neck. He was clearly upset. But he wasn't surprised.

Blake's eyes narrowed. "What the hell is going on, Grandfather? Is Vista being paid to experiment on our horses?"

No reply.

"Shit." Blake's jaw began working. "You do know about it. I kept hoping otherwise, that he was orchestrating this without your knowledge. But, as usual, you're protecting him. Even about something as vile and unethical as this."

A watchful stare. "What are you talking about? Protecting who?"

"James."

"I'm not protecting James. Not in the way you mean."

"Go on."

Edward slammed his fist on the desk. "Fine. You want the truth? This research isn't James's doing. It's mine."

"Yours," Blake repeated flatly. "You're paying Vista to experiment on Sunrise?"

"It's more complicated than that." Edward stared Blake down. "Devon Montgomery was with you when you spoke to Vista?"

"Of course. She was the one who discovered Sunrise's illness. She was furious. She's a veterinarian; her job is to keep animals safe and healthy. How do you think she reacted to Sunrise being used as a guinea pig?"

"I don't give a damn how she reacts. I don't want her sticking her nose in this."

Blake's gaze hardened even more. "You'd better explain."

"There's nothing to explain. I pay Vista. He's a genetic consultant. He's taken a couple of skin samples from our horses to send out for analysis."

"Biopsies."

"Yeah, biopsies."

"Why? What kind of analyses are being done?"

"Evaluative ones. Genetic testing. Vista is assessing for strength, endurance—all the qualities that make an Olympic champion."

Blake frowned. "How does a tissue sample tell him that?"

"How the hell should I know?" Edward waved his arm in the air. "I'm not a scientist. That's why I pay him. All I know is he's working to find the best genetic combination—my mares and to-be-determined stallions. My goal is for him to perform inseminations that result in entries like Stolen Thunder. To secure James's future, and Kerri's."

Some truth. Some glaring omissions.

Blake still wasn't buying.

"If that's the case, then why the secrecy?" he demanded.

"There *is* no secrecy. There's just protecting my interests, and staying ahead of the competition. Vista's doing cutting-edge research. I don't want that information leaking out so some richer bastard can buy him out from under me and beat me to the punch. And the last thing I need is some altruistic veterinarian interfering because Vista's methods offend her principles."

"It's not about principles," Blake responded carefully, studying his grandfather's expression. "It's about medical ethics. And potential illegalities. The drugs in Vista's cabinets are—let's say, unusual."

"How would you know?"

"I wouldn't. Devon would. She didn't recognize the labels."

Twin splotches of red stained Edward's cheeks. "She went through Vista's cabinets?"

"Briefly. He stopped her."

"Big surprise. He's got to be ripping mad. I'm sure he'll be calling soon to read me the riot act. I'm lucky if he doesn't quit." Edward dragged a palm over his face and glared at his grandson. "Don't screw this up for me, Blake. Not now."

Blake bit back his reply. Time to stop. He'd exposed enough of his hand. His grandfather wasn't going to fill the gaping holes or explain the flagrant inconsistencies. That would have to come from elsewhere.

"Fine," he said tightly. "I won't interfere."

"And your girlfriend?"

"What about her?"

Edward rose slowly. "Keep her out of this, Blake. I mean it. Get her to back off. Or I will."

That brought Blake's head up. "Are you threatening Devon?"

"I'm securing my family's future." Edward's eyes were blazing. "You know that nothing stands in the way of that. Not for me. Vista's research is going to make Pierson one of the most prominent names in equestrian competition. That, along with Pierson & Company, is my legacy—one I mean to provide. I won't tolerate outside interference. So divert Devon Montgomery's attention elsewhere." A piercing stare. "That should be easy enough. You're sleeping with her. Take her to bed, and keep her there. Now let's go. Your grandmother's waiting."

He yanked open the door and stalked out of the office.

If cocktails had been a frosty affair, dinner was positively glacial.

Devon choked down each morsel, grateful that Cassidy was there to offset the deafening silence. Other than the snippets of conversation the two of them shared, the dinner consisted of clinking china and blatant noncommunication. Edward's contribution to the meal was an occasional instruction barked at the kitchen staff. Anne sliced her food deliberately, chewing small mouthfuls and darting censuring looks at Devon. James drank more than he ate, toying with his food while lost in moody introspection. Louise slanted assessing glances from Devon to Blake and back again. As for Blake, he was seething. He'd been that way since he'd walked out of his grandfather's office. Devon was dying to hear what he'd found out. But that had to wait till they were alone.

She was beyond relieved when they finally said their good nights and drove to her mother's house.

"Tell me what happened," she said, turning to him in the car.

"Not what I expected." Succinctly, Blake laid out what his grandfather had told him.

Devon frowned. "That doesn't make sense."

"You're right. It doesn't. I'm just not sure how much culpability lies directly with my grandfather, and how much lies in some cover-up for James. I keep remembering how extreme Vista's reaction was when I brought James up."

"He sounded too personally invested in James's career, that's for sure. As for what your grandfather said, it doesn't explain why Vista's trailer is so weighted down. Or why he's so paranoid. Plus, I don't buy the whole biopsies for genetic assessment. They're mating horses, not cloning them." Mentally, Devon consolidated everything Blake had said with what they'd learned from their showdown with Vista. "We've got a slew of question marks. I'd be willing to bet our answers lie behind that curtain in Vista's trailer."

"Maybe." Blake pulled into the driveway leading to Sally's house. "But you're not going to be the one finding out. My grandfather made it crystal clear that any further involvement on your part wouldn't be in your best interests."

Devon heard the hard note in Blake's tone. Her head snapped around, her eyes narrowing as she scrutinized his profile. Even in the dimly lit car, she could see the muscle working in his jaw. "Did he threaten me?" she asked quietly.

"Not in so many words." Blake eased the Jag to a stop. He cut the motor and turned to face Devon. "When it comes to protecting his family, particularly James, my grandfather knows no bounds. So it's time for you to assume a low profile. I'll take it from here."

"What are you going to do?"

"I'm not sure. Maybe contact the horse farm in Uruguay. Maybe go see Vista alone, and try to smooth things over. I'm a Pierson. Ultimately, my family loyalty won't be questioned. Whoever I contact will be more apt to give me information."

Devon gave a hard shake of her head. "That tactic's too passive. We need to do something drastic, before Vista gets rid of the evidence."

"We can't beat it out of him."

"I know." Devon dragged a frustrated hand through her hair. "But we're at a dead end. I'm not getting another word out of James. Any leverage I had with him is gone. I've exhausted all my avenues. At the same time, I feel like we're this close." She held up her gloved hand, her thumb and forefinger extended with just an inch of space separating them.

"So do I. Which is why I'm calling your father in the morning—as per his instructions. We'll tell him what happened. Let him call the shots."

"Fair enough." Devon blew out her breath. "Sorry if I'm short-fused. I just feel like we're in limbo. And I want this to be over."

"I know." Blake's knuckles brushed her cheek. "You're wound up. We both are." Deliberately, he shifted emotional gears. "As luck would have it, that's one problem I know how to fix."

"Really." Devon understood what he was trying to do, and she welcomed the reprieve. "What's your solution?" she asked, her lips curving slightly.

"Come inside and I'll show you."

"You're on."

Monty snatched up the Bat Phone when it rang. "You're late."

"A minute and a half," Sally clarified. "That's not late."

"For you it is. Especially under these circumstances. Listen, Sal, with what's going on, I prefer your busting my chops to making me sweat."

A heartbeat of silence.

"Sorry." Monty realized how sharp he'd sounded. "I didn't mean to bite your head off. I'm just in a lousy mood." He pulled open his kitchen cabinet, banging around until he'd found a clean mug. Then he poured himself some day-old coffee and took a gulp. "I probably need some sleep."

"Don't expect to get any," Sally responded mildly. "Not unless the brew you're chugging down is decaf."

"It is. How'd you know I was drinking coffee?"

"I recognize the sounds—*and* the mood. So instead of apologizing, why don't you tell me why you're so riled up. Is it Devon? Did she call in with something that threw you?"

"Nope. She's still with the Piersons."

"Are you worried about her?"

"Not really. Blake's with her. Plus, no one's going to pull something stupid or reckless right out in the open. Still, I have this niggling feeling in my gut. I'm not sure why—which puts me even more on edge."

Sally didn't argue. She trusted Pete's instincts. They were rarely wrong. "So what are you going to do?"

"Stick around in case I'm needed. Distract myself by working. Review my notes. Double-check a few people on the Pierson enemy list. The usual."

"Which includes waiting for Devon to call."

"*If* she calls," Monty corrected. "Like I said, she's with Blake. I don't expect to hear from them till tomorrow."

"Right." Sally's tone was troubled.

"Hey, don't let that vivid imagination of yours take over." Monty berated himself for opening up his big mouth. "You know very well that I always go into overdrive when I see the end in sight."

"Is that what you see this time?"

"Yes. So take a deep breath and leave the worrying to me."

"Easier said than done."

"Maybe. But try."

"Only if you—"

"I'll call you if there's anything to tell," Monty assured her.

"Okay." Sally didn't sound convinced. "Good night, Pete."

"Sweet dreams." Monty punched off the Bat Phone and shoved it in his jeans pocket. He took another belt of coffee, staring off into space and frowning.

No matter how he sugarcoated things to Sally, he was uneasy. Something was wrong.

He'd stay put until he knew what it was.

Something jarred Devon out of a fitful sleep.

Her eyes snapped open. For a second, she couldn't get her bearings. Then she realized she was in her mother's house, in her old bedroom. Blake's arm was draped across her, his naked body wrapped around hers.

What had awakened her?

She squirmed into a sitting position, whisking her hair off her face and groping around the nightstand until she found the lamp and switched it on.

Soft light filtered through the room, illuminating the digits on the alarm clock. Two forty.

She scanned the room. Nothing. No one.

She slipped out of bed, shrugged into her robe, and padded out of the bedroom. The hall was quiet. So were the stairs. From the landing, she could see that the front door was shut, the dead bolt thrown.

She was about to turn around and return to bed, chalking the whole thing up to her imagination, when she spied the white business envelope lying on the hardwood floor just inside the front door. Heart thumping, she made her way downstairs and over to the door to pick it up.

Inside was a single folded sheet, its message two laser-printed lines:

> Mind your own business. Stay away from the Piersons—all of them. Or your mother won't be the only Montgomery in danger.

Clutching the note, Devon marched forward, unlocked the front door, and threw it open.

There was no sign of anyone.

She went outside, arms wrapped around herself for warmth. She shivered, her breath coming in cold misty puffs as she scrutinized the grounds.

Deserted.

For a long moment, she stood motionless, waiting to see if there was any movement in the woods surrounding her mother's property.

The night was still.

Slowly, she made her way back inside, rereading the note as she locked the door.

"Devon?" Blake was halfway downstairs. "What's wrong?"

"This." Devon ascended the steps and handed him the page, continuing on her way to the bedroom.

"Shit," Blake muttered, reading as he followed behind her.

"Exactly." Devon sat down on the bed, drawing up her knees, resting her chin on them. "Either your grandfather's not wasting any time, or I made someone else feel cornered."

Blake gave a tight nod. "Whoever it was knows you're here. Which narrows it down to my entire family, Dr. Vista, and a chunk of the staff at Pierson & Company." He strode over, picked up the telephone, and thrust it into Devon's hand. "Call your father. Now."

Devon punched in Monty's home number.

"Yeah?" Her father answered on the second ring. His voice was rough with sleep, but his mind was already alert. Years in the Seventy-fifth had done that.

"Monty, it's me."

"I had a feeling I'd hear from you. What's up?"

She told him everything, starting with the threatening note.

"You ruffled somebody's feathers pretty bad," Monty commented. "That means you're close."

"I know. Which is why I've got to get inside Vista's trailer. We can't play this one safe. Time is against us."

"I agree. About everything except you getting into Vista's trailer. That's not happening. Have a stiff drink and go to sleep."

Devon bristled. "Don't get all paternal on me, Monty. You're the one who made me your partner in this case. Well, I'm doing my job. We don't have any evidence, so we can forget getting a warrant. And Vista's scared enough to get rid of whatever he's hiding behind that curtain."

"Yeah, but there are other considerations. My guess is whatever's back there cost a bundle and is at a critical point in development, or experimentation, or whatever the hell Vista's doing for Edward. I agree that it's shady. That's why Edward doesn't want the workstation set up in his stables. But the research obviously means a helluva lot to him. So Vista can't just toss his secret goodies out, not without Edward's okay. As for a warrant, you're right. It's not happening. Not without something more than instinct. So I'm moving on this now. Tonight. I'll get into the trailer before dawn, while it's deserted. Find out where Vista's staying. Ask Blake."

Devon complied. "Is Vista here in Dutchess County?" she murmured to Blake.

He nodded. "My grandfather puts him up at the Best Western."

"Did you hear that?" Devon asked into the phone.

"Yup." Monty was pulling on his clothes. "That's all I need. Go back to sleep. I'll call you later."

It was four thirty when Monty pulled into the dark parking lot of the Best Western motel.

He drove around to the section designated for trucks. There. Vista's trailer. Devon's description made it impossible to miss. And the rear end was definitely low to the ground.

Monty parked to a side, turned off his lights and his motor. The lot was deserted. Still, he gave it a minute or two, just to be on the safe side. When he was sure no one was around, he got out, taking his tools with him.

Collar turned up, he made his way to the trailer. He flicked on his penlight, gripping it between his teeth so the beam was aimed directly on the lock. Grabbing his tension wrench, he slid it into the keyhole and turned. Next came the pick. He yanked it out of his pocket, inserted it into the keyhole, and began lifting each pin in sequence until the last pin had fallen into position. When they were all lined up, he used the tension wrench to turn the lock.

It slid open.

He braced himself for the blare of the alarm. Once that siren started blasting, he'd have a prescribed amount of time to get in and out.

In one fluid motion, he yanked open the door.

Silence.

A wry grin tugged at Monty's lips. That was the nice thing about rural life. Everyone was so damned trusting.

He hopped into the trailer and shut the door.

Quickly, he darted his penlight around, orienting himself and getting a feel for the space. Then he focused the light directly in front of him, keeping it low and steady as he went straight for gold.

He shoved aside the curtain, marching into the back of the trailer and peering around.

The place looked like something out of *Scientific American*—a compact but comprehensive molecular physiology lab. There was a variety of high-tech equipment on the counters, most of which was Greek to Monty, and a lineup of test tubes arranged near a serious-looking microscope.

Monty examined the rest of the area. It didn't take a genius to figure out why the trailer was so weighted down. Two heavy-duty freezers stood in the back corner. Beside them was a whopping uninterruptible power supply and a hefty generator thrumming rhythmically to keep the freezers running. And on the opposite wall was a thick steel file cabinet.

First, Monty went to the freezers, opening the doors and checking out what was inside. Small glass dishes, all neatly labeled and containing samples the size of pencil erasers. Puzzled, he crossed over to the file cabinet, sliding open the drawers and rifling through the manila folders, one by one.

It didn't take him long to see the pattern.

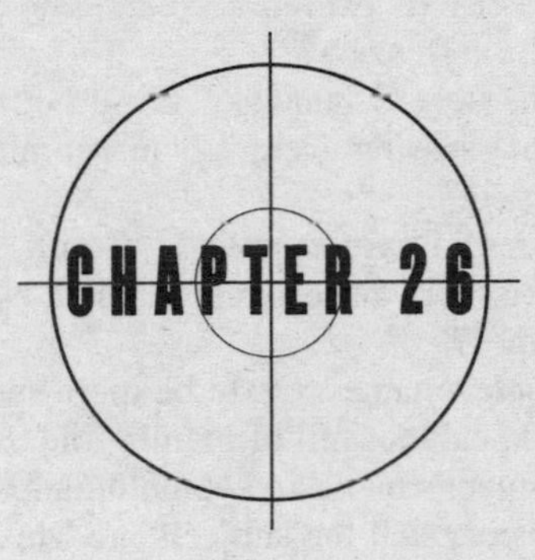

Devon was sitting up, staring out the window and watching the first few rays of sun, when the phone rang. She snatched it on the first ring. "Hello?"

"Mission accomplished," Monty said.

"Are you okay?" Gratefully, she took the mug of coffee Blake pressed into her hand, scooting over so he could sit down beside her.

"Did you doubt it?"

"No. But I worried anyway. What did you find?"

"Frankenstein's laboratory. I didn't know what half the stuff was. But it looked as serious as a heart attack."

"Describe it to me."

Monty plunged into a description of the freezers, the generator, and the UPS. "He's powering a lot more than the average vet needs."

"And a lot more than a consultant who's sending out his tissue samples. Whatever he's doing, he's doing it there."

Devon tucked her hair behind her ear. "Did you check out the contents of the freezers?"

"Yeah. There were a bunch of those petri dishes, filled with what I'm guessing were tissue samples. Thumbnail size, flesh-colored."

"Yup. Biopsies," Devon supplied. "Go on."

"Well, get this. The dishes were labeled. Names, dates."

"Horses' names?"

"Uh-uh. People's names. Or, to be more specific, illegals. Vista's got a file cabinet full of manila folders, each one labeled with a subject's name and containing his personal data and medical history. All the subjects are Mexican. All their social security numbers are 'not applicable.' And all their histories are vague. Now, here's the kicker—all their names match the names on the dishes."

Devon swallowed hard. "He's doing genetic testing on human beings?"

"Sure looks that way. He's paying them enough cash to stay in this country. In return, he's using them for his research."

"That's sickening. But I don't get the connection." Devon raked a hand through her hair. "How will that benefit Edward's horses?"

"I'm not sure—yet. But give me time." Monty paused, and Devon could hear the road noise in the background.

"You're driving home?"

"On my way as we speak," he assured her. "By the way, was Louise Chambers up at the farm last night?"

"Yes. She spent the night. Why?"

"I need to talk to her. When's she due back in the city?"

Devon repeated the question to Blake.

"This morning," he replied. "She and I are both involved in a ten thirty meeting. Which means she'll be in the office before ten."

"Good." Monty sounded pleased. "I'll catch her before that meeting."

"Are you going to tell me what this is about?" Devon asked.

"Later."

Devon sighed. "Fine. Blake and I are about to pack up and head home. I'm due at the clinic at eleven. I'll be out by six. At which time you and I are meeting, either at my place or yours. Pick."

"Yours. I'll cook. Tell Blake he's welcome. So's Chomper. See you later."

At nine twenty that morning, Louise Chambers turned her car over to the midtown parking attendant and walked toward Pierson & Company.

She was in a foul mood. A long drive, a stressful evening, and a sleepless night. And all for what? To see Blake take off with Devon Montgomery for a romantic night alone.

Her last-ditch effort to salvage things was dead in the water before it began.

She rode up in the elevator, unbuttoning her coat and trying to figure out if there was anything she could do to keep her long-term plan from backfiring. A quick fix was out. She'd have to bide her time—again. That had been her course of action for two-plus years. It was starting to get old.

Maybe it was time to give up.

The elevator doors opened, and she headed toward her office, murmuring good mornings to people as she passed.

She paused when she reached her secretary's station. "Hi, Diana. Anything urgent? I've got a ten thirty meeting to prepare for."

"A few messages. They can wait," her secretary said brightly.

"Good. Hold my calls."

Walking into her office, Louise put down her briefcase, hung away her coat, and sank down in her leather desk chair. She had a slew of papers to review before the meeting with

Pierson's key suppliers. Her concentration sucked, and her head was pounding.

She poured herself a glass of water and was swallowing two Tylenol when the door opened and Pete Montgomery strode in.

"Good morning," he greeted Louise. "Glad I caught you."

Something about his choice of words unnerved her.

"I've got a meeting to prepare for, Detective," she informed him. "I should be free late this afternoon. Please check with my secretary and make an appointment."

"That won't work," Monty replied, waving away the curt brush-off. "My situation trumps yours. It's a matter in which—what's that phrase you attorneys use? Oh yeah. Time is of the essence. But don't worry. I won't be here long."

Before Louise could respond, Diana burst into the office. "I'm sorry," she told her boss breathlessly, glancing from Louise to Monty. "I stepped away from my desk for a minute."

"That's all right, Diana." Louise interlaced her fingers on her desk and stared Monty down. "I suspect the detective waited for that opportunity and used it to his advantage." She nodded at Diana. "You can go. This meeting will be brief."

Her secretary left the office, shutting the door behind her.

"Okay, Detective Montgomery, what's this about?" Louise inquired. "I assumed you'd be barking up a more fruitful tree by now."

A corner of Monty's mouth lifted. "That depends on which aspect of this case I'm investigating. The one I'm here about sent me barking right to your office door."

He perched on the edge of a chair. "Here's the scoop. I have a client. A wealthy, decent man who's crazy about his wife. Only she's carrying on with some young stud. He hired me to get the goods on them. So I tailed them, watched them go at it like rabbits. Something about the whole scenario struck me as weird. Talk about staged photo ops. It was like she knew her husband had hired a PI and was trying to be as obvious as possible. Which would mean she wanted to get caught. But why? She and my client had a prenup. She'd never be awarded the hefty settlement she was angling for if he could prove she was screwing around. It just didn't make sense."

"How fascinating." Louise's tone and expression remained impassive.

Monty leaned forward. "Then I met with my client, and it all suddenly clicked. The guy was a mess, thanks to his wife. Physically shot. Weak. Sickly. During our meeting, he shoved a couple of nitroglycerin tablets under his tongue. That's when I realized he had a heart condition. A serious one. The kind that could prove fatal if he were faced with a severe shock. You know, like the shock of seeing porn shots of his wife and her boy toy."

Louise pinned Monty with a cold stare. "That's a shame, Detective—although not exactly a unique scenario. What does it have to do with me?"

"Quite a bit. It got me thinking about Frederick Pierson's wife, Emily. She had a heart condition, too. A serious, debilitating heart condition—not the recently acquired one you indicated during our chat. Because of it, she was a recluse. She stayed holed up in her apartment for years. Saw no one. Oh, except you."

A hard light glinted in his eyes. "When we spoke last week, you told me you'd met Emily Pierson. You also said nothing went on between you and Frederick until after she died. Well, as it turns out, there are some major discrepancies in those statements."

"I'm not following."

"Sure you are. It's true you met Mrs. Pierson, but not as some innocent Pierson employee. You were having an affair with her husband. You knew he'd never leave his wife. So you found a way for her to leave him—permanently."

Louise's eyes narrowed. "If you're suggesting I harmed

Emily Pierson, you'd better have some damned strong evidence, or I'll be suing you for defamation."

"Don't bother." Monty waved away her threat. "I learned a long time ago never to confront lawyers without proof. You see, Ms. Chambers, I did some digging. Turns out you visited Frederick Pierson's apartment the day his wife died. You paid off a doorman to let you upstairs and to forget he ever saw you. I tracked him down. As luck would have it, he regained his memory when I flashed a wad of cash at him. So, incidentally, did the concierge at the hotel you and Frederick used as a love nest for the first months of your affair. As you can see, I've got more than enough proof. Care to fill in the blanks? Or should I?"

He pressed on without waiting. "You walked into Emily Pierson's home and told her you were sleeping with her husband. Maybe you took it a step further and hinted that Frederick was on the verge of leaving her. Whatever you said, it was enough to trigger a heart attack. She died. You got Frederick. And you were on your way to happily-ever-after."

"That's not the way it happened," Louise snapped. Her hands shook as she refilled her water glass and took a gulp. "Yes, I went to see her. And, yes, I told her about Frederick and me. But I did it so she'd let him go, not so she'd die. I was thirty-two years old. It never occurred to me that a blunt talk about a marriage that was in name only would be enough to induce a heart attack."

"But it did."

"It's possible. It's also possible the two events were unrelated. I wouldn't know firsthand. I left."

"That's a lie. You were there when it happened. The nurse who cared for Emily Pierson told me she heard someone leave the apartment as she reached Mrs. Pierson's side. She assumed it was a servant. But it wasn't. It was you. I've got times on everything, right down to the minute. Arrivals. Departures. When Emily Pierson's body was discovered. It's all right here." Monty walked over to Louise's desk and slapped down a sheet of information. "I'd quit playing the denial game. It won't fly. And before you decide to opt for silence, let me remind you that there's no statute of limitations on murder. You're an attorney. You know that."

"I did not murder Emily Pierson." Louise had gone deadly pale. "Okay, you're right—I was there when it happened. I saw her collapse. I'll never forget the look on her face. I nearly died myself. I froze. By the time I got it together enough to react, it was too late."

Monty's brows rose. "You don't strike me as the emotionally fragile type."

"I'm human. I saw a woman die."

"You saw an opportunity. You *let* that woman die."

Louise's chin came up. "That's one charge you can't prove."

"You're right. And even if I could, I'd only be able to get you on failure to render assistance—a misdemeanor, at best, with a two-year statute that's almost up. Unless, of course, there's more. Tell me, Ms. Chambers, what happened when Frederick started seeing Sally? That derailed your plan again. Did you decide to get rid of her, too? Is that what happened at that cabin? You hired some punk to drive up and torch the place. But things didn't go as planned. And the wrong person died. Makes sense. It also explains your sudden interest in Blake Pierson—the rising star of Pierson & Company."

"No!" Louise's voice trembled, and her eyes were damp. "I had nothing to do with Frederick's death. I cared about him." She reached for a tissue. "As for your ex-wife, I wouldn't go to the trouble of having her killed, much less risk my career and my freedom for it. She was a fling, and not Frederick's first. For that matter, I wasn't exactly a saint, either. But he and I always came back to each other. That would have happened this time, too. If someone hadn't murdered him."

"Maybe. Maybe not. We'll never know, will we?" Monty

shrugged. "One thing's for sure: You're one hell of an opportunist. The Piersons didn't know what they were letting themselves in for when they hired you." He glanced at his watch. "We're through here," he announced, turning and heading for the door.

"Wait," Louise demanded. "What are you planning to do?"

Monty paused, glancing back at her. "My job. Figuring out who killed Frederick Pierson."

"So you no longer think that someone was me?"

"Never did. The evidence says otherwise."

"What about my job?"

Another shrug. "That's up to the Piersons. If it were up to me, I'd kick you out on your conniving ass. But it's not my call." Monty's expression hardened and he pinned her with his stare. "One piece of advice. Stay the hell away from my daughter and Blake Pierson. Your grand plan to snag Pierson's head honcho is over. If I get even the slightest inkling you're gunning for Devon, you'll answer to me. And I'm one tough judge and jury."

The note had been insufficient motivation.

It was morning and Devon Montgomery was making no move to stay away from the Piersons—beginning with Blake. The two of them had left her mother's house at dawn, arms around each other as they hiked through the snow to Blake's car. That meant he was her ally as well as her lover. And that made her twice as dangerous. She wasn't giving up on her crusade to find out what was going on in Vista's trailer. And with Blake in her corner, who knew what she'd uncover.

Time to take drastic action.

Devon walked into her living room and dropped her overnight bag on the rug. She sank down on the sofa, dropping her head in her hands.

She was exhausted. She'd had less than three hours' sleep. And she still couldn't figure out what Vista was up to.

There was a piece missing. But what?

Her musing was interrupted by Terror, who exploded into the room, barking and jumping up and down with excitement at her homecoming. He leaped onto the sofa beside her and began licking her face.

"Hey, boy." Devon rubbed his ears, leaning over to plant a kiss on top of his head. "It's good to see you, too."

"Hi, Dev. I didn't hear you come in." Merry strolled into the room, munching on an apple. "But Terror did. He actually abandoned his breakfast *and* an old crew sock to run out and greet you." Seeing her sister's drawn expression, Merry broke off, sinking down on the cushion beside her. "What's wrong?"

"I'm just tired," Devon replied. "The week and a half since the fire seems more like a month."

"I know what you mean." Merry nodded. "But there is a silver lining to all this. You met Blake. He's crazy about you."

"The feeling's terrifyingly mutual," Devon admitted. "I can't believe how intense this relationship's gotten in just a few days. Nothing real happens this fast."

"Mom and Dad did."

A quick sideways glance. "Yes, they did."

"And, speaking of Dad, I can tell he's getting close to solving these murders. Which means Mom will be home soon. And everything will go back to normal. Maybe better."

That was too many pointed innuendos to dismiss as coincidence.

Devon felt her first surge of optimism where this subject was concerned. "Are you trying to tell me something?" she asked her sister.

"Like what?"

"Like the fact that you and Monty are doing better. Like the fact that you're learning to read him. Like the fact that you're starting to believe he and Mom belong together."

Merry chewed a bite of apple, contemplating the questions. "I guess so."

"Which part?"

"All of it. The way he talks about Mom. The way he's on overdrive to save her. It's hard to deny his feelings. And at this stage of his life, yeah, I think those feelings would take precedence over his Evel Knievel nature. As for him and me, we're taking baby steps. Building trust takes time. We're not rushing it. For now, we're just getting to know each other."

"I'm so glad."

"Me, too." Merry finished off her apple. "Have you told Blake about knowing where Mom is?"

Devon shook her head. "That's the one thing I've kept from him. I might be a lovesick idiot, but I'm not risking Mom's safety. Blake will either understand, or he won't." She rose. "I'm jumping in the shower. I've got to get to the clinic."

"No problem. I'm e-mailing my econ assignment in, then starting on my problem set for stats. I've got lecture notes to review, a take-home exam to polish off—I'll probably still be pounding away on my laptop when you get home."

"I remember those days," Devon commiserated. "I was a lot better at coping with sleepless nights than I am now."

"You've got a better reason to stay up now," Merry pointed out with a grin.

"Go do your work." Devon's lips twitched.

"I'm going, I'm going." Merry walked over to the makeshift desk she'd set up downstairs and plopped into the chair. "I'm working down here. It's closer to the kitchen. I'll need sustenance to stay alert."

Devon was heading for the stairs. "Speaking of sustenance, Monty's making dinner tonight," she called over her shoulder. "Blake and Chomper are coming. So don't plan on getting any work done then." She disappeared into her bedroom, Terror at her heels.

Still grinning, Merry turned her attention back to her assignment.

She'd just finished forwarding it when the doorbell rang.

Shoving back her chair, she rose and walked into the hallway. "Who is it?"

"Flowers for Devon Montgomery," a thickly accented voice responded.

"Just a sec." Merry scooted back to grab a bill from her purse. Then she returned and opened the door.

A deliveryman stood on the stoop, balancing an arrangement of pink, yellow, peach, white, and red roses in front of him. There must have been four dozen of them, accented with baby's breath and greens, all in an expensive handblown glass vase. So elaborate was the arrangement, Merry could scarcely see the guy carrying them. All she could make out were his uniformed legs and the top of his balding head.

"Devon Montgomery?"

Merry stared. "Those are gorgeous. Oh yeah, sorry." She reached out and carefully transferred the vase from his grasp to hers. "Hang on a sec." Gingerly, she carried the flowers over to the coffee table and set them down. Then she turned, intending to bring the guy his tip. "Thanks very mu—"

She never finished her sentence.

A handkerchief was pressed over her mouth and nose, and strong arms held her in place. A sickening smell invaded her nostrils, and she struggled to free herself. It was no use. Cobwebs danced in her head as the blackness engulfed her.

Devon noticed the flowers even before she finished walking down the staircase.

Her brows arched, and she went into the living room, checking out the arrangement that was swallowing up her entire coffee table.

"Talk about extravagant," she muttered, searching until she found the card. She plucked it out of its holder, a twinge of uneasiness in her gut. This kind of dazzling demonstration wasn't Blake's style. It was, however, James's style.

She hoped the flowers weren't from him. She wasn't up for another round of cat and mouse.

Anxiously, she scanned the note, which read:

Dear Devon,

As beautiful as these roses are, they pale in comparison to you.
Until later— Blake

Devon blinked. Okay, so she'd been wrong. They were from Blake. How bizarre. Not only were the elaborate arrangement and the effusive words way out of character, but they were the last thing she'd expected, given Blake's present state of mind. Maybe he'd ordered them before yesterday's trip to the farm? Possible. In any case, she'd call and thank him.

Terror had followed Devon downstairs. As she headed for the kitchen, he dashed into the living room and exploded into a fit of barking.

"What's up, boy?" Devon turned to see what was prompting the outburst.

Terror began wildly sniffing a spot on the carpet, his barks becoming more furious.

Devon returned to the living room, squatting down and sniffing the area where Terror was rooted. "Yuck." She wrinkled her nose at the unpleasant odor, which had been masked by the heavy scent of roses filling the air. Up close, the rug smelled like overripe citrus.

"Merry?" she called, standing up. "Did you spill orange juice on the living-room rug?"

No reply.

"Merry?" She turned, searching for a sign of her sister. That was strange. Merry had said she'd be in all day. She'd obviously been here to accept delivery of the flowers.

A quick check of the town house confirmed that she was out.

Puzzled, Devon grabbed the cordless phone and punched in her sister's cell number.

The line rang.

So did the phone.

It trilled right there in the living room, not ten feet away from where Devon stood. She hung up, feeling more than a little unnerved. Merry never went anywhere without her cell, not even to put out the garbage. That Motorola was always glued to her side.

So why wasn't it now?

Devon's home phone rang.

"Hello?" She answered instantly, hoping against hope that it was Merry.

"Just checking on you," Blake said in greeting. "I wanted to make sure you were holding it together."

"More or less." Devon continued scrutinizing the house for a hint of where her sister might have gone.

"You sound preoccupied."

"I am. I can't find Merry. She seems to have vanished while I was in the shower." Abruptly, Devon remembered the flowers. "Oh, thanks for the roses. They're amazing."

"What roses?"

"You have a shorter memory than I do. The dozens of long-stemmed beauties that just arrived with the card that almost made me blush. *Those* roses."

"I'm drawing a blank."

"Very funny. I guess you came to your senses and realized how atypically mushy you'd been."

"I'm not being funny. I didn't send you any flowers."

Blake's tone was too solemn to be teasing, and Devon's smile faded. "But your name is on the card. I don't understand. . . ." Her voice trailed off as an ugly possibility struck. "Oh God." She dropped the phone. "Merry!" She raced through the house, calling her sister's name. "Merry!" She ran to the front door, reaching for the handle.

The door was already ajar.

Devon shoved it open, frantically scanning the grounds around her town house.

There was a heavy set of footprints ground into the snow, leading from her front door to the parking lot.

"Oh no," she whispered. She hurried back inside and scooped up the phone. "Blake, I have to hang up."

"What's going on?"

"It's Merry. I think she's been kidnapped."

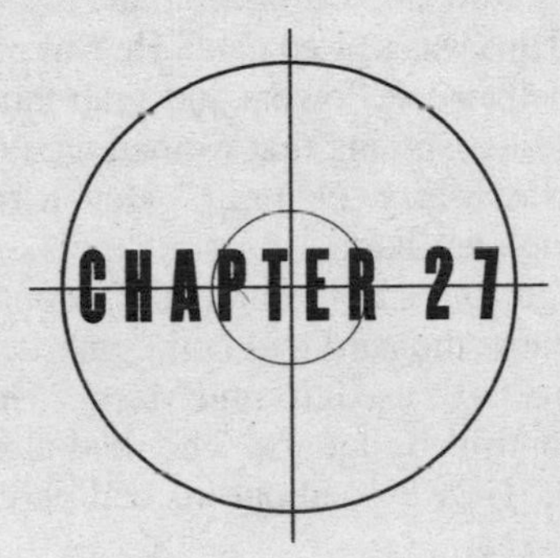

CHAPTER 27

Forty minutes later, Monty burst through Devon's front door, in a scene that was eerily reminiscent of two Saturdays earlier.

"Talk to me," he commanded, striding into the living room without even removing his coat. "Tell me everything that happened."

While Devon talked he squatted down, rubbing his fingers over the area of the carpet where Terror had been sniffing, and bringing his fingers to his nose.

"Chloroform," he stated grimly. "The bastard knocked Merry out before he took her."

"Why would he kidnap Merry?" Devon demanded. "Just to show me he means business? She's no threat. She doesn't know anything."

"It could be a scare tactic." Monty straightened, examining the vase of roses as he spoke. "On the other hand, you're right. It's a lame move. More likely the kidnapper thought Merry was you."

Devon paled. "How do you figure that?"

"Whoever did this was a hired hand. He was probably given instructions to deliver the flowers and grab the woman who accepted delivery—assuming that woman would be you."

"Instead, it was Merry. Dammit." Devon raked a trembling hand through her hair.

"Cut out the guilt. It's not your fault." Monty was reaching for the envelope the card had come in. "Let's not waste energy panicking. Let's use it to find Merry." He scanned the envelope. " 'Beautiful Bouquets,' " he read aloud. "Time to give them a call." He whipped out his cell phone.

The doorbell rang.

In a dazed state, Devon went over and opened it.

Blake stalked in. "Your sister . . . ?" He glanced from Devon to Monty, who was already grilling someone on the other end of the phone.

"There are traces of chloroform in the living room. She was definitely kidnapped. Monty's calling the florist to see what he can find out."

As she spoke, Monty hung up.

"The order was placed two hours ago," he informed them. "The shop manager took the call. She said the caller was a man. She doesn't remember his voice because it was a lousy cell-phone connection. He claimed to be Blake Pierson. He charged the flowers to the company's FTD account. He was very specific, especially about the wording on the card. And he was insistent about the delivery time."

"Two hours ago I was driving down from the farm with Devon," Blake said.

"Exactly." Monty scowled. "Whoever ordered the flowers knew that. Which means he knew when Devon would be arriving home."

"Not based on the time we left he wouldn't," Devon clarified. "Blake and I hit a ton of city-bound traffic. The drive took an extra forty-five minutes."

"Yet the kidnapper knew just when to ring your doorbell. How?"

Blake stiffened. His gaze slid to Devon, and he gave her a hard, meaningful look. "Tell him."

Monty jumped on that. "Tell me what?"

"I meant to discuss this with you sooner." Devon steeled herself for a blowup. "I was on the verge when that whole situation came up with my wearing a wire to trap James. At that point, it slipped my mind."

"Stop backpedaling. Talk."

A resigned sigh. "A bunch of times since Mom disappeared, I sensed I was being followed. Random occasions. Different places. Always when I was driving. I became superalert, watching in my rearview mirror, pulling over to scrutinize the road. I never spotted anyone. So I figured I was just being paranoid."

Monty was every bit as livid as she'd expected. "When were you going to mention this?" He waved away her reply, his forehead creased in concern. "If someone's following you, they're probably watching this place. Which means they know I've been here almost every day since Sally disappeared. It's possible they saw me parked outside the night I taped James's conversation. And they definitely know when you dropped by Blake's place and how long you stayed. Given all that, you're an even bigger threat to them than we realized."

Devon swallowed, hard. "Does that mean they'd hurt Merry? Especially if they think she's me?"

A glint of pain flickered in Monty's eyes. "They've killed already. So I can't rule it out. But my gut says no. The purpose of kidnapping you would more likely be to keep you out of the way while Vista finishes up whatever the hell he's working on. It would keep me out of the way, too, because I'd be consumed with finding you."

Monty paused. "You said this guy tailing you showed up

at random times and places. That means he wasn't stationed outside your house. He knew in advance where you'd be and where you were headed. Which makes me suspect that . . . " Monty didn't finish his thought. He strode out of the room and headed for the staircase leading down to the basement.

"Why the basement? What are you looking for?" Devon demanded as she and Blake followed behind.

Monty had already reached the concrete floor. "Where do your telephone lines enter the house?"

"Over there." Devon pointed at the gray plastic box mounted on the far cinder block wall.

"That's why." Monty made his way over to the box. He tilted back his head to examine the ceiling, spotted the ceramic light fixture overhead. Reaching up, he yanked at the pull string.

The light came on, illuminating that section of the basement.

He removed a Leatherman Micra from his pocket, pried open the flat screwdriver blade, and turned the large captive screw securing the access cover. With the screw hanging, he opened the gray box and peered inside.

"And *this* is what I'm looking for," he muttered.

The miniature transmitter was attached to the inside of the box with double-sided tape. Monty's forefinger traced the wires from the transmitter to the alligator clips that were clamped to the connectors on the main phone line. "That explains how your tail knew so much."

Devon was staring. "He tapped my phone?"

"Yup. He's probably parked nearby, with a pocket receiver and a tape recorder, listening in to all your calls." Monty shut the gray box and retightened the screw. "Let's leave that in place for now, in case we need to manipulate your wiretapper with false information."

Turning, Monty studied his daughter. "What strangers have been in the house? Deliverymen? Repair people? Utility guys to read the meters?"

"Cable." Devon's head came up. "The night of my first date with James, Merry said something about a cable guy being here to fix my reception. I remember being surprised because I'd never noticed a problem."

"That's because there wasn't one." Monty rubbed his face. "Your date with James was a week ago last night. That means we have to mentally retrace your phone calls over the past eight days. Who you spoke to. What you said. Fortunately, I doubt the cable guy had enough time or opportunity to plant bugs around the town house. With Merry home, he probably just went straight for the phone, then got out. But I'll have Sherman sweep the place, just to be sure."

Monty paused, deeply troubled. "We have to figure out how much they know. Especially where it comes to anything you and I discussed."

Devon's gaze met his, and she felt her stomach knot. Her mother. What details had she and Monty discussed on her home line? Did the kidnapper know that Monty had hidden his ex-wife away in a safe place? Williamstown had never been mentioned. That much Devon was certain of. But more than that, she wasn't sure. And if, by some fluke, there were other bugs in the house, then even the calls they'd made on the Bat Phone weren't secure.

With a sick feeling, Devon lowered her gaze and began racking her brain. She could sense that Monty was doing the same.

Blake's stare shifted from Devon to Monty and back. "While you two think, I'll call the police."

"No." Monty shot down that idea in a hurry. "There'd be too much explaining and too much red tape. If necessary, I'll call my own people."

Blake gave him a measured look. "There's something you don't want the cops to know."

"If that's true, be damned glad of it," Monty retorted. "Because there's a helluva lot more *you* don't want them to know."

A muscle worked in Blake's jaw. "I'm not about to protect a murderer and a kidnapper. So if that's what you're implying—"

"I'm not. I'm saying this thing has snowballed out of control. If we turn it over to the cops now, it'll destroy your family and your company. If we go with my approach, we'll minimize the damage and direct the brunt of the fallout to the guilty parties."

"You're being surprisingly fair and levelheaded under the circumstances," Blake commented.

"No, he's not," Devon said quietly. "He wants to handle this himself."

"Yeah," her father confirmed. "I do." His own jaw was working. "That's my baby they grabbed. You don't get more personal than that. I'm driving straight up to Edward's farm and having a long talk with him."

"Go easy, Detective," Blake felt compelled to request. "He's almost eighty. And his heart's not in great shape."

"I'll do my best. No promises. I'm not leaving there without answers."

"What can I do?" Devon asked. "Besides recalling the content of our phone conversations?"

"Go to Beautiful Bouquets on Main Street. Larry Aymes is the name of the delivery guy who was scheduled to deliver your roses. He'll be in the shop until two. I'm willing to bet someone paid him off to take the delivery off his hands—to add a more personal touch. Talk to Aymes. Find out everything you can about that someone—physical description, mannerisms, anything that could help us catch the scum. Remind Aymes that, as of now, he's an accessory to kidnapping. That should loosen his lips."

Monty turned to Blake. "Can you come up with a plausible reason to call that horse farm in Uruguay? We've got to find out what their connection is to Vista and why they're receiving payments from that offshore account."

"The thought of doing that occurred to me last night."

Blake frowned. "The problem isn't coming up with an excuse to call. The problem is communicating. They don't speak a word of English. We rarely deal with them by phone. My grandmother handles all our communications, and it's almost always by fax. She's the only one who's familiar enough with Spanish to get by."

"Devon used to be pretty fluent." Monty's glance flickered back to his daughter. "Can you pull it off?"

"I'm a little rusty but, yes, I think so." Her brows drew together as she speculated where her father was heading. "You want me to pretend I'm Anne Pierson?"

"Yeah. Think about it. She's the only Pierson they've dealt with. And almost never by phone, so her voice is unfamiliar. She's female. She's American. The telephone lines in the rural areas of South America suck. So do cell phones. Let's use that to our advantage. Make your voice a little lower and throatier, and you'll have it. If you're off a little bit, it won't matter. They'll blame the crappy phone connection. So, go for it."

"Done."

"Good. Before I leave, I need to talk to you alone."

With a tight nod, Devon followed Monty a short distance away. She knew exactly what this was about. "What did you decide?" she asked without preamble.

"The Bat Phone's with me," he replied in a low voice. "I have to give her a heads-up. For her own safety. Just in case we're forgetting something we let slip."

"Or in case John Sherman finds other bugs," Devon agreed. "And, Monty, you also have to tell her about Merry."

"I know." Monty looked grim. "You know what that means."

"She'll come home. We can't help that. It might be best anyway, since we now know my calls have been monitored and Mom's safety has been compromised."

"Yeah." Monty headed for the staircase. "I'm leaving the

Pierson file on your coffee table. Use whatever material you need to. And keep me posted."

It was cold.

That awareness drifted through Merry's consciousness as she slowly came to.

She shivered, wondering where her coat was. Her head was pounding. There was a sickening odor in her nostrils, one that seemed vaguely familiar. Her stomach lurched as it rebelled against the smell.

With another shiver, she gathered her strength and tried to stand up. A low cry emerged from her throat as she met with painful resistance. Her arms were secured behind her, and her legs were locked together, bound at the ankles. The ropes cut into her skin, preventing her from moving, and the surface supporting her was rock hard.

A wooden chair. She was sitting on it, and she was somewhere outside. But where? And why?

Instinctively, she began to struggle, trying to blink away the grogginess and the nausea. Neither diminished, but she cracked her eyes open anyway, intent on getting her bearings.

She wasn't outside after all. She was in a woodshed, a maintenance shed, judging by the equipment. Two massive snowblowers, stacks of fifty-pound bags of rock salt, and a row of heavy-duty snow shovels filled the place.

How had she gotten here? What was going on?

It had to be tied to Monty's investigation.

She inhaled sharply, smelled that sickening odor again, and remembered. She'd been kidnapped. That flower deliveryman had knocked her out and taken her, evidently bringing her to wherever this shed was.

She tried to scream. She couldn't. There was a handkerchief stuffed in her mouth. Panic exploded inside her, and she began to battle frantically to free herself. The ropes cut into her skin, but she kept fighting, praying that somehow they'd give.

They didn't.

Weak with exertion, she sagged in the chair, tears filling her eyes. She ordered herself not to cry. She had to keep her nostrils clear. They were her only means of breathing. If she stuffed them up, she'd suffocate.

She tried to calm down. The cold lashed at her, and she began to shake. How long had she been here? There was a sliver of sunlight trickling in from underneath the door. That told her it was still daylight. When it faded, she'd freeze to death.

Her father would find her. He had to.

She was struggling with the ropes again when she heard crunching sounds outside. They were rhythmic, growing closer.

Footsteps.

A key turned on the other side of the door. Merry stared in that direction, not sure whether to be relieved or terrified.

The door swung open, and a man in a parka and boots trudged in. The hooded parka hid most of him from view, but Merry could make out that he was of average height, with a solid build and a dark complexion that suggested he was of Hispanic descent. He was carrying a bottle of springwater, and there were two blankets tucked under his arm.

Without speaking, he tromped over to where she sat and pulled the gag out of her mouth.

Merry began to cough. Her mouth was dry and cottony, and she could barely feel her tongue.

"*Agua,*" he muttered, twisting off the bottle cap and holding the bottle to her lips.

Fleetingly, Merry remembered the accented voice at Devon's door. The same voice. It was the flower delivery guy.

She didn't ask questions. She just drank, forcing herself to swallow small quantities at a time, all the while afraid he'd decide she'd had enough and yank away the bottle.

He didn't. He let her drink her fill, then recapped the bottle and stuck it in his pocket. Next, he shook out the blankets and draped them across Merry's lap and around her shoulders, shoving them into place.

"Eso es mejor." With a grunt of satisfaction, he rose, glancing briefly at her as he wadded up the handkerchief, preparing to stick it back in her mouth.

"No. Please, don't," she whispered, shaking her head. "I can't breathe. Please. I promise not to scream."

He paused, scrutinizing her face with obvious noncomprehension.

"Por favor." She wracked her brain, trying to remember her high school and college Spanish. *"No puedo respirar. Prometo no gritar. Por favor."*

A flash of perception, and a definite hesitation.

He looked around, assessing the danger of complying with her wishes. In the end, he must have decided that no one would hear her if she broke her word, because he gave a hard nod.

Cramming the handkerchief in his other pocket, he walked off.

"Espera," Merry called out hoarsely. *"¿Dónde estoy?"*

He didn't reply. He just turned, staring at her with a brooding expression. Then he walked out.

Merry pressed her lips together, trying to ignore the stinging pain in her wrists. She had to be strong. She couldn't let fear win out over reason. She was an adult, not a child.

Maybe. But all she wanted was her parents.

The minute Sally heard that Pete was on the phone, she knew something was wrong.

He never checked in during the day. They talked alone each night, and with the kids some evenings. Those calls had been her emotional lifeline through this endless week and a half.

Now she hurried into the white clapboard house in Williamstown, thanking Molly for interrupting her walk to summon her to the phone.

She took the call in the den, which was empty and quiet.

"Pete?"

"Hey, Sal. You okay?"

"I am. But you're not. I can hear it in your voice. Your gut was right. What's happened?"

He blew out his breath. "Nothing good. Look, I'm driving up to the Pierson farm. I found a telephone bug in Devon's basement. Someone's been monitoring her calls. It's possible that they got enough to figure out your whereabouts."

Sally processed that. "But if they knew where I was, wouldn't they have come after me already?"

"If they knew where you were, yeah. Hopefully, they don't. Devon and I never mentioned a location. They're probably searching everywhere they can think of and, at the same time, hoping one of us will lead them to you. Still, I don't like it." He paused, and Sally knew there was something else—something bad.

It was even worse than she thought.

"They've got Merry," Pete said flatly.

Sally's insides froze. "Oh God. No." She sank down in a chair, her entire body trembling. "How?"

As calmly as possible, he relayed the details.

"Pete, what are they going to do to her?"

"The first thing they'll do is figure out she's not Devon. Which means they have a huge problem on their hands."

"And how are they going to solve that problem? They killed Frederick. From what you've said, they killed Philip Rhodes. What if they decide to—"

"That's not their agenda. Not for Merry. Not even for Devon. Trust me, Sal. I know what I'm talking about."

"I do trust you. But I'm coming home. Right away. It's not up for debate. So don't bother arguing with me."

"I didn't plan to." Pete sounded wearily amused. "I know what a mother bear you are where our kids are concerned. So I beat you to the punch. Anytime now, Molly should be poking her head in to give you a timetable. She's finding

Rod. He'll drive you down to your house. I'll meet you there. I'd drive up to Williamstown and get you myself, but I've got a date with Edward Pierson."

"Wait for me," Sally commanded. "I'm going with you."

"No way. It's too big a risk."

"That's my choice. Not yours." Sally was finished being protected. "I'm not asking for your permission. I'm telling you. I'll be leaving here in ten minutes. If Rod can't break away now, I'll rent a car. I'll be at the Piersons' farm within a few minutes of you."

Silence.

"I'm her mother, Pete," Sally added quietly. "I need to be there."

"I know you do." Pete sounded resigned. "Fine. You win. But I'll meet you at your place, not the Piersons'. That'll give us the element of surprise. I'm flooring the gas. So tell Rod to step on it."

"I will." Sally fought for self-control. "Do you honestly believe Edward's behind this?"

"He's involved. How much, I don't know. But I'm about to. Game over. No more bullshit. All the players are there. Edward. James. And that slimy veterinarian Edward hired. They're all up to their necks in this. And I'll wring every one of those necks if I have to. I'm finding our daughter."

CHAPTER 28

Devon punched the *end* button on her cell phone and shifted in the passenger seat of Blake's Jag.

"I gave Monty the information we dragged out of Larry Aymes—what little there was." She made a frustrated sound, turning to stare out the window. "Aymes was useless."

"Not entirely." Blake stepped on the accelerator, speeding toward Devon's house. "We know the kidnapper spoke only Spanish. We know he had his instructions written on a slip of paper, and that he read them to Aymes when he gave him that hundred-dollar bill."

"Great," Devon said grimly. "So we know our guy's a hired hand. Did we honestly think your cousin or your grandfather would do thc dirty work himself?"

"Point taken." Blake turned onto Devon's street. "Are you going to open up to me now?"

She tipped her head toward him. "Open up about what?"

"About whatever your father just told you. About whatever you've been keeping from me." Blake paused. "I think we're past the point of secrets, don't you?"

"You mean because this whole situation's unraveling."

"Yeah. And because I'm in love with you."

Devon's breath caught. She stared at Blake's profile, feeling his declaration sink into her gut. She'd known this was happening. But she hadn't anticipated the impact that hearing the words would have on her.

"Are you in shock?" Blake asked, still staring ahead.

"No. I'm overwhelmed, and on emotional overload. How can the most wonderful experience of my life happen during the most harrowing crisis of my life?"

A wry smile tugged at Blake's lips. "I guess that's how love works. We don't get to choose the time or place."

"Obviously not. So much for candles and moonlight."

Blake reached over and took her hand, bringing it to his lips. "We can have those later."

"I know." Devon interlaced her fingers with his. "I love you, too," she added softly.

"Enough to trust me?"

"Yes." She was amazed at how much she meant it.

"Good. Then tell me where your mother is and how's she holding up."

Devon's brows arched. "You figured it out?"

"It wasn't hard. You and your father were much too calm for your mother to be MIA. I assume he stashed her away somewhere safe."

"He did. But she's not there anymore. Not with Merry kidnapped. She's on her way home. Monty's meeting her. Together, they're going to confront your grandfather and company."

Blake's expression turned grim. "That should be quite a party." He pulled into a parking spot and turned off the ignition. "I still can't believe someone in my family is a killer. White collar crime, even what's going on with Vista—all that I can envision, even if it turns my stomach. But murder? Kidnapping? Never. Never in a million years."

Devon squeezed his hand. There was nothing she could say to make his disillusionment go away. All she could do was be there.

Rod Garner's blue Ford Explorer rumbled down Sally's driveway, pulled around, and stopped.

Leaning against his Corolla, Monty straightened and walked toward them. By the time he reached the passenger side, Sally had climbed out. Without a word, she went into his arms.

"It's okay," he murmured, gripping her tightly. "Everything's going to be fine." He gazed past her as Rod ambled over with her bag. "Thanks," Monty told his friend. "I owe you one."

"Nah." The solid, ruddy-cheeked man grinned. "Sally's a pleasure. Molly and I loved having her. Plus, she makes a mean chicken Savoy and was decent enough to share the recipe. So, if anything, I owe you. So, tell me, what else can I do?"

"You can head home. I've got it covered from here."

"You're sure?"

"Positive. If things change, I know where to find you."

Sally broke away from Monty's embrace and turned to Rod. "What can I fix you for the road? A snack? Coffee?"

"Not a thing." He gave her arm a reassuring pat. "Just take it easy. Your ex is a pro. He'll find your girl."

"Thank you." Sally clasped his gloved hands. "Thank you for everything. Tell Molly I'll call as soon as we know anything."

"Will do." He strode back to his car and jumped in. "Hang tough, you two." He drove off.

Sally turned back to Monty, her lashes spiky with tears. "I'm ready. Go ahead and prep me. The sooner I'm up to speed, the sooner we can confront the Piersons."

Edward was on the phone with Vista when there was a knock at his office door.

"What is it?" he barked.

Albert stepped into the room. "Pardon me, Mr. Pierson, but Detective Montgomery just called. He's pulling through the farm gates. He says it's urgent that he see you. He asked that James be included, as well."

A hard swallow as warning bells sounded. "All right, Albert. Find James. Then show Detective Montgomery in." Edward waited until his butler had exited. "Now what?" he muttered into the phone. "What did you let slip this time?"

"Nothing," Vista snapped back. "I haven't spoken to a soul. Not since yesterday when your grandson and Devon Montgomery invaded my privacy. I have no idea what her father's there to see you about."

"That better be true. I'll get back to you." Edward hung up.

A minute later, James knocked and strolled into the room. "You need to speak with me?" he asked his grandfather.

"No." From behind James, Monty grabbed the door, preventing it from being shut. "We do." He gestured for Sally to enter.

"We?" Edward had begun. The word died on his lips as he spotted Sally.

"Hello, Edward." She walked over and sat down in a chair, her back ramrod straight. "You can call off your posse. I saved you the trouble of hunting me down."

It took Edward a moment to recover his composure. "Clearly, you're alive and well."

"I'm alive," she agreed. "But far from well."

Edward started to rise. "I don't understand—"

"You don't need to." Monty cut him off. "We're here *for* explanations, not to give them. Where's our daughter?"

"What?"

Slowly, Monty advanced to the desk, slapped his palms down. "I'm not asking again. Where is she?"

"What is he talking about?" James demanded, turning to his grandfather. "Did something happen to Devon?"

"Not to my knowledge. I don't know what he's talking about." Edward was clearly unnerved.

"Then I'll enlighten you." Monty's eyes were glittering with anger. "You hired me to flush out Sally. You bugged Devon's house and had her followed, not to mention having your grandsons try to seduce Sally's whereabouts out of her. Now she knows too much. So you arranged to get her out of the way. Ring a bell?"

"No." Edward gave an adamant shake of his head. "Your daughter was here with Blake last night. I haven't seen her since."

"And the threatening note?"

"*What* threatening note?"

"The one shoved under Sally's front door last night warning Devon to back off. Still not ringing any bells?"

"No," Edward repeated, waving his arms in a frustrated gesture. "You're not making any sense."

"How about it, James?" Monty turned. "Am I making sense to you? Are you running the show here, or are you just paying off doping control officers for advanced notice of the drug-testing schedule so you can time things right? You know, drug the competition when they're sure to be disqualified?"

James went sheet white.

"That's right, I know all about Paterson. And soon, so will the cops. I'm sure he'll be happy to strike a deal to avoid jail time—one that includes sharing the details of your arrangement. Smart move, picking someone with a gambling problem. Someone between a rock and a hard place. He lets you know the who and where so you can make sure to add diuretics to the right drinks before the right events."

"Shit." James dragged a hand over his face.

"What about the phony blackmail scheme?" Monty continued. "Was that your idea, too? Very clever. You made it look like someone had a vendetta against your whole family, not just Frederick. It helped when you framed Rhodes. The poor guy figured out you were siphoning off money into all sorts of things. Paying off Paterson. Vista's illegal research. Rhodes must have flipped out when he realized what you were doing. And you couldn't have that. So you got rid of him and framed him for Frederick's murder all at once."

"Stop it, Montgomery," Edward ordered over James's sputtering protest. "He had nothing to do with any of that. You're way off base."

"Then straighten me out. You purposely misled me into thinking Frederick was suspicious of Rhodes. The truth was, it was James he was suspicious of. He found out what Golden Boy was up to and he wanted to toss him out on his ass. You couldn't have that. It would screw up everything you'd been planning for—what you *and* James have been planning for."

Edward opened his mouth to refute the accusation.

Sally cut him off.

"A few days before Frederick died, I heard you two arguing at the stables," she said, gripping the arms of the chair. "I remember it, and so do you. Frederick was worried about a loose cannon at Pierson & Company. Someone committing criminal acts that could destroy everything your family had worked so hard to achieve. That someone was James. He was the person Frederick wanted out. Not Philip Rhodes."

"Sounds right to me," Monty agreed. "So, Edward, how far would you go to make sure Golden Boy stayed golden? Would you kill for it?"

"My own son?" Edward lost it. "You think I killed Frederick to keep him from firing James?"

"Did you?"

"Absolutely not."

"But you did steer me in Rhodes's direction, purposely leading me on a wild-goose chase."

"Fine. Yes." Edward rose again, this time pacing around behind his desk. "I diverted you away from James. I made up the blackmail scheme. And I told you it was Rhodes who

Frederick mistrusted. Rhodes wasn't family. James is. I was protecting my grandson."

"Wait a minute." James looked like a cornered rat. "I didn't know about any of this. And I sure as hell didn't kill anyone."

"Yeah. You're innocent as a lamb." Monty glared at him. "Next you'll be telling me you don't know about Vista and his genetic testing."

James's apprehensive gaze darted to his grandfather.

"Ah, so that's your grandfather's project, too." Monty pounced on the opportunity to find out what Vista's research was about. "Experimenting on horses is bad enough. But human beings? Illegal aliens who are too poor and too desperate to refuse? That's criminal and immoral. But you already know that, don't you, Edward? That's why you're paying Vista through an offshore account—the same account Rhodes found an electronic record of the night he died."

A muscle began twitching at Edward's jaw. "I hired Vista as a genetic consultant. Anything else he might be involved in has nothing to do with me."

"I doubt he'd see it that way. In fact, I'm sure he'd be very put off by your lack of loyalty—enough to spill his guts to save his own ass." Monty reached for the phone. "Should I call and invite him over?"

"Put down the phone, Detective." The voice came from the doorway, and Monty turned to see Merry being shoved in at gunpoint. "And while you're at it, put down your weapon, too. You won't be needing it."

Devon leaned back against the sofa, slapping the cordless phone onto the cushion beside her and rolling her eyes.

"That's the third time I've been disconnected," she muttered. "Well, I'm not giving up." She punched up the number again, waiting while the tinny connection went through.

At last, she was rewarded with a mumbled, *"Dígame."*

She sat up straight, signaling to let Blake know she'd gotten through.

"Esta es Señora Pierson." She spoke in the older, throatier voice of Anne Pierson, launching into the simple, direct speech that Blake had prepared and she'd translated into Spanish. *"Tenemos un problema con nuestro banco. El próximo pago quizás será tarde."*

The response she got was a sharp intake of breath, followed by some mumbled words of surprise and then a clarifying: *"Señora Pierson?"*

"Sí."

"Un momento."

Devon covered the mouthpiece while she waited. "I told him there's a problem with his next payment," she hissed. "He's getting someone."

Blake nodded, standing rigidly and waiting.

More background shuffling. Then a different male voice addressed her. *"¿Quíen es?"* he demanded.

Devon's stomach lurched. He wanted to know who she was. The previous guy had asked for her name twice. Had they figured out she wasn't Anne Pierson?

"¿Quíen es?" the new voice repeated.

"Señora Pierson," Devon replied carefully. *"Hay un problema. Su próximo pago será tarde."*

A sharp hiss greeted her ears. *"Usted miente! Yo no soy estúpido. Si usted no manda mi dinero ahora, yo se lo diré a todos que me pagaron empezar ese fuego."*

You're lying. I'm not stupid. If you don't send my money now, I'll tell everyone who paid me to set that fire.

Devon couldn't control the shocked cry that escaped her lips.

At the other end of the phone, there was a muttered oath in Spanish, then a click, and, finally, a dial tone.

"What is it?" Blake grilled her.

"Our answer." Devon stared at the phone, trying to process what she'd just learned. "The second guy I talked to set the fire," she said in a dazed monotone. "Apparently, he was paid off with the promise of more to come."

"He admitted all that to you right off the bat?"

"Yes."

"That makes no sense. Why would he do that?"

"Because he thought he was talking to the person who paid him." Devon raised her head, met Blake's gaze. "Your grandmother."

Anne Pierson stared Monty down with those frosty blue eyes. "Did you hear me, Detective? I said to drop your weapon. Now do it."

"For God's sake, Anne," Edward burst out. "Enough."

"Not quite," she corrected, still staring at Monty. "But almost." She pressed the gun barrel against Merry's head.

"You don't know how to use that," Edward tried.

"To the contrary, I became acquainted with the process the night Philip died. You, of all people, know that. Being an old lady has its advantages. No one ever suspects you. It's ironic. I always assumed that power accompanied youth. Not so. I'm far more formidable now. Why, I'm practically invisible. Everyone assumes I do nothing but fret and peruse old photos. That shows how foolish the world is."

Her forefinger settled on the trigger. "So tell me, Detective, which strikes the floor first—your dead daughter or your gun?"

Merry let out a small whimper, and tears trickled down her cheeks. "Dad . . . " Futilely, she struggled against the ropes that bound her wrists.

"It's okay, baby," Monty replied in a soothing tone. "Stay still." He looked at Anne. "You win." He raised his arm, pointing at his jacket. "I'm reaching for my gun."

"Slowly, Detective," Anne advised. "No matter how good your reflexes are, they won't beat point-blank range." She watched while Monty extracted his pistol and held it out for inspection. "Good. Now slide it toward me."

Monty bent down, placed the gun on the floor, and kicked it over.

"Excellent." She gestured at an empty chair. "Have a seat. Right next to your ex-wife."

"Grandmother, what are you doing?" James croaked out as Monty complied.

"Cleaning up after you." Anne picked up the gun and gave James a brittle smile. "On my own, this time. There have been enough mistakes. Mistakes that cost me my son." Her smile faded, her lips thinning into a grim line. "Stupid illegals. They killed the wrong person. And now they brought me the wrong Montgomery." She glanced at Merry, then turned to stare at Sally, genuine hate in her eyes. "It's all because of you. Bad enough that you turned Frederick's head when you're totally unsuitable. But then you inserted yourself where you didn't belong, and Frederick died because of it."

She was about to say more, when Merry's kidnapper appeared in the doorway.

"Luis—bueno." Anne turned, beckoning him into the room. *"Está aquí."* A brittle smile curved her lips. "I think we're ready."

"For what?" Edward exclaimed. He bolted to his feet and stalked over to her, his step faltering as his blood pressure spiked. "What are you doing?"

Her smile faded. "Calm down, Edward. You're flushed and agitated. It's not good for you. Think of your heart."

"I can't fix this, Anne. Not this time. Not if you hurt these people."

"You won't have to." She lay a soothing palm on his arm. "Don't worry. I'm not planning on hurting anyone." She glanced over at James, who was standing, stiff with shock, beside Edward. "James, take your grandfather to his bedroom. He needs to lie down and rest. And call Dr. Richards. Tell him to drive up immediately. I want him to give your grandfather a thorough examination. Just to be on the safe side."

James turned to study his grandfather. It was true he didn't look well. His color was blotchy and his breathing unsteady. On the other hand, James wasn't eager to see his reaction if he were dragged out of the room. He'd probably go ballistic.

"It's your call," James informed him. "You obviously understand what's going on here a lot better than I do. Do you want to stay or go?"

For a moment, Edward didn't reply. He mopped at his brow, still scrutinizing his wife. "Anne, right now, it's all hearsay, except what's happening in this room. It can be fixed. Detective Montgomery's a reasonable man. He and I can come to an equitable arrangement. But only if you walk away."

"I intend to," Anne assured him. "In just a few minutes. The Montgomerys and I need to have a talk. After that, I'll be in to join you."

Edward's breath was coming in uneven pants. "Have Luis take them home."

"Go rest, dear. You need to lie down. And stop worrying. I have everything under control."

He grimaced, clearly torn between common sense and physical weakness. His chest was tight, and a sharp pain seared through it, reminding him that he was playing Russian roulette with his body. Fighting the pain, he leaned heavily against his desk.

"Enough, Grandfather." James appeared at his side, supporting him and guiding him toward the door. "Stop being stubborn. You can't risk another heart attack; it could kill you. Let's go."

Edward resisted long enough to turn to his wife. "I'm sure you know what's at stake."

"I do." Anne stepped aside so he and James could leave the room. "Pour your grandfather a glass of water," she instructed James. "And stay with him until Dr. Richards arrives."

"I will." James led Edward into the hall.

Anne shut the door behind them. Gesturing to Luis, she pointed at Monty and Sally. *"Ate las manos."*

In response, he yanked some rope out of his pocket and walked over, pausing behind Sally's chair.

"El hombre primero," Anne ordered.

Obediently, he moved a few steps to the left, preparing to tie Monty's hands first.

"Much as I loathe your ex-wife, you're more dangerous." Anne kept the pistol aimed at Merry as she addressed Monty. "Put your hands behind your back, Detective."

Monty studied her for a fleeting instant. Then his gaze slid to Merry. Assessing her terrified expression, he stuck his hands behind his back.

"Wise decision." Anne waited until Monty's wrists were tied. *"Ahora la mujer,"* she instructed.

The man pulled Sally's arms behind her and tied them.

Sally winced as the ropes bit into her wrists. She averted her head, looking over to see why Monty was being so unusually compliant. He was staring calmly ahead. But Sally knew that expression. He was devising some kind of strategy. Her gaze dropped lower, and she saw what that strategy was.

Monty's bound hands had slid down until his fingers were brushing the pocket of his pants—the pocket where he'd stuffed his cell phone. He'd worked a forefinger inside and was grazing the outline of the buttons.

The motion stopped.

He slanted a sideways look at Sally, and winked.

He'd found the number he wanted. Speed dial would take care of the rest.

It had started to snow.

A light dusting already blanketed the highway as Blake's Jag raced up Route 287 en route to the farm.

Gripping her cell phone, Devon stared out the front windshield. "I've tried Monty's cell three times. It's ringing, so I know it's on. He must have it set on *vibrate.* I wish he'd pick up. I want to update him on our call to Uruguay."

"He's probably having it out with my grandfather." Blake's jaw was rigid. "In which case, I doubt he has the luxury of answering his phone. Remember, he's going for my grandfather's Achilles' heel. That means all-out war. I'm sure he's got his hands full." A pause. "I hope he finagles my grandfather into admitting something that makes sense out of what we just learned."

"If he hasn't managed to do so by the time we arrive, he will soon after."

"Yeah." Blake frowned, his expression still as shocked and strained as it had been when Devon first told him what she'd heard. "I'm completely at a loss. My grandfather has never involved my grandmother in any business transactions, much less shady ones. Why the hell was she the one paying off Frederick's killer?"

"That's not business," Devon reminded him. "It's personal."

"Personal? Paying off a hit man?" Blake rubbed his forehead. "A hit man who was hired to knock off her son? Uh-uh. There's no way she'd go along with that, much less play an active role in making it happen."

Devon swallowed, giving voice to the sickening possibility that had struck her a few minutes before. "Maybe Frederick's not the one she paid to have killed."

Blake slanted her a look. "He's the one whose head was bashed in."

"Maybe that was an accident. Maybe he woke up before he was supposed to. Maybe he got in the way. Maybe something in the original plan went wrong."

"You think your mother was the target?"

"It would explain your grandmother's involvement. It would also justify your grandfather's extensive efforts to find my mother. He didn't know what she'd pieced together. He couldn't risk her talking to the cops."

"What motive would either of my grandparents have to order your mother killed?"

Devon drew a slow breath. "A few days before the fire, my mother overheard Edward and Frederick arguing. Frederick wanted someone at Pierson & Company fired. He suspected that someone of criminal behavior—behavior that could jeopardize the entire company. Edward was dead set on protecting that someone. It was serious, a time bomb waiting to explode, according to Frederick."

Blake shot Devon a look. "Your mother told all that to your father?"

"Yes. Right after the fire." Devon pressed her lips together. "That's why I'm so jumpy now. She's over there with Monty. Who knows what your grandfather's reaction to seeing her will be?"

Before Blake could reply, Devon's cell phone rang.

She stared at the display. "It's Monty." In one motion, she punched on the phone and tucked it in the curve of her shoulder. "Finally," she greeted her father. "What did you find out?"

No reply.

"Monty?"

Some indistinguishable sounds brushed Devon's ear, and she frowned. "Monty—are you there?"

Voices. Muted and far away.

Devon paused, listening intently.

"Okay, lady, we're trussed and ready." The muffled words drifted through the phone. "Edward and James are gone. So it's just us. Time to cut the crap."

Monty.

Devon's breath suspended in her throat.

"You aren't letting us go. You can't." Monty's voice was growing clearer, more distinct, as if a blanket were being removed from around his phone. "That speech you gave was nothing but bullshit. A bunch of carefully crafted words to get your husband to leave. I get it. You're not planning to kill us yourself. That's what Luis is for. Any way you slice it, we're dying."

"Don't sound so outraged, Detective. Because of your ex-wife, my son is dead."

That voice belonged to Anne Pierson.

Devon shot a frightened look at Blake.

"What is it?" he hissed.

She didn't answer. Instead, she reached down, groping in her purse. She yanked out a minirecorder. Then she jammed the phone into the hands-free kit, held the recorder up to the microphone, and pressed the record button.

"It's divine justice for Sally's daughter to die, too," Anne was declaring. "It's not what I'd planned, but it is what's known as an eye for an eye."

"Meredith has nothing to do with this."

Devon bit her lip to keep from crying out. *That* was her mother.

"She's totally innocent," Sally continued in a quiet, unsteady voice. "Let her go."

"That's no longer possible."

"Christ," Blake muttered as he figured out what was going on.

Devon responded by leaning forward and pressing the mute button on the phone.

"It was supposed to be your older daughter who was taken," Anne declared. "She'd be kept only as long as necessary, then released unharmed, with only a warning."

"A warning?" Monty inquired.

"To stay away from Blake. There's no way I'd ever allow her to become a member of my family. I tried frightening her off, but that didn't work. She's still latched on to Blake's arm like a leech, and digging around in matters that don't concern her. Well, all that's over. After today, she'll be consumed with her own grief. And I'll make sure it's not Blake she turns to for comfort."

In the car, Blake angled his head, meeting Devon's gaze. He looked as ill as she felt.

"Let's talk about those matters that don't concern Devon," Monty was saying. Clearly, he was pumping Anne for information. "What is Lawrence Vista engineering for your husband? It must be life altering for you to go to such great lengths to protect it."

"I don't worry about protecting the business," Anne snapped. "I worry about protecting my family. In this case, the two are integrally tied."

"Because it impacts both James and Edward."

"Yes. Dr. Vista's been experimenting with gene therapy. He's found a way to transform top-notch riders, and their horses, into unbeatable jumpers without even a trace of his efforts showing up in drug tests. That's an overly simplistic explanation. It doesn't do justice to Vista's genius. But since I'm not a scientist, it will have to suffice."

"So Vista needed human guinea pigs to test and refine his techniques." Monty sounded pensive. "And Edward plans to take the results all the way to the Beijing Olympics. That explains the illegal aliens and all the secrecy."

"He and James have waited their whole lives for this." Bitterness laced Anne's tone. "Right on the brink of it becoming a reality, your ex-wife intruded. Edward completely underestimated the threat she posed. Between the argument she overheard at the stables and the evidence of Vista's experimentation staring her in the face each morning, she became a liability that had to be dealt with. Immediately."

"Sunrise's injured leg," Sally realized aloud.

"Indeed." Anne turned her comments to Sally. "My street smarts far exceed my husband's. Contrary to his one-track thought process, I knew you weren't the type of person who could be bought off. I refused to stand idly by and watch Edward's hopes, dreams, and his very life disintegrate along with James's future."

"Vista was using Sunrise as a pincushion," Sally declared in a sickened tone. "I should have figured it out."

"Your daughter did, thanks to her veterinary training and obnoxious snooping. She had to be stopped. So I sent Luis to waylay her. My plan was to keep her out of commission until Vista's work was complete and he was out of the country. Then she'd no longer be a threat. Unfortunately, your younger daughter opened the front door when Luis arrived. He assumed she was Devon and grabbed her. I didn't realize his mistake until a short while ago. I was on the verge of letting her go when you and your ex-wife charged in here."

"Then let her go now," Sally interrupted.

"No." Anne didn't mince words. "At this point, Meredith knows far too much. Which means she has to die along with you. And you'll have to bear the knowledge that you're responsible for the death of your own child. Just like I have."

Sally made a choked sound.

"Nice plan," Monty commented. "Except how are you going to kill us without it looking like murder? I realize you're a pro at staging suicide, but a triple suicide? No way the cops will buy it. That scraps an encore performance of what you did to Rhodes. The investigation's bound to be thorough, since death by affiliation with the Piersons seems to be contagious this week. And where do you think the cops will start? With the royal family itself. Rhodes isn't around anymore for you to frame. So what's your strategy?"

"You're about to find out." More muffled sounds. *"Luis, vaya adelante. Utilice el chloroform."*

Go ahead. Use the chloroform.

Devon didn't have to translate that one for Blake.

"You underestimate me, Detective," Anne told him, the background noise announcing that Luis was preparing to follow orders. "I'm smart. I'm tough. And I'm willing to do anything to protect my family—even more than Edward will. I'm not afraid of the repercussions. What's life in prison to a woman my age? Besides, I doubt it will come to that. I've got wealth and old age in my favor, not to mention the excellent attorney I'll hire who can capitalize on both. We'll bring the judge and jury to tears. Now relax. This will go easier if you do."

"Leave them alone!" came a horrified girl's voice.

Merry. Devon mouthed her sister's name.

"Meredith—stay still." Monty's voice sliced like a knife. "Don't fight her."

There was an instant of silence, and Devon found herself praying her sister had listened. If ever there was a time for her to trust Monty, now was it.

"Smart girl." Anne's response told Devon that Merry thought so, too.

Devon released a sigh of relief. From her peripheral vision, she saw Blake reaching for his cell phone. He gestured to her, and she understood. He was calling 911.

"You're making it damned easy for the cops," Monty remarked. "Three dead bodies in your husband's office? Pretty open-and-shut."

"I'm not having you killed here, you fool."

"Really? Then before your hit man knocks us out, can I know how and where we're going to die? Or are you planning to wake us up for the show?"

Devon reached over and gripped Blake's arm. "Wait." She understood what Monty was doing. He was grilling Anne so they would know where to send help.

"I doubt you'd enjoy being conscious at the time, Detective." Anne's tone was grim. "The chloroform is my idea of being merciful. I have no desire to prolong your suffering. I simply want you all gone. So say your good-byes. Luis and Carlos—that's the man Edward hired to follow Devon—will tuck you in your car and drive you to Clove Mountain. There's a section of road there that's closed off for the winter. It's thickly wooded and has some marvelously tight turns. The rest you can guess."

"Clever." Monty made an appreciative sound. "It'll be dusk by then. The area's deserted. Hey, you even have the cooperation of the weather. There are a couple of inches of snow on the ground. The roads will be slick—especially on an unpaved road at a sharp turn. You're right. I did underestimate you."

"That's it," Devon hissed at Blake. "*Now* call 911. Tell the sheriff to contact the state police and get as many cars as possible over to West Clove Mountain Road. Tell them to go straight to the wooded section with the dirt road that's closed off for winter. They'll know the spot. It looks like something out of 'The Legend of Sleepy Hollow.' Tell them we're trying to stop a triple homicide."

Blake was already punching up 911.

Devon groped in the Pierson file, extracting a sheet of paper. "And Blake?" she added in a whisper. "Have them pick up Vista. Otherwise he'll take off, along with the evidence. Tell the sheriff we'll give him all the proof he needs when we arrive at the scene." She glanced down at the page in her hand. "Vista's got New York plates, license number XVM-19L."

She shut her eyes, grimacing at the shuffling sounds emanating from her cell phone. She knew what they meant, especially punctuated by Anne Pierson's icy, "Good night, Detective."

The sky had gone dark, and the snow was coming down with blinding intensity as Blake's Jag slipped and slid up the Taconic Parkway. The road conditions sucked, as did the visibility, and the cars were crawling along the curved span of highway toward their destinations.

Devon's nails dug into her palms, and she stared straight ahead, too consumed by fear over her family's well-being to speak. Blake gripped the steering wheel as if it were a lifeline, channeling all his energies into getting them where they needed to go as quickly as possible.

"I wish I'd bought an SUV," he muttered. "It would plow through this faster."

"We're almost at Route 55," Devon replied calmly, as much for herself as for Blake. "East is our exit." She swallowed hard, her composure slipping. "Why doesn't the sheriff call? Why aren't the police there yet?"

"They're battling the same weather we are. But so's Luis."

Blake threw on his directional signal and slowed down as he maneuvered the car to the right. "We'll reach them in time."

"We have to." Devon peered out the window and winced as they skidded off the exit. "My family's counting on me. Monty put their lives at risk by calling me."

"He has faith in you."

"I hope it's warranted."

"It is."

"He had no choice," Devon consoled herself aloud. "His hands were tied—literally. If he tried anything, your grandmother would have shot Merry. But, God, what if it's too late? What if—" She broke off, shaking her head adamantly. "I won't go there. I can't."

"Don't. We're almost at Clove Mountain." Blake slowed down to avoid a collision. Route 55 was completely snow-covered, and the smattering of cars on the road were skidding badly.

It was worse when they turned onto the side streets.

One by one, the drivers thinned out, until there was no one left on the road except them.

West Clove Mountain Road lay just around the bend.

Blake veered onto it.

The initial section was a disaster—slick, snow-covered, and without a single tire tread or car to pave the way. The section they were heading toward would be a death trap.

They had to tackle it, and win.

"There's the roadblock," Devon exclaimed, pointing. "See it?"

"Barely, but yeah." Blake squinted through the pelting snow that was now coming down in a hard, relentless blanket.

"There's a set of tire treads on the other side," Devon reported, spotting the dark lines etched on stark white. "Someone's been here. Probably Luis, since we haven't heard from the sheriff." Grimly, she tightened her seat belt, preparing for a jarring ride. "We've got to hurry."

Blake accelerated, slamming into the barrier and sending it careening down the hillside.

The road was buried by snow. Both sides were thickly wooded, with tree branches that hung over the road. Dark and forbidding, they made the already poor visibility nonexistent. To Devon's right, a steep cliff pitched downward, disappearing past a tangled mass of tree limbs into a bottomless pit.

Devon kept her gaze focused ahead, searching for any sign of movement. She couldn't allow herself to consider the possibility that they were too late.

"I see red lights ahead," Blake informed her, leaning forward. "Two of them. They must be taillights."

"I see them, too." Devon gripped the dashboard, her heart slamming against her ribs. "It's definitely a car."

Blake switched off his own headlights. "I don't want to clue Luis in to the fact that we're here."

"Don't slow down," Devon instructed. "The car's definitely Monty's. And it's stopped. Luis must be getting ready to shove the car over the cliff."

"That's not happening," Blake said flatly. He downshifted and accelerated, blasting ahead. The Jag skidded, but obeyed Blake's command, roaring up to the Toyota.

"There's our guy," Devon muttered, seeing the bulky form of a man standing next to Monty's Corolla and leaning into the driver's seat.

Luis's head snapped around. Panicking, he scrambled out of the way as the Jag lurched forward, shearing off the open Corolla door, and showering him with a spray of snow.

Devon frantically scrutinized the inside of the Corolla. For a fleeting instant, she could make out three human forms—Monty, slumped across the steering wheel, Sally, crumpled and unconscious beside him, and Merry sprawled in the backseat.

Her insides wrenched.

Slamming on his brakes and jerking his steering wheel, Blake skidded, winding up diagonally in front of the Corolla and blocking its forward motion. His front tires came to a halt mere inches away from the edge of the road and its sharp drop-off.

Devon burst out of the Jag before it stopped. She raced after Luis, who was trying to flee, and grabbed him from behind. Spinning him around, she slammed her knee into his groin.

Luis collapsed in agony, choking out a curse in Spanish and crumpling in the snow.

Climbing into the Toyota, Blake leaned past Monty and yanked up the emergency brake. By the time he seized Monty and began maneuvering him out the door, Devon was there, helping him.

Together, they carried her father to safety, then rushed back. Blake went around to the passenger side and scooped up Sally while Devon crawled into the backseat and hauled out Merry.

She'd just lowered her sister to the sheltered snowbank beside her parents when she heard the wail of sirens. From both directions, patrol cars twisted their way down West Clove Mountain Road, skidding to a stop as they reached the scene.

Luis, who'd been limping his way along the road—and toward escape—halted, raising his hands over his head in surrender. Two cops sprang out of their vehicles and raised their weapons, cautioning him not to make any sudden moves. They then made their way over, yanking his hands behind his back and slapping handcuffs on him.

"Any other assailants?" one of the officers called out to Devon.

"No. He's it."

"Are the rest of you okay?"

"Yes . . . I think so." Devon rose slowly, realizing she

was trembling all over, with a chill that emanated from the inside out. "But my family's unconscious. Did you call for an ambulance?"

"Already done. It's on its way."

"We won't need it," a groggy voice from behind Devon declared.

She nearly wept with joy at the welcome sound.

Monty.

She turned, relief flooding through her in huge waves as she saw her father struggle into a sitting position. He took in the scene around him, then shot Devon a wry grin. "Hey, partner. Don't crap out on me now. Get over here and cut me out of these damn ropes."

Devon swallowed hard. "Yes, boss."

"I've got them." Blake pulled out his pocketknife, shifting over and squatting down to slice through Monty's bonds. "There."

"Thanks." Monty rubbed the circulation back into his wrists, then turned to Sally, who was starting to come around.

Blake was already there, severing Sally's ropes and helping her sit up.

"That's it, hon," Monty murmured, reaching over to gently shake her face and stroke her cheek. "You're okay. We all are."

Sally's lashes fluttered and lifted. "Pete?" she managed, blinking and trying to get her bearings. "Where's Merry?"

"Right next to you."

"Next to me—where? Where are we?"

"Safe." He substantiated his claim with a broad sweep of his arm. "See for yourself."

She complied, leaning forward and scanning the area, peering through the falling snow. Her eyes filled with emotion as she focused on her older daughter, now hovering over her. "Devon—thank God."

"Hi, Mom. Welcome home." Devon dropped onto her

knees and hugged her mother, tears burning behind her eyelids. "I'm so grateful you're all right—*and* that you're back here with us."

"Me, too." Sally clutched her daughter for a long minute. Then Devon felt her stiffen and draw away. "Pete, what's taking Merry so long to come around?" she asked nervously.

"She's been knocked out a couple of times today," Monty replied, having crawled around to his daughter. "She's inhaled a lot more chloroform than we have. Give her a minute. She's tough. Right, baby?" He slid his arm behind Merry's back, raising her up and supporting her, as Blake moved around back and sliced through her bonds.

"There you go," Monty murmured, lightly patting her face. "C'mon, Merry. Wake up." He scooped up a handful of snow, letting frosty chunks drop onto her cheeks and forehead.

That did the trick.

With a whimper of protest, Merry averted her face, trying to avoid the chill.

"No way," Monty informed her, his hand following her motion. "You want the cold to go away? Open those beautiful eyes."

Frowning, Merry obeyed, her nose wrinkling as she stared up at her father. "Why are you throwing snowballs at me?"

He gave a relieved chuckle. "Reliving your childhood, I guess. Now sit up and I'll stop."

Merry squirmed into a sitting position, wincing at the discomfort in her wrists. "What's going on?" she mumbled, rubbing feeling back into them. "Oh." Her gaze widened as she remembered what had happened, and fear flashed across her face.

"It's over, sweetie." Devon leaned over to smooth her sister's hair off her face. "No one's going to hurt you, or Mom and Dad."

"Mom's okay?"

"Very okay." Sally reached over to squeeze Merry's arm, then climbed to her feet.

"Where are we?" Merry looked around.

"In a snowbank," Devon reported. "But not for long. Come on. Let's get you home." She helped Merry up, steadying her on her feet.

Monty had made his way over to the nearest cop and was issuing a few terse instructions. He then headed back to his family, giving them a quick once-over to ensure they were fine.

"We're going to your place," he informed Sally. "That way, we'll be able to change clothes and eat something hot while we're giving the cops our statement. The sheriff already sent two cars over to the Piersons' farm. No one's getting away, not in this weather."

"That includes Vista," Devon added. "Blake called in his license number. The sheriff sent a car over to the Best Western."

Monty frowned. "I hope they have enough to hold him."

"They will." Devon pulled out her cassette recorder and waved it in the air. "Blake told them I had a tape of your enlightening chat with Anne Pierson. Also that I have your file, complete with the documentation of Edward's illegal payments to Vista. That's more than enough to issue a search warrant for his trailer. And once they check it out, Vista's toast."

Pride flashed in Monty's eyes. "You did good."

Devon's lips curved. "Like you said, I learned from the best." She turned to Blake. "And I had help."

"Yup. Pretty impressive help." Monty gave Blake an approving nod. "You know that test we discussed? Consider it over. You aced it."

Blake's smile was weary. "Thanks, but I'd be happier if I'd accomplished that under different circumstances. I wish this case had played out any other way but this."

"I know." Monty blew out a breath, then gestured for

Blake to give him a hand. "Let's push my car back on the road and head out. You can either follow us to Sally's or stop at your family's place. It's your call."

"I'll follow you." Blake didn't hesitate. "Before I do anything else, I want to give my statement to the police. I've got time to see my family. I'll call them from the car, make sure Dr. Richards is there for my grandfather. I'll also call Louise. We'll need lots of legal counsel, personal as well as corporate, since so much of this nightmare threads through both. Between the company funds my grandfather siphoned into that offshore account to bankroll Vista and Paterson, and the fact that more of those funds were used to pay off my grandmother's hired thug in Uruguay—state and federal authorities are going to be swarming all over us."

"There's no way around it," Monty agreed. "You're going to have your hands full. But your family's strong. So's your company. Both will survive."

"I'm sure they will."

"As for Louise," Monty said thoughtfully. "You and I need to talk."

"About?"

"Later. Right now, you need a good attorney. And she's it."

"All right." Blake met Monty's gaze head-on. "You must think I'm out of my mind for still giving a damn what happens to my grandparents."

"Nope. I think you're doing what you have to. It's your family."

"Most of whom are good, decent people who'll be stunned when they find out the truth. I have to be there for them *and* for the company."

"Be there for them first," Monty suggested, his tone uncharacteristically raw. "Take it from a guy who screwed up and is just now realizing how much. Family is everything. The rest is icing."

Startled by her father's poignant admission, Devon slanted a quick glance, first at her sister, then at her mother. Merry was smiling, watching Monty with the kind of admiration and love that said she was lowering her walls of self-protection. And Sally was visibly moved, her eyes misting over as she absorbed her ex-husband's words.

Devon found herself crossing her fingers.

Clearing his throat, Monty tromped around his Corolla, picking up the mangled door. "Come on, Blake. Let's toss this in the trunk and get this baby back in commission."

It took only a few minutes of organized pushing for the Corolla to be pointing in the right direction, its engine cranking away.

Monty cleaned off the windshield and punched on the heat, helping his family dethaw by warming up the interior as best he could, given the missing door. That done, he climbed out and gave the car a nod of satisfaction. "There you go," he declared. "Almost like it never happened."

Devon's lips twitched. "You know, Monty, now might not be a bad time to consider getting a new car."

"Why?" He patted the hood. "This baby's still got a lot of life in her. I'll just get her fixed up, and she'll be as good as new. Maybe better. Especially after I'm done with Blake's insurance company." Chuckling at his own dry humor, Monty waved his family over. "All set, gang. Time to hit the road."

Reluctant to comply, Devon stood where she was, watching her mother and sister pile in. "Monty?" she heard herself call out.

He turned, his brows drawn in question.

"I'm riding with Blake."

Monty hesitated for an instant, then gave a satisfied nod. "Yeah. You do that." He snapped off a mock salute, sending a spray of snowflakes sailing through the air. "See you there."

Devon watched her father hop into the car, a smile curving her lips. "You know," she murmured to Blake. "I think you just signed on for a lot more than a driving companion."

Blake bent down, brushed her lips with his. "I'm counting on it."

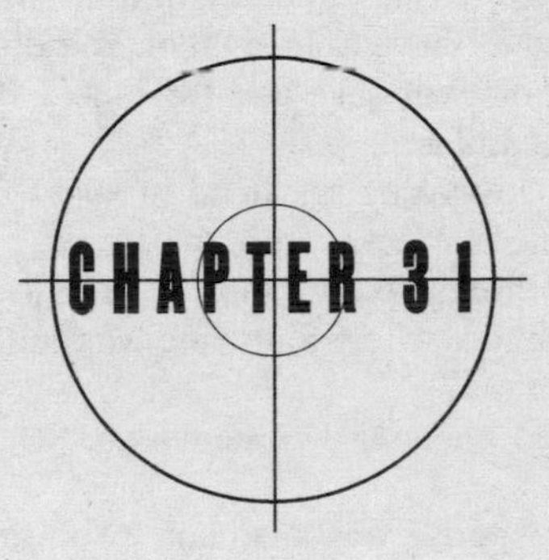

CHAPTER 31

The police took their statements, one by one, verifying all the details. Then they listened to the tape and pocketed it as evidence. Armed with more than enough to make their arrests, they said their good nights and headed for the door.

"Wait." Monty stopped them in the hall, where Blake was already zipping up his jacket, ready to accompany the police.

Tompkins, the younger of the two cops, turned to Monty. "We called over to our guys next door, sir. Dr. Vista's been picked up and brought over there. Between the snowstorm and the overlapping jurisdictions involved, it makes sense to detain all the suspects at the Pierson farm. We're going over there to make the arrests."

"Yeah, I know." Monty grabbed his coat. "I'm going with you."

"So am I," Devon called out from the kitchen. She pushed aside the bowl of soup she'd been swallowing and scrambled to her feet.

Blake frowned as she joined them in the foyer. "Are you sure?" he asked. "I have to face them. You don't."

"I'm sure. For your sake and for mine." She lay a supportive palm on his arm.

He nodded, squeezing her hand in silent understanding, before retrieving her jacket from the closet.

Monty held things up only long enough to poke his head back in the kitchen, where Sally and Meredith were eating. "We're heading out."

Sally stopped chewing her sandwich. "Do you need us with you?"

"No." His response was adamant. "You and Merry stay here. Finish every drop of your soup and sandwiches. Take hot baths. Oh, and call Lane. Tell him what happened and that we're okay."

"All right." Sally gazed steadily at her ex-husband. "Will you be long?"

"Nope." He winked. "I'll be back before you know it."

The Pierson farm was blanketed by snow. Under any other circumstances, it would be a breathtaking view to pause and admire, a veritable winter wonderland.

But not today.

Monty eased the truck up the driveway. In the circular section nearest the front door, a police car was parked. It was covered with enough snow to indicate it had been there a few hours.

The house seemed eerily quiet, although the drone of voices coming from down the hall said that everyone was gathered in the living room.

Blake led the cops in that direction.

At the entrance, they stopped.

Inside were Edward, Anne, and James Pierson, along with Dr. Lawrence Vista and a man Devon didn't know, but quickly determined to be Edward's cardiologist, Dr. Richards.

"Louise isn't here yet," Blake muttered, assessing the room.

"She will be," Devon assured him. "It's only an hour and change since you called her. Metro North takes at least that long to reach the train station nearest here. She's also up against rush hour and a snowstorm. Give her time."

A lawyer and a doctor, she mused silently. Clearly, Edward needed both.

He was sitting on the sofa, gripping a glass of water in a trembling hand. He looked a little out of it, as if he'd been sedated, and there was a blood pressure cuff wrapped around his arm. Dr. Richards stood to his right, listening intently through his stethoscope and pumping the pressure gauge as he monitored Edward's vital signs.

Anne was seated on the sofa beside her husband, her hands folded primly in her lap, her icy gaze fixed straight ahead. Across from her, James was crumpled in one chair, his head buried in his hands. Vista was perched in the opposite chair, his lips pressed tightly together as if to prevent himself from speaking.

The two cops present were jotting down notes, clearly trying to unnerve the Piersons into talking. Just as clearly, the interrogation was getting nowhere.

"Blake." Edward looked up, spotting his grandson and acknowledging him, first with a ray of hope, then—after comprehending that he was aligned with Devon and Monty—with renewed anxiety. "Don't tell me you're part of this witch hunt."

Blake didn't respond. Instead, he looked at Dr. Richards. "What's my grandfather's medical condition?"

"Stable," the doctor responded, having tugged his stethoscope out of his ears. "Earlier, he had some chest pains and muscle weakness. That's no surprise, given the stress he's under. I gave him a mild sedative. The symptoms appear to have subsided. That doesn't mean he's out of the woods. I'm keeping my eye on his vital signs. He shouldn't be agitated."

Blake heard Dr. Richards's warning loud and clear.

"That's going to be tough, considering the circumstances," he responded flatly. He looked like he wanted to say more, then changed his mind. His mouth snapped shut and a muscle worked at his jaw as he struggled for control.

Deputy Tompkins cleared his throat and stepped into the room, heading over to the sofa. "Anne Pierson, you're under arrest for the murder of Frederick Pierson, the murder of Philip Rhodes, and the attempted murder of Peter, Sally, and Meredith Montgomery. You have the right to remain silent. Anything you say can and will be used against you in a court of law. You have the right—"

"To an attorney," Anne finished for him, raising her regal head. "Yes, I know, Officer. And, as I told these two gentlemen, my attorney is on her way. Until she arrives, I have nothing to say."

"Of course you don't." Monty joined Tompkins in the room. "I suggest we all sit down and wait for Ms. Chambers together." He turned long enough to whip out his license and flash it at one of the two cops who'd been detaining the Piersons. "Pete Montgomery, private investigator," he introduced himself.

A flicker of respect crossed the officer's face. "Detective Montgomery, yeah, the sheriff told us about you. I'm Deputy Kearney."

"Kearney." Monty nodded. "I assume I don't need to ask you the status of your questioning."

"No, sir, you don't. Ms. Chambers spoke to us by phone and instructed us to hold off on any interrogation until she arrives."

"Well, there are a few things Ms. Chambers doesn't know. If she did, she'd realize that silence won't help her clients. Not with three witnesses and a tape recording of everything that went down before Luis tried to heave us over a cliff."

"What kind of recording?" Vista blurted out, his eyes as

wide as saucers. His head jerked around toward Edward. "You didn't say anything about taped evidence."

"Shut up," Edward snapped, visibly thrown by Monty's words. He eyed Monty like an animal assessing its foe. "You're lying. There is no tape."

"Yeah, Grandfather, there is," Blake supplied. There was no triumph in his voice, only pained resignation. "I know because Devon made it. Even with his wrists bound, Detective Montgomery managed to press *speed dial* and call her cell phone. She and I heard everything that went on in your office. And now so have the police. We turned the cassette over to them a little while ago."

To corroborate Blake's words, Tompkins pulled out the tape and waved it in the air.

Edward reacted as if he'd been struck. He tensed, squeezing his eyes shut. When he opened them, there was an expression of stunned disbelief on his face. "Blake." The word was an accusation of betrayal. "We're talking about family. Me. Your grandmother. Your cousin. What the hell are you doing?"

"The hardest thing I've ever done in my life." Blake's jaw continued working, but he didn't flinch or avert his gaze. "I can't condone what you've done, or protect any of you. What I can do is preserve the rest of the family. I owe it to them. So that's what I'm doing."

Grandfather and grandson stared each other down.

"Wait a minute," Vista interrupted. Sweating, he pulled out a handkerchief and mopped his face. "If there was anything incriminating about me on that tape, I have a right to know."

"Sounds fair." Monty pursed his lips, seemingly weighing the options. "Then again, fair doesn't matter. Not when we're talking multiple homicide. It's a pity you can't talk to us without your attorney present. Unless, of course, Louise Chambers isn't your attorney. Did she actually tell you she'd be representing you? Because it seems to me she has her hands full. Plus, she's a corporate lawyer. But you probably know that."

"Stop playing mind games, Montgomery," Edward snapped. "Vista's not talking to you."

"I think the doctor should make that decision on his own." Monty shot down Edward's interference with a wave of his hand, never averting his gaze from Vista's. "And Vista? I also think you should stop counting so heavily on the Piersons' lawyer and call a good criminal defense attorney of your own. You're going to need it. Especially after the Piersons hire the best criminal law firm in the country. It won't take long before you'll be set up as the ringleader and the Piersons as unwilling accomplices. But that's your choice."

Edward pointed an accusing finger at Monty. "He's lying, Vista. Don't believe a word he said."

"If you say so." Monty arched a dubious brow. "Okay, Doctor, you want the low-down? Here it is. Between what Mrs. Pierson admitted on tape, and the skin cells and corresponding files the police will find in your trailer, you're going down on more counts than you want to know. Now add kidnapping, attempted murder, and murder charges. That's what you're looking at, if you stay on the current path."

Vista had bolted to his feet, all the color draining from his face. "There's no way you could know about . . . How did you get into my trailer?"

"Whatever you found there is inadmissible, Detective," Anne announced, her gaze boring through Monty. "You didn't have a search warrant. That's breaking and entering. Don't let him rattle you, Lawrence."

Monty's brows rose in feigned innocence. "Now, did I say I saw that stuff firsthand? As for the warrant, it's already been signed. The trailer's being searched as we speak." He inclined his head at Vista. "Listen, *Lawrence,* don't be a jerk. Pierson's only interested in saving his family's ass. Yours is expendable."

Vista wet his lips with his tongue. "What if I'm willing to talk?" he blurted out. "In exchange for some kind of deal?"

"That's up to the authorities," Monty returned smoothly. "But it's worth a try."

"I agree," Deputy Kearney said. "I'll do what I can to make it happen."

"Sounds good." Monty waved his hand in a fait accompli gesture.

"Are you crazy, Vista?" Edward demanded.

Ignoring him, Vista leaned forward, still addressing Monty. "So what happens next?"

"You, Deputy Kearney, and I can stroll down to Mr. Pierson's office and have a private talk. My daughter can join us," Monty added, feeling Devon's insistent stare. "We'll see if we can't help each other."

"Why your daughter?"

"Because she's a doctor. We'll be discussing medical procedures. She can translate."

"Fine. Let's go." Vista was already in motion, despite Edward's sputtering protests.

Before following them, Devon turned to Blake. "I want to be there," she told him softly. "Plus, Monty's right. I will understand more of the medicalese than anyone else. Will you be okay?"

"Yes." Blake nodded. "Go. I have a few things to say to my family anyway."

Squeezing his hand, Devon headed off.

She followed the others into Edward's office. There was a trace odor of chloroform in the air, and Devon wrinkled her nose and grimaced, grateful that Monty was cracking open a window. Snowstorm or not, the fresh air was welcome.

Vista sat down. The others remained standing, clustered around the desk. Kearney gestured for Monty to take the lead.

"Let's cut to the chase. You're experimenting on illegal aliens," Monty announced to Vista. "You're also experimenting on Edward's horses. How do the two connect?"

Silently, Vista lowered his gaze, staring at the oak planks of the floor.

"Your license is gonzo no matter what," Monty informed him, reading Vista's mind and making quick work of his reticence. "But your jail time has yet to be determined. That depends on what crimes you've committed, and how much you're willing to help us."

"I had nothing to do with any murder." Vista's head jerked up, and his frightened gaze darted from Monty to Kearney and back again. "I'm a doctor. A scientist. Not a killer."

Monty nodded. "I believe you. So tell me about your genetic research."

Somewhat appeased, Vista hunched forward, gripping his knees as if to steady his nerves. "There was very little risk involved. Whatever risk existed, the subjects knew about it up front. They signed releases to that effect. It's no different from what drug companies do when they're testing a new product. The subjects in question were my control group."

"Where did you find these subjects?"

"Through Roberto, the Piersons' groom. He lives in Poughkeepsie, where there's a large Mexican community. Many of them are illegals. They need jobs, money."

"And you supplied both. What a guy."

"I provided income for a service."

"Tell us about that service. What type of drug did your subjects have tested on them?"

"No drug. Not in the way you mean. Drugs are detectable. Genetic enhancements aren't."

A lightbulb went off in Devon's head. "You're experimenting with gene therapy. Whatever you're working on for Edward, it's not just for his horses. It's for James."

"Exactly." Vista looked pleased by Devon's response. Clearly, he regarded her as the closest thing in the room to a colleague—one who should be excited and amazed by his accomplishment. "Gene therapy itself isn't new. Nor is the attempt to utilize it in professional sports. But my research goes beyond that. It's unique in its specificity and sophistication."

"Go on." Devon folded her arms across her breasts. She didn't have to fake her curiosity.

Vista converged on it like a moth to a flame. "I've actually managed to genetically engineer skin cells—both equine and human—and reinject them to enhance the exact qualities necessary for a champion jumper." Animatedly, he leaned toward Devon. "This produces both winning riders and winning mounts. In short, I've tailored gene therapy not just for professional sports, but for equestrian jumping."

"How?" she demanded.

"As I said, I harvest then genetically manipulate the skin cells. Those cells are then reintroduced into the body—the horse's cells through the hock, the human cells through the forebrain." Vista indicated the back of his neck. "The procedure results in exactly the enhancements needed for both subjects: improved focus and concentration. Strengthened leg muscles. Decreased nervous tension. And heightened tactile sensitivity, which makes the rider more attuned to his horse and better able to convey instructions to it via his thighs and knees. As a result, a fine contender like Sunrise can become an Olympic winner rivaling Stolen Thunder. And a champion rider like James can become a legend."

"And no drug test can detect the enhancements," Devon concluded.

"Precisely."

Monty let out a low whistle. "No wonder Edward was shelling out such big bucks for you—and from a secret account. Also why your heavy-duty lab is set up in your trailer as opposed to in his stables. Talk about protecting his ass and hanging yours out to dry."

Vista's pride vanished, supplanted by fear. "I haven't hurt anyone."

"I'd call using desperate illegal aliens as human guinea pigs a major violation of medical ethics, not to mention a criminal act." Monty tapped his fingers together thoughtfully. "Did you help plan Frederick's murder? Or just Philip Rhodes's?"

"Neither!" Vista's voice shot up as he took Monty's bait. "Until the police dragged me over here, I had no idea my research was tied to those murders. I would never get mixed up in taking a human life."

Monty wasn't ready to drop the subject. "To your knowledge, was Edward part of his wife's plan? Or did he only jump in afterward, to do damage control?"

"I don't know."

"What about James?"

Vista blew out a breath. "I never can tell what James doesn't know and what he doesn't *want* to know. He was aware of the research I was conducting. That much I'm sure of. It's *all* I'm sure of."

"Anything else?"

"No." Under Monty's rapid fire and blazing glare, Vista began sweating profusely. "I swear I'm telling the truth."

Before Monty could respond, James Pierson appeared in the doorway, escorted by Tompkins. His face was haggard, his hair damp and clinging to his neck. Tension creased his forehead, and his skin was ashen. He looked beaten, as if he'd fought a painful war and lost.

"Can I talk to you?" he asked Monty bluntly.

"Sure. Join the party." Monty waved him in.

"No. Alone." James's jaw set.

Monty considered the offer, exchanging a quick glance with Deputy Tompkins. "We have time to kill before Ms. Chambers gets here," he said. "Any problem if I meet with Golden Boy for a few minutes?"

Tompkins's lips quirked at Monty's reference to James. "No problem. I'll stand outside the door."

"I'll take Dr. Vista back," Kearney said, gesturing for Vista to accompany him. "We'll be in the living room with the others."

Devon watched them go, hanging back for a minute.

"Go ahead, Dev," Monty instructed. "It'll be easier if James and I talk one-on-one."

She nodded, following the others to the door.

James caught her arm as she passed. "I'm not a killer, Devon," he said, his panicky gaze on her face. "You must realize that."

"I do," she agreed. "You're not a killer. Just a coward, a felon, and a spoiled, self-centered son of a bitch."

He flinched, releasing her arm and letting her leave.

"I guess you expected Devon to be an ally," Monty commented when they were alone. "Think again. She's got a core of steel when it comes to her family."

"I understand." James swallowed. "I don't know what Vista told you, but I can give you a lot more. But it has to be off the record. No cops, no tapes, no notes."

"In other words, you want to be able to deny having said any of it."

"For the time being, yes. Look, I can't go to jail. It's that simple. Until I figure out the best way to accomplish that, I'm keeping my options open. So, do you want to hear what I have to say or not?"

Monty folded his arms across his chest in a formidable stance. "I'm listening."

James sank down into a chair. "I didn't know any part of what I'm about to tell you until a few hours ago, when I walked into this room and saw my grandmother pointing a gun at you. I was as stunned as you were."

"Yeah." Monty nodded. "That much I believe."

Stark relief registered on James's face, and inspired him to continue. "My grandfather was very shaky when I settled him in. He needed to talk. The more he said, the sicker I felt. He told me my grandmother was responsible for what happened at the cabin in Lake Luzerne. She knew what your ex-wife had overheard between Frederick and my grandfather at the stables. She was hell-bent on preventing her from ruining things. So she hired one of Vista's illegals—some guy with a criminal background—to kill Sally. The plan backfired. Frederick came face-to-face with the guy and wound up dead instead. My grandmother promised to pay the guy fifty thousand dollars and gave him a one-way plane ticket to Uruguay. He was supposed to vanish into the woodwork."

"Your grandfather had no part in this?"

"Nope. Not until afterward, when my grandmother confided in him. He's been protecting her from the get-go. He was desperate to flush out your ex-wife so he could hand her a blank check and put the whole fiasco to bed. He hired that guy Carlos, who'd done some electrical work and who spoke English. My grandfather paid him to keep tabs on Devon and to bug her phone, just in case she had any contact with her mother."

"But your grandmother wasn't satisfied," Monty surmised.

James nodded grimly. "She didn't think my grandfather was being aggressive enough. She thought it was naive to assume your ex-wife could be bought off. She was also worried about all the poking around Devon was doing. Apparently, she was outside this door, listening, when Blake confronted my grandfather and told him how much Devon knew. My grandmother wanted her stopped. So she delivered that threatening note, warning Devon to back off. When that didn't work, she resorted to kidnapping."

"And attempted murder."

"Yeah. That, too."

"What about Philip Rhodes?" Monty pressed. "Your grandmother took care of his murder herself. She announced that while she held us at gunpoint."

"I know." James rubbed the back of his neck. "It seems that Philip dug up the information documenting those funds my grandfather used for his payoffs."

"*His* payoffs?" Monty interrupted, his brows arching dubiously.

"Okay, fine, *our* payoffs." James gave an impatient, and defensive, wave of his hand. "Look, Detective, I never claimed to be an altar boy. Sure, I greased a few palms along the way. I was also in on the ongoing arrangement with Paterson involving the Antidoping Agency's drug-testing schedule."

"And, in the process, you drugged a few riders."

"Yeah, that, too. You want the rest of my list of transgressions? I helped my grandfather fabricate the extortion scheme to throw you off track. I knew about Dr. Vista's research. Hell, I applauded it. Why wouldn't I, realizing how much it would benefit my future? And I left this room when you, Meredith, and your ex-wife were being held at gunpoint—although I deluded myself into believing my grandmother would let you go. So there you have it—the beginning and the end of my culpability. You can argue that any of it's criminal. But none of it's murder. Not even close."

Monty didn't comment. Instead, he asked, "What about the payments to Uruguay?"

"What about them? I assumed they all related to Vista's research. It never occurred to me that a portion of it was payment to a hit man, if that's what you're asking."

"All right. Let's get back to Philip Rhodes."

James blew out a breath. "After finding that spreadsheet and poring over it, Phil called my grandfather. He meant to have it out with him."

"But your grandmother intercepted the call."

"Right. She told Philip she'd give my grandfather the message that he'd called and urgently needed to speak with him. She never did. Instead, she went to the office, shot Rhodes, and typed up the suicide note." James swallowed, shaking his head in appalled shock. "I'm saying all this, but I still can't believe it. My grandmother . . . anyway, that's what happened."

Monty absorbed all that in silence, intentionally keeping the tension high.

"Now what?" James demanded.

"Now, nothing." Monty shrugged. "As long as this is off-the-record, there's not a damned thing I can do for you. Want my advice? Come clean. It can only help you. Your grandparents will get off easy. They're elderly. They'll win the sympathy vote. You won't. If you're implicated in these homicides—especially killing your own uncle—you'll wind up being somebody's bitch in jail."

"You're right." James shuddered, dragging a palm over his jaw.

"The evidence will support what you and Vista each told me. Do the right thing—you'll be doing everyone a favor."

At that moment, there was a commotion outside the door, and Louise Chambers burst in.

"James, don't say another word," she ordered, staring grimly from him to Monty and back.

Monty straightened, the stare he leveled at Louise coolly detached. "Not to worry, Ms. Chambers. Your client and I are finished." He crossed over, stopping in front of James. "Think about what I said. Any way you slice it, the good doctor won't be winning the Nobel Prize, and you won't be winning gold at the Beijing Olympics."

Devon pulled the prime rib out of the oven, took off her oven mitts, and stepped back to admire her handiwork. She might not cook often, but when she did, she did a damned fine job. Whether or not it was enough to best Blake's salmon remained to be seen. But the ten pound beauty in front of her faced a challenge that Blake's salmon hadn't. It had to feed all the Montgomerys *and* Blake.

Terror barked, scratching eagerly at her legs to ensure that his name was added to the guest list.

"You don't need to remind me you're here," Devon told him. "I know. Besides, there's more than enough. But just to be on the safe side, I'll put your portion aside. Okay?"

He yipped his approval, then rushed off as the front door slammed.

"It's me," Lane called out, making his way to the kitchen. "I didn't miss dinner, did I?"

"Nope," Devon assured him as he gave an appreciative

sniff. "You're right on time." She checked on her scalloped potatoes, added some spices, and put them back to simmer. "Are you really leaving tomorrow?" she asked her brother.

"For the fifth time, yes." He leaned past her and swiped a slice of tomato off the salad.

Devon slapped his hand. "You could sound a little unhappy about it. You just enjoyed a three-week reunion with us. I thought you'd be a little ambivalent about flying three thousand miles away."

Lane licked his fingers, his expression remaining nondescript. "I would be. If it wasn't for the move."

"What move?" Devon demanded.

"The one to New York." He grinned as Devon's jaw dropped. "I just finalized a book deal with Time-Life. They're publishing a compilation of my photo essays on survivors of natural disasters. Besides, I've had enough sun and sand. So I'm moving back east in three weeks."

Devon let out a shriek and threw her arms around him. "You miserable creep. Why didn't you tell me?"

"What, and ruin the fun of torturing you? Nah."

"Does the family know?"

"Mom and Dad do. I went up to Mom's place today and told them."

Devon smiled as she pictured that announcement. "They must have been thrilled."

"Actually, they were caught off guard. But *you're* going to be thrilled."

A puzzled shrug. "You lost me."

Lane plucked out an olive and munched on it. "Let's say I dropped by at an inopportune time."

Devon stared. "You didn't."

"Oh yeah, I did. Mom was in the bedroom, indisposed. Monty was in the kitchen, wearing a towel and throwing together some breakfast in bed. We collided in the hall."

Stifling her laughter, Devon caught her lower lip between her teeth. "I don't know who I feel sorriest for."

"Me," Lane supplied. "I waited for them in the living room like a kid who'd gotten caught with his hand in the cookie jar. Mom finally came out in a bathrobe. She couldn't look me in the eye for ten minutes. All she did was blush. And Monty—his jaw was clenched so tightly, I half expected him to pull out his Glock and blow me away."

"So what did you do?"

Lane gave her a crooked grin. "*Now's* the part where you'll be thrilled. I told Monty he'd better make an honest woman out of Mom. He told me that was the plan."

"Really?" Devon gripped her brother's arms. "He said those exact words?"

"Sure did," Monty confirmed, strolling in out of nowhere and snatching an artichoke off the salad. "And I meant them. Now all I need is a little time—and some privacy—to convince your mother." He rolled his eyes, chomping on the artichoke. "And here I thought only little kids interrupted their parents at the wrong time and that grown-up kids had more smarts. Guess I was wrong. By the way, Dev, do a better job of locking your front door. Anyone could walk in."

"Thanks for the tip," she replied, fighting the urge to cheer. "I will."

Monty sniffed. "Smells good. Your mother and I are starved. Oh, and cut the conversation. Our relationship is off-limits—the same way all of yours are. You know, what's good for the goose is good for the gander, and all that. Besides, it wouldn't hurt to show your parents a little respect." Whistling, he left the room.

Devon and Lane stared at each other and cracked up.

"We're going to get a ton of mileage out of this one," Devon gasped out, her shoulders shaking with laughter. "I don't care how cavalier Monty's pretending to be. He'll move heaven and earth not to upset Mom during this courting stage. He knows how easily she embarrasses. The last thing he needs is for us to make sexual innuendos. He'll be on his best behavior. For a while, anyway."

"Damn straight," Lane agreed. "That means no snide remarks about the women in my life having to take a number. And no sentry duty for you to face after spending a night with Blake." Abruptly, Lane paused, a glint lighting his eyes.

"Uh-oh, I know that look."

"You sure do." A corner of his mouth lifted in a smug grin. "Like you said, this reprieve won't last long. Especially since it'll take Monty about a New York minute to convince Mom to remarry him. After that, it'll be bye-bye leverage. We'd better strike now, while the iron's hot."

"You've got a suggestion about the best way to cash in our chips?"

"Not a suggestion. A brainstorm."

From out in the foyer, Merry's voice drifted in, mingling with her parents'. At the same time, the doorbell sounded, followed by a flurry of footsteps and three sets of barking—one deep, two slightly higher, but no less forceful.

"Chomper's here," Devon determined. "That's his, Terror's, and Scamp's idea of saying hello and competing for the role of alpha male."

"Chomper? Good. That means Blake's here." Lane grabbed the salad bowl and gestured for Devon to follow. "Time to eat."

Devon opened the fridge, took out the tray of fresh fruit she'd prepared, and scooted after Lane. Whatever her brother was planning, she didn't want to miss it.

"Finally," Monty noted drily. He was standing next to the dining-room table, an arm draped around Sally's shoulders. "I was about to send out for a pizza."

"No need." Devon set down the fruit tray. "I made enough even for you." She bent down to pat Chomper, then turned to Blake, her gaze intimate. "Hi."

"Hi yourself." He caught her hand, pulled her closer, and kissed her. "Judging from whatever smells so great in that kitchen, I'm afraid I'm about to lose another contest."

"I'm a gracious winner."

"And a lousy loser," Lane supplied, picking up the salad tongs and doling out leafy servings. "Don't ever get into a card game with her, Blake. It's a lose-lose situation."

"That's only because you're such an arrogant winner," Meredith retorted, jumping in with both feet. "No one can stand losing to you. You're so . . . so . . . so *male*."

Lane arched a brow. "Is that supposed to be an insult?"

"Yes," Merry, Devon, and Sally said simultaneously.

They all laughed. Then, amid the guys' sarcastic comebacks, everyone filed around the table to settle down and eat.

Devon took the opportunity to pull Blake aside.

He looked haggard. Then again, he'd had a hellish couple of weeks. Sixteen-hour workdays, seven days a week, with no hope of things letting up for months to come. Not to mention a barrage of mental, emotional, and financial pressure.

Right after Edward's arrest, Blake had been named interim CEO of Pierson & Company. Under the most grueling of circumstances, he'd assumed responsibility for all the company's day-to-day operations. His days were spent locked in nonstop closed-door meetings with outside counsel and public relations firms who'd been hired to manage the fallout from the impending allegations of improper business dealings. In the midst of this turmoil, he'd called an internal meeting of all Pierson employees, in which he'd tried to put the staff at ease about their job security, asking for their support during this stressful time. And then, finally, he'd broken away from the in-house pandemonium to jump on the corporate jet and make a whirlwind trip to all Pierson's customers, assuring them that Pierson & Company would survive this crisis while continuing to earn their current and future business.

Then there was the personal side of things.

Edward and Anne were ensconced at the Pierson farm, under house arrest and awaiting trial. They'd hired David

Lange, one of New York's most prominent criminal attorneys, to represent them. Given their age and Edward's physical condition, Lange was serving their best interests by making sure the proceedings dragged on as long as possible. As for James, he was out on bail and cooperating fully with the authorities. Therefore, in lieu of jail time, Lange was angling for a hefty fine and community service. In the meantime, James was following his advice and keeping the lowest possible profile. The show circuit was out; the only riding he was doing these days was for personal enjoyment.

The rest of the family was all on overdrive, but the brunt of the hard work and damage control fell to Blake.

Devon searched his face, hurting for the lines of stress and fatigue she saw there. "You look beat," she murmured, her voice drowned out by the sound of the chairs scraping the floor.

"I'm hanging in there."

"What about your grandparents? How are they holding up?"

Blake's shoulders lifted in a resigned shrug. "Healthwise, they're fine. My grandfather's not showing any more signs of a second heart attack. And my grandmother's a steamroller—but only in private. When she talks to the cops, she's a broken, elderly woman. She's paving the way for Lange to argue diminished capacity or undue duress or whatever the hell he plans to argue so her confinement will be at some gracious convalescence facility rather than prison."

Devon sighed. "Have they softened up toward you?"

"Nope. They're civil. They know I'm the best person to run the company. But they'll never forgive me. So don't hold your breath." He rubbed a strand of Devon's hair between his fingers. "Don't look so upset. I expected this. I knew what I was doing. It was the right thing. The *only* thing. I can live with myself. It amazes me that they can."

"What about the rest of your family? Are they supporting you?"

"Across the board." A trace of dry humor. "Except for James. Big surprise. Then again, he's a lot more subdued than usual. So he might not sing my praises, but he doesn't get in my way, either."

"I guess that's a plus." Devon paused. "Any word from Louise?"

Blake's jaw tightened. "Not since I told her to pack her things and get out. After hearing what your father learned—frankly, I couldn't stand the sight of her."

Devon couldn't argue that one. "How's the interviewing for her replacement going?"

"Pretty well. I've seen a couple of strong candidates. The change will be good for Pierson & Company. A clean sweep of the broom is what we needed after all the corruption. And frankly, I feel good about heading up that campaign. Restoring integrity to the Pierson name—it's a goal I can be proud of. And I have you to thank for it."

"Me?"

"Actually, all the Montgomerys. You gave me a crash course in what family's all about."

"A crash course—that's a good choice of words." Devon grimaced at the clatter going on behind her.

"Hey!" Lane called out, interrupting them. "Private time is later. Now's dinner."

"Leave them alone," Sally admonished. She rose, glancing over at Devon. "Why don't I start serving?"

"Good idea." Monty jumped up. "I'll slice the prime rib; you serve it. It'll be just like old times."

"What old times are *you* remembering?" Sally asked, flashing him a teasing grin. "Prime rib wasn't in our budget."

"It's still not in mine," Devon admitted. "I'd be eating Cheerios for the next two weeks if Lane hadn't kicked in."

"Yeah, well, you had a bet to win." Lane gave her a broad grin. "And priorities are priorities."

Meredith watched their parents disappear into the kitchen.

Then she glanced quickly and assessingly at Devon and Blake. "Hey." She poked Lane. "Would you help me pack up my computer? It'll be one less thing for me to do after dinner."

Chuckling, Lane came to his feet. "In other words, give both couples some time alone. Gotcha, Dear Abby." He joined Merry and crossed over toward the staircase. "You've got five minutes," he informed Blake as they passed. "Then we're eating."

"Thanks for the warning," Blake replied. "And Meredith?" He winked at her. "In your case, just thanks."

"Don't mention it." She followed Lane up the stairs.

Devon smiled, turning back to Blake. "Merry's driving up to the house with Monty and Mom tonight," she explained. "They're taking her back to school in the morning. And Lane's flight leaves tomorrow afternoon. So, after that, it'll just be me and my pets."

"Hmm." Blake wrapped his arms around her and pulled her against him. "That has possibilities. Our marathon nights in my apartment are starting to wear thin."

"I'm too much for you, huh?" Devon's eyes sparkled as she smiled up at him.

"Uh-uh." He lowered his head and kissed her. "Not even close. What's too much for me is having you to myself for just five hours a night."

"That's because of your crazy schedule, not my family."

"I know." Blake regarded her intently, threading his fingers through her hair. "But I want more."

Devon studied his expression, her smile fading. "So do I."

"We'll have to probe the options." He kissed her again, this time more explicitly. "Tomorrow night?"

"Tomorrow night," she murmured. "Consider it a date."

At that moment, there was a commotion from the kitchen. First, a shout from Monty. Then a "Pete, grab the tray!" from Sally, followed by a grunt, a splat, a few yips, and the *pad-pad* of running paws. Finally, Terror darted out, a slice of meat dangling from between his teeth. He peered from left to right, spotted Devon and Blake, and veered away from them, bolting down the hall. Scamp burst out on his heels, jumping and snapping in an attempt to grab the piece of prime rib. Seconds later, Chomper exploded into the room, also in hot pursuit of the meat, his chunky little legs sliding out from under him as he sprinted after Terror and Scamp. Behind the vying male canines, Connie exited, her feline expression the picture of disgust as she gazed after them. She turned to blink at Devon, gave an exasperated meow, and headed in the opposite direction.

"Talk about a bucket of ice water in the face," Devon said with a rueful shake of her head. "I think they're telling us not to count on *too* much quiet alone time tomorrow night."

"Great," Blake muttered. "Any chance that SUNY Albany would be willing to start an undergrad program for matriculating pets? We could send the whole bunch of them up with Meredith."

"Nice thought." Devon's lips quirked. "But doubtful."

Monty poked his head out of the kitchen. "Your dog, your portion," he informed Devon, glaring after Terror. "Expect to see one less slice on your plate. And be grateful that I have lightning reflexes, or your whole dinner would be on the floor. By the way, your mother and I are about to carry out the food. So lip-lock time's over." He disappeared back inside.

Devon rolled her eyes and glanced from the three dogs—who were now in the hall playing tug-of-war with the meat—to Blake. "Those five hours alone at your place are starting to sound good."

"Uh-uh." Blake gave her a heated look, then released her. "Like I said, I want more. And I don't just mean time."

Something in his tone struck Devon, a profound note that told her that whatever he had on his mind was significant.

Unfortunately, it would have to wait.

The entire family reappeared at once, this time along with

platters of food, as Sally and Monty placed Devon's meal on the table for all to admire and enjoy.

Devon served, and everyone dug in, offering their high praise in between mouthfuls.

"I didn't taste Blake's salmon, but I still say you win," Monty announced.

"Then that's that. I win." Devon put down her fork, giving her father a teasing look. "The judge has spoken. And he can overrule the jury, no matter what verdict they come back with, right?"

"Yeah. Right."

"Lane just told me the incredible news that he's moving back east," Merry interceded, her eyes bright with excitement. "Isn't that fabulous?"

"It's wonderful," Sally agreed, gazing affectionately at her son. "We've all been angling for this for five years. Looks like we finally wore him down."

"Yup." Lane chewed a bite of meat and swallowed. Then he shot a swift glance at Devon—purposeful enough for her to realize he was about to set in motion the plan he'd alluded to earlier. "Problem is, I've got nowhere to stay."

"Of course you do." Sally waved away that nonsense. "There's more than enough room at my house."

A flicker of displeasure crossed Monty's face. It didn't take a genius to figure out that he'd be less than thrilled to have Lane move in right now. Or why.

"True." Lane pretended not to see his father's displeasure. "And I really appreciate it, Mom. But that won't work. You've got a life to get back to. You need your privacy. . . ." A hint of a pause—just enough to make Devon wonder if he was about to embarrass Sally.

Judging from Monty's scowl, he was worrying about the same thing.

"Plus, I'll be spending most of my time in the city," Lane concluded, visibly stifling a grin as he let them off the hook. "The commute would kill me."

"You could stay here." Devon watched her brother's face as she made the offer.

"Thanks, doc." Lane rose to the challenge. "But the same problem exists here. Not the long commute, but the privacy. I think it would be easiest if I lived right there in Manhattan. Assuming I can find a place."

"My brownstone has a ton of room," Blake suggested. "And these days I'm rarely there. You're welcome to share it."

Lane's response told Devon this was the opening he'd been waiting for. "I have a better idea. How about if I sublet it?"

Blake started. "Sublet—you mean the whole brownstone?"

"Yeah. You won't be needing it for long. I'll save you the time and trouble of listing it with a broker. Let's do it now. You can bunk down there as long as you need to. *If* you need to. Otherwise, you can move in with Devon right away."

Everyone's head snapped around, all eyes on Devon. Monty, who'd been drinking water, began sputtering, glaring at Devon between coughs.

"Dev?" Merry was the first to speak. "You didn't tell me Blake was moving in."

"I . . ." Devon had no idea what to say. She'd expected a lot of things from Lane, but this?

"You didn't mention it to me, either." Having recovered from his choking bout, Monty was all over Lane's announcement. "Was it supposed to be some kind of surprise?"

"Pete." Sally ran interference, her tone and expression telling him to restrain himself.

"What? I just want to know—"

"She's a grown woman," Sally interrupted quietly.

"I realize that. I'm just asking when all this was decided."

"It wasn't," Devon announced loudly. Whatever game Lane was playing, she wanted no part of it. "Lane was just pulling your chain. Blake has no plans of moving in here. So everybody just calm down and . . ." Her voice trailed off as she saw the strained expression on Blake's face. "Blake?"

Lane was also staring at him, looking totally baffled. His shoulders lifted in a questioning shrug.

"We haven't had a chance to talk yet," Blake answered.

"Shit." Lane dragged a palm across his jaw. "You'd said . . . So I assumed . . . I just thought this would expedite . . ." He blew out a self-deprecating breath. "I'm sorry."

"About what?" Monty demanded. "What the hell is going on?"

"Nothing," Lane said, looking totally miserable. "I screwed up. Leave it alone."

Devon blinked. "That's not likely. What secret are you two hiding?"

"No secret," Blake assured her. "I ran into Lane in midtown the other day. I asked his opinion. He gave it to me. I was supposed to discuss the idea with you last night. By the time I left my office, it was after midnight. The timing was wrong. So I decided to wait until tomorrow, when things here settled down. That's what I was referring to before."

"Oh." The pieces fell into place, and Devon's heart skipped a beat.

"You wanted Lane's take on the idea of your moving in with Devon?" Monty sounded incredulous. He turned to his son. "And *you* thought it was a good idea?"

"Pete—enough." Sally had abandoned subtle for direct. She kept her gaze lowered, and she gestured at the bowl of scalloped potatoes on the other side of Monty. "Could you pass me those, please?"

"Yeah." Monty handed her the serving bowl. "Here." He was still glaring at Lane. "Before I shut up, I'd like an answer."

"Okay, as a matter of fact, yes. I thought it was a good idea." Lane reached for the green beans. "Now can we change the subject?"

"No, we can't change the subject."

"Yes, Monty, we can." Devon underscored each word with as much emphasis as she could. "This is not a topic for family debate."

Monty didn't reply, but a muscle was working in his jaw. "Blake, your sister Cassidy's a pretty girl. How would you feel about her shacking up with a guy she met less than a month ago?"

Devon dropped her head in her hands and groaned.

"Not too happy," Blake admitted. He sounded more amused than intimidated. "Like Lane, I'm a little overprotective where my sister's concerned."

"Is that what you call it? You could've fooled me. At least when it comes to Lane. He's suddenly become the epitome of broad-mindedness."

"No, Detective Montgomery, he hasn't. Not about his sisters." Blake chuckled, then waved away Lane's attempt to cut the conversation short and spare him the public display. "It's okay, Lane. I didn't plan on this being a roundtable discussion, but I'll risk it. I think the cat's out of the bag, anyway."

Lane frowned. "I feel terrible."

"You should," Monty informed him.

"He's right. You should." Devon shot her brother a look. "But not for the reason Monty thinks."

"I have an idea," Sally said brightly. "Why don't you and Blake go into the kitchen and have a word alone?"

"That depends on what that word is." Blake's stare was fixed on Devon. "Will you?" he asked, searching for his answer.

"Yes." Tears glinted in her eyes, but she didn't miss a beat. "I will."

"Wow." Merry's eyes were damp, too. "I can't believe how romantic that turned out."

"Me, either." Lane exhaled sharply, watching in relief as Blake pushed back his chair and walked around the table to tug Devon to her feet and kiss her. "It was one for the books. And it really saved my ass. Talk about open mouth, insert foot."

"Yeah," Devon agreed from inside the circle of Blake's arms.

Monty frowned as Sally rose and went around to hug Devon. "This isn't just about moving in together, is it?"

"Nope." Lane answered his father's question with a grin, simultaneously giving Blake a congratulatory handshake. "You know what a consistent guy I am. Blake's crazy about Devon. So I told him to make an honest woman out of her. Those words ring a bell?"

Devon reached over and playfully punched her brother in the arm. "Quit while you're ahead."

"Good idea," Monty echoed. He stood up and walked around, folding his arms across his chest as he eyed Blake. "Just so we understand each other, we're talking about marriage, right? Rings, vows, the whole nine yards."

Blake's lips twitched. "That's exactly what we're talking about."

"Good." Monty nodded. "You know you'll answer to me if you hurt her."

"Monty," Devon warned.

"Somehow I expected that," Blake replied. "But I'm not going to hurt her."

"I know you won't." Monty nodded again, a hint of emotion glistening in his eyes. He stuck out his palm, shaking Blake's hand. "Congratulations, Blake. You're a lucky man."

"Thank you, Detective. I know I am."

"Cut the formalities," Monty instructed. "Call me Monty." He turned to Devon, wrapping her in a tight, paternal hug. "Be happy," he said roughly.

"I will, Monty." Devon hugged him back.

"Hey." He recovered himself, emotions back in check.

"See? I told you that our being partners would be worth your while."

"You were right."

"As always," he prompted.

Devon smiled. "As always."

"Good. Now that we've got that settled, let's eat."

The nightmare crept through her like a slow-acting toxin, paralyzing her as it insinuated itself into the darkest recesses of her memory. There was no escaping the devastating finale, no looking away from the horror.

She couldn't bear to see them. Not their broken bodies. Not their vacant stares. And not the pools of crimson blood that kept oozing beneath them as their lives drained away.

With a low moan, Morgan forced herself awake, jerking upright. Her muscles were rigid. She pressed back against the solid oak headboard, letting it cool her perspiration-drenched skin. Her heart was slamming against her ribs, her breathing fast and shallow.

This was a bad one.

She squeezed her eyes shut, concentrating on the muted sounds of predawn Manhattan. The intermittent *thump-thump* of cars making their way down pothole-ridden streets. A distant siren. The hum of 24/7 just outside her brownstone window. It connected her to life, to the comfort of what was real and familiar. She drank it in, fighting to drown out the images of her nightmare before they engulfed her.

It was an exercise in futility. The nightmares might be sporadic, but the vivid memories had been seared inside her head for the past seventeen years.

She shoved back the covers and swung her legs over the side of the bed. Her nightshirt was damp and clinging to her body. Her hair was plastered to the back of her neck. She gathered it up, twisting its shoulder-length strands into a loose knot and pinning them to the top of her head with the clip she kept on her night table. A winter draft blew past her, and she shivered.

She'd half expected tonight's episode. It was that time of year. The nightmares always came fast and furious around the holidays. But exacerbating the situation had been her own damned fault.

Morgan glanced at the clock on her night table: 5:10. No point in trying to go back to sleep. Not that she could if she tried. But it wasn't even worth the effort; not with only fifty minutes until her alarm went off.

She pulled on a robe and padded into the dimly lit hall, crossing over to the spare bedroom. The contents of the box she'd been going through were on the ottoman just as she'd left them—memorabilia in one pile, photos in another, and the working journals she'd only recently discovered off to a side.

Still haunted by her dream, she flipped on the light and went straight for the photos, kneeling down beside the ottoman to peel back a layer of history.

The top snapshot meant the most and hurt the most. It was the last photo of the three of them together. Wistfully, Morgan studied it. Her mother, gentle and elegant. Her father, intense and dynamic, one arm wrapped protectively around his wife's shoulders, the other hand gripping the shoulder of the skinny little girl in front of him—a girl who had her mother's huge green eyes and fine features and her father's sharp, probing expression.

Morgan turned the photo over. The handwriting at the bottom was her mother's. It read: *Jack, Lara, and Morgan, November 16, 1989.*

She'd penned those words a month before the murders.

With a hard swallow, Morgan put down the snapshot and sifted through the others. Her mother in college, posing with her best friend and roommate, Elyse Shore—then Elyse Kellerman. Law school graduation day for Morgan's father, both her parents standing in front of Columbia University, brandishing Jack's diploma. Their wedding day. The day Morgan was born. Family photos of happy occasions, from Morgan's first birthday to summers at the beach with all the Shores—Elyse, Arthur, and Jill. Last were the photos Elyse had developed for Morgan months after the funeral—photos taken at Daniel and Rita Kellerman's lavish Park Avenue penthouse on Christmas Eve, where Morgan's parents had dropped by for the holiday party being hosted by Elyse's parents in honor of Arthur and those who'd contributed heavily to his political campaign.

Those were the final photos taken of Lara and Jack Winter alive. The next ones were snapped in a Brooklyn basement later that night by the crime-scene unit.

With a shiver, Morgan put down the stack of photographs and rose, tightening the belt of her robe. Enough. She was allowing herself to be sucked into that emotional vortex all over again. Her mental health couldn't withstand it. Dr. Bloom had cautioned her about this very thing.

Time to listen to his advice. Be proactive. Focus on the present.

She'd get a jump start on the day; brew a pot of coffee, shower and dress. Then she'd head downstairs to the office. She had a slew of early morning phone calls to make in the hopes of catching her clients before they left for work, and a mountain of paperwork to attack. At eight-thirty, it would be time for her therapy session—which worked out well since Dr. Bloom's office was just a block away from the Waldorf-Astoria Hotel, where she had an eleven o'clock new-client interview. After that, it was back to the office for a one o'clock follow-up appointment with Charlie Denton—attractive, forty-four, married to his job in the Manhattan D.A.'s office. With very specific criteria and a crazy-busy life, he was still looking for Ms. Right. And it was Morgan's job to find her.

She turned off the light and left the room—and her past—sprawled out on the ottoman behind her.

The deal was cut.

No one in the Brooklyn D.A.'s office was happy about it. Another scumbag who'd turned on a fellow inmate to save his own neck. Another case where the rule of law converged with Darwin's survival of the fittest.

Having to go easy on that drug-dealing punk, Kirk Lando, was a rotten break. But they had no choice. He'd given them a cop killer in exchange for a lighter sentence. The NYPD was happy; Nate Schiller would pay for killing one of their own.

Schiller would probably have his throat slit once word got out at Sing Sing why he'd lied about shooting Sergeant Goddfrey. Normally, killing a cop would have made him a hero there. Not this time. Schiller had screwed himself—bad. When he'd tracked Goddfrey down in Harlem and blown him away, he'd also blown away the perp Goddfrey had been cuffing at the time, figuring he was eliminating the sole witness to his crime.

Bad move. That perp had been gang leader Pablo Hernandez. Once the gang members inside Sing Sing got this news, Schiller could kiss his ass good-bye.

The whole trade-off sucked—for bigger reasons than leniency for Lando or the inmates taking out Schiller. Lando's story was true. It had been corroborated by a couple of neighborhood teens, now adults, who'd spotted Goddfrey's killer fleeing the scene. Originally, they'd provided a description. Now they'd each picked Schiller out of a lineup. So there was no doubt that Schiller had killed Goddfrey and Hernandez. Which meant he couldn't have committed the double homicide in Brooklyn he'd been convicted of as part of his killing spree.

The ripple effect was going to be felt far and wide. The daughter. The congressman. The staff over at the Manhattan D.A.'s office.

And one really pissed-off retired cop.

Pete Montgomery swerved his car into the driveway, glaring at the semi-attached house that served as his office as if it were the enemy. He was in one foul mood. He'd purposely left Dutchess County at eight forty-five to avoid rush hour. Still, it had taken him three hours to get to Little Neck. It should have taken half that time. Except that it had started snowing—just a dusting with the threat of an inch or two to follow. But that was enough to transform all the drivers on the road to pitiful, scared-shit wimps who drove with their noses pressed to the windshield and crawled along at a snail's pace.

He hopped out of his faded maroon 1996 Toyota Corolla, which had a hundred thousand miles on it and had been put back together again more times than Humpty Dumpty. Still, Monty—as everyone called him—insisted that it had another good decade of life left in it. Besides, it was the perfect car for a private investigator—ordinary, unpretentious, the kind of vehicle that could blend in anywhere.

His phone was ringing as he unlocked the office door, and he strode over to grab it. "Montgomery."

"Hey, Monty." It was Rich Gabelli, his old partner at the Seventy-fifth Precinct in Brooklyn. They'd worked together for a dozen years, right up to Monty's retirement at age fifty. Gabelli was younger—and more tolerant—so retirement for him was still a ways off.

"Yeah, Rich, what's up?" Monty was already shuffling through his files, putting his cases in priority order.

"You working half days now? I called your cell three times, and there was no answer. I guess being a newlywed takes up lots of time. And energy."

Monty grunted. He'd been taking good-natured flack from his buddies since he'd remarried his ex six months ago. "I wasn't home with Sally. I was on the Cross Island, cursing out the other drivers. Besides, I saw your number pop up. I ignored it. It's time to get a sex life of your own and stop living vicariously through mine."

"That's easy for you to say," Gabelli retorted. "Sally's still a babe. Have you taken a good look at Rose lately? She's put on twenty pounds."

"And you've put on thirty. That gut of yours needs its own desk. So be grateful Rose doesn't dump you. Now what do you want? I've got work to do."

"I called to give you a heads-up." There was a somber note in Gabelli's voice that Monty couldn't miss.

"About?"

Gabelli blew out his breath. "The D.A. cut a deal with Lando. He gave them the name of Goddfrey's killer."

"Good. It sucks about Lando, but Goddfrey's killer deserves to rot."

"I agree. But there's more."

"I'm listening."

"The guy who shot Goddfrey—it was Nate Schiller."

"Nate Schill . . . Shit." Monty ground out the word. "Are you sure?"

"Yeah. Schiller was bragging at Sing Sing about popping a cop. He was dumb enough to mention it was Goddfrey. Which means he killed Hernandez, and figured out who he was too late. There's evidence to corroborate it, so he'd confessed to killing Jack and Lara Winter. Killing an A.D.A. would mean rotten treatment at Sing Sing, but killing a gang leader would mean being carved up like a chicken.

And since Goddfrey was killed that Christmas Eve in Harlem around the same time as the Winters were murdered in Brooklyn, Schiller couldn't have killed them."

"Son of a bitch." Monty slapped his file on the desk. "You were right all along."

"I didn't want to be. I still don't. But I won't lie and say I'm surprised. The Winter double homicide didn't follow Schiller's pattern. The crimes felt too personal. And the Walther PPK? Not exactly Schiller's style."

"You know he loved throwing us off track. Anyway, the Manhattan D.A.'s pushing to reopen the Winter case."

"Big surprise. Jack Winter was their golden boy. They'll want to nail his killer's ass. Problem is, the ball was dropped the minute Schiller confessed. Now it's seventeen years later. No matter how much noise the Manhattan D.A. makes, who's gonna jump? With no leads, no witnesses, and a skimpy list of potential suspects—most of whom are either dead or vanished into the woodwork—they might as well try pulling a rabbit out of their ass. Talk about a cold case."

"You're right. We already dug out the file. There's nothing. But the captain wants us to go through the motions."

"Of course he does," Monty agreed drily. "He's got his ass to cover. Man, he must be thrilled I'm gone. He knows I'd be all over this if I were still on the force." Abruptly, Monty broke off, his voice taking on a rough note. "What about the daughter—Morgan—has she been told yet?"

"That's the reason I'm calling. This whole deal just went down. The D.A.'s office is scrambling to get their shit together. They're not looking forward to the fallout. But they can't risk a leak. So they're notifying her today." A pointed pause. "As soon as our precinct finishes dotting our *i*'s and crossing our *t*'s to give them the okay. Which I'm doing as we speak."

Monty got the message. "That gives me time to get to her first."

"Right. If that's what you want."

"It's what I want." Monty fell silent. He could visualize the hollow-eyed child who'd grown old in the space of a heartbeat just like it was yesterday. Even now his gut wrenched when he pictured the scene he'd walked in on.

Most cases didn't get to him. This one had.

And still did.

"She was in bad shape," Gabelli murmured. "You were the only one who was able to reach her."

"Yeah, well, I was in pretty bad shape myself at that time. That's why she and I connected."

"I remember." Gabelli cleared his throat. Partners or not, there were still some subjects he shied away from. That bumpy time in Monty's life was one of them. "You'd better move fast. I can only hold up the process so long. And I don't need to tell you that you didn't hear this news from me. The captain would hand me my ass on a platter."

"Not a problem. We never spoke." Monty grunted. "But between you and me, I'm doing him a favor by being the messenger. I might be able to do some damage control."

"With Congressman Shore, you mean."

"Hell, yeah. He's going to have a cow. When the murders went down, I'm the only one he didn't threaten to sue."

"He wanted answers. I can't blame the guy. He and his wife had just lost their best friends, *and* been handed custody of their kid."

"Blame him? He was more controlled than I would have been under the circumstances. Seeing that poor little girl, what she was going through—hell, I would have resorted to more than threats to get my answers." Monty shoved his pile of paperwork aside and grabbed a pad and pen. "What's Morgan Winter's address? I want to get to her before anyone, including the press, does. She's going to be freaked out enough by this news without being ambushed by reporters."

The rustle of paper. "She lives in that brownstone her parents left her on the Upper East Side. She runs a business out of there, too—some kind of high-class matchmaking service." Gabelli read Monty the address.

"Thanks, Rich. Give me an hour. Then let the dogs out." Monty blew out a breath. "I hope Morgan Winter can handle this."

"She's not a kid anymore, Monty. She's a grown woman. She'll be fine."

"You think so? I'm not so sure. She didn't just lose her parents that night. She found them, murdered. The kid was traumatized. The only thing that kept her from going completely over the edge was knowing the killer was caught, locked up, and given life without parole. Now I have to tell her he wasn't."

It was one o'clock, and Morgan's stomach was growling as she hurried back into the brownstone. She hadn't eaten a thing all day. In fact, she hadn't had a minute to breathe since she'd unlocked the doors to Winshore LLC five hours ago. Business at the boutique social agency was hopping. The phones had been ringing off the hook when she left her newest employee, Beth Haynes, and dashed out for her eight-thirty therapy session. They were still ringing when she called to check in a short while ago. The good news was that Beth had informed her Charlie Denton was running late and had pushed back his appointment until three o'clock. That gave Morgan a window of opportunity during which to cram down her sandwich—assuming it was delivered in the next hour.

She brushed the snowflakes off her coat and hung it up, rubbing her arms as she glanced around. Done in rich woods and Oriental rugs, the ground floor was the business hub of Winshore. The second floor, also designated as part of Winshore's office space, was equally elegant but much cozier. It consisted of a cushy sitting room for interviews and a large, airy living room for photo shoots and fashion consultations.

Upstairs was for relaxation and comfort.

Downstairs was all business and bustle.

Well, not *all* business. There were personal touches, too: recent client wedding photos on the credenza, some funky art pieces on the desks, and—thanks to Jill Shore, Morgan's partner and dearest friend—an array of eclectic holiday decorations purchased on her travels. This included an eight-foot Christmas tree that barely cleared the ceiling, a handcrafted Hanukkah menorah Jill had found in Israel, and a Kwanzaa display.

Morgan smiled as she squeezed by the tree to get to Beth's desk. "No one can accuse us of shortchanging the holidays."

"That's certainly true." Beth blew a few pine needles off her pink cashmere sweater. "And Jill's still not finished yet. She said something about bells to commemorate the winter solstice, and books to explain its ancient roots."

Morgan's amused gaze flitted around the room, settling on the nook beside the fireplace. "Well, we do have one empty corner. I guess that's the one that'll take on the winter solstice theme." She grimaced in response to a loud growl from her stomach. "Any idea if Jonah's on his way?" she asked hopefully.

Jonah Vaughn was the delivery guy for Lenny's, the best *and* the busiest Kosher deli in New York. Located on Delancey Street, Lenny's delivered overstuffed sandwiches to offices all over the Lower East Side and Brooklyn. And while Winshore was clearly outside that delivery zone, Morgan and Jill had a special "in" with the owner. Lenny was Jill's grandfather. And since Morgan had grown up as a member of the Shore family, he was like a grandfather to her, too.

Beth gave her the thumbs-up. "You're in luck. Jonah called from the truck right before you walked in. He should be here in ten."

"Thank goodness. I'm about to pass out from hunger."

"Well, hang on. Reinforcements are on their way." Beth swiveled her chair away from the computer and stretched. She was a fresh-faced young woman of twenty-two with a sharp mind, great people skills, and a psychology degree from Northwestern. Morgan had met her at a seminar and snatched her right up. After six months of training, Beth was well on her way to being a fantastic interviewer.

"Anything urgent I should know about?" Morgan picked up the stack of phone messages and began sifting through them.

"A slew of new inquiries." Beth jotted down a few additional notes. "Speaking of which, how was your meeting at the Waldorf? Rachel Ogden is barely older than I am, but she sounded like a dynamo on the phone."

"She is." Morgan handed Beth the information forms Rachel had filled out, together with Morgan's notes from their interview, ready to be organized in a new client file. "At twenty-five she's already a high-powered management consultant. I have a few guys from our database in mind for her. Starting with Charlie Denton. He's in his forties, but Rachel prefers that. I think they'd really hit it off."

The phone rang again, and Beth blew out her breath. "Break over. Probably another new client."

"Part of why these calls are coming in fast and furious is Elyse's doing," Morgan replied, grinning. "She makes commercial announcements before every spin and aerobic class, and pitches Winshore while perched next to every Lifecycle and treadmill." Affection laced her tone when she spoke of Jill's mother, Elyse Shore. The woman was a pistol. She ran an upscale gym on Third Avenue at East Eighty-fifth Street, where the term "word of mouth" took on a whole new meaning.

The front door of the brownstone opened and Jill burst in, shaking snow off her coat. "It's coming down hard. That's the bad news. Now the good news. I saw Jonah's truck. Lunch has arrived. Not a minute too soon, either. My stomach's growling like something out of a horror movie."

Shrugging off her coat, Jill continued to talk as she ran her fingers through her hair to dry it. She was more striking than beautiful, with red-gold hair, dark eyes in contrast, and a wide, sensual mouth. And when she smiled—which she did often—her entire face lit up.

"It's a good thing corned beef has renewing powers," she informed Morgan. "My afternoon's going to be crazier than my morning. Back-to-back meetings, first with our accountant, then with our new software designer. Pushed to save money, then pushed to spend it. By six o'clock, my brain will be fried." She waved away any outstanding concern. "Not to worry. I'm picking up the winter solstice decorations on my way home. The last of the office will be decorated tomorrow morning. Oh, and I'm meeting Mom for dinner. We're going over the final party details."

Jill rubbed her palms together for warmth, her eyes sparkling as she contemplated the holiday celebration Winshore was hosting for its clients. "You won't even recognize Mom's gym when we're through with it. Lighting, music, decorations. And enough food to sink a ship. It'll be fantastic. Before I forget, Dad left a message on my cell. He's flying in from D.C. tonight. So save some time."

At long last, Jill stopped to catch her breath, and Morgan found herself marveling, yet again, at her friend's tireless energy. That was Jill—the whirlwind. She lived life to the fullest, and pushed all the boundaries in the process. She was all about reveling in whatever the world had to offer, and if anyone existed who didn't like her, Morgan didn't know about it. Jill was a proverbial breath of fresh air, a sister in all ways but blood, and Morgan adored her.

"Morg?" Jill was eyeing her speculatively, her brows knit with concern. "You okay?"

"Fine. Just hungry."

With a quick sideways glance, Jill verified that Beth was on the phone with a client. Then she crossed over and pulled Morgan aside, lowering her voice as she spoke. "No, you're not just hungry. You're exhausted. It's no wonder Dad's worried about you. Which, in case you haven't figured it out, is why he's coming here straight from the airport. Did you have another bad night?"

Morgan shrugged. "I've had worse. Then again, I've had better. It's par for the course these days."

Jill frowned. "Maybe I should cut back on the whole decoration thing, at least for this year."

"Don't you dare. Your holiday spirit has nothing to do with my nightmares. If anything, it diverts me."

"Not really. You're a mess."

"I know." Morgan didn't try denying it. "I'm not sure why they've hit me so hard this year. Dr. Bloom says it's a subconscious vicious cycle. Reading my mother's journals triggered a stronger-than-usual connection to her and my dad; that connection prompted me to delve deeper into her journals, which, in turn, triggered more nightmares."

"But the nightmares were worse than usual even before you found those journals buried in that box of your mother's things. It's been weeks since you were yourself."

Morgan sighed, massaging her temples. "I just have this weird, creepy feeling. I can't seem to shake it."

Before Jill could reply, the front door buzzer sounded, followed by a rhythmic knocking and a bark of "Lunch!"

No second announcement was needed. Jill hurried over and yanked open the door. "Hey, Jonah," she greeted the teenager who tromped in.

"Hey." Tall and gangly, Jonah was swallowed up by his down parka and boots, with only a lock of sandy hair and the puffs of cold air he was exhaling visible. But the telltale aromas of deli meat wafting from the brown bag he carried were the only ID required.

"You're a lifesaver." Jill snatched the bag, opening it for

an appreciative sniff. "Corned beef on rye with mustard, and a Dr. Brown's cherry soda. All's right with the world."

Shoving back his hood, Jonah acknowledged Jill's statement with a nod. "I've heard those words about ten times in the last hour."

"I'll bet." Jill dug around in her purse and pulled out a bill, stuffing it into Jonah's gloved hand. "Get some pizza instead."

"Thanks." Gratefully, he pocketed the tip. "But I already ate. I had two pieces of your grandmother's noodle pudding—*kugel*—" he amended, using the Yiddish word Lenny had taught him. "After all, I have a reputation to uphold."

Despite being Welsh, Jonah had been gobbling up Rhoda's kugel since he was old enough to take the subway to Lenny's by himself. Everyone teased him about it, but his addiction had landed him this delivery job. Lenny had hired him on the spot, offering him decent pay and unlimited kugel, while affectionately labeling him "The Kosher Kid."

But the best perk of his job had been Lenny introducing him to Lane. Interning for a photographer with Lane's skill and notoriety was the opportunity of a lifetime.

"I'll bank this," he murmured on that thought.

"Ah," Morgan ventured. "Another donation to your camera fund."

"Yeah." Anticipation flickered in Jonah's eyes, and his customary monotone took on new life. He was a quiet kid, and a bit of a geek. But he was a whiz at computers. As for photography, Morgan knew that was his passion, as was this new internship of his. Anytime those subjects came up, he lit up like Jill's eight-foot Christmas tree.

"I saw a cool digital on eBay," he announced. "An Olympus E-300. It's got shading compensation, antishock—anyway, if it's still there after Lenny pays me on Friday, I'm bidding on it."

Jill waved her arm at the three computer stations. "If you need extra money this month, our system could use a few software updates and a maintenance check. How about it?"

"Sure." He scratched his head. "I've got two weeks' vacation from school starting next week. I can put in a few days here."

"Great."

Jill and Jonah lapsed into computer jargon, and Morgan used the opportunity to pluck her sandwich out of the brown bag and head for the kitchen.

She was halfway there when the front door buzzer sounded again. She looked over her shoulder in time to see Jonah open it. A tall man in a wool overcoat stepped inside. His features were concealed by a turned-up collar, but he had dark hair and a no-nonsense stance.

He folded down his collar and unbuttoned his coat. There was something decidedly familiar about him. Which meant he must be a client. And *that* meant she could kiss her pastrami good-bye.

"Hey, Jonah," he greeted the boy. "Making a lunch delivery?"

"Yeah." Whoever the guy was, Jonah looked surprised to see him here. "I've got a couple of extra sandwiches. Did you want one?"

"Nope. Already ate. But thanks." The man's dark gaze eased from Jonah to Jill. "I'm looking for Morgan Winter. Is she in?"

"Do you have an appointment?" Jill responded in her friendly-but-noncommittal tone that said Winshore didn't accept walk-ins.

"No. But it's important that I see her. Is she around?"

His voice—Morgan recognized it. And it didn't belong to a client. Or a walk-in.

It was a wrenching memory from the past.

"I'll check," Jill was carefully saying. It was obvious she'd picked up on the urgency in his tone. "May I ask your name?"

Morgan had already begun retracing her steps when he replied.

"Yeah. Tell her it's Pete Montgomery."